PEELER

KEVIN MCCARTHY

MERCIER PRESS
IRISH PUBLISHER – IRISH STORY

MERCIER PRESS
Cork
www.mercierpress.ie

Trade enquiries to CMD BookSource,
55a Spruce Avenue, Stillorgan Industrial Park,
Blackrock, County Dublin

ISBN: 978 1 85635 659 6

10 9 8 7 6 5 4 3 2 1

A CIP record for this title is available from the British Library

Printed and bound in the EU.

Mercier Press receives
financial assistance from
the Arts Council/An
Chomhairle Ealaíon

1. Whereas the spies and traitors known as the Royal Irish Constabulary are holding this country for the enemy, and whereas said spies and bloodhounds are conspiring with the enemy to bomb and bayonet and otherwise outrage a peaceful, law-abiding and liberty-loving people;

2. Wherefore we do hereby proclaim and suppress said spies and traitors, and do hereby solemnly warn prospective recruits that they join the RIC at their own peril. All nations are agreed as to the fate of traitors. It has the sanction of God and man.

By order of the GOC,
Irish Republican Army.

Men like my father were dragged out, in these years, and shot down as traitors to their country. Shot for cruel necessity – so be it. Shot to inspire necessary terror – so be it. But they were not traitors. They had their loyalties, and stuck to them!

Sean O'Faolain,
Son of an RIC man.
Vive Moi!

Friday
26 November 1920

Word of the body had come from the wife of a shopkeeper in Ballycarleton. It was only a rumour, she had told the young RIC constable as he collected the barracks' newspapers from the rear of her husband's newsagents. But she hadn't the heart not to pass it on. Imagine, she had said. Some poor soul lying alone in the gorse and the heather, in the wind and rain of late autumn. Unclaimed. A young woman, she had told the constable, her hand resting on his forearm, speaking quickly in a breathless whisper, eyes darting left and right lest someone should see her speaking to a Peeler. Just a rumour, mind. Passed on by the friend of a cousin who grazed sheep in the hills.

The same hills where they were now searching. Eleven cold, wet men in the open back of a Crossley Tender. Acting Sergeant Seán O'Keefe of the Royal Irish Constabulary bumped shoulders with a Private from his escort of eight Essex Regiment soldiers out of Bandon. With him from the barracks were Constables Logan and Keane, O'Keefe only bringing the recently sworn-in Keane because it was he who had been given the tip on the body by the newsagent's wife.

The Crossley's engine strained, gears grinding as it climbed a rutted boreen used by farmers and their livestock. O'Keefe scanned the landscape for any sign of the body. The squaddies scanned the sky for rain through the chicken wire mesh that shrouded the back of the Crossley. The chicken wire kept out grenades, but not the weather.

O'Keefe knew the soldiers resented being there; dragged away from a warm fire to run escort for three Peelers searching for a body that probably didn't exist. They smoked, cupping cigarettes in down-turned hands, their Lee-Enfield rifles resting between their knees. O'Keefe considered ordering a pair of the men to stand watch to the front and rear of the lorry bed, arms at the ready, but didn't have the heart. He wasn't sure the soldiers would obey a Peeler's order anyway.

Fifty-five policemen killed in the previous four months in Ireland. Forty-nine disarmed and countless others wounded, shot at and beaten. West Cork had been the worst affected in the country. The constabulary needed army escorts to move around the county and the army relied on the constabulary for local intelligence, but neither was willing to cede authority until something went sour. Until someone was killed on patrol or a shop was looted and torched, when suddenly it was the other lot who had been in charge. O'Keefe remained silent.

Hills of deep green, mottled with rusty patches of dying bracken, clumps of spiny gorse and rock, and studded with grazing sheep, rose gently on both sides of the boreen. Halfway up the hill to the west were the abandoned remains of a small cottage, most of the structure's rotting thatched roof collapsed inwards.

'There! Down from the cottage, there.'

O'Keefe saw it a second after Keane did. Rumour become truth, some two hundred yards up the hill to the west, to the left of the ruin. The sheer, fleshy whiteness of it. The black, rifling attention of crows.

The soldiers followed Keane's pointed finger, one or two taking up their rifles, assuming the young constable had spotted a sniper or party of ambushers. O'Keefe reached over into the cab, tapped the Crossley driver's shoulder and the Tender squeaked to a halt. The men jumped off the tailgate, leaping over the ditch at the edge of the narrow track, fanning out in rough, defensive positions.

O'Keefe followed them down from the Crossley and paused behind it, studying the landscape. It was an odd place to dump a body, he thought, even if it was left as bait for an ambush. The only places an attack could come from were the ruined cottage or the hilltop, where there was a ruck of wind-worn boulders that could act as a firing position. He would be exposed while he did his examination of the scene, but O'Keefe had seen far better ambush sites: bodies laid at bends in roads bordered by high blackthorn hedges and dry-stone walls; bodies left in front of derelict buildings, darkened windows nesting snipers. This felt different. He waved over the Essex Lance Corporal in charge of the escort. The man came slowly, ducking low in the ditch but in no hurry. He was a hard-looking man, a tracery of fine white scarring on one side of his face. O'Keefe guessed this wasn't his first war.

'The boulders there, and the ruins ...' O'Keefe pointed. 'Can you send a few lads up to clear them? Maybe leave two in wide positions and a couple with the Lewis gun on the Tender. Doesn't feel like an ambush, but ...' he felt a fool saying it, 'better safe than sorry.'

The Lance Corporal looked as if he might disagree, then shrugged and bellowed four names. The men received their orders and began to trudge up the hill while the Corporal set his remaining squad in positions facing north and south, up and down the boreen, with two men manning a Lewis machine-gun on the Crossley's bonnet.

A breeze cooled the damp wool of O'Keefe's bottle-green uniform. Gooseflesh dimpled his back. Constable Keane jogged over and squatted beside him, gently setting an oiled leather camera case on the grass at the ditch's rim. Not every murder scene in Ireland was photographed, but it was becoming increasingly common. Juries and coroner's courts were requesting photographic evidence on a regular basis and O'Keefe, a keen amateur photographer, could not imagine examining a crime scene – particularly a murder – without his Kodak Box Brownie.

'Will we head up, Sergeant?'

'No,' O'Keefe said. 'Wait 'til those boys clear the area. The body's not going anywhere.'

Keane nodded, rummaging in his trouser pocket for a tattered paper bag of sweets. He held it out to O'Keefe, who shook his head.

'Queer spot to leave it, all the same,' the young constable said, palming sweets into his mouth and returning the bag to his pocket. 'Have to lug the body a fair stretch to get it up there. And left in full view of the whole valley.'

'No sense plugging someone if others can't learn from it.'

O'Keefe watched as the Essex scouts disappeared into the derelict cottage halfway up the hill. Moments later they re-emerged, signalling an all clear and O'Keefe continued to track them as they climbed towards the boulders at the hilltop, the soldiers moving in a loose group of four instead of spreading out and working around from each side of the crest. They ambled, upright, Enfields held loosely at their hips. Like Sunday hillwalkers, O'Keefe thought. Too young to have fought in the war or they'd know better. 'Where's Logan?' he asked.

Keane nodded back towards the Crossley. Constable Logan was leaning up against the lorry's bonnet, pipe stem wedged in his mouth under the cover of a thick, white moustache. O'Keefe didn't need to see his mouth to know that he was yarning to the soldiers. It was what Logan did. The man could talk paint off walls.

O'Keefe could hardly believe the old constable hadn't taken a bullet since the Troubles had started. Logan was from a different age of policing in Ireland. A time when a constable stopped for a natter with the people he served, for a hand or two of cards with the bachelor farmer, a short whiskey on a cold night patrol, a mug of tea and a look-in at the dairyman's newborn calf. Now, O'Keefe reflected, we travel in packs and kick in the dairymen's doors and hunt down their sons, while their sons hunt us. Logan had taught O'Keefe a lot of what had been good about the job in the days before the killing had started. He decided to leave him where he was, hoping that Logan would hear the shooting, if there was any, over the sound of his own voice.

The four Essexes reappeared from behind the boulders and again signalled the all clear.

'Right so, Constable.' O'Keefe rose stiffly from the ditch.

Keane picked up the camera case and took long strides up the hill, boots pressing a trail in the damp grass for O'Keefe to follow. As they climbed, O'Keefe took note of the ascent and estimated the distance from the Crossley to the body. The gradient of the hillside was enough to make a reasonably fit man break into a sweat. A fitter man than himself, he thought, the scar on his face tensing with the effort of the climb. He rubbed it with his palm. Like the Lance Corporal, O'Keefe had his own curio from the war: a dark-pink rope of knotted tissue, from under his right eye down to his neck. It played up when he was under physical or mental strain. If RIC regulations had permitted, he would have grown a beard to cover as much of it as he could. Instead, he wore a thick brown moustache, in a vain attempt to distract from what the war had left etched into his skin.

'It's a fair climb, Sergeant.'

Keane was only twenty-two years old, a Donegal lad, six months in the police. He had sharp blue eyes, sandy blond hair under his peaked uniform cap and the wispy beginnings of his own *de rigueur* RIC moustache. He was an athletic, handsome, if shorter, version of the thousands of men who had clamoured to join the RIC for over a century. When the IRA had begun shooting RIC men, recruitment to the constabulary had understandably dropped. Out of necessity, age-old standards for height, girth, reading, writing and arithmetic had been relaxed, allowing men under five foot nine, such as Keane, to enlist.

'It is,' O'Keefe answered. 'You'd reckon more than one to do the job – to haul it up there.'

'And a motor,' Keane said, 'or an ass and cart to get the body up the boreen. Sure, the village there …' the constable turned back from his climbing and pointed south-eastwards, 'must be a mile or more away.'

O'Keefe stopped and looked. The hamlet was clearly visible from where they stood on the hill.

'Drumdoolin,' he said. 'Two of our lads were killed just outside it on cycle patrol last summer. O'Rourke and Cotton – good Cons, God rest them.' *Con*. RIC slang for constable. O'Keefe had heard that *con* was short for convict in America. He enjoyed the irony. 'They boarded up Drumdoolin barracks shortly after. Divvied up the men between Bandon barracks and ourselves. IRA burned the shell of it last Easter.'

Keane shook his head but wasn't surprised. It was all in the run of things for new RIC men and the rabble of Black and Tans brought in from across the water. Barrack mates shot in the face from behind stone walls, their guns and ammunition taken while they lay twitching and bleeding on the road. Men kidnapped from dance halls and executed by moonlight, their bodies dumped in bog holes or left on the wet cobbles of town squares as a warning to prospective recruits to the constabulary. Keane had never known West Cork when it wasn't a place hated and feared by policemen.

Peeler

'You think the body had anything to do with the village?' Keane asked, turning back and continuing to climb.

O'Keefe shrugged and followed. 'If it did, we'll probably never find out. Sure, murder's as common as rain round here these days. And no one knows anything about it, even when they do.'

They reached the body and several crows flapped and rose from it, angry at the intrusion. Even then, it appeared as if one had refused to flee its roost on the body's mid-section. *Odd colouring for a crow*, O'Keefe thought, or maybe it was a different bird altogether. Only as he moved closer could he see that it was not a bird covering the young girl's hips and thighs.

Keane blessed himself. 'Jesus *wept*. Look at her ...' He swallowed. 'Are those ... feathers?' The young constable turned then and vomited into a scrag of heather.

While Keane finished retching, wiping his mouth with the sleeve of his tunic, O'Keefe reflected on his own reaction to the body. He felt a general, detached sense of sorrow and with this, a rising anger at the way the body of the young woman had been abandoned to the elements, but none of the horror he knew he should feel. In the war he had seen so much death in so many of its manifestations that it had ceased to shock him. Bodies turning to mush at his feet. Bits of shattered bodies leathering under a relentless Turkish sun. The body of his own brother floating face down in the water of a Turkish tide.

But Keane hadn't been to the war and O'Keefe wasn't sure if the lad had been present at any of the recent shootings in the district. It was possibly the first time Keane had been close to a life destroyed by violence.

'Are you all right?'

Keane nodded and spat, turning away from the body.

'If you feel poorly again, just head back down the hill. I can't have the area disturbed by outside elements. Understood, Constable?'

'I'm all right, Sergeant.'

O'Keefe turned his focus to the victim. She lay on her back, naked and white against the grass, arms out as if awaiting an embrace, her legs spread wide, bent at the knees. Across her chest a crude sign on a piece of plank read *TRATOR*, the letters rendered in what appeared to be tar or black paint. O'Keefe crouched down and carefully lifted the plank. Under it, the right breast was missing. There was a similar gaping wound where the left breast should have been, but there was no blood on the body, almost as if it had been washed. Probably by the rain, O'Keefe reckoned and wondered how long it had been on the hill. There didn't appear to be too much bloating, in the abdomen in particular, indicating sluggish decomposition or recent death. However, it had been cold the past few days, particularly at night. On the hillside, here, it would be colder again. There was no way of estimating time of death, O'Keefe realised, until the surgeon did the post-mortem. He lowered the sign and took in the girl's face.

The crows had been at her eyes and there was a pulpy mess around the sockets. There was also some wounding to the lips which O'Keefe assumed the birds had done, but could have happened during the violence that led to her death. Despite the injuries to the face, O'Keefe could tell that this had once been a beautiful young woman. She had a full mouth, straight white teeth, an upturned nose, long, dark lashes on her one undamaged eyelid, and a smattering of dark freckles on her high cheekbones. Her thick, brown hair was spread out around her head, a few stray strands around her forehead shifting in the gentle wind. He estimated her age to be late teens or early twenties.

There was no sign of discarded clothing in the immediate area and it struck O'Keefe that the body had been deliberately arranged this way. Too much care had been taken in the positioning to be the random work of gravity or rigor mortis. The pose reminded him of the French picture postcards of whores or North African harem girls that soldiers had bought and traded during the war.

O'Keefe lowered his gaze. The hips and pelvic area of the body were painted with tar and carefully covered with a profusion of feathers. At first glance these appeared to lend an element of modesty to the body, except that, on closer inspection, O'Keefe realised that the victim's genitalia had been left open and exposed. *Left on display*, O'Keefe thought, stooping to examine more closely for obvious signs of sexual assault and finding none apparent.

'She's been tarred and feathered?' Keane's voice was a welcome intrusion.

'She has, but not in any way I've seen before.'

O'Keefe recalled other women he had attended in the district who had been tarred and feathered by the IRA. It was usually a slapdash affair – the woman held down while scalding tar was smeared onto her skin. Handfuls of feathers were then scattered over her as she writhed in pain. And almost always, the woman had her head shaved, marking her as a 'whore of the Crown' for having the audacity to keep company with soldiers or policemen. No, he thought, this was something different from the common branding of a woman as a collaborator or spy, despite the feathering and the crude sign laid over her chest. Informers were often shot and 'labelled'. *Spies and Traitors Beware. SPY – Shot by Order of the IRA.* O'Keefe had seen the signs before, but never misspelled.

He squatted again and placed his hands under the young woman's left shoulder, lifting the body slightly, noting the purple stippling of the skin on her back, buttocks and the backs of her thighs. He made a note in his diary to ask the surgeon about this at the post-mortem, but he was fairly certain that this indicated that the young woman had been left on her back in the hours immediately following death. It would also mean that the body had been posed as it was after rigor mortis had left it. Otherwise there would have been greater evidence of lividity in the lower calves and heels owing to the downward slope of the hill. Pure speculation, of course. He would have to wait for confirmation. Before the shooting war had started, a doctor would have attended the scene of a murder, along with the assigned investigators. Now, O'Keefe thought, there was no doctor in the whole of County Cork who would risk his life to attend such a scene.

Letting his eyes scan back up the body, O'Keefe noted a single pearl earring worn in the left ear and the ugly, purple-brown bruising around the girl's throat. At least he wouldn't need to wait for the post-mortem to determine cause of death. Asphyxiation by manual strangulation. The wounding to the breasts, he guessed, had been done after death. O'Keefe formed the assumption that the girl hadn't been killed on the hillside since there were no marks in the earth around the body. Throttling someone to death was a brutal act, requiring strength and a relentless commitment. O'Keefe had seen it in the war and shuddered at the memory. Ammunition spent, bayonets still sheathed, men battering and strangling each other as if to repudiate all the savage advances of modern warfare. No, he decided – and scratched it into his diary – the girl had been killed elsewhere and brought to the hillside.

He stood and climbed to the ruins of the cottage, some twenty-five yards away. Grey stone showed through the time-faded whitewash and O'Keefe had to stoop to enter the abandoned dwelling. Inside, he stayed to the left of the empty doorframe where roughly half of the thatched roof remained standing. Even in the gloom he could see fresh ashes in the fireplace and, in a corner, a makeshift table of rotting planks set on rocks from the crumbling wall. There was staining on the table, but it was difficult to tell what it was. Blood? He didn't think there was enough of it to be from the girl, even if she had been mutilated after she was strangled. And there was no sign of any tar, feathers or a bird carcass in the room. Even if the killer had done his work here, foxes and the wind would have carried away any trace of the birds used; the tar, he imagined, the killer would have carried away in the bucket or tin in which he had brought it. O'Keefe imagined the cottage was used by local farmers as a shelter while they were tending their sheep and that there was no way of knowing if the murder had been committed within, but he decided to photograph the interior anyway, just to be safe. He had worked seconds and thirds on several murders in the past year and a half, but had never worked lead. He would cover his tracks. Photograph and measure, note anything and everything. Catch the devil in the detail.

Returning to the body, he entered its location, the time of its discovery and the constables present at the scene in his diary, making a note to get the name of the Lance Corporal and his men later. Then he drafted a description of the body, making careful mention of the tar and feathering and the misspelled sign, the bruising at the throat and the deliberate pose. He described the body as facing east, towards the village of Drumdoolin. Without looking up, he asked Keane to get the tape wheel and measure off the distance from the boreen to the body and then from the body to the cottage.

About ten yards down the hill, Keane stopped and turned back.

'Sergeant, do you think I should get a blanket from the Tender to cover her up? It doesn't seem right, her being … left out like that.'

The young constable rose in O'Keefe's estimation.

'You're right. Get a blanket from the medic's kit. We'll cover her after I'm done with the photographs.'

Keane nodded and jogged down the hill to the Crossley.

O'Keefe knelt beside the body and unpacked the camera. As he stood up, he had the uneasy sensation that he was being watched. He glanced down the hill at the Tender. The Essexes had stood down and were eating tinned rations and smoking around the Crossley. None of them paid him any heed. Unable to shake off the feeling, he looked up to the boulders at the crest of the hill. Above them slate-coloured clouds lowered in the sky, shunting, reshaping, exposing the odd blast of blue. He noticed a lone kestrel suspended on a shaft of wind, hunting, and remembered the old saying: *Long before you've seen the kestrel, the kestrel has seen you.* He gave the surrounding hills a final scan and saw nothing to account for his unease. Sudden motion. O'Keefe's gaze shot back to the kestrel, the bird dropping from the sky on its prey like a mortar round, and ascending again, something small and dead in its talons.

———

With the Lance Corporal's reluctant help, O'Keefe had the body carried down the hill on a litter and organised a search of the hillside and boreen. He watched as the cold, tired soldiers lolled through the task in the desultory manner he had expected. Shaggy-fleeced sheep oversaw the search impassively until the soldiers came too close, then scattered, trotting a few yards away to safety.

As they began loading the body onto the Crossley for the return to barracks, it suddenly became apparent how it had been brought to the hillside. Logan spotted it first. Not wanting to have anything to do with the body, he had strolled some yards away from the Tender and was filling his pipe when he saw the tracks.

He called O'Keefe over. 'You might want a gander at this.'

Logan pointed to the side of the path, fifty feet behind the Tender. The earth in the ditch was churned and scraped from its bottom to its rim in two parallel strips. O'Keefe could picture the scene. A motor car, attempting to turn on the narrow path, its rear wheels rolling back into the rain-soaked depression; the driver spinning the wheels in an attempt to free the car but succeeding only in burying the wheels deeper into the soft, boggy earth. And on the opposite rim of the ditch, there were footprints, the earth heel-gouged where someone – the killer, O'Keefe would swear it was him – had attempted to shove the car free. The footprints, however, were indistinct, the topsoil too loose and loamy to hold a good impression.

It was Logan again who spotted how the car had been shifted. 'See here, Seán, how they done it, got the motor out.'

Clear as day, O'Keefe thought. The car's wheels spinning away the covering of loose earth on the rim of the ditch and digging down to the thick, black mud beneath. Impressed in this mud was the perfect negative image of a slat of wood. O'Keefe thought of the scraps of wood in the ruined cottage and the crude sign on the girl's chest. Or perhaps the killer had the wood in the car already. It was common enough for motorists, particularly those outside the cities, to carry a plank or two of wood in the boot to aid them in their negotiation of the largely unpaved, and often muddy, roads of rural Ireland. Here, the wood had been placed under one wheel – there was only evidence on one of the two tracks – to give enough traction for the car to get over the rim of the ditch. The forward momentum would have taken care of the rest.

Logan's blue eyes smiled and his privet hedge of a moustache moved around his pipe stem. O'Keefe called to Keane.

'Keane, get the camera kit. We need a shot or two of this.'

The Essexes chorused a groan and lit cigarettes, slumping to the ground, reluctant to climb into the Crossley with the body until it was necessary. O'Keefe ignored them. He smiled back at Logan, the scar on his face tensing, something savage in the smile underneath the fleeting joy of discovery.

The Crossley drew up in front of the barracks in fading daylight. Some fool of an official in Dublin Castle had been quoted in the *Cork Examiner* some months previously as saying that Ballycarleton RIC barracks was 'as near to impregnable as any barracks in Ireland'. O'Keefe was sceptical of the claim and glad that it had yet to be tested.

It was situated to the north of the town, on Macroom Street, between a feed warehouse and grazing fields owned by the local creamery. Across the rain-softened road from the barracks – a wide stretch with a water pump, trough and hitching post for horses in its centre – was the normal array of businesses found in any small Irish town: five pubs, a draper's shop, grocery, solicitor's office, newsagent's, undertaker, cabinet maker, petrol pump and garage. A redbrick hotel built in 1904 towered above these establishments at the end of the thoroughfare.

The barracks building was a sturdy, two-storey house set back from the road, with an attached yard, purchased for the RIC from the widow of a cattle dealer in 1886. There was room in the barracks for ten police to work and be billeted comfortably. At present, twenty-four men – a district inspector, head constable, two sergeants, nineteen constables and Tans, and a retired constable – resided in the building.

Until Easter 1919, the building had been recognisable as a former domestic dwelling. It was built of solid grey stone, fitted with three windows on the first floor and two on the ground floor flanking the main entrance. However, recent events had transformed it into a fortress. Its windows were closed over with steel shutters, the outside world visible only through firing slits, called loopholes. A section of roof had been cut away and sandbagged so that a Lewis machine-gun could be fired from the barracks' highest vantage point in the attic. The front garden was a tangle of barbed wire choked with ragwort and overgrown bramble.

The main access to the barracks was through a solid steel gate operated by an armed sentry in a sandbagged post. This gate opened onto a yard of worn cobbles, the whole of which was enclosed by a ten-foot-high brick wall, festooned with more barbed wire. To the rear of the yard and forming the back wall, original cowsheds and stables had been converted into a garage, a cottage billet for two constables and a cold storage room for meat and produce. The cold storage room contained a recently installed refrigeration unit, paid for out of the District Inspector's family coffers. It was here O'Keefe intended to place the body of the young woman until the post-mortem.

The Crossley driver blasted the horn three times and waited. O'Keefe jumped off the tailgate and approached the sandbagged sentry post, finding it deserted. He slipped his baton from his belt and rapped on the gate, making sure he was covered by the bulk of the rumbling Crossley. As he waited, O'Keefe turned and cast an anxious glance at the row of houses and shops some fifty yards across the road. A lone, tethered horse dipped its head in the public trough. A woman carrying a basket of groceries hustled past the back of the Tender, avoiding his gaze. Dusk had arrived and there was a damp chill in the air.

O'Keefe's muscles tensed and his heartbeat jabbed at his ribs. He banged on the gate again, then slipped his baton back into his belt. He unholstered his Webley revolver, keeping it low at his thigh, and decided that he would have to discommode the soldiers once again. Approaching the passenger side of the Crossley cab, he asked the Lance Corporal to deploy his section about the Tender. The Lance Corporal smiled and elbowed the Crossley driver. Turning back to O'Keefe he said: 'Why don't you ask them your fucking self, Sergeant?'

O'Keefe ordered the men out of the Tender. The men groused and swore, and one of them flicked a cigarette end dangerously close to O'Keefe's face as he turned away from the back of the lorry. He would never find the man who had done it, but some bastard, he thought, was going to pay for the vacant sentry post. O'Keefe drew his baton again and beat a tattoo on the steel. He checked the road behind him for a second time, half-expecting a sniper's bullet to snap out from behind lace curtains through the waning light.

Keane appeared delighted with the chance to heft a loaded weapon in earnest and was hunkered down behind one of the Tender's wheels. His special model RIC Lee-Enfield carbine was raised to his shoulder, aimed now at the windows across the muddy street, now at the horse lifting its head from drinking, hot breath streaming from its nostrils. Logan stood upright, lazily resting his carbine on the bonnet of the Tender while he continued a one-sided conversation concerning race-fixing in his home county of Mayo with a young, nervous-looking squaddie. O'Keefe slammed again on the shutter, thinking how Logan wouldn't have lasted a hot minute in the war for all his blather.

'Get the head down, Logan.'

Logan waved O'Keefe's words away with his pipe stem. 'Ah sure, we're grand as we are, Seán.'

'That's an order.'

O'Keefe turned and was about to approach the front door of the barracks when the grating of metal hasps and lifting bolts stopped him, and the gate creaked open on its hinges under the power of a Black and Tan constable named Finch. O'Keefe waited until the Tender and the men were safely inside and the gates locked shut, watching as Finch accepted a light for his cigarette from one of the Essex soldiers. There was nothing approaching contrition or shame about the man. O'Keefe stepped forward, rage charging his blood. 'You,' he said to the Essex, 'help them with the body.'

Finch raised his eyebrows at the soldier and turned lazily towards O'Keefe.

'Where were you, Constable?' O'Keefe asked. 'We were in full view in the street for the last five minutes.'

Finch let smoke trail from a half-smile. He had a hard, thin face, dark eyes and at least two days of sandy stubble on his jaw. He was of average height – several inches shorter than O'Keefe – and on the thin side, but possessed the wiry strength and speed of a boxer. O'Keefe had often seen him sparring with his mates in the courtyard and had been grudgingly respectful.

'I was in the jakes if you must know,' Finch said. His accent was heavy Cockney. 'Sitting out 'ere on watch and nowhere for a man to shite. Do me a favour, mate. And nobody fucking came when I called 'em.'

O'Keefe noted the man's uniform tunic was unbuttoned at the neck and dusted with cigarette ash. The Black and Tans wore the regular, dark-green uniforms of the RIC, but had acquired their name when they had arrived eight months earlier and there had been a shortage of full police uniforms. They had been kitted out with surplus army khaki tunics and RIC bottle-green trousers or, in some cases, the reverse. Some wit in Limerick had noted the similarity they bore to a local pack of hunting dogs – the Black and Tans – and they had been graced with the name. Many of these men – from England, Scotland and Wales – were war veterans. They had probably been brave soldiers, a credit to the Crown. It didn't make them good police constables. Not by a long shot. Most Irish RIC men reckoned the Limerick hounds would have served better.

O'Keefe holstered his Webley, deliberately fastening shut the holster's clasp, unsure of what he might do if the gun was in his hand. 'You're aware, Constable, that in the army you'd be shot for quitting your post?'

Finch dragged on his cigarette and exhaled a thin stream of smoke. O'Keefe noticed Logan and Keane and some of the soldiers from the Tender gathered on the cobbles to watch the dressing down. Finch appraised the crowd as well and smiled like a music hall man on the verge of a dirty punchline.

'And *you're* aware, mate, this ain't the bloody army …'

O'Keefe threw a sharp jab, crushing the cigarette butt against Finch's lips, sparks showering the Tan's tunic, the *thap* of knuckles on flesh and bone and tooth. Finch staggered back, bumping the sandbagged guard post, knocking down several of the bags, one of them bursting, bleeding sand onto the cobbles. He righted himself, wiping ash and tobacco off his lips, a claret trickle from his upper lip, smiling again, his eyes locked on O'Keefe's. He brushed down his tunic and presented himself in a loose approximation of parade rest. 'Right, Sergeant,' he said. 'Point taken.'

O'Keefe held his gaze on the Tan for a long moment, his right hand on the butt of his Webley, then turned away, confident for the moment that, with the crowd present, he'd be safe enough showing the Tan his back. Over his shoulder he said, 'Refill that bag and replace the others, Constable.'

In reception, O'Keefe greeted the constable on barrack orderly duty – another Tan. He received a grunt in reply, the man never looking up from his days' old copy of the *Sporting News*, his feet propped on a chair in front of the fire. O'Keefe considered hauling the man up but left it, stepping behind the reception desk and reflecting that, for all the fortress-like exterior that was Ballycarleton barracks, there was a paper thin structure within. Discipline and morale, once two words synonymous with the RIC – making it the model for police forces from Canada to Burma – had descended to the point where guard posts were left idle and sergeants thumped constables in full view of other men. His own morale, he thought, was hardly model, his discipline more habit than virtue. *Discipline.* He laughed to himself, thankful he had managed to avoid cutting his knuckles on Finch's teeth.

In the converted cupboard behind reception, he used the wireless to contact the British naval communications post at Bandon army barracks. They in turn would radio 6th Division HQ at Victoria barracks in Cork city, forwarding on O'Keefe's request for the services of an army surgeon to perform a post-mortem examination on the body. It was an indirect process, but necessary. Dogs in the street knew that the telephone, telegraph and postal services were infested with rebel spies. Telephone operators were demons for gossip at the best of times. Since the shooting had started, this propensity had been pressed into lethal service.

If Liam Farrell had been a better soldier, he never would have become involved in the case of the body found on the hillside.

'You've done fine work in the Newcestown Company, Farrell. Fine work for the Cork 1st as a student as well. Grand fine work. But the flying column is a different pot on the fire.'

Farrell was standing before Tom Barry in the kitchen of the O'Sullivan house. The O'Sullivans were an old republican family in the Ahilina area of West Cork and the elderly Mr O'Sullivan had taken many the whack of an

RIC baton across his skull in the days of the Land League actions of the last century. He had purchased the twenty-acre farm in the acts of redistribution that followed the Land War. Now O'Sullivan allowed the land to be used as a safe house and training camp solely, it seemed to Farrell, for the purpose of having men around to argue with as to who were the greater Irish patriots – O'Sullivan himself and his few remaining Land Leaguer comrades or 'ye new shower of fellas, not having mettle enough to cut down weeds and nettles'. The IRA men who used the house humoured the old man, telling him that things were only getting started; that soon there'd be much cutting done and it wouldn't be nettles falling under the swing of their scythes.

The house served that week as HQ for the 3rd West Cork Brigade IRA flying column training camp. Outside the house Farrell could hear a section of Volunteers marching drill. A lump rose in his throat. The past week he had been among those drilling, listening to lectures on tactics, practising close formation movement and rapid retreat, engaging in mock battles in the hedges, the furious clacking of dry-fired rifles like kindling taking light. It had been a week of what he'd always dreamt of: training to fight for his country, for the freedom of his people. And now it had come to this.

Tom Barry – with his small dark eyes and oiled dark hair unruly on his forehead – served as Training Officer for the 3rd West Cork Brigade. He was in command of the exercise that week, despite the presence in the camp of Charlie Hurley, the Brigade Commandant, and Seán

Brennan, Brigade Intelligence Officer. Both sat with Barry at the table.

Had Farrell been thinking of anything other than his dismissal from flying column duty, he might have wondered about the presence of two high-ranking officers such as Hurley and Brennan, both in attendance at the passing out of a week's training camp. The two of them in the same place at the same time was a risk. Raiding parties of British soldiers had twice come within two miles of the farm in the past week.

'Mr Hurley …'

'Call me Charlie, Liam, for the love of Christ. How long have I known you, boy?'

Hurley smiled at Farrell. He was a kindly man, despite his aggressive reputation, and seemed older than his twenty-eight years, a fine net of wrinkles about his eyes, flecks of grey in his light brown hair.

'Charlie, I've been on two raids already. Ten revolvers, six Enfields and God only knows how many rounds of .303 and .455 from the ambush on that army section. And not a shot fired.'

Barry cut in. 'Probably a good thing that, going by your shooting.'

Hurley smiled benignly at the interjection. Tom Barry was a harsh, intimidating figure. Farrell could picture him in the deserts of Mesopotamia, gutting enemy assassins with a trench knife, boxing street fighters from his regiment. The IRA viewed most former members of the British army as spies, informers. Many were shot and very few were allowed into the ranks of the IRA. Barry had been welcomed with open arms. Admired and feared by those who served with him and those who fought against him, at that moment Farrell felt only hatred for the man.

'I … we all here recognise what you've done as a Volunteer,' Barry continued. 'But I need men who can shoot straight. Even with your specs on, Farrell, you came nowhere near to hitting any of the targets today from any range. Static targets. Sure, what would you do if they were moving?'

Farrell was aware of his failings. His eyesight was poor and he was a slight, unfit twenty-one-year-old. The Lee-Enfield rifle was heavy and seemed a wayward, stubborn weapon for forging a nation. It refused the commands he gave it, kicked and bruised his shoulder, flung lead high and away from the paper targets pinned to hay bales on the firing range. Only four live rounds per man for musketry training. Given more, Farrell felt he would improve.

'Charlie?' Farrell could hear the pleading in his voice and shame warred with the desperation he felt. His face burned with it and tears welled in his eyes.

Seán Brennan, who until now had been a silent observer, spoke. 'You were reading law in Cork, Mr Farrell?'

Compared to the rest of the men, Brennan – in his mid-forties – seemed ancient to Farrell. He had greying hair and the face and solemn demeanour of an undertaker.

'Yes, sir. And I scouted for D Company, 1st Corks while I was at college. I gave up my studies last June to devote myself to the Volunteers. I went back to Newcestown and have been active since.'

Brennan nodded and lifted a paper from the table, appearing to read from it. 'You were in your third year?'

'Yes, sir. But …'

There was a brisk knock on the door. Without waiting for an invitation to enter, two men Farrell had never seen before came into the kitchen. They brought in with them the cold and damp of late November along with an unkempt, wild smell, as if they'd been living rough.

'Jesus, the cold of it. Would you not put on a fire, Tom? You'd think it was bullets you were burning, ye mean bastard ye.' The man shed his filched British army field coat and tossed it over the back of a free chair. He then opened the breach and removed the live round from the box magazine of his Enfield, rolling the .303 round carelessly onto the table in front of Barry.

'See,' he said. 'Nine more in the box. Count 'em if you doubt me.'

Farrell was surprised at the easy familiarity with which the man spoke to Tom Barry. The IRA were more informal about rank and title than a conventional standing army, its members made up of lads who had been friends for years, had played football together, courted one another's sisters and worked one another's farms. Men were democratically elected to lead sections, companies and battalions. The trappings of rank were largely absent, and some officers were even elected out of command if their leadership was found wanting by their men. Still, it was unnerving to Farrell to see the returned stranger so undaunted by Barry.

'It's not bullets, but it's not our peat and coal to burn either, Donal. You need to remember that when you're billeting in the homes of the good people of Ireland, boy.'

The man winked at Hurley across the table. 'Well then, do you think the good people of Ireland would spring for a cup of tae for a man's spent the last two days sprawled out in bog water on a hillside, Tom?'

Hurley cracked a smile. Noticing Farrell, the man called Donal flicked a friendly salute his way. Farrell nodded in response, not feeling part of the banter, already outside it. He watched as the second man carefully removed his trenchcoat and a pair of field glasses from around his neck, hanging them both from a peg on the back of the kitchen door. He removed the live round from his rifle – an American-made P14 Enfield, fitted with a sniper's scope – leaned it against the wall and pulled the last free chair up to the table. 'Tom, Charlie,' he said. 'And *Monsieur* Brennan, still with us thank God. Make us a cup as well, Donal, if you can stop your messing long enough.' He nodded at Farrell.

The first man took the kettle from its hook in the fireplace, testing its heat with his hands. 'Jesus, I'd like to, Mickeen, but you'd be hard pressed to make mud with this.'

Barry sighed and smiled. 'Farrell, would you fetch a few sods for the fire? I think I might just shoot Donal Cahill here if he doesn't get his tea.'

Farrell could have resented the order – one minute, firing

an Enfield on the range and the next, demoted to fetching turf – but the spirit of the times presided against it. The truth was he'd seen Barry himself fetch turf and coal, and make tea for the men. Charlie Hurley was known for giving up his bed to men coming in from a long stretch of scouting.

When he returned to the house, one of the Cumann na mBan girls was cutting thick slices of bread at the sideboard, slathering them with butter from the O'Sullivan's larder. Barry was speaking.

'… and they passed by the same time, each day?'

'Same time, same road,' the man called Mickeen Cope said. 'Two lorryloads. Nine men in each and moving fast.'

'Like hell's own riders, by fuck – sorry Aoife,' Cahill apologised to the young woman.

Farrell placed the turf in a loose pyramid on the fire and stood to leave. He decided on a last appeal. 'Tom, Charlie, I can do another camp.'

Brennan spoke first. 'There'll be no need for that, Liam. We've other things we'll be needing you for, boy. Sit down there and listen.'

Farrell did as he was told while Brennan turned in his chair. 'We'll get our own tea, Aoife. Your mother will thank me some day for sparing your ears the injury.'

When she had gone, the men at the table proceeded to discuss locations, numbers of men and armaments. Farrell remained silent, listening in as the other men finalised plans for an ambush he would never see. When this was done, Brennan turned to Mickeen Cope, holding his heavy-lidded eyes on the scout. 'And what about the other matter?'

Donal Cahill answered. 'It was there all right, like the lad from the poultry house said. On the hillside, a young woman. Not a stitch on and labelled.' He looked at the rising flames of the turf fire. 'We didn't touch her. I couldn't have touched her if the Devil himself had given me the order. I don't know what she done, boy, but it's not right at all, how she –'

Mickeen Cope cut in on Cahill, as if concerned he might say something he shouldn't in front of Brennan and Hurley. 'Peelers arrived shortly after we did. About noon, so my guess is word reached them a day or so after it reached us. They sent a party of tin hats up to the top where we were watching from but they never saw us.'

'You didn't shoot?'

'Thought you wanted all your precious bullets back, Tom,' Donal Cahill said, smiling.

Mickeen Cope shot Cahill a harsh look. 'There were too many of them. The whole area'd be too hot for the job on Sunday if we'd fired on them.'

'How many were there?' Barry asked.

'Three police and eight soldiers. I'd say they reckoned on an ambush. They could barely fit the body in the Tender for all the boys they brought. They were Essex.'

'And the Peelers were from Ballycarleton,' Cahill said. 'I recognised one of them. Lazy auld shite called Logan. Had me up years ago for snipping the tail off the Penforth's bullock in pasture.'

Brennan seemed to consider this, then turned to Hurley. 'Charlie, are we sure none of ours did this?'

Hurley shrugged. 'You're Intelligence, Seán. It's ye root out the touts. Do we even have a name? Know who the girl is … was?'

The two scouts shook their heads. 'No, nor heard a peep.'

Barry addressed Hurley and Brennan. 'We've not shot any women yet, have we? Or do we now? We've been given damn all direction from Dublin on things like this. Forced to make up rules of engagement as we go along. For all we know, some locals heard she was informing and had her shot.'

'She wasn't shot,' Cope said.

'What do you mean?'

'She was strangled, I think. And then she was cut, like.' Mickeen Cope looked away, sipping his tea. He touched his chest to indicate where the young woman had been mutilated.

His partner said, 'Her throat was black and purple with the bruising, so it was. And her … her chest … butchered. None of ours could've done it, I'm telling you. Informer or not, no girl should be left like that.'

Brennan stared at Cahill for a long moment after he'd finished, then turned to Farrell. 'You're to start in Drumdoolin, Liam. Seems the most logical place. They're a useless shower, the Drumdoolin mob, but you never know what some lads might get up to. Talk to O'Higgins, the company commander there. He might know something. See can you get the girl's name at least.'

Donal Cahill pointed at Farrell with a crust of bread. 'And you may ask them lazy *dahs* what in the name of God they're using the six lovely Lee-Enfields we gave them for.'

Hurley and Brennan smiled without warmth.

Farrell moved to speak and Hurley raised his hand to silence him. 'You've always been a clever fella, Liam. You read the papers. The people of the country may want a republic, but they're hardly ready to tolerate strangling young women to get one. Do what Seán says. It's now we need you.'

Brennan took over. 'You'll billet with Stephen McGowan in Ballycarleton. He's a solicitor there and one of ours. Works the republican courts outside of Macroom and Bandon alongside his normal Crown business. You're his new clerk. We'll get you set up with the proper cover tomorrow, the papers and all. The position will give you the freedom of movement you'll need. Report to him after you've seen O'Higgins. Any questions?'

Farrell thought for a moment. 'What do I do if I find out what happened, who killed this girl?'

Brennan looked to Hurley and then back at Farrell. 'Just you get back to us, boy. We'll deal with it from there.'

———

A late dinner of cold beef and potatoes, smeared with a paste of chutney he'd found in a jar in the kitchen, lodged in O'Keefe's stomach like a rebuke. He sat at his desk and lit a Player's cigarette from a dented tin in his drawer, sucking in smoke as if it might calm the foulness brewing inside him.

The letter was waiting for him on his desk. It was his first piece of mail in over a month that wasn't an anonymous death threat or official missive. He picked it up, his stomach seeming to settle in anticipation of reading it. His sister's handwriting.

Posting a letter to a policeman was risky. For writing to your Peeler brother you could be marked as a spy. People had been shot for less. Women tarred and feathered. O'Keefe thought of the body out in the cold storage shed. He stood up from his desk and removed his damp tunic and undervest, pulling on a dry vest and thick cotton shirt.

Two desks took up most of the space in the office, pressed against each other in the middle of what had once served as a child's nursery. Most of one wall to the side of the desks was covered by a cork noticeboard papered with blurry photographs of suspects and a fading, pin-scarred map of West Cork with Ballycarleton district outlined in red wax pencil. There was one window behind O'Keefe's desk, its steel shutters silent now for lack of wind. Ashes were cold in the grate.

It had been three months at least since he'd heard from Sally, his beloved older sister. She was thirty-one to O'Keefe's twenty-nine and a schoolteacher in Balbriggan, County Dublin. The town had been sacked little more than a month before by Auxiliaries and Tans from Gormanstown barracks after a head constable and his brother – a sergeant – had been shot in a pub. O'Keefe had contacted Balbriggan barracks as soon as he had heard and had been assured that the school had escaped the burning and that Sally was fine.

As long as she was safe, the whole of Dublin could burn. He opened the letter carefully.

Dear brother,
I hope this letter finds you well and in good health –

Before he could read further, Sergeant Jim Daly crowded into the office, all bulk, bluster and pipe smoke. 'Well now, Seán. Heard you found a wee girl on your travels.'

Slipping the letter back into its envelope, O'Keefe watched Daly slump into the creaking wooden chair at the desk across from his own. Daly lifted his legs, then dropped his huge boots onto his desk, scattering weekly reports, mess bills and half-read issues of *Hue and Cry* – the constabulary newspaper.

'Nineteen or twenty years old, I'd guess. In a bad way, she was,' O'Keefe said.

O'Keefe had been promoted from the exam pass list to acting sergeant when his predecessor, Sergeant O'Bannion, had been shot and wounded escorting a prisoner to Dublin. He had taken the sergeant's exam before the war, back when he'd thought such things as rank and promotion mattered, and was as surprised as anyone when he'd been conditionally promoted in May 1920. His appointment to acting sergeant was dependent on there being no man of longer service or higher examination score available to take up the post in Ballycarleton. Six months later, O'Keefe was still in the job. No right-minded constable volunteered for a posting in West Cork. No more than they'd volunteer for a bullet.

With the acting sergeant's post came the first-floor office, shared with Sergeant James Patrick Daly. O'Keefe was as tidy as Daly was cluttered, but they had been friends for years, having patrolled the town streets and countryside of the Ballycarleton district before O'Keefe had gone off to the war. They were well used to each other's habits.

Daly shook his head and took out his pipe and tobacco from his tunic. 'Poor thing. There's a line off the wire for you, by the by. Surgeon's coming Sunday. And look at this.' He held out a day-old copy of the English *Daily News*. 'There's one for you now. The boyos are in the shit, so they are. Shot up a heap of His Majesty's horses and donkeys up your way. Ambushed some supply wagons. You'd think the Shinners would've known better. No way at all to conduct a war, plugging drays. God knows the reading public won't like it.'

O'Keefe took the paper from Daly and read the story, then skipped to the editorial. Bad enough, it seemed to say, shooting Peelers and Tommies. Slaying innocent nags and asses was taking the conflict to a new and more barbarous level.

He tossed the paper back onto Daly's desk. 'An *outrage*, I'd say.'

Daly nodded, continuing to pack his pipe with Walnut Plug. 'Should finish the IRA off for good. Lost the war with the reading public right there, the bastards. *Heinous crime.* No army can get on with proper killing with the papers shouting "heinous".'

'*Heinous*,' O'Keefe repeated, thinking how, after the war in Europe, words had no way of matching the things men did and saw. The newspapermen used words they had no right to use. It was almost funny. None of the scribblers had landed on V Beach at Gallipoli. He lit another cigarette. None of the scribblers had seen the brutalised body of a young woman left on a hillside.

He shunted aside the black train of thought and looked over to Daly. 'Have you seen the bossman?'

'I haven't, though I can't say I've looked.'

O'Keefe rose and made his way down the hallway to the District Inspector's office. Walter Masterson was in command of the three remaining barracks in the Ballycarleton district. There had been nine before the Troubles had ignited in earnest, but the more isolated of them had become impossible to defend from attack and had to be absorbed into the larger barracks. Masterson, in turn, was responsible to the County Inspector in Cork city.

The job required that he be out of barracks often, visiting other stations on inspections and supply and manning matters, and reporting on these to the County Inspector. And yet the other two barracks in the district saw about as much of the man as O'Keefe and Daly did. As he'd expected, Masterson was absent from his office and O'Keefe returned to his own.

Daly was leafing through O'Keefe's patrol diary when he returned. 'And you thought there'd be nothing up the hills there at all,' he said.

'Nothing but an ambush. Instead, we found the girl.'

'She was labelled?'

O'Keefe nodded. 'T-R-A-T-O-R'.

Daly exhaled a stream of pipe smoke. 'All the schoolmasters are slinging Lee-Enfields these days. Spelling in this country's going to shite and all for the sake of independence.'

O'Keefe didn't laugh and Daly didn't expect him to.

'The queer thing, though,' O'Keefe said, 'was how she was tarred and feathered. Only round her waist and hips. And left bare, down around her …' He wondered how to put it. It didn't seem right somehow, using any of the common vulgarities and yet, with Daly, it would have been just as odd applying the proper anatomical terms.

'*Country mile?*' Daly said, sliding the patrol diary onto O'Keefe's desk. 'Pair of feather knickers with the important bits missing?' Daly rarely stood on the niceties of language.

'Something like that. It seems too deliberate for your run of the mill "out the tout" job. The girl wasn't shot, not that I could see. Throttled, it looked like. We'll know for sure come Sunday, I suppose.'

'Shinners are short of .303, so they say. Maybe she wasn't worth the bullet?'

O'Keefe considered it. 'But she was worth strangling and butchering and stripping naked? Worth setting up on a hillside like a dirty picture?'

'They're not all monkish types, the Shinners. Sure, it's well known there's a few priests among them and, Lord knows, them padres do be up to all sorts.'

Daly went to Mass with his wife and children any Sunday he could get home. And when he couldn't get away, he attended in Ballycarleton, no matter that an RIC man had been shot entering church five miles away in Bandon just two months earlier. He was as devout a Catholic as O'Keefe was an atheist, but could never resist a jibe at the priests of the country. O'Keefe imagined that Daly confessed the jibes to his own priest, just for the opportunity to repeat them. A low-minded chuckle was always worth a few laps round the Rosary or the odd Act of Contrition.

'Jesus, Jim. Only you'd find a way to link the priesthood to a sex crime.'

And as he spoke, O'Keefe became convinced that what they were dealing with was just such a crime. Yes, the young woman might have been murdered for some political reason, some real or imagined slight against the Volunteers. She may have stepped out with a soldier or been seen coming out of an RIC barracks. Perhaps leaving a dancehall on a constable's arm. But whoever had done the killing had done it in a sexualised way and O'Keefe was willing to bet he had enjoyed it.

———

As a child he'd been told his father was away at the war, fighting the boars. He used to picture him in thick forest, fending off the charging beasts, tusks bared, his father with cutlass and revolver drawn. Like the picture on the painted sign hanging over the door of the Boar's Head tavern.

His father had been gone for less than a month when it started. At first, his mother used to ask him to go out and play while she and her friend talked about grown-up things. New friends, always with a bottle of something. Soldiers in uniform. Officers, gentlemen, some of them, she told him once, her new friends. Soon she began to forget about him, outside, alone in the dark and he took to sleeping in the hen shed when his mother entertained her friends. He found comfort there. Comfort in the musty, uric smell, in the guttural clucking and dry scratching of the birds. And there was fascination. Eggs dropping from the hens' backsides, stretching the skin, pushed into the world under a garland of feathers.

Saturday
27 November 1920

O'Keefe had slept fitfully, his usual nightmares infused with images of the dead girl on the hill. He rose finally – a fleeting ray of sunshine slicing through the firing slit in the steel-shuttered window – his fatigue bringing with it the resignation he felt about most things since his return from the war, the black cloud of negativity that blotted out hope. That cloud had momentarily broken the previous day, had been blown away by the anger he'd felt for the girl on the hill. But it was back now, sheer habit and force of will the only things driving him to complete his duties in the barracks and then set out for the village of Drumdoolin.

The village sat at the foot of the hills they had searched the day before, hunkering in a valley and bordered by the Bandon river. It was a republican stronghold according to intelligence reports, boasting an active IRA company. To date, none of the company had been lifted for anything other than questioning, indicating that they were either very good or very lucky. Still, as O'Keefe approached the first of the village's two pubs, he wished he'd brought more men with him.

Constable Aaron Senior, DI Masterson's batman, was more suited to parade and inspection than a scrap, and O'Keefe had been surprised when he'd volunteered to accompany him that morning. Thin, tidy, with dark hair and eyes, a weak, carefully shaven chin and a thin moustache, Senior was a cadet constable, a young man from a landed family accepted directly into the RIC as an officer. He was currently serving as a constable and would remain so until a head constable's post became vacant. In the current climate,

O'Keefe didn't imagine it would be long before one came up, if the DI was willing to let go of his personal valet. Rumour had it their fathers were members of the same club up in Dublin. O'Keefe accepted Senior's offer to accompany him because he couldn't think of a valid reason not to.

Also in attendance were Keane and Logan, who were waiting by the Ford in uniform, carbines hanging lazily over their forearms. O'Keefe paused before he entered the pub – O'Neills it said over the low door, in faded lettering under a moss-coated thatch. He sensed no danger on the bright Saturday morning. A scan of the street: barefoot children kicking a football against the gable end of the pub, women chatting in open doorways as they swept the steps of their cottages, another carrying a basket of eggs covered in a tea-towel, men leaning on gates, smoking pipes. All of them ignored Logan and Keane.

In the end, it took him less than five minutes. His questions about the girl on the hillside resulted in one verbal response, from the publican himself – a balding man in a stained shirt and collar. 'And what girl would that be you're talking of, Sergeant? Sure, we've heard of none of our girls dead and lying in the grass.'

Back in the Ford, Constable Senior said, 'They were lying I suppose?'

O'Keefe shrugged as Keane cranked the hand starter and the car coughed into life. Senior studied him. 'Do you really think there's any way to tell if people like these are lying or telling the truth. I hardly think they know themselves.'

Keane climbed into the Ford and they pulled away from the pub, O'Keefe chewing over the meaning of Senior's words: *people like these.* He could taste the disdain. To Constable Senior, 'people like these' were as distantly related to a man like himself as the apes of Africa. And by association, so were O'Keefe, Keane and Logan. Catholic. Irish. The IRA were fighting attitudes such as Senior's every bit as much as they were fighting the reality of British rule. Their struggle was as much about equality as it was about independence. And where did that leave Catholic, Irish RIC men? It left them as targets, O'Keefe reckoned, as if every dead constable would make any single Irishman more equal, more free.

———

When Major Thomas Mathew-Pare first met 'O', the man was performing surgery on a horse.

A chap Mathew-Pare had met in the Dublin Castle officers' mess – a secret serviceman he'd crossed paths with in Palestine – had commented that O bore a striking resemblance to a little, wicked, white snake. The secret serviceman had also told him that Ormonde had chosen his own codename on his arrival in Dublin. They'd had a good laugh at that one. O for Ormonde. Ormonde de l'Epeé Winter, an artillery man made Chief of Combined Intelligence Services. It seemed a proper War Office plan. When intel had dried up in Ireland to the point of being non-existent, appoint an artillery man to run the show. Nothing surprised Mathew-Pare any more.

He had been summoned to Dublin Castle from where he had been staying for the last week in Beggar's Bush barracks, keeping the head down, doing a spot of interrogation work for the Auxiliaries in return for their hospitality. The Auxies had got their claws into one of Mick Collins' shooters, a lad who'd been involved in the massacre of Crown intelligence men the previous Sunday. At present the prisoner was being rested for further questioning.

A young officer dressed in riding gear greeted Mathew-Pare at the entrance to the Castle stables.

'Sir,' the officer said, 'would you be so kind …' The man sounded worried. 'Are you here to see the Colonel? Would you be so kind as to enquire after Milly, sir? My mount. She's been in surgery for hours now and the Colonel insisted he knew what ailed her.'

Mathew-Pare gave the man a kindly smile and assured him that he would enquire.

Inside the stables, O had his shirtsleeves rolled up. He had supplemented the weak electric lights in the stables with several lanterns strategically placed around the stall where he was working. There was a stink of blood, paraffin and fresh bedding hay. O didn't look up when he spoke. One of his hands held a surgical clamp, the other was inside the horse's abdomen. 'One of Henry Wilson's boys, eh? I thought you lot caught a packet last Sunday, courtesy of Mr Collins.'

Michael Collins' Squad – his 'Twelve Apostles' – had put the lights out on most of them that Sunday. Seven members of Mathew-Pare's Cairo Gang had been killed. They didn't get all of them, though. Mathew-Pare and two others had been too good for even Collins and his boys. Later that day the Auxiliaries had killed fourteen spectators at a football match in Croke Park. It was claimed the dead were IRA men. Not that anyone, anywhere, believed that they were.

'Not all of us, sir.'

'I'd heard you're a canny one.' He twisted the clamp within the horse's belly.

'Lucky, sir. Allow me to introduce …'

'One moment.'

O reached his hand further inside the horse. His forearms were coated with blood. Mathew-Pare watched as he released the clamp and shifted it within the horse's belly.

Milly was laid on her side, an impressive bay, a noble splash of white on her brow. One of her hind legs was raised and suspended by a rope and pulley, allowing O access to her innards. She was a cavalry horse, Mathew-Pare assumed, having met her master outside – one of the army's ornaments. Trench warfare had put paid to the notion of any more horses fighting His Majesty's battles. Bit of a bother, sending a horse over the top of a trench.

'There,' O said. 'No need for introductions. Wilson recommended you personally. Had a gander at your file.'

O continued to focus on his task, applying a spreader to the incision, cigarette lodged between his lips, a monocle in his right eye, squinting through the smoke with his left. He was a small, wiry sort, with thinning blond hair, a sharp nose and light-blue, hooded eyes. A wicked white snake. Mathew-Pare smiled to himself. 'Very good, sir.'

'Nasty business, last week,' O said. 'Bloody Sunday they're calling it. Two fine men from the Royal Veterinary Corps caught it as well. Bloody shame. Shinner Intelligence not up to much, shooting vets in hotel beds.'

'No, sir,' Mathew-Pare said, thinking that Shinner Intelligence must be up to something, having plugged ten Crown spooks in *their* beds along with the vets. He kept this to himself. Instead: 'I wasn't aware of your skills in the surgical line, sir.'

'Not many are. Bit of a hobby, veterinary medicine. Pastime, if you like. Came in handy in India.'

'I'm sure it did, sir.'

O worked in silence for some minutes before speaking again. 'Thought you'd be best for the job, Mathew-Pare. Hush, hush job for the "hush, hush men".' He laughed through his nose, adjusting the spreader and widening the incision.

'Job, sir?'

'Yes,' O said. 'Not, however, what you might think. Bit of a cushy number this. None of your more sinister skills needed I shouldn't think.'

'Glad to hear it, sir.'

'There's been a small problem. Some bint, apparently. Isn't it always? Found dead in the county of Cork. Most likely the Shinners. In fact, let's just say it *was* the Shinners.' O looked at Mathew-Pare for the first time since he'd entered the stables, light reflecting in the monocle.

'Shinners it was, sir.'

'Kind of thing that would play well on the mainland, don't you think?'

Mathew-Pare rode along with O's line of argument. 'Certainly would, sir. Play well, indeed.'

'The "Murder Gang" angle pleases readers – notwithstanding the *Manchester Guardian*'s view of things. Republican army? Rebels? Bloody corner boys with stolen Webleys, more like.'

'Couldn't agree with you more, sir. One outrage after another.'

'Throttled the poor bitch to death. Cut off her tits. Poor gal left stark naked on a hillside. Sinn Féin outrage, I'd say.'

'*Sensational* outrage, sir. And do we have any particular Shinners in mind?'

'Any will do, just so long as it's them. I've arranged for you to be assigned to the investigation. There's a young acting sergeant in charge at the moment. Make sure he gets his man, will you?'

'Yes, sir.'

O grunted and reached once again into the horse's abdomen.

'I don't …' he laboured inside the horse, '… need to stress … the importance of this, do I, Major?'

'No, sir.'

With a clamp in his free hand, O reached deeper into the beast, twisting, manipulating. The clamp snapped shut, making an audible 'click' inside the horse. O carefully withdrew his hands, slick with blood, and stood back to admire his work.

'There,' he said. 'That should about do it, eh?'

Mathew-Pare watched as the abdominal incision distended slightly, then widened as the spreader lost its hold, and the horse's intestines spilled out in a steaming mass onto the hay-covered floor, sliding over and around O's feet. The horse began to convulse, its eyes rolling in their sockets. Soon the animal went limp, expelling a last wheezing breath.

'Will there be anything else, sir?'

Ormonde de l'Epée Winter dismissed him with a bloody wave of his hand.

Outside the stables, Milly's master accosted Mathew-Pare once again. 'Milly, sir. Did you …'

Mathew-Pare couldn't help himself. 'Milly? Oh yes, Milly will be just fine. Right as rain.'

―――――

At half-past six in the evening, O'Keefe came into the office after presiding over the routine interrogation of a patrol that had been fired at on the outskirts of Bandon. Only the Tender had been hit, a clean shot through the grill, forcing it to limp back to barracks spraying steam and boiling water from the radiator. He'd radioed Bandon, requesting an army patrol be sent out, but he knew that whoever had shot at the Crossley was long gone by now. The IRA man was probably sipping a pint in some pub, yarning about how he had plugged ten Tans with one bullet. O'Keefe didn't have time for a pint or stories.

He looked across at Daly, his feet up on the desk as usual. 'You finish the provisions list and mess bills?'

Much of any RIC sergeant's day was spent on barracks' paperwork. The rest was spent ensuring that the constables in his charge were doing their jobs, were in proper uniform and keeping up to date and legible in their patrol diaries. Often, O'Keefe felt that a copper's job of investigating crime was secondary to signing chits once he'd been promoted to sergeant.

'Now now, Seán,' Daly said, puffing on his pipe. 'That'd be telling, wouldn't it?'

'So you haven't then?'

'Course I haven't. I've more important things, by far, to be doing than taking grub orders from that rabble downstairs. They may boil their fucking boot leather for all I care.'

Before the Troubles, provisioning had been a simple task, most often done by the one or two unmarried constables who were billeted in the barracks, but since it had become unsafe for police to live in the towns and villages of Ireland, RIC sergeants were now charged with the requisitioning of food. This task was made more difficult by the general boycott against members of the RIC and their families, in place since 1918. Started by local Sinn Féiners in County Clare and approved the following year by the provisional Dáil government, the boycott had spread throughout the country. At first it had been only loosely enforced. The merchants who had done business with the barracks over the years had been reluctant to lose a steady source of trade and had continued to serve the police. But when a shop or two was burned out, most of the businesses began to comply with the order. Which is to say many of them continued to sell their wares to the police but discreetly, not serving them directly or delivering goods to barracks.

This required the barracks to send men to the shops for provisions under cover of darkness and often under risk of ambush or sniper fire. It also required that the exact amount of money be left for goods taken, a concept lost on many of the Black and Tans.

O'Keefe took out the previous week's lists and mess bills. 'Here.' He slid them across the desks to Daly. 'Just tick the same order as last week and get one of the Black and Scums to collect the money off his mates. I'll get our lads later and a pair of them can make the run tonight.'

'Collect from that shower? That'll be a first. Sure, half of them are Scottish. Blood from a stone …'

'And that's coming from a Cavan man.'

Pointing his pipe stem at O'Keefe, Daly said, '*Careful* with the money is a different thing from being mean with it.'

'Some call it careful; others call it tighter than a gundog's arse.'

'I told you I'd buy you a pint, so I did …'

'At my funeral. Give me the bloody sheet. It'll be quicker if I do it and easier on the ears than listening to you moan about it.'

'Well spoken, man.' Daly slid the sheets back to O'Keefe.

O'Keefe ticked items on the list. *Bacon, corned beef, baked beans, milk, tea.* 'All these years I've known you, Jim, and I'm not sure you understand the concept of work at all.'

'I understand I'm *supposed* to do it.'

Rashers, sausages, ju-jube sweets.

'Only lazy Cavan man I've ever met. Who put ju-jubes on the list?'

'The young lad, Keane. And that's untrue and you know it, Seán, about the work. Point of fact, I spent the entire afternoon drafting letters to our fellow members of the Police Federation so that – all justice being done – you, my good man, will earn more squodge for the *work* you do.'

'*Letters* plural? Flour? Do we need flour?'

'All right, letter singular. And no, no flour. Reams of it, there is.'

'So you spent the day *not* working at trying to convince the brass to pay you more money for the work you don't do? Was the cost of living allowance we got last month not enough to keep you and yours in the style accustomed?' *Cheese, bread, stout.* O'Keefe crossed stout off the list. The men could buy beer for themselves.

'Cost of living allowance? That's what they called it. Nothing more than a getting-shot-at-allowance, that was. And that payment is non-pensionable, mind.'

'You get shot at enough times, you won't need a pension.'

'The wife will want some reward for the work I've done when I'm gone.'

O'Keefe smiled and shook his head. 'If work were in bed, you'd sleep on the floor.' *Butter, brack, eggs.*

'Not at all. There's more than sleeping done in bed.'

Eggs.

O'Keefe sat up and looked at Daly. 'Do you remember, during the summer, that case – the woman who supplied eggs to Bandon barracks?'

Daly rummaged in his pockets for his pipe, frowning in an effort to remember. Finding his pipe and plug, he said, 'If she was selling eggs to the Bandon lads, why didn't they take the case?'

'Because she lives in our district. Murray worked it, I remember that. I was second on the Twoomy murder then with that chap from the Castle.' Twoomy was an alcoholic ex-soldier from Ballycarleton who had been shot and labelled for informing. The case was still open, but nobody in the RIC had any illusions about it ever being closed.

O'Keefe stood up and crossed the hallway to Head Constable Murray's office. Murray had been gone from the barracks for more than a fortnight – though he had only taken a week's leave to attend his father's funeral – and O'Keefe wondered briefly whether Murray would mind him rooting through his files for the information he needed. He didn't imagine the man would, but resolved to brief him when he returned to duty. *If* he returned to duty. It was becoming common for RIC men to head home for leave and never return. Some felt they had to be at home to protect their families, though O'Keefe reckoned that their families were probably safer without an ex-Peeler in the house. Some had been given assurances by the IRA that they would be safe if they resigned from the constabulary. Still others never made it home and were never found.

O'Keefe located the file he was looking for in the second cabinet drawer. The egg-woman was named Katherine Sheehan. The IRA had warned her several times to stop selling eggs to Bandon RIC barracks and the British army post in the town. When she refused, two men had gone to her house and assaulted her. They had inserted a pig ring in one of her buttocks as punishment for aiding the Crown and Murray's notes showed that he assumed, based on a doctor's report which he had included in the file, that the woman had also been raped.

Flicking through Murray's notes at the back of the file, he read that the woman had refused to identify the men who had assaulted her, claiming she did not know them. He made a mental note to contact Bandon barracks in case they had received any intelligence on possible suspects for the crime but doubted that they would have. He closed the file, disgust welling inside him, competing with the shame he felt for how he and his constabulary had retreated behind the steel shutters and barbed wire of the barracks and allowed terror to reign in the county. A woman – one who did business with the RIC in a time when few would – attacked and violated for the crime of trying to put bread on her table and all there was in response was a file gathering dust in the back of an absent copper's cabinet.

He returned to his shared office and began to strip off his uniform. There was a small side room that served as a place to store files and in it O'Keefe and Daly had installed an army cot and dresser, each taking turns to sleep downstairs in one of the day rooms that served as billet for the men, while the other had the storage room cot.

O'Keefe dressed in his civilian clothes – a grey woollen suit and white shirt with a dark blue tie. Inspecting the two collars he owned, O'Keefe found them frayed and yellowing. He couldn't remember when he'd last bought a new one; before the war probably. He found one of Daly's ironed white collars in a dresser drawer and put it on.

'That's right, don't bother asking. Poor Muireann hasn't enough to do with five whelps under her feet but to wash and iron collars for you to wear at your leisure. Go right ahead, son.'

O'Keefe smiled. Daly's wife was a Kerry woman he'd met when he was based in Tuckey Street barracks in Cork city. She had been caring for an invalid aunt, who had encouraged their courtship, telling Muireann she could do worse than hook a Peeler, what with the job for life, salary, pension and respectability the constabulary provided. That was in the years before the shooting started. O'Keefe wondered whether the aunt would still recommend a police constable as a husband to her niece. Given the times, a job for life in the constabulary might be a short one.

Even so, O'Keefe imagined Muireann still would have married Jim. They were made for each other. She could be as scandalous in her own comments as he could and yet was as kind and patient as any wife of Jim Daly would need to be. When O'Keefe was recovering from his wounds and the almost inevitable blood poisoning that accompanied them, it was she who had visited him every day in the Army Hospital in Cork, a child or two in tow, another in her belly. It was she who kept him from falling back into the black pit of numbness, of terrors relived. He would never be able to repay her for the kindness she had shown him and she would never want him to.

O'Keefe took his goggles from the press and hung them around his neck.

'Bit dark for a spin,' Daly said.

'Just dark enough for one, you mean.'

Daly smiled around his pipe stem. 'You still look a right Peeler even in mufti, Seán. You could kit up in one of Muireann's frocks and you'd fool no one at all.'

O'Keefe put his arms through the leather straps of his shoulder holster, took his Webley from its belt holster and slipped it under his arm. Memory washed in. He had just joined up, the Royal Dublin Fusiliers, better known to soldiers as the Bluecaps. Late winter 1915, a pal of his – a Dublin lad from the tenements of the Liberties – had said the same to him. *All copper, you are. Spot it a mile off. Feel like I'm up for something just lookin' at you.* A young man who'd known his share of coppers, O'Keefe would have trusted him with his life if he'd ever got the chance. The Liberties lad was shot as he stepped off the pontoon bridge after the *River Clyde* had grounded at V Beach, his reed-thin body sinking like a stone under sixty pounds of kit and rifle. He had never fired a shot in anger and his war was over before it had even started. Just like O'Keefe's own brother, Peter.

What *was* the lad's name? Suddenly, it seemed crucial that he recall it. *What in the name of Jesus was that fella's name?* Unable to remember, he tried to force the other memories back down. Rising memories filled with the bodies of dead men, stray rounds, shattered bone, mangled viscera. *What was the fella's name?* Memories now leaking forth, diffuse and murder-red, like the blood in the water off V Beach, staining the hour, washing up with tides of random thought.

Daly sensed the change in him. 'Keep the head down, so.'

O'Keefe shrugged on his trenchcoat and leather helmet. He nodded, not wanting to catch Daly's eye, human contact somehow anathema to him when the darkness flooded in.

Night pressed down as O'Keefe rode away from the barracks, wind battering his goggles, tugging at his scarf. His Triumph's headlamp carved a clear path of light on the road ahead. He had bought the bike after the war with money an aunt – his father's sister – had left him. O'Keefe had intended to use the small legacy one day as down payment for a house where he would live with a wife and children. But then the war had come and he had been foolish enough to volunteer. And so had Peter.

When he got out of the Army Hospital in Cork, all he'd wanted to do was move. The faster the better. The Triumph Type H 'Trusty' motorcycle had seemed the best way there was. He'd bought it from a Milltown lad who'd got his leg blown off at the Somme.

Already, the speed of the machine – the sound of the two stroke, pistons hammering, wheels spitting crushed gravel beneath him – had lifted his spirits. O'Keefe could sense more than see the sheep behind the hedges and bare stone walls. The wiry outlines of trees, shorn of leaves, bent near prostrate by westerly Atlantic winds in the glare of the half moon, now covered by cloud, now exposed. It was crisp, cold and dry. Perfect for an ambush. Too early in the evening yet, he hoped.

Suddenly, on a slow bend, the glare of headlamps. A Crossley-load of Auxiliaries, roaring towards Ballycarleton or Macroom. O'Keefe let go of the breath he'd held as he passed them. They didn't stop. Or shoot.

All experienced combat veterans and all officers, the Auxiliaries had been brought over to Ireland on wages of a pound a day. They were to serve as an elite, anti-guerrilla force. Not for the Auxies the constraints of arrest or due process of law. They were feared and hated by republican and loyalist alike. O'Keefe assumed the lorryload that had passed was out of Macroom, billeted in the hotel there and, at present, officially running amok. Three weeks earlier the IRA had kidnapped two of their number. Their bodies had not been found. The Auxies, least of all, had no illusions as to their fate. No quarter given, none asked in return.

O'Keefe shifted gear and accelerated, putting as much distance as he could between himself and the Auxiliaries. Five miles south of Ballycarleton, on the Timoleague road, he slowed and pulled the Trusty over in front of the Sheehan place. The house was typical of the area. An isolated, whitewashed cottage with a thatched roof, tucked under the dark shadows of the hills that rose steeply behind the small farm. Light glowed from two windows on either side of the front door.

He shut down the bike and dismounted. Halfway to the woman's door, a dog began barking. A cow lowed in its stall.

'Who's there? Show yourself!'

Katherine Sheehan stood framed in the doorway of the cottage, light spilling out of the open door. She held an axe. 'Come no further!'

There was fear in her voice, but resolve too, as if she would use the axe if whoever was there came closer. O'Keefe stopped twenty feet from the house and removed his leather helmet and goggles.

'It's all right. Mrs Sheehan? My name is Sergeant Seán O'Keefe. I've come from the barracks in Ballycarleton. I got your address from Head Constable Murray's file. I didn't mean to –'

'Nice of him to leave directions to my home in his papers.' Katherine Sheehan lowered the axe.

O'Keefe had never thought his visit might frighten the woman. He suddenly felt foolish. 'I'm sorry, Mrs Sheehan. I wanted … I wonder if I could ask you a few questions?'

A young boy joined the woman at the door, wrapping his arms around her waist. She pulled the child closer to her.

'I won't be long, Mrs Sheehan. I know it's a difficult –'

'You know nothing, Sergeant.' She set the axe inside the

door and took the boy by the hand, leaving the door open behind them. 'I'm giving the child his dinner.'

O'Keefe stood for a moment on the stone path, unsure if he should enter.

'Were you expecting me to bring your tea outside to you then, Sergeant?'

The inside of the cottage was warm and smelled of boiled potatoes and cabbage, of lamp oil and turf smoke. The ceiling was low, inches only above O'Keefe's head. A man of roughly O'Keefe's own age was slumped in a chair by the fire, staring blankly at the glowing turf. Steam rose from the spout of the kettle hanging from its iron hook over the grate.

'A fine evening,' O'Keefe said to the man. 'I'm Sergeant O'Keefe, out of Ballycarleton barracks. I hope I haven't disturbed your evening, sir.'

The man didn't move.

'Gerard can't hear you, Sergeant. Gone with the fairies, he is.'

The woman flashed a bitter, challenging smile, as if daring O'Keefe to mock the notion. Fairies, in this age of gunmen, motorbikes, telephones and long-range artillery shells that could blow a man into a million pieces so that his teeth became shrapnel. Fairies snatching the fit and healthy, leaving withered husks of men, women and children in their place. O'Keefe had lost his belief in most things, but he knew that farmers still ploughed wide, reverent berths round fairy rings in their fields. He had no mind to mock anything any more.

Katherine Sheehan seemed to read his thoughts and softened a little. 'Since the war. His body's better but his head's not right. God help him.' She blessed herself.

O'Keefe nodded. 'There's many came back like him. More than you'd think.'

He had seen them in the Army Hospital, the ambling, weeping remains of men whose heads would never again be right, no matter what the doctors did or said. The fairies would never let them go, no matter the white horses ridden round the fairy mounds or all the gallons of yearling's milk left on the doorstep.

The woman waited for O'Keefe to say more and when he didn't, she turned away. O'Keefe turned his eyes too, away from her husband at the fire. He noticed the cottage's similarity to every labourer's cottage he had ever entered. A wooden table draped with an oilcloth, the centrepiece of the main room in which he stood. A fireplace and next to it a cast iron range for cooking. To the right of this was a tall dresser filled with mismatched china, a wedding photograph in an ornate frame, a few books and a postcard of the sacred heart, and a paraffin lamp hanging from a beam, cast a gentle, yellow light on the room. There was a set of rough-cut stairs to the left of the fireplace, leading to a loft. Every inch of space in the cottage was used for living. He noticed last the cheap, framed print of the martyrs of the 1916 Rising on the bare, white wall beside the dresser.

The irony of it, he thought: a country where a woman could revere the dead heroes of one vain uprising and then be assaulted by local 'heroes' of the same organisation several years later, because she had sold eggs to Irish policemen. Where was the logic in it? Where, for that matter, was the logic in his own desire for a home-ruled, independent Ireland and yet his taking a wage to hunt the men who thought murder was the surest way to achieve this?

The woman's child – small and delicate-looking, with a pale complexion and tousled blond curls – was dunking a crust of buttered soda bread in a steaming bowl of stew.

'You're a fine big lad,' O'Keefe said to him. 'And what age are you?'

The boy lowered his head and continued to eat in silence. His mother busied herself at the range, shifting pots from one ring to another. 'He'll be five in January. He doesn't talk much either, so he doesn't. Not to strangers.'

O'Keefe could understand why, if the poor child had witnessed his mother's assault. He forced himself to smile. 'I'd say he's a divil running the fields and the hills. Fine life in the country for a young fella.'

The woman turned to O'Keefe. She was younger than he had expected, not at all like the egg-monger he had conjured in his mind when he'd read Murray's report. Katherine Sheehan was a fine-looking woman. Tall, with thick, light-brown hair pulled into a loose bun off her face, her cheeks flushed rose with the heat from the range. Good country stock, O'Keefe's father would have called her and laughed as his wife scolded him.

'Fine life,' she said, 'when his mother can put meat on his plate.'

O'Keefe nodded, still standing, holding his helmet and goggles in front of him. There was a soft pop of turf from the fire and the kettle hanging there began to sing in a low whistle. 'I was hoping to ask ...'

'When the boy's finished his tea.'

'That's grand, Mrs Sheehan.'

She looked hard at him again, a rigorous, assessing gaze that made his face flush. 'And do you prefer standing to sitting, Sergeant?'

He smiled at her, genuinely this time. 'I'll sit, so. Thank you.'

Katherine Sheehan turned back to the range and returned with a bowl of hot stew and a hunk of bread. 'You'd better be getting that in you while you're waiting. You're too thin to look a proper Peeler.'

He ate with relish, his and the boy's spoons against their bowls the only sound in the small kitchen. When the boy had finished, he disappeared up the stairs to the loft, a rabbit, O'Keefe couldn't help but think, taking to its hutch. 'I'm sorry about your husband ...' he began, feeling a sudden urge to tell her about his own brother. His throat tightened again and he looked away. *Jesus, O'Keefe, what's wrong with you, man?* He clenched his fists under the table, searching for something to say.

'Not as sorry as myself, Sergeant.'

O'Keefe was silent for a moment. He cleared his throat. 'Thanks again for the feed, Mrs Sheehan. Lovely, it was.'

'It keeps the wolf from the door. Which is why you're

here isn't it? Come to ask about the wolves who came to my door?' Hands on her hips, direct gaze, proud stance.

'I … yes.' He took his notebook from his trenchcoat pocket and, as he did, the woman folded in on herself and collapsed into the chair across from him. She was exhausted. Any fool could see it, O'Keefe thought. *What am I doing here?*

He wrote the date, time and location of the interview while Katherine Sheehan took a McIvor's boiled sweets tin filled with loose tobacco from her apron and rolled a cigarette. She lit it then and exhaled at the ceiling. Women in the city smoked cigarettes. It was becoming more fashionable by the day, but countrywomen, if they smoked at all, did so rarely in front of strangers and usually then, they smoked a pipe. This woman's smoking was bold, an act of defiance and O'Keefe had to stop himself from watching her.

She slid the tin across to him. He smiled. 'Thanks, I will. Must stop, but there's always tomorrow.'

'Why?'

He looked up from rolling. 'Why?'

'Why would you bother stopping?'

'Well, they're bad enough for the chest.'

'So are bullets.'

He licked the paper. 'So they are. I'm hoping not to catch one.'

She studied him for a moment. 'You have to think that, don't you, Sergeant?'

'Sure, the pay's good,' he said, lighting up.

'Not good enough to die for.'

He shrugged. 'Somebody's got to do it.'

It was another common saying in the Peelers, repeated so often it had lost its meaning. It was used by men who felt, like O'Keefe, that there wasn't much else they could do. He'd heard it during the war as well. Why take that beach, that hill, that trench? *Somebody's got to do it.* One of those somebodys had been Katherine Sheehan's husband. Another had been his brother.

They smoked in silence, using the upturned tin lid for an ashtray. Katherine Sheehan stared into the fire and O'Keefe took the opportunity to study her more closely. She had clear blue eyes, long lashes, a long, strong neck. He could see where her dress had been mended. The stitch marks of the hard-working poor, he reflected. The thrift and fatigue. The meatless stews and early mornings. She yawned and O'Keefe watched her fingers go to her mouth. They were long and graceful, the skin hard and cracked from work around the smallholding. They were the hands of a pianist or a harpist under a sentence of hard labour.

She held her eyes to the flickering firelight as she spoke. 'So why come here, Sergeant – after curfew?' She turned to him. 'Looking for eggs for the barracks, are you?'

'No, no. I need to ask –'

'Questions. So you said.'

O'Keefe looked down to his notebook, wondering where to start. He had Murray's file on the crime tucked into the Trusty's saddlebag. An apology was as good a place to start as any. 'First, let me tell you how sorry I am about what happened. At any other time we would have been able to make an arrest. Find the person, the people, who hurt you.'

He was indeed sorry. The RIC should have been protecting the people of West Cork. Policing. Instead it spent its days behind sandbagged gates and steel-shuttered windows or haring around the countryside in Crossley Tenders and armoured cars with carbines and army escorts, while decent people were left victim to thugs with stolen guns and pig rings.

Katherine stubbed out her cigarette and rolled another.

'At any other time, Sergeant, it wouldn't have happened. My Ger would have told those bastards where to take themselves. He was a fine, strong man who took nothing from no one. You should have seen him before the war got through with him.' She looked over to her husband. If the man had understood anything, he gave no indication. It was like having a ghost in the room, O'Keefe thought. She lit her new cigarette and turned back to O'Keefe, her voice growing in passion.

'Any other time there would be no boycott and no cornerboys with guns to tell me who I can or can't trade with. Young thugs who'd hold a woman down and ...'

There was real anger in her voice. Perhaps the terror of the crime had left her. The terror of memory replaced by rage. Perhaps she would help him. Perhaps she would let him help her.

'Mrs Sheehan, I understand you're –'

'You understand, do you? Were you in the war, Sergeant?' She reached across the table suddenly and touched the scar on his face. O'Keefe turned away and she let her hand fall to the table. He looked over at the silent husband, the man's eyes still fixated on the low flames of the fire. He felt the heat of her fingertips where she had touched him.

'Yes, I was. Gallipoli. With the Royal Dublins. Your husband?'

'The Dirty Shirts. Royal Munsters. V Beach, they called it.'

O'Keefe turned back to her. 'I was there. He was lucky to come off it. A thousand-odd Irish lads didn't.'

'I wonder was he lucky? I pleaded with him not to go, that we'd be grand with the farm here.'

'A lot of women told a lot of men the same thing, I'd say.'

She smiled bitterly. 'He said we could use the money and that the Kaiser couldn't be running into the small nations of the world as if he owned them. Said it wasn't right and that Irishmen needed to do their bit to stop him. And he believed Redmond when he said the Irish serving in the war would help bring Home Rule to Ireland. Fool that he was.'

O'Keefe nodded but said nothing. He imagined the man might have half-believed the reasons he'd given.

'The truth was Ger never liked the farming. He loved town and the fairs and the hubbub of the city. He'd been to Dublin and came home saying there was no place on earth like it with its bustle and life.' There were tears in her eyes now. 'The truth was we were not enough for him – myself and the boy. That man wanted to see the world. And he saw it, so he did. Saw too much of the world.'

'Many men did, Mrs Sheehan. Saw every ugly bit of it.'

There was a flash of intensity in her eyes. She leaned forward and wiped her eyes with her hands. 'What was it like, Sergeant? On that beach. What was it like?'

It was his turn to stare into the fire. Memory rose up and lapped at his consciousness. Turquoise sea turned red with blood, fading to pink with the shushing tide. Bullets like a hailstorm, Turkish machine-gun rounds so thick in the air, you could see them. Men face down in the water, floating, rising and falling with the gentle heave of the surf. Good men torn to pieces. Men half in the water, half in the boats or on the pontoon bridge leading them to the shore from the *River Clyde*. Curious sharks beginning to nose the dead in the blood-dense water. His brother …

'What was it like?'

The room had closed in on them, the woman's husband lost to distant violence, leaving the woman and himself alone with the dying fire and the pain of a war nearly two years finished but never really finished. The two of them bearing the scars of it.

'Mrs Sheehan, how many men came here that night?'

'Please,' she said.

Her husband had closed his eyes and looked as if he were dozing. Suddenly, the fever of wanting to know left Katherine Sheehan and she leaned back in her chair. 'Sergeant, why are you here? What does this have to do with anything – what happened to me? Sure, they're shooting two of you Peelers a week. Shot dead that poor sergeant going into Mass in Bandon. If you can't catch the boys killing your own, why do you give a tinker's about the ones who hurt me? I'm a "traitor" after all. I should be dead by rights, shouldn't I, Sergeant? I should consider myself lucky.'

Lucky, O'Keefe thought. The woman was right: sometimes it wasn't the ones who lived who were lucky. But the woman had her son; that was something.

'I'm here because I found a young woman on a hillside yesterday.'

'A girl on a hillside. Not so lucky then, was she?'

He looked hard at her. 'No. She was dead. Left there exposed for anyone to see. Someone had hurt her too, Mrs Sheehan. And I want to find the men who hurt her – who murdered her.'

'And you think it might be the same men?'

'I've no idea. But I've nothing else to go on.'

'And so you thought you'd start with me.'

'I thought there might be a connection. The Volunteers don't usually harm women.'

'Making me one of the lucky few.'

It occurred to O'Keefe then that the woman might be unhinged. The loss of her husband's sanity, of her livelihood, the violation she'd suffered – these had been just enough to bear without the likes of him coming into her house and asking her to relive it all.

'How many men were there, Mrs Sheehan? You could help me.'

She stood and walked over to the range, taking a pan from one of the cold rings and placing it in a basin of water on the floor. Then she turned back abruptly to face O'Keefe. Her voice wavered.

'Two men. Do you know how to pierce a pig's nose, Sergeant?'

'I –'

'You take a long needle and you scorch it against infection. Did you know that? But sure, a pig's worth more than the likes of me. They didn't bother with the scorching.'

'Mrs Sheehan –'

'And then you hold the pig down, Sergeant. Two men, sometimes three for a big sow, one that fights, and drive that needle through the flesh, just run it out the other side so there's a clean hole for to hang the ring.'

She was growing frantic. O'Keefe felt the same at times and his heart could bled for her. He stood up.

'Mrs Sheehan, you don't have to –'

'Why don't you call me Kate, Sergeant? Those boys did, when they held me down and put a needle through the flesh of my backside. *Kate*, they said, *you like that, Kate? You need to do what you're fucking told, first time round, Kate*, they said.'

The anger left her then and she started to weep. She gathered her apron in her hands and covered her face.

'Mrs Sheehan …'

'Go,' she said. 'They're not the same men at all. Away with you, out of my house.'

There was nothing he could do for her at that moment. He looked to her husband then, still unmoved, eyes closed, a thin tracery of spittle on his chin reflecting the firelight. O'Keefe left her with her memories, closing the cottage door gently behind him, her demons still loose and roving the hills and villages. She has her son at least, he thought, kicking the Trusty to life, adjusting his helmet and goggles. She'd keep going for him. But what did he himself have? What hope? A meagre one at best – catch the bastards who had killed the girl and left her on the hillside. Maybe find the men who had hurt Katherine Sheehan. Show the woman that justice hadn't gone entirely from Ireland. It had just lost its way for a time.

———

Liam Farrell went to O'Sullivan's cowsheds to sleep, but found it impossible. Despite his promotion to Intelligence under the command of Seán Brennan, his gut still ached at his expulsion from the flying column. In the sheds he listened to the preparations the men around him were making in the lantern-light – cleaning rifles and loading rounds into magazines, smoking, chatting, giddy with anticipation of combat. Three young men said the Rosary. When he could take it no longer, he got up and sat by a friend of his from home.

Diarmuid O'Shea looked up at him. 'Well, Liam, heard you're in with the bossmen now. First feckin' off to college and now joining the top dogs at the table. Secret missions and all, boy.'

Farrell shook his head and offered him a cigarette. 'Not something I went looking for. Wish to God I was going with you fellas. Tear the arse out of the Auxies.'

O'Shea caught the note of bitterness in his voice. 'You never know, Liam. They could tear the arse out of us, so they could. You could be lucky sure, not going at all.'

'Do you really think that will happen, Diarmuid? And would you trade places with me?'

O'Shea ran the cloth cleaning plug through the barrel of his Enfield one last time. Farrell wondered was it one of the guns they had taken from the coastguard station, together with the Kilbrittain lads, the summer before. O'Shea was two years younger than him. Back then, he had looked up to Farrell, followed his lead, as Farrell followed that of the older lads. But O'Shea had proven himself to be a fierce and loyal Volunteer in his own right, able to walk tens of miles of countryside in any weather, fervent, cheerful and alert on odd hours of snatched sleep, while Farrell had been away at college. How soon things changed, Farrell thought.

'No, Liam. I figure we'll paste the Auxie bastards and then Lloyd George and the King and the whole shaggin' lot of Peelers, Tans, Tommies, Auxies, spies, traitors, touts, taxmen, magistrates and fuckin' friends to the Crown will all feck off home, boy, and leave us to run our own affairs. That's what I believe.' He pulled on his cigarette. 'And no, I don't think I'd want to trade places with you for the world. No disrespect, *sir*, but you officer lads make me nervous.' He shot Farrell a mock salute.

Farrell smiled sadly. 'I'm no officer, Diarmuid. Just a failed gunman.'

'You wait.' O'Shea clapped him on the shoulder. 'You were made for it, boy. Dishing out orders, poring over maps and all.'

'Sure, going by what Tom Barry thinks, I could hardly see what's on them. What's more, Diarmuid, no matter how soon the Brits feck off and leave us to the running of Ireland, there'll always be a taxman.'

'You're not serious, Liam.'

'If you don't get yourself shot, sure you can sign up for a tax collector's job in the new republic.'

'And you can get a lovely new pair of specs on your IRA pension. Quick, Liam! How many fingers?'

'I'll give you fingers, boy.'

Diarmuid laughed and began loading .303 rounds into the Enfield's box magazine. Each man on the ambush would carry thirty-five rounds. Thirty-five rounds Farrell would never fire for the liberation of his people. O'Shea stood, held out his hand and pulled Farrell to his feet. Without letting go, he pumped his friend's hand. 'Liam, I wish you were going. You know that, don't yeh?'

Farrell's grasp was hard and firm. 'Just plug one of the bastards for me, Diarmuid.'

O'Shea fired off another mock salute as he left the shed,

his precious Enfield slung over his shoulder like he'd been carrying it all his life. Farrell watched him leave, his chest tight with longing and envy.

'Farrell.'

Startled, he turned to the voice. Farrell knew Seamus Connors from his time at University College in Cork. Connors had been studying medicine, though Farrell could hardly have imagined a more unlikely man to succour the ill or help bring new life into the world. He was tall and gaunt, with pale skin drawn over knife-sharp cheekbones and dark, deep-set eyes that seemed to soak up and extinguish light. He had the welt of a recent wound on his forehead.

Connors had been two years ahead of Farrell in his studies, but he too abandoned them for the cause. He was a younger son from a large farm and, like Farrell, the first of his family to attend college. But all similarity between them stopped there. Connors was a gunman through and through. Most of the medical students who joined the IRA were used as medics. But Connors, it was discovered early, had a gift. And his gift was taking life, not saving it. It was rumoured that he had shot seven, some said up to ten, soldiers and policemen. He had been a member of the 1st Cork City Brigade's heavy boys. People said that he had just returned from Dublin, that he'd been working for the Big Fella himself and that Collins had wanted him as member of his Squad, but that Barry had convinced him there'd be more fighting done in West Cork. Farrell had also heard that Connors had fired the shots in the Cork City and County Club which killed Lieutenant

Colonel Bryce Ferguson Smyth, Munster RIC Divisional Commissioner.

But though they knew each other, Farrell and Connors had had no contact within the camp that week. Connors socialised little, being silent and sullen by nature.

'Seamus.'

Connors gazed unblinking at Farrell. It was a habit he had and Farrell wasn't the only man in the Brigade unnerved by those eyes. Then Connors asked bluntly, 'What do you know of the girl they found on the hillside?'

For a second, Farrell was taken off guard. He hadn't really thought much about the girl in the past few hours. And then two things struck him. The first was: how had Seamus Connors come to hear of the matter? Farrell knew that his demotion – or promotion, depending on one's perspective – was common knowledge within the camp, but at no time had he mentioned the girl on the hillside to anyone. He had taken it as a given that her existence and his orders to investigate her murder were not fodder for camp gossip. Brennan himself had impressed upon Farrell the importance of discovering if a fellow IRA man had been responsible for her death.

The second thing that struck Farrell about the question impressed him as the more sinister by far: why did Connors want to know? Unconsciously, he answered Connors' question with one of his own.

'And what have you heard, Seamus? Have you heard anything yourself, man?'

Connors' eyes narrowed. Instinct dictated that Farrell hold his gaze, keeping on his face an expression that strove to appear neutral, unchallenging.

'You were promoted, so you were. Lieutenant Farrell is it now?'

Farrell nodded. 'For all it means, I was, Seamus,' he said, realising that, although he was younger than Connors and despite the man's lethal reputation, he was now Connors' equal in rank and thus not obliged to share operational details with him unless ordered to by someone of higher rank.

'Intelligence?' Connors said, as if reading Farrell's thoughts.

'The Spooks and Question Men, Seamus.' Farrell smiled, as if he were making a joke of it, all the time aware that as a Corkman himself, Connors understood innately that there is nothing so serious as a joke. He returned Farrell's smile, his angular features unmoved by the effort.

'You're good ones for the questions, you law boys, so you are. You know I heard you speak one time, back at college? For the Law Society. A debate on physical force republicanism. You remember it, Farrell?'

Farrell did remember it, but not what side he took or how he had performed. 'I think I do, Seamus, but –'

'You were good at the auld questions then, Farrell. Tore strips off the other fella. Had even me thinking there was no use for force in the cause of freedom. That to use it was to lower ourselves to the ... how did you put it? Something about how we'd be drowning with the Crown in the same pool of blood? And that our hands would be stained red, much the same as our oppressors. You remember that speech, Farrell?'

He didn't remember what Connors had quoted but, embarrassingly, they sounded like his words. His face reddened. But then, that had been years ago, before all hopes of Home Rule had been so thoroughly abandoned. Before he'd been searched and beaten by foreign soldiers, lads younger than himself, on the streets of his own county town. Never mind that he'd been assigned his position in the debate on the House's motion through the toss of a coin. He could have, Farrell reminded himself, not without pride, just as convincingly have argued in favour of physical force republicanism had the King's head landed up instead of down. Anger, stoked by vanity, rose in Farrell's chest.

'I take it you didn't much care for my argument, Seamus?'

Connors appraised Farrell coldly. There was something so outside the bounds of normal human interaction, Farrell thought, to stare so directly at another person. Then Connors' lips twitched, as if he could look into Farrell's head – into his heart – and was amused by what he saw there.

'Sure it was only a debate, Farrell. One side against another. Could have been tennis. A sport, like. You must think we're not up to much intellectually, us medical boys, as to take a law student's empty words as anything but the heap of shite they are. I knew you were spouting, Farrell. Of course I did.'

'I never thought you didn't, Seamus. I was only –'

'Pay no mind Farrell. If I'd thought you were serious I would have put you first on my list for a bullet when it all kicked off. But sure ...' his lips twitched again, no light in his eyes, '... we're on the same side now boy, aren't we?'

———

Returning from Katherine Sheehan's house, O'Keefe entered Ballycarleton barracks through the rear door that opened onto the stable yard, and headed downstairs to the kitchen in the hope of a cup of tea. The kitchens were located on the lower ground floor of the barracks, across the hallway from a short corridor of four cells and a small day-room, which some of the more enterprising young constables and Tans had converted into an exercise room. There was always a set of barbells and a medicine ball around the barracks, even in the days before the men had been forced to billet in, but Ballycarleton now had a weights bench, exercise cycle and canvas heavy bag, as well as a table tennis table made from a sheet of painted board resting on two sawhorses, the net and bats brought over from England by one of the Tans. The sport was a recent import to Ireland and was proving addictive to constables around the country. The distinctive tick-tocking of bat and celluloid ball was as common a sound in barracks as the flutter of playing cards being shuffled. O'Keefe heard the sound now and went towards it. He had been a messy, if relentless, handball player when he was younger and could see the appeal of a game that could be played indoors and behind barbed wire; a game that would erase the outside world for the time it took to play a match. Wipe the mind clean with the metronomic rhythm of the rallies.

Young Keane was playing against a Tan called Heather-field. They were both about the same age and had formed a fast friendship in barracks. O'Keefe reckoned that this could be either a positive or a negative development, depending on who influenced whom, but it was the way of things in the police. You hung around with the fellas of similar age and rank. In the days before the shooting war started, you'd go to dances together, court women, drink in the pubs and go to race meetings and football matches. Now you played table tennis and watched each other's back on patrol.

He watched the two of them, in uniform breeches and cotton undervests, sweat beading on their foreheads as they leaned in, pushing, chopping the ball over the net. Keane noticed him first and caught the ball in his hand, ending the rally. In the sudden silence O'Keefe could hear a gramophone playing upstairs, but couldn't make out the song.

'Sergeant,' Keane said, wiping his brow with a threadbare towel hanging from his belt. He took a crumpled bag of sweets from his pocket and held it out to O'Keefe. 'Ju-jube, Sergeant?'

O'Keefe was embarrassed that they had stopped because of him. He had hoped to watch them play and now he'd interrupted them. It hadn't been long – eight months – since he'd been made acting sergeant and he was sometimes still surprised by the respect shown to the rank. It wasn't real power, like that wielded by the officers of head constable rank and above. But it was the power to make a constable's life in barracks a misery if he wanted to. Or make it a lark if he so chose, if such a state was possible in the times they were in. He wasn't used to the deference shown to him, by the Irish cons at least, and sometimes he wondered whether or not he deserved it. Were the men under him happy? O'Keefe realised that he had no idea. He thought to ask Daly and then imagined the answer he'd get.

'Sorry to break it up, Keane, Heatherfield. I was just watching. Carry on.'

Keane seemed unsure whether or not to begin playing again. He swallowed one of the sweets. 'Any developments on the case, Sergeant?'

'No, none at all so far. We'll get a jump on it once the girl's identified. That's the important thing now.'

Keane nodded, his face serious. 'Anything I can do to help, Sergeant? I'm on a late tomorrow, but I don't mind working the morning for you.'

O'Keefe smiled, thinking that young Keane might be a positive influence on the likes of Heatherfield after all. 'That's grand, Keane. I can pull you after drill if I need you.' He made to leave them. 'Good work today, Constable. Well done.'

Before he turned away he thought he saw Keane blush. Outside the room he heard the ball tock back into play and the deep Geordie voice of Heatherfield. 'Bloody boot-lick you are, lad.'

Smiling a little, O'Keefe thought, *Nothing I wouldn't have said myself once.* He heard Keane laugh and tell his friend to go and shite. *Would have said that too.* He mounted the stairs.

As he reached the ground floor hallway, the music he'd heard from below grew louder. The song was a popular one with the war veterans among the Tans, a group that numbered four or five who stuck fairly close together in barracks. O'Keefe recalled that Heatherfield had also fought in the war, but that he kept away from the Tan mob that centred on Jack Finch and another Londoner, Derek Bennett. The song was 'Stony Broke in No Man's Land'. A sentimental number, the lads tended to play it more when they were on a spree. O'Keefe realised that while he'd been downstairs, the record had been repeated several times. DI Masterson must be out, he thought, and wondered again if Head Constable Murray would ever return from his leave. Murray wouldn't tolerate the heavy drinking and singing that had sprung up in his absence. He only just put up with some social supping in barracks as an alternative to the lads being out smashing up pubs or giving the barracks password away to IRA spies and getting sniped at as they weaved home.

'Sergeant?'

O'Keefe turned to see that evening's Barrack Orderly, William Dunn, approaching him from reception. Dunn was one of the older Irish constables. He had always billeted – even before the Troubles – with his mate, Constable Slainey, in the labourer's cottage that adjoined the cowsheds. He was close to retirement and wanted an easy life. Did things by the book, not out of any great devotion to duty, but because twenty years of RIC life had taught him that there was less bother in barracks if everyone followed the rules.

'Constable?'

He came up close to O'Keefe, raising his voice, partly in annoyance and partly to be heard over the din. 'Do you hear that rabble? How's a man supposed to catch a wink of kip with those …' Dunn searched for a word and found two, 'bloody eejits in there, playing that poxridden gramophone record fifty times twenty. And the same song, over and over. It's not right for a barracks, Sergeant, it's not, and them as drunk as mice fallen in a keg of stout, the fuckers.'

O'Keefe held up his hand to indicate that he should go easy. Dunn wasn't much of a man for cursing, so O'Keefe knew he was at the end of his patience. And no doubt, being years senior to him, he felt that, despite the difference in rank, he could speak freely to O'Keefe and he would listen. Still, much as O'Keefe agreed with Dunn, there was only so much of calling a man's fellow cons 'fuckers' one could take. 'That's grand, Dunn. Is Sergeant Daly not in?'

Dunn made a face and threw out his hands in a gesture of futility that spoke volumes. O'Keefe's own patience was starting to fray. Jim Daly had a reputation for idleness – one he promoted best himself – but he was a full-striped sergeant and a good copper. He'd earned his rank through years of fair, tough policing and a fine knowledge of law and procedure, garnering several commendations for bravery. O'Keefe gave Dunn a look back that told the man he would brook no disrespect for Sergeant Daly.

'He's up in his office, *Sergeant*.'

O'Keefe ignored the sarcasm and headed for the stairs. It occurred to him to break up the party himself, but he wasn't sure whether or not Daly might have sanctioned it for some reason. Two steps up, O'Keefe met the man himself coming down.

'There's Seán. Good to see you back in one piece. Bring us any eggs?'

O'Keefe raised his voice over the volume of the gramophone, the song starting again. 'No, I didn't. Are you letting that shower off the leash for a reason or will I shut them down?'

'Reason?'

'Yes, Jim. Any particular reason?'

Daly considered the question. 'I'd rather they changed the song, but otherwise, sure, they need a knees up now and again. No harm at all, at all.'

'They're jarred, Jim.'

'Better in here than out there. Out there, they might hurt someone.'

'They might hurt someone in here. Have they locked away their arms?'

Daly ignored the question. 'They got another anonymous letter today. Said they weren't welcome and should feck off home to England before they're butchered in their beds and their heads sent home to mammy in a Heinz beans' crate. And one of their Tan mates ate a bullet in Cork. Not sure if he did it himself or had help. Of course, the fella was up on murder and robbery charges, so I suppose his passing could be considered a good thing for all concerned. Still, you can hardly blame them for waking their chum.'

'Mind while I get me handkerchief. Did they lock away their guns before they started drinking or not?'

'Their what?' Daly cupped a hand to his ear.

'Their guns, Jim.' O'Keefe's tea had gone cold in its mug and he was tired. The Tans were roaring, more than singing, along with the song.'*I can't get the old job, can't get the new/Can't carry on as I used to do …*' They were nearing a crescendo. Daly appeared amused by it all. O'Keefe said again, 'The guns?'

The singers hit their stride and O'Keefe could hear the heavy, drunken dance steps of booted men. A chair fell over and Dunn once again appeared from reception in the hallway, glaring. O'Keefe waved him back into reception. The words to the song bellowed out.

'*I look all around me and daily I see/Thousands and thousands of men/A lot worse off than me …*'

Daly turned to O'Keefe and mouthed the words the Tans had added themselves '… *and so I joined the FUCKING RIC!*' Then he said, 'Their guns? I haven't the faintest. You'd think they'd have put them away themselves. They're not children.' He smiled as he said it. 'Come on then, you always knew how to spoil a good hooley, O'Keefe.'

Daly and O'Keefe entered the ground floor day-room and were faced with four men standing, arms flung round one another's shoulders. Cigarettes dangled from the lips of two men, long fingers of ash ready to drop down uniform tunics to blend in with the egg yolk and chop grease smeared there already. Two bottles of Dewar's scotch whisky sat on a small card table surrounded by chairs, one of them upended. The Tans and many other war veterans never drank Irish whiskey if they could avoid it, thinking – correctly or not, O'Keefe didn't know – that the Irish distilleries had sent the dregs of their product to the men in the trenches after the 1916 Rising while the Scots had sent their best spirits. It was the kind of trench story that became truth after a while.

Daly leaned in to O'Keefe. 'You know what Churchill said about the Tans? That they were the best of a fine lot of applicants, chosen "on account of their intelligence, their character and their records in the war".' Daly winked and then righted the fallen chair. The Tans appeared to become aware of Daly only now, his massive frame filling the door. Daly's was that unique country strain of hugeness that was easily masked by his genial demeanour. O'Keefe himself was considered a big man, but was slight compared to Daly. The Tans, however, after marking O'Keefe and Daly's presence in the room, dismissed them.

One of the Tans, Taylor – a wiry Scot from Glasgow – untangled himself from the throw of arms and shoulders and, without acknowledging Daly or O'Keefe, began cranking the Victrola gramophone for another run at 'Stony Broke'.

Daly said, 'Now lads, I think we've had enough of that one for tonight. Time please, gents, time please. Have you no beds to go to?' He smiled as he spoke. O'Keefe scanned the room for weapons and saw two Sam Browne belts abandoned in the corner. They were behind the men and, he hoped, forgotten. But Finch was wearing his belt, Webley in its holster, the holster's fastener and flap loose.

Taylor continued to crank the Victrola. Finch looked at O'Keefe and smiled. 'All right, Sergeants Daly and … you. You come to apologise for smacking me in the mouth?' He reached out and grabbed one of the whisky bottles from the table. 'It's all right then, mate. 'Ave a fucking drink and let's settle it right fucking now, eh? Eh, Sar'nt?' He swigged from the bottle and then held it out.

O'Keefe said, 'Party's over, lads. That's it, cork it and stow it.'

Taylor looked from Daly to O'Keefe, then manhandled the needle onto the record. Crackling static filled the room.

Daly said, 'Turn that fucking thing off. Now, Taylor.' He didn't say, 'Or you'll be written up or docked pay and reported for insubordination.' He knew better than to waste his breath. The Tans didn't care about such punishments and, even if they did when they were sober, they certainly didn't now. The war had made them men for whom the minor details of normal life mattered little. The big things – staying alive, your mates, a bottle of whisky – were the only things that mattered. O'Keefe sometimes wondered how he had avoided the bitter nihilism and impulsive violence that afflicted many of the veterans when they drank. Perhaps because, drunk or sober, he didn't care about anything at all. And then, strangely, he remembered Katherine Sheehan and thought how disappointed he would be if one of these idiots shot him and he never saw her again.

Bennett, the other Cockney, spoke up. 'There's no need for that now, Sar'nt. We was only 'aving a laugh. One more time and we'll knock it down a notch. Promise we will … Right, lads?' His smile was slow and obvious.

O'Keefe opened his mouth to speak when, over the scratch and pop of the record, Daly intervened. 'I'll give ye one more chance to turn that off and go to your beds. *One.*' He looked at each of the men. The fourth Tan, a Scouser named Reid, appeared to have passed out, hanging from his mates' shoulders, eyes closed.

Finch took another long sup of whisky and held his rheumy gaze on O'Keefe. O'Keefe crossed his arms and felt the comforting heft of his own Webley in its shoulder holster. Still staring at O'Keefe, Finch raised his voice.

'And I'll give you two stuffed cunts one more chance to fuck off out of my sight.' He turned to Daly and roared, 'ONE!'

Bennett laughed and Taylor began to sing. '*I can't get the old job, can't get the new …*'

Daly took his Webley from its belt holster and put two bullets into the Victrola.

The shots were stunningly loud in the confines of the room. Acrid powder smoke hung at eye level for a moment, then hooked a draught and began to clear. Reid fell from Finch and Bennett's shoulders and banged his head off the card table on his way down. Bennett stood stock still and

Taylor was cowering in a corner of the room, his hands over his ears.

O'Keefe saw Finch go for his sidearm. Drunkenness made him slow. O'Keefe grabbed the second bottle from the table and whipped the remaining whisky into Finch's face. The Tan's hands went instinctively to his eyes and O'Keefe, skipping around the table, moving faster than he'd done in ages, grabbed Finch's gun hand and brought it up and around his back in a wrist lock. Finch went down on his knees.

'My eyes! You bastard, I'll fucking gut you, you Irish bastard!'

The hallway outside the day-room suddenly filled with half-dressed constables, some holding guns.

Daly cuffed Finch's hands behind him while O'Keefe took the Webley from the Tan's holster and opened the cylinder, letting the six rounds drop to the floor. O'Keefe then told Bennett to lift up his mate while Daly took a handful of the cowering Taylor's oiled hair and shoved him next to the others. Holding his revolver on Finch, Daly turned to Taylor and Bennett, 'Ye two daft planks take your mate here down to the cells. Put him in three ...' He turned to O'Keefe. 'Is there anyone in the cells at the moment?'

'Not the last I heard.'

Daly turned back to Taylor. 'You. Bring me up the key to cell three after you've locked this fool in it and then you sit jailer. If you fall asleep down there, I'll rip your head off and send it home to *your* mother in a Heinz beans' crate. You ...' to Bennett now, 'take Reid to bed and sit by him 'til he wakes. He might have a concussion and if he starts sicking up, he's likely to choke on it. If he dies, you die, Bennett. Understood?'

Bennett nodded, not meeting his eyes.

'And you,' Daly said, jerking his chin at Finch. 'You sit on your arse 'til I decide if you're to be court-martialled.'

Finch's reddened eyes flared like Verey lights. 'On what fucking charges?'

Daly placed the Webley's barrel on Finch's forehead. 'On what fucking charges, *Sergeant*.' He was smiling now, digging the barrel into the skin of Finch's brow. 'Well, Constable Finch, why don't you think about that one yourself? If you can come up with a set of three charges that more accurately reflect the nature of our problems this evening than I can, I'll let you off when you sober up. How's that for a laugh, Finch?'

Finch said nothing but held Daly's eyes. The gun barrel against his forehead didn't seem to scare him in the slightest. Daly lowered the gun and holstered it. He took out his pipe and began tamping tobacco into the bowl. Looking up at the Tans, he said, 'You three *dahs* still here?'

The Tans left the day-room and the men in the hallway drifted back to bed or to their cards or table tennis. O'Keefe made half an effort to clean up the fragments of gramophone and vinyl. Daly took up Finch's bottle of whisky. Miraculously, it had survived the mêlée. He poured drinks into two of the empty glasses on the table.

'Now,' he said. 'Problem solved. Drink, Seán?'

O'Keefe set the pieces of broken disc on top of the splintered wooden gramophone case and sat down. He took up the glass and raised it. 'To a spanking new Victrola.'

———

As he grew older, his mother stopped caring whether the boy was in the house or not when she entertained her friends. Sometimes he watched what they did together, his mother and her friends.

Most days, he was forced to scavenge for food. Stealing apples from the orchards outside of town, vegetables from kitchen gardens, loaves of bread cooling in open windows. He had asked her only once for food and she had beaten him so badly, he'd never asked again. She still kept her chickens and used the money from the eggs she sold to buy her medicine. It came in bottles, and he was nine years old when he realised it wasn't medicine at all. It seemed as if his father had been gone forever, fighting the boars. He'd asked his mother about it once and once more she'd beaten him, so he never asked again and his father had never come home.

Sometimes he used to sleep in the hen house, but it wasn't the same now that he knew. He could hear them inside and picture what they were doing. The rough grunting men, his mother's high, piercing laughter, her imprecations and pitiable pleading for more. More drink. More pleasure. More than life had seen fit to give her. And in the half-dark of the silent hen house, moonlight shafting through cracks in the walls, he listened and gathered stray feathers caught in the straw. Cupped them in his hands and brought them to his face. Listening.

Sunday
28 November 1920

'Surgeon wants you now, Sergeant. Says he's ready,' Constable Keane said, putting his head around the doorframe.

O'Keefe started at his voice and realised he'd been nodding off at his desk, the hillside murder file open in front of him. He wondered had Keane noticed.

After the Victrola incident, O'Keefe had spent the night in the curtained-off section of the barracks' attic beside the sandbagged Lewis gun emplacement, developing the photographs he had taken of the body *in situ*. He sniffed at his fingers now and noted that they still smelled of Acid Fixing Powders, despite his having washed them several times.

When he had hung the photographs to dry, he finished the duty rosters for the following two weeks and typed out a preliminary report on the murder, so that it would be ready for the surgeon and the army court-martial officers when they arrived, leaving a duplicate copy on the DI's desk. It had been after three when he had tried to sleep on the cot he'd dragged into the ground-floor day-room, setting up camp beside the shattered gramophone player.

By half-past four, the nightmares had him, and he'd risen again at six, beaten from sleep by the dreams, fading images of V Beach, Sedd-el-Bahr and Hill 141. Katherine Sheehan had been in his dreams too, among the blood and the dust and the carnage.

Coffee then, and a solitary wait for the night patrol to return. Daly had been scheduled for a routine interrogation of the constable in charge of the night patrol, but O'Keefe blessed him with another hour in bed and did it himself. Sleep was a luxury O'Keefe enjoyed vicariously. The interrogation was short and to the point. All men accounted for, two obstructions moved from the Bandon and Dunmanway roads, no shots fired, no contact with the enemy.

The rest of the day O'Keefe spent briefing the surgeon who had arrived from Cork and tending to the daily duties of a barracks' sergeant: supervising drill, uniform and weapons inspections, lecturing constables in their one hour of school and study of parliamentary acts, law and policing procedure.

He checked the clock on his office wall. Twenty past three. Outside, the weak winter sun was descending over West Cork. He yawned.

'Long night, Sergeant?' Keane asked.

'Tell the surgeon I'll be there shortly. Is the DI back yet?'

'He is. He's there with some swells in mufti, in his office. *Sasanaigh*. Closed the door when they went in.'

Sasanaigh. Englishmen. O'Keefe remembered that Keane came from an Irish-speaking area in Donegal. He also noted how comfortably the young man had taken to the culture of the constabulary, remarking, *sotto voce*, the comings and goings of the DI and visiting strangers. Some things never changed. Nothing like a visit from strange men in suits to start the gossip wheel spinning. All cons loved a sniff of scandal.

O'Keefe let the matter drop. He'd find out soon enough who the men were. 'Notify the surgeon I'm on my way, will you?'

Keane left, but O'Keefe couldn't bring himself to rise. One more minute. He lit a Player's cigarette and picked up a copy of Friday's *Evening Standard*. Daly had left it for him, folded open at the editorial, before heading into Cork to see his wife and family. O'Keefe smoked and read:

Age-Old Conflict Reaches New Low

In the centuries of history shared between Ireland and her closest neighbour and sovereign protector, foul means have been employed by some to advance the cause of Home Rule or independence. Never in this time, stretching back to Diarmuid McMorrough and Strongbow and the abdication of the High Kings of Leinster, has one party opted for the slaughter of innocent beasts to further its cause …

Never, O'Keefe thought, unless one considered the dead dog they buried with Diarmuid McMorrough's father. Never, unless you considered some of the RIC men and Tans shot recently. Pure beasts of burden, a few of them, God rest them. Pure innocent, as Daly would have said, and not in the virginal sense. O'Keefe smiled bitterly and stubbed out his cigarette. Horses and asses and newspapermen's ire. It was a grand thing to know one's place in the grand scheme of things.

'Ah, Sergeant O'Keefe, just the man, just the man.'

District Inspector Walter Masterson was smiling with

welcome. Beckoning O'Keefe into his office, dosing out avuncular pats on the back. Visitors always brought on fits of spontaneous good cheer in the DI. O'Keefe was surprised he hadn't called him 'Seán'.

'Inspector,' O'Keefe said, allowing himself to be guided, deciding to suffer the act just long enough to see if he was staying on the case. Looking around the room at the suited gathering of men, he reckoned his odds of doing so had dropped since yesterday.

DI Masterson was 'Castle Kidney': connected to the governing class of Ireland through ancestral title, marriage and religion. A tall, large-gutted man in his late forties, with thick brown hair peppered grey and worn oiled, he had a smattering of tiny red veins around his soft, puttyish nose which seemed to increase in number each time O'Keefe saw him. It was a face O'Keefe associated with too much rich food and drink. The face of a Lord Such and Such, O'Keefe had always thought. And no wonder. Masterson had come from an estate near Slane in County Meath and, like his batman, Constable Senior, had joined the constabulary as a cadet on the recommendation of the local magistrate, a close friend of his father's.

O'Keefe said, 'The surgeon is ready to report on the post-mortem, sir.'

'All in good time, Sergeant. All in good time. There's not a lot he can report if the lead in the investigation and his superior aren't present now, is there?' Masterson chuckled warmly.

O'Keefe forced a smile and inwardly noted two things. First, Masterson had called him the lead on the investigation. His prospects were on the move. Second, his use of the word 'superior'. The word galled O'Keefe but also drove home the fact that the investigation was staying local. Many murder cases were taken over by the County Inspector and assigned to men hand-selected by him. Sometimes, if the murder was particularly bloody or notably political, special detectives from Dublin Castle – Murder Men – were brought in. But this looked as if it was staying in the district. And if the DI was keeping it, he must see himself benefiting from it somehow.

'Yes, sir.'

'Good, good. Now, a progress report, Sergeant. But first …' Masterson indicated the man who sat in the leather-backed chair in front of his mahogany desk. 'First allow me to introduce Detective Sergeant Thomas Mathew-Pare. One of us, O'Keefe. Scotland Yard. Here to lend us a hand in the investigation. Thomas, Sergeant Seán O'Keefe.'

There were two other men on a leather couch against the wall that matched the chair and O'Keefe noticed one of them smile at the mention of Scotland Yard. Masterson's batman, Constable Senior, sat on a couch against the opposite wall, his eyes fixed on O'Keefe.

O'Keefe held out his hand and Mathew-Pare stood and took it. The first thing that struck O'Keefe was that he didn't look like a proper copper. Like many policemen, O'Keefe was guilty of categorising people, slotting them into handy boxes. This one, civilian. That one, soldier. Fellow cop. Shopkeeper's wife. Cornerboy. Tinker. Poitín-maker. Young one. Wrong one. He would admit the system had its shortcomings and was highly prejudicial – often he found his judgements not wrong, but oversimplified, and was forced to amend them.

He'd stand by it this time, however. Detective Sergeant Thomas Mathew-Pare didn't fit the box marked 'copper'. He looked to be in his late thirties, was of average height and weight – five foot nine, eleven stone, O'Keefe reckoned – and his face was smooth and boyish. It hardly looked to O'Keefe as if the man had ever shaved, and yet there was a thatching of fine wrinkles around his eyes which gave his age away and suggested heavy smoking or time spent under harsh sunlight. The eyes themselves were a watery grey that seemed to take on the light of their surroundings, making O'Keefe question their actual colour. In all, it was a face that lacked any one definable feature; a face that could blend in anywhere. O'Keefe realised that despite not looking like a policeman, the man couldn't be easily labelled anything else either.

'Sergeant,' Mathew-Pare said, releasing O'Keefe's hand. 'Walter was just giving me a brief take on the case. Hope we can be of help.'

We? O'Keefe had noticed the 'Walter' as well. Being on Christian-name terms with the DI meant one of two things: this Mathew-Pare was related socially to Masterson, most likely via the informal but exclusive network of landowning families throughout Ireland and England, or – more likely

– he was a Castle man. One of the many men assigned by Dublin Castle or Whitehall or both to keep an eye on things in the outer reaches of Ireland. Castle men reported directly to Ministers and Lords Lieutenant. With a word, they could scupper your career.

O'Keefe studied the 'we' now: the two men sitting on the leather couch. The smiling man sat on the left smoking a cigarette. He was unhealthily thin, with diamond sharp features, dark slits for eyes, a nose that resembled a scythe in every way except that it had been broken at least once and had a pronounced lump of scar tissue on its bridge, a thin moustache, and thinning, sandy blond hair oiled and combed back from his forehead. His hat rested on his knee, the brim as sharp as his eyes.

O'Keefe's gaze shifted to the second man. Also smoking, he was much bigger than the first, with a large, protruding jaw padded by hanging jowls and shadowed in black whiskers. His skin bore the blemishes of childhood illness or acne. The sleeves of his suit jacket strained against his bulging arms. These two slotted better into the box marked 'copper'.

O'Keefe turned back to Mathew-Pare. 'I think we're coping all the same, Mr Pare.'

'Detective Mathew-Pare,' the DI corrected. 'And we're glad of any help we can get, aren't we, Sergeant? The Yard understands the task we have here with the rebel … with the problems we're having. How difficult it's made the investigation of crime as such. Jolly good of them to lend us your expertise, Thomas.'

The DI had caught himself, but O'Keefe noted the slip. He had heard it called 'the rebellion' – the revolution, the war that it actually was. No doubt the DI's superiors – Mathew-Pare's as well, come to think of it – felt that a war by any other name ceased to be a war, but the men who took the bullets knew otherwise.

Mathew-Pare gave a smile of perfect blandness while addressing the DI. 'I'm not sure, actually, how much help we can be, not knowing the local ropes, as it were. I'm here as a favour to the bureaucrats, Inspector. Spirit of co-operation and all. Some extra legs.' He turned to O'Keefe, 'I assure you that is all that we are. In from the neck down, as they say. The Inspector has made me aware in no uncertain terms, Sergeant, that you're the lead on this. And I wouldn't want it any other way frankly. Like to get back to Blighty with my head attached, what?'

'The mandarins know best, so they do,' O'Keefe said.

Still the bland smile. 'You fought in the war, Sergeant? Possible we crossed paths somewhere along the Front?' Nothing behind the smile in the eyes, O'Keefe thought, but he had to admit that the man was shrewd, letting O'Keefe know whose side he was on.

The DI tried his best, his own smile locked in place. 'Thomas here fought in the big three at Wipers, then in Mesopotamia wasn't it?'

Mathew-Pare turned to Masterson. O'Keefe could sense the amusement from the couch. The room was full of loaded smiles.

'Ypres,' Mathew-Pare said, properly pronouncing the Belgian name.

'Indeed,' the DI said. He stood corrected and the bonhomie faded a little on his face.

Mathew-Pare turned once again to O'Keefe. 'Shall we go then? I expect the surgeon and the wigs will be waiting.'

'Indeed, indeed …' Masterson said again, allowing Mathew-Pare to hold the office door open for the others as if it were his own.

O'Keefe stayed where he was. 'Actually, Detective, I would like a quick word with the Inspector. You don't mind heading down yourselves?'

'Of course.' The smile again, bright and as unfeeling as the crocodiles O'Keefe had seen on the Nile while holding over in Alexandria on route to the Dardanelles.

When O'Keefe turned back, Constable Senior was still there. The DI had seated himself behind his desk, his smile extinguished, no longer any need for it.

'A private word, sir?'

Anger flashed in the DI's eyes, but his voice stayed calm, as if he'd thought better of letting it loose. 'Constable Senior is privy to all matters concerning this investigation. Indeed, all matters that occur within this barracks or any I'm responsible for. So unless it's a personal matter you wish to discuss, Sergeant, Senior will attend. Is that clear?'

O'Keefe nodded. 'Sir.'

'Get on with it then.'

The other side of the DI was coming out now, no need for

the happy-barracks act with a lowly acting sergeant. About the only thing that could recommend the man, O'Keefe found himself thinking, was his constant absence. It had allowed Daly, Head Constable Murray and himself to run the shop with minimal interference.

'I was wondering, sir, do we really need this Mathew-Pare on the investigation?'

The DI stared at him for a long moment and O'Keefe was conscious of Senior doing the same from his place on the couch. Finally Masterson said, 'What you mean is, you don't want him on it. Is there any particular reason why that might be, Sergeant?'

'No, sir. It's just that I might be able to manage better on my own. With men from this district who know the ropes …' He caught himself using Mathew-Pare's words and winced inwardly. 'It's hard enough getting information from people without the imposition of strange accents. Murder Men from the Castle are one thing. They're Irishmen at least. We know, roughly, their intentions. But these men?'

Again, the DI stared. But this time it was Senior who spoke. 'Is it possible, Sergeant, that your intention is to allow this case to remain unsolved? That it would be uncomfortable for you should you be forced to investigate it properly?'

Stunned, O'Keefe turned to him. 'And why would that be? What are you saying, *Constable*?' He stressed Senior's lower rank, but knew it counted for nothing, either within the RIC or out of it. Aaron Senior might be a constable now, but his rank in society would always count more than anything else.

Masterson asked, 'When were you planning on informing us of your sister's plans, Sergeant?'

O'Keefe turned back to Masterson. His sister? What were they talking about? He remembered her letter, still unread, in his desk drawer.

'Sir?'

Masterson took a thin file from a stack on the desk and opened it. 'I received word from "I" Division that your sister is to marry into one of the most active republican families in County Dublin and I'm left waiting for you to come to me with this intelligence. I realise we can't but bear up to some of what our families subject us to but …'

'My sister –'

'You can see how it might look, O'Keefe,' Senior joined in, deliberately not addressing him by rank. 'This is a case that will need exceptional police work and, I might add, exceptional luck to solve and here you are rejecting expert help from a trained detective; a man with a good deal more experience in the investigation of murder than you, notwithstanding his "strange accent".'

O'Keefe was silent for a moment, unable to respond. His sister? Getting married? To a known republican? It was too much for him to take in. 'Sir, I want to solve this crime. How could I want to do otherwise?'

The DI leaned back in his chair. The smile threatened to return. 'I've never thought differently, O'Keefe, never. I've specifically selected you to lead this investigation because you've the cut of a fine Peeler. I've heard grand things about your work on the bank manager's murder in Navan some years ago. And the job you did assisting the Murder Men on the Twoomy shooting. That was good work, result or not. But you must understand my position. How it would look if we rejected the help offered by Mathew-Pare and it got out about your connection to …'

'*My* connection?'

'All right, your sister's connections to the Volunteers.'

O'Keefe swallowed his gathering rage. He'd be the first to admit he had his faults, but disloyalty was not one of them.

Senior continued. 'Of course, we have no control over what our families do. There are many fine and honourable men with … unfortunate connections to the IRA. This in no way affects their standing in the, O'Keefe. But their work, the vigour with which they pursue the enemy, is perhaps subject to more scrutiny than that of others. For this reason we've decided to accept any help Mathew-Pare and his men might provide. Really, it was good of the Castle to offer his services, considering how stretched things are around the country.'

Masterson stood up and came around the desk to where O'Keefe was standing. 'Look, Sergeant,' O'Keefe noticed it was back to 'Sergeant' again, 'I'll tell you this and you didn't hear it from me …'

O'Keefe nodded, his gaze set straight ahead.

'Absolutely confidential and for high eyes only, if you get my meaning, Sergeant?'

'Sir?'

The DI leaned towards O'Keefe, resting his hand on his shoulder. 'The Castle has intelligence. Bloody good stuff too, the word is. The Shinners are upping their efforts. All out push in the new year. The thing is, "I" division says the boyos need to clean out the touts in advance of the big push. Loose lips sink ships they've realised, somewhat late in the game, what?'

'And how does this affect my investigation, sir?'

Masterson smiled again, a cheeky, conspiratorial grin. O'Keefe could feel his breath in his ear. 'They're topping women now, Sergeant. Makes sense, doesn't it? Whose lips could be looser? Tar and feathering itself won't always do the job, but a bullet will, fairer sex be damned.'

He stood back and clapped O'Keefe on the shoulder. 'So you see why this is important. The papers get wind of Volunteers plugging bints, Sergeant, and one front of their fight is finished.'

'The propaganda war,' Senior chipped in, 'which, after the Black and Tans' burning of Balbriggan, they are most decidedly winning. All the world's Press is on the side of the republicans against the "savage, sanctioned outrages of Crown forces". What the rebels did to that girl you found was savage.'

'We don't know who killed her,' O'Keefe said.

The DI again clapped him on the shoulder. 'And that's

exactly what you and Mathew-Pare are going to find out, isn't it? Turn over every rock in this county and find her killer. For just the reasons Constable Senior has outlined for you.'

O'Keefe had an overwhelming urge to lash out at Masterson, to throw him and his fawning batman through the steel-shuttered window. He let the urge drain from him, but kept his eyes on the wall behind the DI's desk, afraid to look at either man for fear the impulse might return.

'Any questions, Sergeant?'

'No, sir. Things are much clearer to me now.'

'Shall we go then?' It was the DI who held the door open this time.

Before the shooting started in 1919 and prior to the passing of the Restoration of Order Act, suspicious deaths in Ireland were subject to a coroner's inquest, requiring the attendance of a magistrate judge and twelve civilians as witnesses. Now such deaths were investigated by British army courts-martial in Military Courts of Inquiry. It was yet another of the hazy, grey regions of the Troubles policemen were forced to operate in and O'Keefe, like many others, didn't like it. The RIC was expected to investigate crimes in the manner in which they were trained and accustomed to and yet, when – if – a suspect was arrested in County Cork, the police were obliged to hand that suspect over to the custody of the army to be tried at court-martial.

Common law, the basis on which the RIC had operated for nearly a century, had been suppressed in the name of security.

O'Keefe didn't object to this part of the inquiry, however – the post-mortem and death pronouncement required only that it be witnessed by five or more army or police. He had heard that the surgeon was proficient in his work and there was little way for politics to enter into a surgeon's report on cause of death. Politics entered through other doors, which he would deal with when it happened.

The cold storage shed was twelve by sixteen feet long, lit by a single, bright, hanging electric light. Its walls were heavily insulated and lined with tin. At the back of the room, in front of the steel-boxed refrigeration unit, four meat hooks hung from a beam. Stacked against the walls were wooden crates of provisions. Someone had been thoughtful enough to remove the sides of bacon and mutton from the hooks before the young woman's body had been placed on the waist-high butcher's table in the centre of the floor.

The room was perfect for a post-mortem, the table having recessed troughs for fluids running along its edges, and underneath it was a slight gradient to the floor, leading to a drain. The bodies of two constables had been examined here in the last few months and O'Keefe reckoned there would be more to come before the fighting ended.

A surgeon from Cork Army Hospital, Major Giles Wells, Royal Army Medical Corps, stood at the head of the long table. He had with him a young male nurse as his assistant and a subaltern clerk to minute the post-mortem. The latter sat at a portable camp desk of a type O'Keefe hadn't seen since the war, a typewriter and pot of ink in front of him, pen and notebook in his hands.

With O'Keefe were District Inspector Masterson, Detective Sergeant Thomas Mathew-Pare and two court-martial officers. These had been introduced to O'Keefe as Lieutenants Wiley and Lambert. It occurred to O'Keefe that they were hardly the type of officers sent to a case of any importance. He would have expected the presence of a court-martial judge or a captain attached to division staff at least. But the road from Cork to Ballycarleton was dangerous and perhaps a decision had been made not to risk the lives of any high hats. Or maybe the case mattered less than Masterson thought it did.

He choked back the anger he still felt after his conversation with Masterson and Senior, and counted those present in the room, noting in his diary their names and ranks and the fact that there was a quorum for a pronouncement on cause of death.

The young woman's body was covered with a sheet, preserving whatever modesty was left after the invasion of the surgeon's knives. O'Keefe felt sadness surge through him, replacing the anger he felt at his own predicament. This had been someone's daughter, he thought. Wife perhaps. Sister. Left naked on a hillside, mutilated, tarred and feathered; now laid out on a butcher's table like a side of beef among crates of tinned stew and beans.

The men circled the table and the surgeon folded down the sheet, exposing the young woman's head and shoulders. It was cold in the room and their breath streamed out in lazy billows. There was a faint, almost sweet, odour of putrefaction, but the refrigeration had reduced the rate of decomposition as well as could have been expected. O'Keefe turned the pages in his diary to a list of questions he had drawn up earlier.

'Gentlemen,' the surgeon began, and it struck O'Keefe how much like a play a post-mortem and inquest was, the surgeon narrating, the sheet covering the body to be swept back like a stage curtain, revealing to the gathered audience the tragedy befallen. The victim was one of two leads in the play. Offstage, somewhere, there was another player. Waiting.

'We have here the body of a well-nourished young female, aged in her late teens or early twenties. There is no evidence of the victim having borne any children and she was in average to good health at the time of her death. Time of death has been estimated, based on average air temperature in the region of the body's discovery and progress of decay, to have been some time between the twenty-second and twenty-fourth of November.'

O'Keefe noted this. Roughly five days earlier. Six at the most. Four at the least. Sunday to Tuesday at the latest.

'Gentlemen,' the surgeon said again, looking at each of the men around the table, 'it is my strong belief, as to be recorded by this Military Court of Inquiry, that the subject we have before us was murdered.'

O'Keefe noted the time and date of the announcement.

'And the cause of death, Major?' the DI asked.

The surgeon gave Masterson a sharp look. O'Keefe thought of the DI as a heckler shouting out lines from the stalls. Wells answered Masterson, however, turning to O'Keefe as he did.

'Sergeant O'Keefe's preliminary report and photographs, of which I have copies, recorded extensive bruising around the neck,' the surgeon pointed to the young woman's neck and the two court-martial officers leaned in to take a closer look, 'indicating attempted strangulation to be the cause of the bruising.' He gestured to the nurse to assist him. 'Initially, I also assumed manual strangulation to be the cause of death.'

'However?' Masterson again.

The surgeon had moved to the side of the table and begun to raise the victim's shoulders as if to turn her. Now he stopped and looked at the DI. O'Keefe studied the surgeon's face. Wells' eyes were deeply inset in his skull and were cast in shadow by the hanging bulb above him. His gaunt, angular features were a florid collection of burst capillaries and deep ridges carved, O'Keefe assumed, by excessive consumption of alcohol and tobacco and regular proximity to death. O'Keefe put him at about forty years of age, but he could have passed for fifty or more.

'Are you in a hurry, District Inspector?'

Masterson mumbled his apologies. Standing behind and to his left, O'Keefe could see the back of Masterson's neck redden.

'You said you *initially* assumed death was caused by strangulation?' O'Keefe said now, surprising himself, his voice sounding loud in the small room. He had been impressed by Wells' preliminary questions when he had met him earlier, and the surgeon had in turn complimented O'Keefe on his photographs of the scene and body. O'Keefe was aware, however, that he was speaking up so as to further drive the knife into the DI's wounded pride.

The surgeon nodded at O'Keefe and then to his assistant. The two turned the young woman onto her side, the sheet slipping and exposing her back, mottled purple with lividity. The assistant adjusted the sheet to cover the buttocks.

'Yes Sergeant, I did think so at first. She was, I believe, throttled to the point of grave injury prior to but not, in fact, to the point of death. Despite the bruising and soft tissue damage to the throat and neck, the hyoid bone is intact and the trachea shows none of the heavy internal injury we might expect to see with strangulation. Her death was, in fact, caused by this.'

Wells lifted up the victim's long, limp, brown hair. Underneath the hair at the back of her head, a patch had been shaved away. O'Keefe stepped forward and leaned in to get a closer look, noticing the thin line of stitching that circled her head just below the hairline, where the surgeon had cut and peeled back the scalp and then – sawing a planar cut into the casing of bone – had removed the top of the young woman's cranium. His eyes followed the surgeon's pointing finger. There was a puncture mark at the base of the girl's skull and surrounding the puncture wound was more livid bruising.

'Cause of death,' Wells said, 'was subdural haematoma caused by a blow from a thin, sharp object of approximately six inches in length. Something like an ice pick, gentlemen, or a stiletto of some sort. This is only speculation, however. I nearly missed it, but after determining that death was not caused by strangulation or the lacerations on the chest – committed post-mortem, incidentally – I looked her over more closely and found this. I've estimated the length of the weapon based on the bruising around the wound and the channel of the internal injury to the brain, which suggests that the weapon was inserted – thrust – violently up to its hilt or handle.'

O'Keefe's mind flashed to Katherine Sheehan and her description of the needle used to pierce a pig's or bull's nose. 'Could the wound have been made by a needle of some sort? A knitting needle or some type of livestock tool?' he asked.

Major Wells considered the question for a moment before replying. 'It's possible. But I believe, based on the bruising here,' he pointed again to the wound, 'that the instrument was attached to a hilt or hand-guard of some sort. Speculation, of course.'

The subaltern continued to minute the inquiry and, for some moments, his pen nib rasping the ledger on the desk was the only sound in the room.

'How did you conclude that she didn't die from strangulation first?' Mathew-Pare asked.

'Your name sir, once again for the record?' the surgeon asked him.

'Detective Sergeant Thomas Mathew-Pare, Major. Scotland Yard.'

The surgeon took a long look at the DS and seemed to decide something about him. O'Keefe wondered what it was. The subaltern entered his name into the minutes.

Wells said, 'I determined this because, in cases of death by strangulation, the blood vessels in the eyelids show signs of profound oxygen deprivation. Our victim's one eyelid that remained undamaged by scavengers shows none of the burst capillaries one would expect to find in cases of death by asphyxiation. This young woman continued to breathe for some time after she was strangled and was killed by a single blow from a sharp object, severing her first vertebra and entering the brain stem, causing disruption of mid-brain nerve pathways, extensive bleeding, paralysis and almost instant death. Silent death too, I imagine.'

The room was quiet before Mathew-Pare spoke again. 'You say a single blow. Indicating …'

He had taken the words from O'Keefe's mouth. Maybe, O'Keefe thought, the Yard man would be of some help after all.

'Indicating,' Wells replied, 'that the killer was either exceptionally fortunate – or unfortunate, as the case may be – in his first thrust. Or …' and here the surgeon paused, 'as I'm inclined to believe, the killer knew what he was doing and has done it before. More than once, if I were to hazard a guess.'

The words shunted through O'Keefe's mind like the echoes of the dreams he had at night. *Silent death. Night work. Body-snatching.* 'Major Wells,' he said, 'have you ever before, by chance, come across a person suffering this type of injury?'

'Not a living person, Sergeant, and not by chance.'

O'Keefe nodded, knowing exactly what he meant.

One of the court-martial officers spoke up. 'Meaning what, Major?' He was a young man, perhaps in his early twenties.

'In the war, Lieutenant,' Wells answered, 'a quick and quiet way to remove a sentry on a night raid was a single thrust to the base of the skull with a very sharp knife or pick. The men used to fashion their own. Ugly things. The innovation of men and their means to kill shouldn't surprise one, I suppose.'

'But you said, forgive me, Major,' Masterson wasn't going to risk humiliation again, but there was an urgency in his voice that seemed to override his caution '… you also said it could have been a lucky blow? An accident even?'

'Yes, District Inspector. I did say that, but if this was an accident, it was an accident a trained assassin would be proud of.'

'Indeed,' the DI said, nodding to himself. 'I've heard that the IRA have recruited German war veterans into their ranks to swell the numbers, add some combat experience to the rabble of country boys.'

'Their very own Auxiliaries, Inspector? Imagine.' It was

Mathew-Pare. O'Keefe smiled inwardly. He was beginning to like the man.

Wells said, 'There were hundreds, thousands, of our own chaps who were rather proficient at this type of killing, Inspector, though I suppose, yes, the wounds could have been inflicted by a German. However, as I stated before, it could have been a lucky blow struck by an angry amateur. Not my line, I'm afraid, the "who done it" side of things. I'm in the "how it's done" line, Inspector.' O'Keefe caught the barest traces of a sad smile on the surgeon's face, a bunching around the eyes.

'Indeed,' the DI said again, nodding.

Masterson was right about one thing, O'Keefe thought: the IRA was in need of men with combat experience, but he dismissed the idea of German killers. It was ludicrous. There were plenty of Irishmen around the country who had fought in the trenches and plenty of those who could handle a knife. It was common knowledge that, although a history of service in the British army was cause enough to get a man shot as a spy by the IRA, the republicans nonetheless had among their ranks men who had served in the war. There had been mention in recent dispatches of a Rosscarbery man who had fought in the Mesopotamian campaign, in charge of training and ambush parties in West Cork, and no doubt there were others. There was also talk of Irish-Americans returning to the 'Old Country' as they called it, to do their bit for the struggle for freedom. This was pure speculation since none had been captured, but O'Keefe reckoned the returned Yank theory to be far more plausible than Boche assassins stabbing their way around the Irish countryside.

There was more to come from the surgeon. O'Keefe watched as he and his assistant rolled the body onto its back and drew the sheet up to the shoulders. Before recommencing with his findings, Wells said, 'Gentlemen, feel free to smoke. The smell could use some masking.'

The men in the cold storage shed welcomed the suggestion. Wells himself took a pipe from a pocket underneath his white surgeon's smock and proceeded to stuff it with plug tobacco. O'Keefe accepted a Gold Flake from Mathew-Pare and lit a match, holding it out for him and DI Masterson, extinguishing it and lighting another for himself. Mathew-Pare smiled.

'First to spot, second to get the wind …'

'Third to get the bullet,' O'Keefe said. It was a soldier's superstition. The sniper's curse. Never take the third light from a match.

The nurse folded back the sheet, exposing the gaping wounds on either side of the Y-shaped post-mortem incision where the young woman's breasts had once been. A white rib bone, O'Keefe noticed, was visible in one of the wounds. Cut to the bone, he thought.

Wells continued: 'The victim was also, I'm sure you'll be aware, mutilated about the breasts. I have determined that the mutilation was caused by an extremely sharp blade. The cuts were clean. No tearing about the edges of the incision, suggesting a cutting tool such as might be used by a butcher or surgeon. There were also no cut marks on the breastbone or ribs, suggesting, perhaps, an experienced hand at work. Speculation again, gentlemen.'

O'Keefe noted down: *Butcher? Surgeon? Combat exp.?*

The older of the two court-martial officers spoke now: Lambert, O'Keefe remembered. 'What ...' he said, unsure of how to phrase his question, 'what did the killer do, ah, with ...' He gestured towards the wounds on the chest.

'Couldn't begin to tell you, Lieutenant Lambert. We may never know. Unless Sergeant O'Keefe has the good fortune to catch the person who committed this crime and asks him.'

I'll need more than good fortune, O'Keefe thought, exhaling smoke.

Wells puffed on his pipe for a moment and then went on. 'The victim was tarred and feathered about her midsection, lower abdomen and thighs. I removed the feathering prior to autopsy, but photographs have been taken and will, of course, be entered as evidence in the case file. As well as this, the young lady was found to be wearing one earring in a piercing in her left ear. It has been photographed and entered as evidence.' He pointed at two cardboard boxes sitting on a large wooden crate of bully beef in the corner of the room.

'Only one earring, Major?' O'Keefe asked, remembering the earring as he'd seen it on the girl when they had found her.

'Yes, Sergeant. You might consider having another look around the site where the body was found, but I think it more than likely that it was removed or fell off at the scene of her actual death, as opposed to where she was left. Perhaps the earring was dislodged by the blow that killed her. Or perhaps she only had one and had lost the other.'

The young subaltern scribbled. Smoke gathered in lazy swirls about the hanging bulb as the surgeon carefully folded down the sheet, exposing the girl's abdomen and lower extremities. The pubic area, which had been so elaborately tarred and feathered before, was now starkly naked, the area of skin a cleaned, deathly grey. The surgeon explained how he had used a chemical solution to dissolve the tar and how he had retained the feathers as evidence. O'Keefe asked him why he had done this.

'Because the feathers struck me as unique, Sergeant. From more than one type of bird, I'd venture. Some of them quite beautiful, and deliberately arrayed about the pubic region in a pattern of light-coloured feathers at the outside,' he pointed to the girl's hipbones with his pipe stem, 'to a brown and black speckled dark selection closest to the genitalia. The choice of feathers seemed both deliberate and carefully arranged.'

O'Keefe nodded. 'So it would have taken some time to do, Major? The feathering?'

'Yes, exactly. Hours at best guess, and hours he had, I'd say. There was no burn trauma to the skin where the tar was applied.' The surgeon stopped and pulled again on his pipe, exhaling a thin stream of smoke into the arc of light above the body.

Mathew-Pare broke the uneasy silence. 'Meaning what?'

The surgeon nodded at his assistant, who folded down the sheet. O'Keefe had known doctors far less considerate of the dead and was thankful that Wells had seen in the young woman the life that had once been, the innocence maybe, which demanded respect, reverence, even in death. For a man who had no doubt seen as much carnage inflicted on the human form as he had, the surgeon had retained his sense of humanity. O'Keefe wondered if he could say the same of himself.

'Meaning,' Wells said, 'that, like the cuts to the breasts, she was already dead when the tarring was done.'

The surgeon went on to describe minor lacerations to the victim's genitals, which he allowed could have been caused during consensual sexual relations. There was ante-mortem bruising and some slight tearing in the lining of the vaginal walls.

'So was she raped?' asked Mathew-Pare. 'Was this a sex crime as well as an execution?'

Masterson shook his head slowly, as if in disgust.

The surgeon said, 'I'd lean more towards a sex crime than execution, myself. But there's no reason to say that it wasn't both. Rape and war have come as a matched pair for as long as they have existed. Sometimes, I imagine, it's rather difficult to separate the two.'

'Was there … evidence of emission?' Masterson asked, apparently having conquered his squeamishness.

'If there was, it was too degraded by the elements for us to say. If I were to guess, however, I'd say that whoever did this had a more than normal sexual interest in the young woman, God rest her soul.'

O'Keefe waited for Wells outside the shed.

'Major, could I ask you one or two more questions, if you wouldn't mind, I ...'

'Is there a public house in this town that still serves our like, Sergeant?'

'There is. Sure, there's always a publican who's not troubled with the choice between politics and money.'

The surgeon smiled. 'Whiskey doesn't know the difference between left and right, does it?'

'No, it doesn't. Let me change out of uniform and I'll take you.'

Ten minutes later, O'Keefe led the surgeon to the gate and a young constable let them out of the barracks' compound. He walked with the surgeon down Macroom Street, passing the darkened shop windows, soft rain peppering the tops of gas lamps. There was no one on the street, though the curfew was still an hour away. People tended to begin the curfew early. Trigger-happy army patrols were known to do their own timekeeping, once darkness fell.

They passed several blacked-out public houses, front doors shut, curtains and shades drawn. At the third, the surgeon touched O'Keefe's arm and stopped.

'Sounds as if there's life in this one, Sergeant.' O'Keefe noticed the surgeon licking his lips and imagined 6.45 in the evening was long past the hour Wells normally had his first drink.

'There is, Major. But that's not a pub we'd want to go into now. One of the first to bring in the boycott and one of the few to take it seriously. The publican's uncle was killed in a baton charge by one of our boys years back, during the land wars. The odd time some of the lads from barracks stop in, just to make a point that they've a right as Irishmen to drink anywhere they please. Not that the constabulary is supposed to take a drink in the first place, mind. But the publican won't touch their money, so they serve themselves and leave their money on the counter and sit in the bitter silence with the flaps of their holsters open. I've heard the measures are generous.'

The surgeon shook his head and walked on. 'I'll never understand your country, Sergeant.'

O'Keefe smiled. 'What's not to understand, Major?'

They entered the Ballycarleton Hotel by the rear entrance, avoiding the restaurant and lounge, and made their way to the residents' bar. It was a separate room with a small oak bar where they seated themselves on high stools. As if by magic, the owner of the hotel, Dominic Murphy, a stocky man in his fifties with the ability to please Peeler and Volunteer alike, appeared through swing doors behind the bar. O'Keefe asked Wells what he was drinking and the surgeon told him Bushmills. Murphy frowned and shook his head in a pretend show of sadness.

'Now Bushmills, sir. Of all the whiskeys a man could want,

it's the one I can't give you. Made up north, it is, I'm sure you know. Subject to the boycott on Ulster-made goods.'

The surgeon's face fell. 'But they've got it still in Cork. Surely …'

Murphy smiled and went on. 'Shame, the whole thing. Imagine, the boys putting a boycott on Protestant-made goods in Ulster, when it's their own that suffers through lack of work? Not right at all, it isn't.'

'But …'

'How much will it run us, Mr Murphy?' O'Keefe asked, tired of the charade. The Murphys of the world had ways of getting whatever they wanted, whenever they wanted, for the right price.

Murphy smiled. 'For yourself Sergeant, eighteen bob would do me just fine. Fair enough, gentlemen?'

'Fair's not a word I'd use, Mr Murphy, but it'll do.'

It was nearly a day's pay for the average Peeler. The true cost of the bottle was a quarter of the price. The hotelier smiled and left to get the whiskey.

Over the past months, the hotel had developed into a kind of free zone that welcomed both sides in the conflict. The RIC men and soldiers used the residents' bar; IRA men and their political representatives in Sinn Féin, the main lounge. There had never been any trouble in the hotel and O'Keefe didn't expect there ever would be. He explained this to Wells as Murphy was fetching the bottle. Murphy returned and enquired after their health and welfare as he poured out two glasses of the Bushmills, commenting on the weather and the football from England. O'Keefe imagined he did the same with the local boys out front, substituting some comment about the weekend's Gaelic matches for the soccer.

Wells gulped his whiskey and put his glass back down on the bar, taking his billfold from inside his overcoat. O'Keefe took out his own and his money was halfway to the bar when Wells handed the publican his price.

Murphy took the money and wedged it into a pocket of his waistcoat. 'Now, gentlemen, I'll leave you to your bottle. It's black with people out front it is.'

O'Keefe nodded and tipped his glass to the publican.

Wells spoke up. 'Thank you, Mr Murphy. One question, if you don't mind?'

'Certainly not, sir.' He smiled benignly.

'The Bushmills, Mr Murphy. Do you sell much of it in the lounge?'

Murphy, still smiling, replied, 'Of course, sir. A most popular whiskey, Bushmills. The boys would hardly do without it, would they?' He left through the swing doors.

Wells took another drink, then turned to O'Keefe. 'I'm beginning, I think, to understand your country a bit better, Sergeant.'

O'Keefe raised his glass, 'To my country, Major, a bit better.'

The surgeon laughed and drank, and O'Keefe did the same. O'Keefe liked the man. He seemed adaptable, non-judgemental.

'One more question, Sergeant – forgive me.'

O'Keefe nodded for him to continue.

'If you know there are active IRA men in the front bar, Sergeant, why don't you simply arrest them?'

O'Keefe lit a cigarette from a crushed box of Players' Navy Cut. Exhaling, he said, 'If I did that, who'd Murphy sell his bootleg Bushmills to?'

Wells laughed. 'Seriously though, why don't you?'

'Me personally?'

'No, but surely there are only so many of them. Why doesn't the RIC and the army simply arrest them all, lock them up and ship them off to their cousins in America or some other bloody place?'

'There's many who'd like to, believe me. Lock up every Irishman of fighting age. It would be one way of dealing with the problem. But *your* countrymen wouldn't stand for it. Imagine the letters pages to the *Manchester Guardian* and *The Times*: citizens of the Crown arrested on mere suspicion of being involved in insurrection. The public wouldn't tolerate it because they'd know it could be themselves next. The army interning every miner, dockworker or railwayman who went on strike or who was suspected of being a union member? They find the curfews and courts-martial of the Restoration of Order Act bad enough as it is, and I can't say I disagree.'

'But this is a different situation to striking miners, Sergeant. This is a war ...'

'It is? Do you see a war on, Major? I don't. I see what the readers of the morning papers see. I see British citizens under curfew, arrested and placed under courts-martial, citizens like any other in England, Scotland or Wales. Citizens assumed to be innocent until proven guilty and a free Press to keep an eye on it all. The fellas on that side of the wall can't be arrested because the good people of England wouldn't stand for it.'

The surgeon thought it over for a minute. 'Unless you suspect they've done something, committed a crime?'

'Of course then we can arrest them. Readers of *The Times* are against crime as a rule. Law and order types. Crime won't do, sure it won't?'

'Something tells me it's not just the breakfast readers of the British Press who restrain you from putting bracelets on the lot of them. You seem different to the average head-breaker.'

'More average than you might think, Major. And hardly any different from any of those men in the front bar but for the uniform. I want an independent Ireland the same as them. I just think there's a right and wrong way to go about getting it, that's all.'

'And a right and wrong way of preventing it as well?'

O'Keefe laughed. 'It's a steady wage and don't all the lovely schoolteachers want a fine Peeler for a husband?'

Wells laughed with him. 'And will you be allowed to arrest the killer of the young woman I opened up today?'

O'Keefe looked at him, the laughter gone. 'Sure, why wouldn't I be?'

The surgeon shrugged and drank again before speaking. 'Then I suggest, Sergeant, that you do your best to find the man who killed her. Because if you don't, he'll do it again.'

'Like he's done it before?'

'Just like that, Sergeant. Just like that.'

A silence settled over them. After some time O'Keefe asked, 'Do you think she was killed because she was an informer?'

'Not my job, the why of it.'

'As you said, "only the how of it". But I'm asking you, in your own opinion.'

The surgeon took time to light his pipe, then poured himself and O'Keefe more whiskey. 'If she was executed for political reasons, why bother tarring and feathering her after she was dead? And leaving her on the hillside?'

It was O'Keefe's turn to shrug. 'A warning to others maybe? To further terrorise the locals?'

'Is it necessary to terrorise them any more? A bullet and a body left in a ditch would do the same. Nobody talks these days anyway. This is a very popular insurrection, Sergeant. Surely you know that. Leaving the girl on the hillside like that would be excessive to say the least. It would cause the people of the area, who already, for the most part, support the IRA, to wonder what kind of boys they'd be supporting who could do such a thing to a young woman.'

'You're right. It doesn't make sense.'

'And you're forgetting one thing.'

'What's that?'

'That whoever did it took a lot of care to get it just right. That in my opinion – personal, you understand, not medical opinion –'

'Yes.'

'In my opinion, the body was the point of the killing – the possessing of it. The way the feathers were arranged, the way the body was laid out on the hill. Just think what kind of man it would take to do those things to the girl and then spend so much time with the body afterwards. Bad men, like your District Inspector imagines? A bad *man*, most likely. And no local cornerboy, I suspect. Political killing?' Wells shrugged again and sipped some more. His words were beginning to slur. 'All politics are personal, Sergeant. Don't forget that.'

O'Keefe swallowed the last of his second glass. 'I won't.'

'Don't,' he said. 'It's everywhere, politics. Murder is its own form of politics.'

Wells was losing O'Keefe now, the several whiskeys taking hold of him. A young army Private in Essex colours entered the bar and approached them.

'Major Wells sir, you're needed right away. We've a Crossley out front.'

'Needed for what? What could possibly be the matter at this time …'

'There's been an ambush sir, up the Macroom road. Near a place called Kilmichael. Loads dead, sir.'

'Loads?'

'Loads of ours, sir. Shot to ribbons, so the word is.'

Wells stood up and pulled his overcoat over his shoulders. 'Politics, Sergeant, remember that,' he said, placing a steadying hand on O'Keefe's shoulder. 'Murder is an extension of politics by other means – someone said that, or something like it.' And then he left, weaving a little as he followed the Private out of the bar.

O'Keefe poured himself one last glass of whiskey, replaced the cork and slipped the bottle into the pocket of his trenchcoat. There was a quarter of the bottle left. His mind drifted to Katherine Sheehan and how she too had been violated, mutilated. Bad men, the surgeon had said. One man, most likely. A bad man. O'Keefe would remember.

———

Politics.

It was half-past eight that same Sunday evening when O'Keefe arrived at the Ryan house. After leaving the hotel, he'd stopped at the back door of Casey's pub and undertaker's and convinced Casey to tend to the body of the young woman back at the barracks. He would need photographs of the victim's face that showed a likeness to life. The boycott meant the undertaker couldn't minister to the body of an alleged informer openly, and so O'Keefe had smuggled Casey into the barracks, his hat down, collar up. Casey would be paid for his work, but he did it more as a favour to O'Keefe, who had pulled the undertaker's son out of more than one scrape before the war. The dead needed tending and O'Keefe was well aware that he and Casey served the same master.

Now he was calling in another favour. He expected more resistance to this one.

'Come in, Sergeant. Come in. Nothing wrong I hope?'

Councillor Ryan's wife was a short, nervous woman. She wore her hair pulled back so tightly, it struck O'Keefe as more punishment than style. He assured her that there was no problem.

'A social call then?' she asked, leading him down the hallway of the house she and her husband, Sinn Féin Councillor Edward Ryan, had inherited from her father, along with a large creamery and dairy herd. Other than Murphy in the hotel, the Ryans were the only real wealth in Ballycarleton and it had been a natural move for Edward to enter county politics. He had been elected in the November 1919 local government elections, where Sinn Féin had taken an overwhelming majority of the seats. O'Keefe suspected that the Councillor's republicanism was a convenient sham, but Ryan – as Daly had once remarked – was a man with a knack for knowing which side his bread was buttered on, him being a dairyman after all.

O'Keefe also reckoned that if a fella like Ryan knew that Sinn Féin was the real future of Ireland, then the King could have spared himself the trouble and signed off on a republic right then. It was men like Ryan – who married into money and then made more – who told anyone who asked all they needed to know about the future of Ireland. The men with the money rarely got things wrong, O'Keefe believed.

Except once, when Ryan had got it badly wrong – proving to O'Keefe at the time that men with money might be sharper about most things, but that they were as dull as any man when it came to the fairer sex. And he half thought

Ryan's wife knew this as well as anyone. O'Keefe pitied her a little.

The Ryan's parlour was stiflingly warm, a coal fire crackling brightly, lace collars on the backs of stuffed, upholstered chairs. One of Ryan's daughters, a girl of sixteen or so, was playing a melody on an upright piano. O'Keefe recognised the tune: Thomas Moore's 'The Last Rose of Summer'. It was a most popular piece in Ireland and he remembered his mother singing it when he was a child. Somehow, he couldn't picture his mother singing it now, after all that had passed since then.

Ryan sat with his eyes closed, the *Cork Examiner* draped across his lap, a contented smile on his lips. O'Keefe wondered what he was dreaming about and then decided he would rather not know.

'Edward, you've someone to see you.'

The girl stopped playing and looked up at O'Keefe. She was pretty in a conventional way but, like her mother, wore her hair drawn severely back from her forehead. She smiled at him and O'Keefe smiled back, unable to avoid the notion that the young woman on the butcher's table back at the barracks was only a few years older than this one.

Ryan sat forward in his chair and blinked. There was a look of momentary panic on his face and just as quickly it was gone, buried behind a politician's smile that was buttressed by two well-fed chins spilling over a starchy white collar. He stood up, his hand extended. This man, O'Keefe had to remind himself, was once a small dairy farmer.

'Sergeant O'Keefe. To what do I owe the pleasure? Fierce damp aul' night to be out in!'

'Could be worse, Councillor. You're looking well.'

Ryan threw back his head and laughed, patting his large belly. 'Public office suits me, Sergeant. That and Lizzie's stews.'

His wife chipped in now, a brittle smile on her face. 'Sure, Sergeant, he'd eat four men's share and then ask when dinner was!'

The three Ryans laughed and O'Keefe wondered, as he conjured up a polite smile, what kind of life the daughter must lead, amidst all the bluster and money. O'Keefe allowed Ryan to guide him out of the parlour and further down the hall to his office. He heard the Councillor's wife calling out that she would bring tea, but Ryan told her not to bother.

'I think it's late enough for the real stuff, don't you, Sergeant?' Ryan closed the door to the office and indicated a chair in front of his desk. The room was as stuffy as the parlour, the dying embers of a fire in the grate still giving off heat. Shelves full of creamery accounts books and animal husbandry manuals lined the walls. Ryan's desk, with papers neatly aligned and a tall, thick accounts book open to a page of figures in ruled columns was set before a window overlooking the darkened farmyard and dairy. To the left of this was a smaller desk, piled high with papers, an overflowing ashtray, invoice sheets, receipts and more ledgers. Ryan saw O'Keefe looking at the desk and picked up the ashtray, emptying it into the fireplace. He stirred the embers with an iron poker.

'Colbin,' he said, pointing to the desk beside his. 'My accounts man. Manners of a tinker, but a damn fine bookkeeper. Those bloody Churchman's he smokes – stink like Satan left the doors to Hell open, boy. He's a good man, though. Indispensable. The business suffered greatly when he was away.'

Colbin, O'Keefe remembered, had been 'away' in Mountjoy Prison, lifted in Crossbarry with a stolen Enfield in one of the creamery trucks. He had been released in April when Dublin Castle, in its wisdom, had decided it would be a good idea to free one hundred and twenty republican prisoners because a number of them had decided to stop eating their porridge. It was just one of the many things the Castle had done to let Peelers know how low down they stood in the scheme of things. The RIC locked up the bastards, took bullets in the head for their troubles, while the government let the same bastards go again because they were afraid of the stir in the Press if some of them lost a few stone on hunger strike.

O'Keefe tried to picture Colbin but couldn't remember ever meeting him. He was no longer a particular problem for the police, however, because he was a known entity. It was the gunmen about whom they had no knowledge – the young men with no photos or names in a file – they needed to worry about.

Ryan opened a cupboard beneath the bookshelves and took out a bottle of Power's whiskey. Setting a glass in front of O'Keefe on the desk, Ryan poured out a generous measure and then sat down behind the desk and poured himself one.

'Sláinte, Sergeant.' He smiled and raised his glass. O'Keefe half-raised his and drank. Ryan gasped and pursed his lips with the pleasure of the sup. O'Keefe felt the bite at the back of his throat and then the warmth as the whiskey snaked its way into his belly. He said, 'He'd want to be good, your bookkeeper. What with the troubles ye've had.'

During the summer, workers in Ryan's creamery had demanded better wages. There had been talk of inviting in a trade union to organise a branch. Ryan had refused to countenance his workers joining a syndicate and a short strike had followed, during which the milk and cream had curdled under the warm August sun. In the end, rumour had it that Ryan arranged for some of his pals in the Ballycarleton IRA to speak to the workers. Rumour again: several of these 'labour negotiators' had since been employed by Ryan to keep an eye on things. There was nothing like having an army to break your strikes, O'Keefe reflected.

Ryan smiled and waved off the notion of trouble. 'Nothing really. Bolshevism comes in many guises. Just last week Father McCartney warned of its materialism as a greater threat to holy Mother Church than –'

'Republicanism?'

'I didn't see you in church, Sergeant O'Keefe.'

'I wasn't there. Not safe for us to attend, you may have heard, what with the brave boys of the IRA shooting Peelers on the way into Mass.'

'Ah Sergeant, you know yerself. There's a war on. So people tell me.' He winked at O'Keefe, as if it were all a little joke.

O'Keefe's face remained blank. It was never the Ryans of the world who mopped up the blood of their dead friends, he thought. Never the well-stuffed likes of Ryan who ended up shot to pieces on a hillside or in a trench, in the blood-dyed sea. He could sense the black numbness on the fringes of his consciousness. He set his whiskey down on the desk.

'Cornerboys' revolt, I've heard people call it,' he said, forcing down the blackness, replacing it with a quiet anger that would allow him to do what he had come here to do.

'Now now, Sergeant. A legitimate army, led by a legitimately, democratically elected government.'

'An army that threatens to shoot priests if they give the holy sacraments to Peelers? Shoots men who survived four years in the trenches in their beds as spies –'

'Acts of war as carried out by a small army in the face of an enemy with overwhelmingly superior numbers. The Crown has over five thousand of its bullyboys in County Cork, Sergeant, armed to the teeth and well paid for their trouble. Unfortunate things happen, but one can hardly find cause to complain of David attempting to slay Goliath using any means at his disposal. There's nothing reprehensible in the use of stone and sling, surely?'

'Maybe to Goliath there was. Had Goliath been going into Mass, unarmed, or was just back from a foreign war, bothering nobody, David would be seen as a murderer, not as a hero.'

The Councillor laughed. 'Sergeant, you should be a magistrate rather than a policeman.'

'Crime is crime. Doesn't matter where a man sits.'

'At the bench or in a straw lodge, Sergeant?'

O'Keefe shrugged, picked up his glass and drank more whiskey. He was tired of the thrust and parry. Ryan represented an enemy he was coming to hate more each day. Not because of their cause – that of a free, independent Ireland – but because of their methods. He thought of the young woman on the hillside and of Katherine Sheehan, and was certain in his heart he had been right to call on Ryan.

'So then, Sergeant, I can see you're not in uniform, so I'm assuming this is a social call of some sort? Some matter for the council perhaps?'

Ryan was still smiling and for a moment O'Keefe wondered if maybe he'd dreamt the whole thing; wondered if his life before the war had been a fabrication, a muddle of dreams and whispered rumours blasted into fact on the beaches and dusty hills of Turkey. Ryan looked for all the world as if he had no shame, as if he thought nothing of what O'Keefe knew of him and had seen; of what Jim Daly and he had done on Ryan's behalf six years before.

O'Keefe swallowed another sup and looked hard at Ryan. 'I've come to ask you for a favour.'

Ryan continued to smile at him. It was the slick, emotionless smirk of the professional politician. This smile would tell you what you thought you wanted to hear and tell you nothing at the same time. O'Keefe had a flashing memory of a member of the general staff on the deck of the *River Clyde*, grounded off V Beach. A poncing, jumped-up lieutenant-colonel from some big house in Wicklow with that same fucking smile on his face, telling the men of the Royal Dublins and Munsters that the beach was as clear as the water; that Abdul had hit the high road at the first salvo of the accompanying battleships' big guns the night before. Smiling like Ryan was now. *Clear as the water*. The water didn't stay clear for long. O'Keefe shoved the memory aside and decided that Ryan was going to help him, one way or another.

'Well, Sergeant, you know that as an elected representative I am here to serve the people of this district and county to the best –'

'I know the speech, Mr Ryan. Save it. You remember a woman outside of town, on the Timoleague road, was attacked, three months or so ago? Her name was Katherine Sheehan. She was selling eggs to the barracks in Bandon.'

The man closed his mouth and the smile shifted a little. It was still there, but it had lost some of its sheen. Perhaps, O'Keefe thought, Ryan was thinking of a way he might paint what had happened to the woman as the 'legitimate act of a legitimate army'. Ryan nodded, taking a cigarette from a silver box on his desk and lighting it. O'Keefe pressed on. 'Some of your boys didn't like it –'

'Now hold on there a tick.'

'Let me finish.'

'I have no power over the actions of –'

'I said let me finish!' His voice was hard and sharp, and the smile dropped away from Ryan's face. 'She was assaulted, probably raped, by some of your mob. Two brothers mainly. One is named William Skelly. The other, we think, is his younger brother Thomas. I don't know if they were official or not, but they had sanction.'

Ryan pointed at O'Keefe with the lit end of his cigarette. 'There *was* a boycott on, Sergeant O'Keefe. The woman was defying a Dáil government order. A government which was elected by the people of Ireland, lest you've forgotten.'

O'Keefe reached down into his briefcase and withdrew two files, opening the one he had taken from Head Constable Murray's cabinet. He began to read aloud from the Major's report: '... *infection of wound to left buttock. Patient refused examination of genital area but cursory inspection during cleaning of buttock wound would indicate bruising about and around genitalia, indicating possible sexual assault ...*'

Looking up from the page he saw that the smile was back on Ryan's face. The Councillor took a pull on his cigarette, exhaled and said, 'An unfortunate event no doubt. Excessive, to be sure. But what exactly do you want from me, Sergeant?'

O'Keefe opened the second file. Bandon barracks had posted it on in response to his query with a handwritten note from the head constable there explaining his reasons for suspecting the Skelly brothers for the assault, along with the information that they were no longer living in the family home. From inside it he removed an old arrest photograph of William Skelly – he had been prosecuted for malicious wounding of livestock in 1913 as a fifteen-year-old – O'Keefe laid it down on Ryan's desk. He did the same with Thomas Skelly's; a lad who'd spent more time in Bandon court than he had at school, for various petty offences. The boys in the photos were young men now, respectively twenty-two and nineteen.

'These two bastards, the Skelly brothers,' O'Keefe said. 'I want you to find out where they are and tell me.'

Ryan's smile stayed locked in place, but the skin on his face had taken on a mottled, angry flush. 'I have no truck with the IRA, Sergeant. I am an elected representative of the people. And even if I did know who to ask ...'

O'Keefe stood up, taking his briefcase from the floor. 'Find out where they are and tell me.'

'Sergeant, I don't know how you got it into your head that I could help you.'

'I still have the photographs.'

Ryan looked as though O'Keefe had slapped him. 'But, Jim ... Sergeant Daly said that he'd given them all to me. He ...' Some strength returned to his voice now. 'Does Daly know you're here? Does he? He made a promise to me. A gentleman's promise that I didn't think he would break.'

'It was he told me to come to you.'

'But we had an agreement. I paid –'

'He told me to tell you all bets were off. Haven't you heard, Councillor? There's a war on.'

Ryan slumped down in his chair, hatred in his eyes.

'You have two days or the *Examiner* gets the photos. Or maybe I'll just give them to your wife. As an elected

Peeler

representative, you'll understand the importance of obtaining justice for those of your constituents who've been in some way wronged.'

'Get out of my house, Sergeant.'

'Two days,' O'Keefe said and saw himself out.

Mathew-Pare and his two men had set up in the servants' cottage at the back of the stable yard, temporarily displacing two older constables – Dunn and Slainey – who had billeted there since long before it had become necessary. The pair were very put out, having to move into the barracks with the other constables and Tans. They wanted an easy life and had found one, living together in the cottage like an old married couple. They did as little as possible on their patrols, since they were both nearing retirement, leading their escorts of soldiers into the most obscure and IRA-free areas in the district before returning to the cottage where they brewed tea, read day-old copies of the racing papers and played endless games of thirty-five on a low table they placed in front of the turf fire.

There were two beds in the cottage. Mathew-Pare had taken one and his men would sleep end to end in the other. Eakins, the larger of the two, sat down on the bed and said, 'I've slept with uglier cunts, me.'

The second of Mathew-Pare's men, the lean, knife-faced Starkson, replied, 'Just keep your paws to yourself, Eako, and mind you don't eat beans.' He laughed and took from his bag a Winchester pump-action shotgun with its barrel and stocks cut down.

'Nice feed of beans and I'll blow your bones out the rack, Starks,' Eakins replied.

Mathew-Pare smiled. They were good men. He had served in the trenches with Eakins and had met Starkson on a job in Fallujah. Together they had fixed so many problems that Mathew-Pare couldn't put faces to most of them now. Sorting out problems for the King was how he viewed his work. Good for King and country. He doubted if Starkson and Eakins thought much about their work at all, but they liked it, wherever it took them. Behind the lines in the shell-pocked towns and villages of France and Belgium. Down fly-blown, labyrinthine streets in Mesopotamia and Egypt, into the stout and smoke-charged backrooms of Dublin. Both were handy with a blade or a gun.

There was a knock on the cottage door. A young constable stood on the doorstep, shifting nervously from foot to foot. 'Detective Mathew-Pare? There's a woman and her husband here. The DI, sir, he told me get you.'

Mathew-Pare met the woman and her husband at the gate and had the constable on guard open it to admit them and their cart. The evening air was damp and cold, and the donkey's breath puffed from its nostrils.

'Your daughter,' Mathew-Pare said. 'You say your daughter's missing, is she?'

The woman nodded. 'This last week, sir, she's missing. She always comes to us on a Sunday and brings us a small something. And Sunday last she didn't come. And then a young man came, enquiring after her, like. A man says she's not been in work the week past.'

'And was this man from her place of work?' He questioned the couple gently as he led them, taking the ass by its harness into the barracks yard.

'He didn't say. But he looked ... he didn't look like a man from the Barton's Works.'

'In what way, Mrs ...?'

'Costelloe. My daughter's name is Deirdre.'

'Deirdre. Well, I certainly hope the girl we have is not your Deirdre.' He gave a bland smile, stopping now in front of the cold storage room. 'You said your daughter worked in the Barton's factory? Isn't that in Cork?'

'She does, sir. She rooms in the city with her friend from home.'

Mathew-Pare noticed her insistence on the present tense. But in her drawn face, and in the bleary, reddened eyes of her silent husband, he saw resignation, as if they had somehow known they would one day find their daughter laid out before they'd the chance to die themselves.

'Deirdre's a good girl, sir,' Mrs Costelloe said. 'A good girl; always something for us from her packet, each week.'

Mathew-Pare wondered if they would miss their daughter more than the money she brought into the house. Jobs in the Barton and Sons' plant were hard to come by, he imagined. All jobs in Ireland and Britain were, for that matter. A young girl would hardly leave one unless she had good reason.

'Of course she is,' he said, already knowing he had found out who the girl was.

District Inspector Walter Masterson heard the woman's high, keening wail and opened the steel shutters in his office to look down onto the stable yard. He heard the keening rise and carry, like wind through a gap in a window frame. Watched as Mathew-Pare led the old woman and her husband from the cold storage room back out into the yard, holding the woman by the arm. He felt a vague sense of sadness for the couple's loss, triggered no doubt by the woman's keening. It was a sound he had heard any number of times as a child when one of his father's tenant farmers had passed away. There were women, when he was a boy, who travelled to wakes around the adjoining countryside as paid keeners, hiring out the shrieks of grief that marked the death of a man, a woman, a child. The girl in the shed, Masterson realised for the first time, had been someone's child. Though so obvious, the realisation struck him like a hammer blow.

He pushed the young woman's image from his mind; the image of the last time he had seen the girl before today. Then, the girl had been lively, laughing. He pressed closed his eyes and steadied himself. Opening his eyes again, he looked on as the parents followed Mathew-Pare across the yard and entered the barracks on the floor below him. Mathew-Pare would make them tea and ask them questions. District Inspector Masterson wondered what the old couple could tell him. And then he wondered what Mathew-Pare would want to know.

O'Keefe recalled the incident as he walked the curfew-quiet streets back to the barracks.

Edward Ryan had met the woman through a lonely hearts' advertisement in the back of a 'journal of men's affairs'. It was an under-the-counter publication reputedly printed in Paris but more likely grafted together on a cellar press in Putney or Preston. Only Jim Daly could help him, Ryan had explained. As a distant cousin by marriage to Jim's wife Muireann, he considered Daly family and believed he would be sympathetic. A delicate matter. Off the books, of course. A generous fee. Blushing, Ryan had shown Daly the torn copy of the lonely hearts ad. *'Strict lady wishes to meet generous gentleman for gentle guidance.'*

Daly had agreed to clean up Ryan's mess and enlisted O'Keefe to help. 'Sure,' Daly had said to O'Keefe at the time, handing him the photographs that had arrived at Ryan's creamery by post, 'if that's "gentle guidance", I'm not sure I'd want to see the rough.'

In the pictures, Ryan was nude and tied to a four-poster bed. In each of the photographs he was in a different position: hands and feet spread and bound to each bedpost in one; feet drawn back and tied to the same posts as his hands, exposing his privates in another. In one photo, there was a shiny, black object inserted in his rectum. In another, the woman – whose face never appeared in any of the prints – was nude from the waist down and squatting over Ryan, appearing to urinate on him.

The thing that struck both Daly and O'Keefe as odd was

that Ryan's face was unmasked and perfectly identifiable in each photo. When they asked him about it, Ryan told them that he had no idea how he'd been photographed because there had only ever been himself and the 'lady' in the room.

The pictures had shocked O'Keefe at the time. He supposed now that he had been a naïve lad, the same as most young Peelers. But the most notable thing for him by far was the look on Ryan's face. His was a visage of such pure rapture as he'd never seen before or since. On his face in each of those photographs was a smile that was profoundly different from the one he wore in public. O'Keefe would bet a year's wages that it was a smile Ryan's wife had never seen.

Daly and O'Keefe went first to the room where the pictures had been taken, the master bedroom of a brothel in Queenstown. They questioned the madam of the house at length, but ultimately believed her story that the woman and her fiancé had merely rented the room from her on several occasions. They had not wanted any of her girls and had paid a more than reasonable rate for the room in what were generally off hours for the brothel.

Asked why they wanted the room, the madam had replied that the woman's fiancé enjoyed watching her *frolic* with other men. Inspecting the room, Daly and O'Keefe found the means by which the photographs had been taken – a floor to ceiling false mirror that was accessed via the wardrobe. It was a popular room, the madam said, though if she had known the kind of carry-on she had seen in the pictures had been taking place, she would never have rented it to them. *Watching an old frolic is one thing, but that* – the woman had pointed to a photograph – *bless us and save us, that's just not hygienic, now, is it?*

Daly had instructed Ryan to respond to the letter included with the pictures. He did as they told him, replying to a numbered box in Cork general post office, asking the blackmailers to meet him in person since he was afraid to send such a great sum of cash through the post and, to be fair, he didn't trust the woman and her fiancé to send on the photographs as they had promised.

The couple were greedy amateurs and took the bait. Daly and O'Keefe met them and took them for a spin in Ryan's Talbot motor car. Stopping at the Old Head of Kinsale, they left the car and walked the couple to the edge of the cliffs at revolver point. It was then that the couple admitted the scam and told Daly and O'Keefe where they could find the copies of the photographs in their rented room near the harbour in Queenstown. When Daly and O'Keefe had gone there with the couple, they had found many more than the four that had been sent, but they were all of a kind.

After putting the two on the mailboat, they took the pictures back to Ryan, who burnt them, one by one, looking at each of them in a private way so that O'Keefe thought he might just be a bit sorry to be destroying them. When he had finished, Ryan asked Daly if there were any more of them, anywhere, and Daly had acted surprised, saddened by the question. How could he imagine something so low of a man who was nearly his own blood? Had he not gone to great risk to keep Mr Ryan's reputation, his marriage and possibly life from the most savage of tarnishes? Hadn't he? Daly could lay it on. Ryan apologised for the question.

O'Keefe received ten pounds for his help, with which he bought his Box Brownie. He liked the irony of it at the time, being paid to reclaim photographs and using the money to buy a camera. It was the same camera he had taken with him to the war. He still had it, though he used it now only at crime scenes. He sometimes wondered if he would ever be able to look through the lens of a camera again and see anything but death.

———

Mathew-Pare was leaning in the lit doorway of the cottage, smoking and smiling blandly. O'Keefe had a flashing sense of danger from that smile. It passed quickly enough. Mathew-Pare called him over across the barrack yard.

'Enjoy your chat with the Major, Sergeant?'

O'Keefe shrugged, non-committal. 'Never hurts to keep the medics sweet, Detective. Never know when you might need one.'

Mathew-Pare tossed his cigarette onto the cobbles. 'Never a truer word.'

O'Keefe could see one of Mathew-Pare's men moving about in the cottage. The man seemed to be cleaning weapons. O'Keefe nodded towards the interior. 'You fellas seem fairly well geared-up.'

Mathew-Pare nodded. '*Si vis pacem, para bellum.*'

O'Keefe translated using his schoolboy Latin. *If you want peace, prepare for war.* Used, he remembered, by Georg Luger in the naming of the parabellum pistol he had invented.

'Can't be too careful,' Mathew-Pare continued. 'You heard about the ambush up the road? Kil-something? Pack of Auxies, fifteen, twenty of the fellows in two Tenders, gunned down. Not a single survivor, so the word is.'

'I heard. Wells was taken away from his whiskey to attend. Sounds bloody.'

'Collins and his lads, two weeks ago up in Dublin and now this?' Mathew-Pare shook his head, lit another cigarette and held the packet out to O'Keefe, who took one.

'Some say there's a war on, Detective. Bad things happen in wars.'

Mathew-Pare smiled. 'A war? This?' He held his hands out as if to take in the whole of West Cork. 'No, this isn't a war. Cushy number, this.' He sucked hard on his Gold Flake.

'You sound like the DI. "*This is not a war. This is nothing but a collection of criminals intent on levelling anarchy on the emerald jewel of the Empire!*"'

Mathew-Pare laughed through his nose. 'I suppose you're right, but that's not how I meant it. I didn't say the IRA weren't an army and that they didn't *want* a war. I only said this wasn't it.'

'What's a war then?'

Exhaling smoke, Mathew-Pare said, 'A war today involves distance. Industrial production of armaments, mass destruction. A war eats economies. Requires the devastation of the landscape and every bloody living thing in it. You were there.'

'Dardanelles,' O'Keefe said.

'Same as the Western Front, I'd think. And yet look at this place. Most beautiful place on earth, County Cork. Landscape as rich and green as ever and the place crawling with my fellow man just going about his business, paying no heed to the few idiots like ourselves and the great republican army.'

'Tell that to those Auxies. Or those lads dead in their beds in Dublin.'

A shadow crossed Mathew-Pare's eyes. O'Keefe could see it even in the half-light that came from inside the cottage. Almost before he was aware of it, the shadow was gone.

'You're right, of course, Sergeant. You could tell it to the young woman we looked at today, as well. She might think differently.'

O'Keefe nodded.

'Deirdre Costelloe,' Mathew-Pare said.

'What?'

'Why I called you over, Sergeant. I've been working while you were away. That girl in there,' he pointed to the cold storage shed, 'her name is Deirdre Costelloe.'

Mathew-Pare had even thought to hold the body for another day in case the surgeon wanted further access to it, telling the parents to return for it the next morning. He had told them that O'Keefe, as the lead investigator, might have questions for them as well. O'Keefe asked him had the undertaker done his work before the parents had come and was told that he had. A small mercy, he thought. He hoped Casey would not get shot for his troubles but it had been the right thing to do. Besides, O'Keefe needed a photograph of the victim's – Deirdre's – face, without evidence of the ravages of the violence done to it, to show potential witnesses, though perhaps now he could get one from her parents.

It was a clever move, O'Keefe was forced to admit, to keep the body for another night as a means of having the parents return for questioning in the morning. Whatever Mathew-Pare's reasons for being in County Cork, he thought, the man had done well by the case.

'I appreciate your help, Detective.'

Mathew-Pare tipped an imaginary cap. 'Think nothing of it, Sergeant.'

Turning to go back inside the cottage, the Detective stopped and looked back at O'Keefe, 'You know another reason why I think this is no war, Sergeant?'

'No.'

'Because in a proper war, someone's always willing to bury the dead. Maybe not right away, but eventually. We buried Boche. They buried our lads. Civilised behaviour all round. Cricket, real war. But here? Here, the parents of a dead girl have to take away their daughter's body on an ass cart because even the undertakers are afraid to lay out the bodies of informers. Imagine that.'

Again O'Keefe shrugged. 'Laying out is still done at home here. Maybe ...' But he was too tired to argue the point.

Mathew-Pare shook his head and smiled as if he were remembering a joke. 'No, this isn't war, Sergeant. This is something worse. Can't have a war without rules. Then you have anarchy, like your DI says.'

O'Keefe smiled wearily back at him. 'Oh, there are rules to this war. It's just a matter of working out what they are.'

———

Liam Farrell arrived in Drumdoolin after dark, clutching his bag of legal papers as a cover against any Tan or Tommy who might question his presence on the streets. The documents were a convincing collection of legal briefs and contracts drafted by his contact and employer in Ballycarleton, given to him the previous evening by Seán Brennan. The documents would work with both the Peelers and the regular army. With the Auxiliaries, you took your chances. They were just as likely to shoot you as waste time checking credentials. *The bloody bastards.*

Soon after thinking this, on turning a corner into the village square, he was forced to duck into a doorway and press himself close to the frame – where to his disgust, he found himself praying – as a patrol of soldiers accompanied by two constables passed, their bootsteps and clanking equipment heralding menace, like thunder from an approaching storm. He was still shaking minutes after the patrol had departed from the village, equal parts fear and anger at his own cowardice rattling his slender body.

The low rumble of conversation stopped when Farrell

entered the low-ceilinged pub. Farrell smiled nervously, his face reddening, tipping his cap to the gathering. He received no response from any of the drinkers and made his way to the bar.

'Fine evening,' he said to the bartender, a balding man with a florid face and a filthy collar worn over a threadbare shirt. The man's eyes were deep-set, pinpricks of mean light in a fleshy, drinker's face. Farrell instantly dismissed him as a drunkard. Like his own father, he thought, and then felt shame in the thinking.

The bartender nodded. 'What can I get you, boy?' His face remained unmoved.

Farrell felt his face burn. *Boy*. The word was a common, meaningless end to many sentences in Cork, but in the barman's usage Farrell felt a rebuke, a judgement. Unconsciously he shot a look at his reflection in the tarnished mirror behind the bar. His face was young and smooth-skinned, even to his own eyes, the lenses of his spectacles thick and smudged. He looked a student, and maybe not a college one at that. 'Pint of Murphy's, please,' he said, his voice sounding as young to his own ears as his face looked. He cleared his throat and lowered his voice an octave. 'A sup would do me nicely so it would. Long walk I've had today. All the way from …'

He was about to say Inchigeela, but stopped himself. He realised he was speaking to cover his nervousness, but still had the presence of mind to catch himself before he let slip operational details. Already the dictates of intelligence work had started to take hold. It occurred to Farrell that perhaps

Hurley had seen this in him. Had been shrewd enough to spot a talent for the combat of smoke and mirrors Farrell himself had never known he possessed. On thinking this, he became convinced of it and felt a certain pride.

The barman set the pint in front of him and made to turn away.

'Sorry,' Farrell said, 'I couldn't have a word with you, could I?' He smiled in what he thought was an ingratiating manner.

The barman made it clear with a dismissive wave of his hand that he was not interested in any kind of chat. Farrell was stumped. He needed to find a man called O'Higgins, the officer-in-charge of the Drumdoolin Company, but assumed he should be circumspect in his use of the name. But the barman's lack of co-operation was making this difficult.

Farrell leaned across the bar and as quietly as he could while still being audible, asked the barman where he could find O'Higgins. The barman stared at him for a moment and Farrell thought for a moment that he might be simple. He waited for the barman's answer and when it didn't come, asked, 'You do know him? Bernie O'Higgins? Where can I find him?'

When the barman finally spoke, his words were almost what Farrell had expected.

'And who would it be that wants to know?'

Farrell smiled that smile again. *Here we go lads*, he thought. He leaned in further, notching up the conspiratorial drama he and the barman were performing for the pub's patrons.

'The proper lads want to know, that's who, boy. Now get him for me, would you?' Farrell fixed him with his hardest stare, a look he was sure would convince the man of the seriousness of his mission. The barman stared back with a neutral, almost gormless expression before finally nodding.

'I'll get him for yeh. You wait there and I'll get him.'

Farrell nodded with satisfaction, the nervousness he had felt upon entering the pub evaporating into the smoky air.

He had finished his pint and was thinking how much he could do with another, when the barman returned through the doorway behind the bar, closing it softly, waiting for the audible click of the latch. He moved to the taps then and poured another pint, topped it off carefully and set it on the bar in front of Farrell. Barely moving his lips he said, 'That one's on O'Higgins himself, boy. Get it down you. He'll be along shortly.' He gave Farrell a stagey wink and turned to his other customers.

Some minutes later there was a knock on the door behind the bar. The barman turned to Farrell. 'That'll be him. Come now and you'll meet him, so you will.'

Farrell got up from the stool and followed the barman, passing behind the bar and through the doorway into the kitchen of the cottage that backed onto the pub. He had enough time as he passed through the kitchen to notice an old woman sitting in front of the fire, a long-stemmed pipe hanging from her lips, a black, knitted shawl around her shoulders. He wasn't sure, but he thought she blessed herself as he passed out of the kitchen and into the small stable yard behind the pub.

The barman stopped in front of him and, as his eyes adjusted to the darkness, Farrell noticed that the man was pointing to the small, whitewashed cowshed across the yard.

'You'll find him in there,' he said, in a harsh, excited whisper. It was the most animated the barman had been since Farrell's arrival. 'Don't keep him waiting, boy,' he muttered under his breath as he turned and went back into the pub, leaving Farrell to grope his way across the yard to the cowshed. The door to the shed was ajar and Farrell could see a sliver of yellow light from an oil lamp flickering unevenly in the draught.

'O'Higgins?'

There was no reply and he called out the name again. He pushed open the door and stepped over the threshold into the shed. The blow came from behind, lightning fast, to the base of Farrell's skull and he felt unconsciousness take him.

He was woken by a bucket of cold water thrown in his face. He started and tried to stand, only to fall onto his side in the musty straw, unable to gain his balance, his hands bound behind his back. The pain in his head was intense and he closed his eyes and waited as a wave of nausea rose in his throat and then slowly subsided. When he dared to open his eyes again, three men were standing over him, blocking out the light from the lantern. His spectacles were missing, so their faces were blurred.

One of the men leaned down and Farrell could smell beer and tobacco on his breath. He extended a hand and slapped Farrell's face playfully. 'Wakey, wakey. Time to talk so it is, yeh soft cunt.' He smiled and slapped Farrell harder in the face. 'Get yer arse up on that stool, boy. And do it now before I get cross.'

Farrell struggled upright and two men lifted him onto a milking stool. When he was sitting, a gruff voice ordered him to turn and face the wall. Farrell's body began to shake. He started to speak and could hear the terror in his own voice. 'I was sent here by Seán Brennan, Brigade Intelligence –'

'Turn around and *whisht*!'

The voice was like a whip, cracking across Farrell's nerves. It had come from the shadows, beyond the remit of the lantern light and belonged to a fourth man. Farrell thought he had heard it recently, but his mind was so muddled he couldn't place it.

'So you're looking for Bernie O'Higgins, are yeh, boy? Well, you've fucking found him you have.'

It was the voice of the barman, Farrell realised, a man he had dismissed as a simple, rustic sot. A stab of shame pierced him. It was a physical sensation, a wound to his pride almost as painful as the throbbing in his head.

'Look,' he said, 'my name is Liam Farrell. Lieutenant Liam Farrell, 3rd West Cork Brigade Intelligence. I've been sent here by –'

'By Brennan himself. So you said.'

Farrell heard the smile in the voice and felt the cold steel on the back of his neck, the place where his neck joined his skull.

'And do you think the man himself will appreciate my service to the cause, boy? I hope he does. It'd make me fierce glad, to be recognised like.'

Farrell heard the other three men laugh and listened as one of them struck a match and lit a cigarette, and thought there was nothing in the world he wanted now more than a smoke. He was about to ask for one when he thought how much like a last request it would sound.

'Now,' Bernie O'Higgins said, 'tell me who you really are and I mightn't shoot you.'

Farrell swallowed and clenched his hands into fists to try to stem the shaking. 'I am who I told you. Did you look in my bag? Those papers in there. Those were given to me by Brennan as cover against any patrols I met on the way. I've come today from the column training camp at O'Sullivan's farm in Inchigeela. Honestly.'

'If you've been sent by Brennan, where's the letter from the man? I saw no letter, no orders from the man in your papers.'

Farrell was surprised by the question. And in his surprise, he was suddenly angry. 'Letter? What do you mean *letter*? What do you think I am, the bloody postman?'

'Get smart, boyo, and you've had your chips. Now where's the letter if Brennan sent you?'

'I told you, I'm a member of the Intelligence Squad. Do you think he'd send a letter with his name on it for any shite of an Auxie or Peeler to pull me on? None of us would be in this business very long if we went carrying signed letters round the place like summer sweethearts. Now untie me.'

O'Higgins snorted. 'You tell us who you're jobbing for and I'll not start with your jewels, boy.' He took the gun barrel away from Farrell's neck and reached it down over his shoulder, pressing its barrel firmly into Farrell's crotch.

But Farrell's voice was suddenly confident. He could still talk. No one could take that away from him. 'I order you to release me right now,' he said, 'or you'll be held up on court-martial charges. Charlie Hurley would himself be a witness in the proceedings, as would Tom Barry and Seán Brennan. So if you –'

'There'll be no court-martial if I plug you and sink you in a boghole, will there, boy?' The amusement was gone from the voice. Farrell could feel the barman's breath on his neck. It occurred to him that if this O'Higgins really wanted to kill him, he would have done it already and had him halfway to the boghole by now.

'If you plug me, Brennan will send somebody else. Or he might send for you, O'Higgins. Then you'd have some explaining to do, wouldn't you? About what happened to the fella he sent to ask you about that girl on the hillside. Now cut me loose, so I can ask you the questions I was sent here to ask.'

'What questions? What about the girl?' It was the man who had slapped him, standing to Farrell's left. 'What questions are you on about, boy?'

Farrell detected doubt in his voice. 'The questions –'

'Lads, I'm going to shoot this fucker,' O'Higgins said. 'He's a Tan spy, he is. The county's fat with them. Listen how he talks.'

But there was hesitation in O'Higgins' voice for the

first time. Farrell had hit a nerve at the mention of the girl. O'Higgins again raised the gun to his neck. Farrell changed tack.

'If you shoot me, make sure you use one of the six Enfields you Drumdoolin boys took delivery of, courtesy of the raid on the Royal Mail van last August. I imagine they're getting rusty and could use the firing.'

The gun barrel pressed harder into his neck and Farrell wondered had he pushed too hard. He could hear the breathing of the men behind him and then the bated silence, as if in expectation of the gunshot.

'Bernie, he knows about the girl on the hill.'

'Of course he does. Every fecker in the town saw them Peelers ask me about it in the bar.'

Another of the voices spoke now. 'And how did he know about the rifles? Only the four of us here know how many we took off Brigade.'

'The four of us and who knows what fuckin' Crown spies. I say we plug the fucker. Nobody will find him.'

'Tell me about the girl.' Farrell was persistent if nothing else. A part of him was surprised by his newfound assertiveness and another part of him was very much at ease with it. He had a sudden memory of his father ordering about one of the serving girls in his draper's shop. 'Did you or your men execute her, O'Higgins?' Farrell swivelled around on the milking stool so that he was facing the barman. 'As officer-in-charge of the Drumdoolin Company, did you or any of your men execute the woman Crown forces found on the hillside?'

Even in the dim light, Farrell could see O'Higgins' face redden with anger. His eyes bright with violence, jaw rigid, O'Higgins stuck the gun in Farrell's mouth, the barrel clacking against his teeth.

'Bernie,' one of the men said, 'you saw the girl. What if Brigade thinks we done that to her? We should hear the lad out.'

O'Higgins clawed down the hammer of the gun and cocked it back again. Farrell could smell the sharp tang of his terror sweat.

'Bernie,' the man said again and gripped the barman's arm. 'We'd better hear him out.'

Watching O'Higgins, Farrell could sense his growing uncertainty. Suddenly he lowered his gun and moved to cut Farrell's bonds.

'Fine,' he said. 'Let's go back into the bar and hear what he has to say. But know this, boyo. If I don't believe you, your body won't be as easily found as that girl's.'

The absurdity of the situation didn't strike Farrell until he tried to sleep, later that night. He was in the master bed of a small labourer's cottage in Drumdoolin – its owners, Dessie O'Driscoll and his wife, exiled, against Farrell's will, to share a bed with their two young children. His clothes were freshly washed and hanging in front of the fire to dry. His belly was full and the cottage and bed were clean and warm. A delicious feeling of comfort was creeping over him, despite the dull ache in his head, and yet the oddness of it all made him want to laugh. He was sleeping in the house of the man who had knocked him unconscious earlier in the evening.

Over bottled stout they had taken from the pub after Farrell had finished answering questions and asking his own, he had sat with Dessie O'Driscoll at his table while his wife served them eggs and the previous night's spuds fried into a hash, and the man had apologised for hitting him: O'Higgins had ordered him to do it and, like any good Volunteer, he'd followed orders. Mind you, O'Driscoll had said, he couldn't have done *that* to no young girl, not even if Michael Collins … not even if de Valera himself ordered him to. Still, a whack in the aul' loaf never did much harm.

'And what did you hit me with?' Farrell asked.

'A hurl. But the flat of the blade, like. Sure if I'd used the edge you'd be dead instead of horsing down eggs and poppies.' Mrs O'Driscoll had smiled at this and shortly afterwards there was a knock on the cottage door. Without waiting for it to be answered, one of the men from the shed entered and theatrically set down a bottle of Paddy whiskey on the table.

'Glasses, Dessie,' the man said, his ruddy, labourer's face glowing red with drink and obvious excitement. O'Driscoll called for his wife to bring them and she did, setting down three mugs taken from the dresser.

'What's the scandal, Stephen boy?'

The guest glugged whiskey into the three mugs and called for Mrs O'Driscoll to take a sup as well. He raised his mug.

'A toast.'

Farrell, O'Driscoll and his wife raised their mugs. 'Who is it to, Stephen, in the name of Jesus?' O'Driscoll asked.

'To the boys of Kilmichael is who. To Tom Barry's flying column which is only after sticking the boot to two lorryloads of Auxie bastards – forgive me, Margaret – on their way back to Macroom. Twenty-odd dead and all! A bloody great miracle of a massacre!' His smile lit the room and the O'Driscolls smiled along with him.

So, it had gone off, Farrell thought. A pang of bitterness seized his throat and he swallowed it down. 'And our lads,' he asked, 'were there any losses?'

'Not that I heard, boy. Word is Barry and Connors and the lads tore into them Auxies with their bayonets, like … like spades into soft ground, by fuck – sorry Madge.'

Connors. Farrell remembered his conversation with the man in O'Sullivan's barn the previous evening. What a long time ago it seemed. Goose pimples crawled up his back. Seamus Connors. Running a bayonet like a spade into soft ground.

'To the boys of Kilmichael,' Dessie O'Driscoll said, and Farrell, Mrs O'Driscoll and Stephen from the shed repeated it and swallowed down the whiskey, the burn of it welcome in their throats. In his mind Farrell could see Connors, his eyes black and his bayonet bloody.

After O'Driscoll and his wife had gone to bed, Farrell drafted a brief report in a code of his own devising, leaving a key to the code with his host to be collected by a Cumann na mBan messenger later. Women did a lot of collecting and transporting of messages for the IRA. They had the advantage of voluminous skirts and dresses to hide things under and were much less likely to be thoroughly searched by soldiers or police.

He had been told that the solicitor for whom he'd be jobbing as cover would provide him with the standard and most recent code produced in Dublin. But the dogs in the street knew that the code was usually long broken by the time it reached Cork from GHQ and that it was used more as a means of passing bogus information on to the enemy than imparting genuine intelligence to IRA units around the country. So Farrell invented his own. He was sure Brennan and Hurley would be impressed.

In his code he wrote that he believed the story told by the men of Drumdoolin Company. Yes, they had seen the body on the hill and no, they had not ordered the young woman's execution or taken part in it in any way. He believed them when they said they could hardly abide the thought of the type of men who could do that to any woman, spy or not. In fact the only men in the country they could imagine doing something of the sort were the Auxiliaries and some of the Tans they had met around the place. But, as Farrell had suspected, they were worried that the body would be assumed to have originated in Drumdoolin since it was found so close to that town. Again, Farrell believed them when the men said they had never laid eyes on the girl in life and that they would have known the young woman if she was from the area. His conclusions were: 1) The Drumdoolin Company of the IRA, West Cork Brigade No. 3, had no part in the death of the young woman and had no part in her placement on the hillside north-west of the village of Drumdoolin in the state of disarray in which she was found; 2) The young woman did not come from Drumdoolin or from any of the surrounding villages, and her identity remained unknown.

Farrell went to sleep that night in Dessie O'Driscoll's best bed more than proud of how he'd handled the investigation thus far, telling himself that he was cutting it nicely – if he did say so himself – in this job of work that was intelligence.

———

The boy grew older.

His mother was bad for the drink by now, cracked in the head, haggard and wild. She'd lost a front tooth to one of her 'friends'. And now the boy knew what she did. Whoring, the older boys in St Crispian's Terrace called it. His mother. A whore for the drink. The boys stayed away from him, beat and chased him when the fancy struck them. He was smaller than they were, his clothes ragged. Their parents were disapproving of his presence. A silent, watchful soul at the margins of any group of children. Watching. Wondering what other lives might be like and unable to imagine.

It wasn't long before he began to wander the streets of the garrison town alone. He was at home with the night sounds of the town, listening to the drunken soldiers stumbling back to barracks; listening to the songs bellowed behind the doors of pubs; listening under other families' windows. Listening and watching.

There was a serving maid in one of the big, redbrick houses three streets over and a world away from St Crispian's Terrace. From the high wall at the back of the house he would watch her as she readied herself for bed. It was always after she had finished in the kitchen, swept the last crumbs from the tabletops, set bread dough under a towel to rise, fresh bread for the master in the morning. And his eyes would follow her as she moved upwards, her candlelit presence appearing briefly in each of the staircase windows, then moments later in the light of her bedroom at the top of the house.

Her garret room was so small, no view of her was impeded. He watched as she slipped out of her maid's uniform and pulled her white slip over her head. She wasn't much older than him – maybe sixteen – and her skin seemed to glow in the light, her nakedness emanating a warmth that was as distant as the sun. And each night, when she turned to take her nightdress from under her pillow, when she turned and bent down and her buttocks and back were exposed, displayed, framed by the window, he stiffened. And his mind erupted in images of eggs, distending hens' cunts, the servant girl's body covered in feathers, white, dappled brown, black. And he pictured the girl, in his hen house, alone with him, where he could bide his time and look at where the eggs came from.

On top of the wall, at the end of the garden, he watched, he touched himself and spattered the hydrangeas at the base of the wall with his seed.

Monday
29 November 1920

Before he had gone to bed, O'Keefe contacted the wireless station in Bandon in order to forward the details of the murder and post-mortem findings to other RIC barracks in the county, along with a request for any information concerning similar murders or assaults on young women. This was routine procedure and one he thought necessary. The constabulary, for all its faults, still possessed men who had an encyclopaedic knowledge of local crimes and intelligence. Many of the RIC's opponents, in fact, accused it of being nothing better than the eyes and ears of the Crown in Ireland. There was some truth to the accusation. By 9.30 that morning, O'Keefe had received official intelligence reports from two different barracks in the county.

The first one – taken off the wire – concerned the murder of a known prostitute, found dead in a lane off Merchants' Quay in Cork six weeks previously. It did not detail possible similarities with the hillside murder, but listed the name of the RIC Crimes Special Branch sergeant who had investigated, out of Tuckey Street barracks. O'Keefe had heard of the man – something of a legend in Cork city – and decided it would be useful to meet him.

The second message was more immediately useful, he thought, being from the head constable in Ballincollig barracks. O'Keefe knew the man personally. Kieran Synott was an aggressive copper, a man with so large a bounty on his head that he rarely left his fortified barracks and only then under the escort of some of the hardest Auxiliaries you would never want to meet. There was a certain irony to it,

O'Keefe thought: the Peeler now the imprisoned. O'Keefe wondered, as he read the transcript of the telegram, why the man bothered staying in the constabulary, concluding that Synott must feel safer in than out. Ex-coppers were just as sweet a target for Volunteer gunmen as active ones.

Synott's message read: *Costelloe family strong republican background. Daughter only child. Late birth to parents. Michael and Mary née O'Regan. Michael Costelloe involved as youth in Land League actions in district. Assumed to have been party to arson attack on Bridgeton House, Bridgeton, Co. Cork, 14 July 1879. Arrested and held. Not brought up. Assume active distrust of constabulary. Hope this helps. Best regards. KS.*

There was a knock on his office door. It was Keane, the young constable looking as if he had slept a full eight hours in the finest hotel, instead of the maximum of four hours kip O'Keefe knew he'd had after patrol and another table tennis marathon with Heatherfield.

'Sergeant, the girl's … the victim's father and mother are here to collect her. Detective Sergeant Mathew-Pare said I should give you the nod first.'

'Good man, Keane.'

Keane waited until his sergeant stood. 'Sergeant O'Keefe?'

'Mmm?' O'Keefe shrugged on his dark green uniform tunic and buttoned it to his neck. He gave each of the buttons a good wipe with a handkerchief. He wanted to look his best for the parents, as much out of respect for their grief as what Synott had said in his wire about their republican sympathies. *Assume active distrust of constabulary.* O'Keefe assumed as much of everybody lately, but most civilians would relax a little if it was safe to do so and if they felt the constable in front of them was there to serve them and not the Crown. Ninety per cent of Peelers were Irishmen like the people they were entrusted to protect. Pariah status was a recent phenomenon and one that could, O'Keefe vaguely hoped, be countered with professional and fair service. Or maybe, he thought, giving his black boots a final swipe of the brush, I am as naïve now as I was when I signed on.

Keane said, 'Sergeant, I was wondering if I could sit in on your questioning of the family. I just thought that …'

'Of course you can. I could use the help. I'll need you to get the tea, assuming they'll take it, and then watch and listen. I'd like you to just listen. I'll be taking notes, so I want you to be able to confirm or reject any assumptions I make. It's important to always have two people in an interview because two impressions of the same situation are never the same. Do you get me?'

'Yes, Sergeant. Serve the tea and just listen. I can do that.'

'I know you can, Constable. You've been doing good work lately.'

'Thank you, Sergeant.'

'Go and show the family up.'

Deirdre Costelloe's parents looked much as O'Keefe had imagined they would, her father a typical small farmer in his worn, patched, canvas coat and flat cap, his face ruddy and riven with weathered gullies. He had several days of grey stubble on his chin and jaw, and his eyes were red-ringed with grief. There was a cloying, stale smell of drink emanating from his dishevelled clothes. O'Keefe figured this, as much as his grief, could account for his bloodshot eyes. The Costelloe woman wore a black shawl, wrapped tightly around her shoulders, and a thick cotton skirt. Like her husband's, her face was lined by years of poverty and exposure to the elements. It was a face that appeared to O'Keefe to have seen more than its share of sorrow.

He guided the couple to chairs he had arranged beside his desk, and introduced himself and Keane. They sat in silence, the man fidgeting nervously with his cap, the woman plucking at the frayed ends of her shawl. There was little resemblance between mother and daughter that O'Keefe could see, but countrywomen grew old before their time, pretty faces and fetching figures destroyed by physical labour and child-bearing.

'First, Mr and Mrs Costelloe, I want to say how sorry I am for the loss of your daughter, God rest her. I know this is a very hard time for you both.'

They nodded but only the wife looked at him. Her husband kept his eyes firmly on the floor. O'Keefe offered them some tea. Perhaps some bread and jam? Mrs Costelloe seemed about to say yes when her husband looked up. There was bitterness in his voice.

'We want nothing from you but our daughter.'

'I understand, Mr Costelloe, but you have to realise I'm trying to catch the person or people who killed your daughter and I need your help to do it. It's crucial I ask you these questions, do you see that?'

O'Keefe turned to the man's wife.

'Can I ask you, Mrs Costelloe, where did Deirdre live during the week? She was at the Barton and Sons' plant, wasn't she?'

The woman swallowed. 'Yes, she was. A grand job and a grand wage in these days when there's so little work to be had. She was so pretty, I'm sure she got the job because she was so pretty, so …' O'Keefe finished the sentence in his head. *So full of life.*

The image of the young woman's body on the butcher's table flashed through his mind.

'And where did she live, Mrs Costelloe?'

'She shared a room with a girl from Ballincollig, in a fine house on the quays in Cork. Thick friends for years they've been, our Deirdre and Anne. Anne had got the job in Barton's first, on account of her uncle working there. It was she arranged it for Deirdre. Deirdre done lessons – typing lessons. She was a good girl, and clever that way.'

O'Keefe noted the address and thought about asking after suitors but decided he could get the information from her girlfriend more easily. 'And this girl's surname?'

'Duffy. Anne Duffy. A kind friend to Deirdre all these years.' The woman choked back a sob, her voice breaking for the first time.

'Are we finished now?' It was the father. A smell of stale whiskey wafted across with his words. 'Can we not take our girl now, Sergeant?'

'I've just a few more questions.'

'Why? Your English friend last night asked them all already, didn't he?'

O'Keefe appealed to the wife. 'Mrs Costelloe, you mentioned to the Detective last evening that a man came by your farm three days ago, asking after your daughter.'

She nodded, looking to her husband before answering. 'Yes, he did. A grand, long fellow he was.' The woman knotted the shawl ends in her hands and gathered them into white-knuckled fists.

'And was he a soldier, do you think?'

Her husband answered for her. 'He was no British soldier. My daughter didn't run with soldiers. Or Peelers.' His eyes burned red and shone with fresh tears. He would have heard about his child being labelled a traitor. 'She was a good girl, Deirdre. She was no informer.'

O'Keefe nodded in sympathy. 'Can you give us a description of this man, Mrs Costelloe?'

The woman shot a look at her husband, but he was again staring at the floor, his Adam's apple rising in his throat as if he were forcing back sobs. O'Keefe thought of the army surgeon's Bushmills in his desk.

'Can I offer you a short glass of something, Mr Costelloe? I know this must be hard.'

He didn't look up but O'Keefe saw him considering the

offer. After a moment, he said, 'I told yeh, boy. I've come for my daughter and not to take soup from Crown spies like yerself.' He swallowed again. His refusal to take the whiskey was costing him dearly.

O'Keefe reached into his desk anyway, taking out the bottle and telling Keane to fetch glasses. The man's ignorance angered O'Keefe. He was trying to help him and his wife, and all the farmer could do was dredge up the rebel posturing of his youth. It crossed his mind to ask Mr Costelloe if he reckoned the IRA was doing anything to help discover who had killed his daughter. Instead, he turned back to the wife.

'A description, Mrs Costelloe?'

'Yes,' she said, nodding, understanding that she had no one to turn to but himself, and O'Keefe was forced to admire how women had the power to weigh matters in a way men didn't. The freedom of Ireland could wait. The RIC might be Crown spies but maybe – just maybe – they could find the man or men who had killed her daughter.

'He was tall and thin and he spoke like he was a Corkman. His clothes like a labourer's. And he'd a scar ...' the woman pointed to her face and drew her finger across the skin over her eyes, 'a red welted scar, it was. Like it'd happened not long ago.' She pointed to the scar on O'Keefe's own face. 'Not like yours. Fresher, like.'

O'Keefe made a note of this and looked up to see Keane returning with three glasses.

'Are you sure you won't have some tea, Mrs Costelloe. Sometimes a cup helps.'

She shook her head. 'No. As soon as we can be gone with our Deirdre, the better, Sergeant.' Out of the corner of his eye, O'Keefe saw Mr Costelloe staring hard at the bottle on the desk.

'And what did this man ask of you, Mrs Costelloe?'

'Only, where was Deirdre? He said she hadn't been to work on the Monday. That's when I started to worry, Sergeant. She didn't come home to us on the Sunday and then this stranger came with news that she hadn't been at the factory.'

Tears welled in her eyes and began to roll down her cheeks. O'Keefe's stomach knotted with compassion, a vision in his head of how his own mother must have looked when she had heard about his brother's death. He shoved the image aside, writing in his diary. *No show, home, Sunday. No show, work, Monday. Confirms post-mortem chronology?*

'Did he tell you his name, Mrs Costelloe? Or say how he knew your daughter?'

She shook her head. 'No, only that he was called Seamus. Never saying why or how he knew her. Sergeant, he put the fear of God in me.'

'Did he threaten you?'

'No, no, it was the scar. But not only that. His eyes, it was. Like bogholes. They were brown and green and near black, they were. And he wore a soldier's coat.'

'An army coat? Long or short, Mrs Costelloe?'

'Short. With the big pockets.'

'But you don't think he was a soldier?'

Again the woman looked to her husband, a heavy

pleading in her eyes. *Please*, the look seemed to say. *For Deirdre.* Suddenly her husband reached across, took the bottle of Bushmills and poured a full measure into one of the glasses. He handed it to his wife. She took a sip and grimaced, tears rolling down her face. When she set down the glass, it was as if her husband had given her permission to speak for them both. O'Keefe felt a sudden respect for the man. He wasn't going to help, but he would let his wife do so. Taking the bottle, O'Keefe poured another large measure in the second glass and handed it to the farmer. The man accepted it without a word and drank.

'No,' his wife continued. 'He wasn't that kind of soldier.'

'What do you mean, Mrs Costelloe "that kind of soldier"?'

She looked at her husband again. 'He wasn't the King's army like. But he might have been …' She stopped, as if afraid to go on.

'Might have been what?'

'Might have been a Volunteer soldier.'

'And did he give you a surname, any message for Deirdre?'

'He said to tell her Seamus called for her, if she came back.' The woman covered her face with her hands and sobbed.

If she came back. It could mean anything or nothing. As he was thinking this, O'Keefe sensed a presence outside the office and glanced over at the door. 'Hello, is someone there?' The couple and Keane turned and looked at the closed door. It opened a crack. 'It's only me, Sar'nt. Keane's after telling me ye might be wanting tea.'

O'Keefe shook his head. Tom Reilly, a retired constable allowed to live in barracks for his own safety, was a decent if awkward presence in the barracks, pitied and scorned in equal measure by the new generation of young policemen and Tans.

'No, Reilly. I don't think we'll be needing any tea.'

'Grand, Sar'nt. Just if I could be of any help.'

'Actually, you can.' O'Keefe stood up and went out to him in the hallway. 'Can you run down to Casey's for me, Tom? The parents are to take away the girl's body and –'

'Casey's won't take her, y'know. She's been labelled and Casey's his business to think of.'

'I know he won't take her and I'm sure the family will want to lay her out at home. But they have to have something to take her in.'

'In, Sar'nt? Sure, didn't they come with a cart?'

'A coffin, Tom. Go round the back entrance and talk to Mr Casey. Take Keane with you. Get a coffin from them. If it's herself answers, tell Mrs Casey we'll pay the going rate for it. She's an anvil, but a decent woman at heart. You can tell her who it's for. And help get the girl's body in it for them. It's enough to ask them to cart home their only daughter without having to heave her off a butcher's table.'

Reilly nodded. 'And if it's himself?'

'What?'

'Mr Casey.'

'Tell him I'll pay double the going. He's done enough for us already, the poor bastard.'

'Nothing poor about an undertaker these days, Sar'nt.'

———

After he'd seen the Costelloes off with the coffin roped down in the back of the cart, Keane returned to the office. He sat down at Daly's desk but waited for O'Keefe to speak.

'Right, Keane,' O'Keefe said, looking up from the interview notes he was re-reading for the third time. 'If you were in charge, what would you do next?'

Keane thought for a moment. 'I'd go to Cork, I think, and interview her friend at Barton's. That's what I'd do first. If anyone knows about any fellas she might have been seeing, it'd be the girlfriend, aye. Then I'd search her digs and interview the landlord.'

'Go on.'

'I'd also get on to "I" division in Dublin Castle as well, soon as I could, and see if the Raid Bureau have anything on a Seamus something with a scar on his face. That's assuming it was his real name.'

O'Keefe nodded and said, 'And assuming the scary lads in the Castle are able to tap up suspect files on Christian name only. Lot of Volunteers go by "Seamus" I imagine.'

Keane's eyes flared and O'Keefe smiled. Every copper had the odd eureka moment. There were few feelings that matched it. 'But,' Keane said, leaning forward now, 'what if they're able to cross-reference rebel files by area and then pull all the Seamuses from Cork city and West Cork. Then, if they could add the scar, we could show any photographs they come up with to the Costelloe woman. She might put a finger to one of them.'

'Good man, Keane.'

'Will I put it on the wire?'

'Do that. And then shift yourself into mufti.'

'Sergeant?'

'Civvies, Keane. And bring a sidearm and spare cartridges. Never know what you might come across in the big city.'

O'Keefe's plans to take Keane and make a quiet run into Cork to question the flatmate, stopping into Tuckey Street barracks on the way back, were disrupted when he entered the yard and found that the barracks' only functioning car – a dented Ford Tourer with steel plates riveted to the inside of the door panels as makeshift armouring – had been requisitioned earlier that morning by the DI and his batman, Senior. Keane looked devastated and, as if to raise his spirits, threw some ju-jubes into his mouth.

The barracks was due delivery of two more Fords, one a half-car with armour and an open back, as well as another Crossley, but these had been held up in Dublin because of striking dock workers who had refused to unload ships carrying provisions for the Crown forces in Ireland. O'Keefe thought of Daly's petitions to the police trade union and wondered, if he joined, would he have to strike in sympathy with the dockers. Stranger things had happened. Would continue to happen, he reckoned.

With a pang of bitterness, he noticed the DI's personal car, a gleaming black Daimler, sitting unused in the yard.

Typical, he thought. Didn't want to risk bullet holes in his own lovely motor. He walked to the sheds and pulled open a large steel door on runners. There was a smell of grease, motor oil and cigarettes. The barracks mechanic had the bonnet up on the Crossley that had taken the bullet in the grill; the guts of its engine were laid out on a tarpaulin on the floor. Seeing O'Keefe, the mechanic said, 'Don't even fuckin' ask, Sergeant. No offence.'

None taken. One man could only do so much. The mechanic went back to work and O'Keefe shut the door without uttering a syllable. He returned to Keane, who was standing on the rain-slick cobbles, chewing sweets. Mist hung in the air, amplifying the cold.

'We could wait for one of the patrols to come back and lift us in as far as Bandon or Crossbarry,' Keane said.

'It would take too long. Sure, we could be stuck all day in either place with no guarantee of getting back, even if we did make it to Cork.'

Aware of Tom Reilly coming through the gate, busily packing his pipe with tobacco, O'Keefe called over to him. 'Tom, did the DI say where he was taking the Ford?'

The man took his time lighting his pipe, then looked up. 'Sure, why would that puffed-up cunt tell me a thing like that?'

Reilly had a point. It had been a stupid question and O'Keefe himself was no different from the majority of constables in his resentment of the cadet system and the generally Protestant officers from ascendancy families who benefited from it. Still, Reilly was living in the barracks on the goodwill of the DI.

'There's no need for that, Tom.'

Reilly continued walking towards the barracks, pulling on his pipe as if he hadn't heard.

'In need of a car, Sergeant?'

Mathew-Pare was standing in the doorway of his billet. His own Ford, moisture beading on its black polish, sat idle in front of the cottage.

'I was going to take the barracks motor but …'

'But some puffed-up cunt beat you to it?'

O'Keefe shot an angry look at Reilly's back. 'Looks like it,' he said.

The Englishman smiled, motioning with his head at the Ford. 'Hop aboard, gentlemen.'

O'Keefe hadn't intended bringing Mathew-Pare, never mind his two heavies, but a journey of any kind through the countryside could be dodgy. Even if some local Volunteer mob didn't know you were a Peeler, the IRA had taken to requisitioning cars for the cause. O'Keefe supposed it couldn't hurt to have them along.

———

Just past noon, the secretary to the general manager of Barton and Sons' Tractor Works on Marina Quay met them in reception, a wood-panelled room with a fire in the grate and framed agricultural scenes on the walls. O'Keefe was aware from the newspapers that Barton and Sons' had suffered a slump with the end of the war, the demand for tractors dropping off significantly. Indeed, Fordsons – a much larger factory further down the quay – was winding down its production of tractors to focus on producing Model Ts for Ford. This shift had led to Bartons taking almost sole control of Irish tractor manufacturing and so, despite the drop off, they were doing well enough filling the demand that Fordsons had left them. O'Keefe had read something about contracts to make parts for Ford cars as well, but he knew little enough about it. He didn't imagine it would matter.

The secretary, a thin, angular woman in her forties wearing a tweed skirt and jacket, led them down a hallway that ran to the side of the shop floor and up some stairs to the accounts and general manager's offices. She stopped outside an office marked General Manager and knocked on the clouded glass window. The hallway had a bird's eye view of the factory floor below and they watched as the shiny red shells of Barton and Sons' famous tractors were craned onto steel chassis. Further down the line, blue sparks showered the floor as other workers spot-welded joins. The noise was constant but purposeful. A job in the Barton and Sons' plant was coveted in Cork. Few places of work in the city paid better.

After a moment, a voice called, 'Come in!'

The secretary gave them a nervous smile as she opened the door. 'Mr Barton,' she said, 'it's the police. They're here to interview one of the girls. I thought it best if they spoke with you first. Sergeant O'Keefe and Detective Sergeant Mathew-Pare.'

O'Keefe watched through the open door as Barton cleared away what appeared to be a deck of cards from his blotting pad and stood up. 'Of course, Miriam. Of course. Gentlemen, please …'

O'Keefe and Mathew-Pare entered and Barton came around his desk, hand extended. Keane and Starkson waited on the landing outside the office. The big man, Eakins, had waited outside with the car.

'Thank you for seeing us, Mr Barton,' O'Keefe began.

'Please, call me Richard. Around this place, my father is Mr Barton. Now, what is it I can do for you, gentlemen?'

'We don't really need talk to you, sir. We're looking to speak to one of your typists, a Miss Anne Duffy.'

Barton indicated a velvet upholstered sofa. 'Please, Sergeants, have a seat. I'll get the girl you're looking for now.' The plant manager paused at the doorway, a smile playing around his lips, his thick, dark eyebrows raised. 'She's not in any kind of trouble is she, Sergeant?'

O'Keefe realised that Barton might not have even known Deirdre was missing. 'Mr Barton, one of your employees has been murdered. Another typist, Anne Duffy's friend, Deirdre Costelloe. Were you aware of the fact?'

The smile faded. 'No … no. My God. What happened to her?'

'Would you send for Anne Duffy, please?'

The manager paused as if he wanted to ask something

further and then thought better of it and left the office. A moment later he returned. 'My secretary is fetching the girl, Sergeant.'

O'Keefe thanked him, then asked, 'Did Miss Costelloe get on with everybody here at work, Mr Barton?'

'As far as I know. I don't personally supervise the employees, Sergeant, as you'd well imagine. But from what Miriam – my secretary – has said in the past, I'd say she was a popular girl. Pleasant, hard working …'

Barton was a big man in his early thirties, going soft around the middle, with dark, oiled hair and thick eyebrows. He wore an expensively cut suit of grey wool-silk mix. His mouth was tweaked at its edges with a smile. O'Keefe put the smile down to the general nervousness people felt around police and the detached, grateful discomfort people felt when tragedies struck close by but, blessedly, not close enough to do damage.

'Competent,' Barton continued, 'quite a pleasant young thing from what little I saw of her. I was surprised when Miriam told me she hadn't come to work last week.'

In his diary, O'Keefe wrote: *Good worker, regular attendance.* 'Did she, as far as you know, go around with any of the fellas from your factory, Mr Barton?'

Before he could answer, the typist was ushered into the office. Barton arranged a chair in front of the sofa. He hovered behind it as if reluctant to leave the young woman alone with the policemen. O'Keefe indicated the door with a nod. Barton opened his mouth, but then smiled again and left the office.

The girl didn't sit down right away. 'Is this about Deirdre?'

'Yes,' O'Keefe said. 'I'm afraid it is.'

'She's not in any trouble, is she?'

'Why don't you have a seat, Miss Duffy. I'm Sergeant O'Keefe and this is Detective Sergeant Mathew-Pare.'

She acknowledged both men with her eyes and sat down. O'Keefe couldn't think of a way to soften what he had to say. 'Miss Duffy, I'm sorry to inform you that Miss Costelloe is dead. She – '

'Dead?' Anne Duffy blessed herself instinctively. 'But how? How did she …'

'I'm sorry you had to hear of it this way, Anne.'

O'Keefe called her by her first name. He didn't sense any resentment of the police and wanted to establish a bond with the girl, knowing that if she saw him as someone whom she could trust, she would be less likely to withhold information for political or moral reasons.

'Now, Anne, what I'm going to tell you will be hard to hear. I want you to know that. I also want you to understand how sorry I am. Mr and Mrs Costelloe told me you two had been friends since you were young girls.'

Anne Duffy wiped her eyes with a handkerchief pulled from the sleeve of her dress. The blue wool suited her, O'Keefe thought, highlighting her pale skin, flushed cheeks and blonde hair. She was short and plump, however. Nothing like as pretty as her friend. O'Keefe wondered if Anne had envied Deirdre. The young woman sniffed and swallowed her tears, nodding.

'Deirdre was murdered, Anne. She was killed by someone, and my job is to find out who did it.'

She wasn't looking at O'Keefe or Mathew-Pare. Her gaze was focused on things far outside the confines of the stuffy office. 'The bastard,' she said.

'Sorry?'

'That bastard.' She looked up at O'Keefe. 'It was that bastard, Shay Connors. I know it was!'

O'Keefe chanced his arm. '*Seamus* Connors?'

The girl nodded.

'He was after her no end.' Tears began to run down the girl's cheeks. 'He was a bad one, Sergeant.'

'How was he a bad one?'

She looked at him and almost smiled. 'Sure you should know him well. Heaven knows he's shot enough of you.'

He circled the name on the page several times and noted the new information.

'And why do you think this Seamus Connors killed her, Anne? Why would he do a thing like that to Deirdre?'

'You really don't know him, do you Sergeant?'

'No, Anne. Tell me what he's like.'

'He's evil is what he's like. Though he thinks he's God's and Ireland's own man in Cork. There's a pure black soul in him, never mind the raw knees and his Rosary beads worn down to nubs.' She was crying now, her voice breaking with the effort not to sob. 'I told her she'd regret stepping out with the likes of him, but she wouldn't listen. Deirdre, she liked that kind of a fella …'

'The religious kind?' Mathew-Pare asked, his voice gentle. The girl shook her head.

'What kind, Anne?' O'Keefe asked.

She wiped away her tears and looked into O'Keefe's eyes. 'The dangerous kind.'

Barton's secretary returned with tea and they sipped in silence for a moment. Mathew-Pare surprised O'Keefe by recommencing the questioning.

'Miss Duffy, did you share rooms with Miss Costelloe?' His voice was as bland as his face. A half-smile – a futile attempt at warmth – played on his lips.

'Yes, we do …' the tears came again and the girl placed her cup back on the tray, 'did.'

Mathew-Pare nodded and confirmed the address. She again began to weep and he waited for the girl to compose herself. 'And were you not concerned when she didn't come home for several days? Surely you must have been worried?'

Anne Duffy looked up at him. 'Of course I was worried, especially when she didn't come to work. She'd never missed work before. But it wasn't like it was the first time.' She hesitated and O'Keefe sensed she was worried about damaging her friend's reputation.

'Wasn't the first time she'd stayed away from your lodgings?' Mathew-Pare prodded, in a light, non-judgemental tone. O'Keefe conceded the man was doing a fine job. He was an experienced interviewer; that much at least was clear.

The girl nodded and lowered her head to stare at the wrinkled handkerchief balled in her fist. O'Keefe asked her,

'Did she stay with Seamus Connors, Anne?' Sometimes it was easier to speak of things if you were asked.

'She had done,' she said, still looking down, 'but he was always going from room to room. On the run, like. Sure, he used show up at the oddest hours; any time at all. Our landlord, Mr Timulty, said he wouldn't put up with it any more and that we'd be evicted.'

'So he stopped calling then?'

'Oh no. He still called whenever he could.'

'And why, then,' Mathew-Pare asked, 'did your landlord not throw you out?'

She looked up. 'Because Seamus told him he'd put a bullet in him if he did.'

O'Keefe caught Mathew-Pare's eye and the Detective returned a look O'Keefe couldn't interpret.

'And so they were lovers, Miss Costelloe and Mr Connors,' Mathew-Pare continued.

The girl's face flushed red. 'Yes, but they never, I don't think they ever …'

'Were intimate?'

She nodded, looking down at the carpet. 'Deirdre was fierce frightened of having … of getting in trouble. She always says … said that life ended when a baby comes. She wanted to live. To see Dublin, maybe even London some day. You couldn't do that if you got yourself landed with husband and child. And anyway, she'd grown tired of him. He was so …'

'So what, Anne?' O'Keefe asked.

'I'm not sure. He wanted everything from you. From

Deirdre. Like he wouldn't take only the half of you, Deirdre said once.'

'And what did she mean by that, do you think?' Mathew-Pare asked. 'Did he want to marry her, Anne?'

'I don't know, but I know she'd not have had him. I think it was exciting for her at first, courting a gunman. But she said that he scared her sometimes and that she was worn down by him. He wouldn't only take the nice part of you,' she crinkled her brow, searching for the words, 'the part of you you give a fella, like. The part you like when you look in the mirror. Deirdre said it that way. *The part of you you like when you look in the mirror.* I remember it because I spent days afterwards looking in the mirror for that part of me.' She smiled sadly.

O'Keefe said, 'What part did he want then, Anne?'

'She said he wanted the dark part of you. The part you'd show nobody. The black part of your soul you keep hidden from the world.' She flushed again. O'Keefe couldn't imagine the black part of her soul; she seemed too young to have one.

'And Deirdre thought this was … too much?'

'Yes, she did. Deirdre liked men who were bad and a bit wild – the gallivanters. But only because they were fun to be with. They kept her laughing, she used to say. But Seamus Connors couldn't have made a madman laugh, the graveyard face on him. Anyway, he hadn't called in a while. Deirdre'd said he was on the run in the hills and good riddance to him.'

O'Keefe asked her to estimate the date Connors had last called on Deirdre and noted this in his diary. Next to the dates he scratched: *Approx. 6 wks. Courtship ended?*

Mathew-Pare asked the question before it formulated in O'Keefe's mind. 'And who was Deirdre seeing then, Miss Duffy? She was stepping out with someone new, wasn't she?'

Anne Duffy nodded. 'She was coming home with lovely presents. I was jealous.'

The tears flowed freely and she didn't bother to wipe them away. 'Lovely earrings and a beautiful dress, a dress suit like, with a pointed French collar.'

O'Keefe remembered the one earring. 'Were they pearl, Anne, the earrings?'

'Yes, how did you …' She seemed then to understand.

'We found only one.'

'She looked a picture, wearing those earrings and her hunched over the typing. We had a laugh over that, myself and the other girls in the office. Deirdre wearing those earrings to work. Making a show of herself. We meant no harm, we only …' Her voice cracked and the tears coursed down her cheeks. O'Keefe thought of an expression his mother used: *The tears cutting ditches in her face.*

'What was this man's name, Anne?' O'Keefe asked.

But she shook her head, wiping the tears again with her handkerchief. 'She never told me and I never saw him. *My card-sharpie chappy* she called him.' Anne Duffy smiled through the tears. 'She said he bought her all the things from the money he made playing cards. And she said he lived in a smashing big house in Montenotte and he used to call for her in a lovely blue motor.'

Montenotte was one of the wealthiest areas of Cork, where the merchant princes looked down on their city and subjects from their mansions on the hill. The man had money. He noted on his page: *Montenotte. Blue car. Wealthy. Card player. Gifts.*

'Do you know what kind of car it was, Anne?'

She shook her head. 'I know nothing about cars. I only saw it from the window. He used park in front of the house and press the horn. He never called to the door. It looked like …' She shrugged. 'It was shiny blue and longer than a normal car. And it had a tan top that folded back in the fine weather. Deirdre called it his "Fancy Spaniard", whatever she meant by that.' The girl laughed sadly at the memory.

O'Keefe noted the details.

'And is he an Irishman, this card player? Do you think maybe he is a nationalist?' Mathew-Pare asked. O'Keefe noted his use of the neutral term. This was good interviewing, he thought, because they did not know where the girl's sympathies might lie. The girl shook her head.

'She never said but that he was a gentleman. And a rogue. She laughed when she told me. *A proper gentleman rogue*, she said once.'

'And did Connors know about this new man, Anne? Had he found out?'

She didn't hesitate. 'Obviously he did. And now Deirdre's dead, God rest her.'

The two of them gave Anne Duffy time to wipe away her tears. 'We're almost finished,' O'Keefe said. 'Anne, why did Miss Costelloe and Mr Connors part company? Do you remember why it was?'

The girl paused. 'He wasn't a laugh any more. He'd gone too serious for Deirdre and she was sick to her teeth of talk of a republic and all the wash that Connors was forever going on about. God and Ireland and the bloody English.' Her eyes darted up to meet Mathew-Pare's. 'No offence, sir.'

'None taken, Anne.' Mathew-Pare smiled and lit a cigarette. 'And do you know any of the houses where Mr Connors may have stayed when he was seeing Deirdre?'

'No. I don't think Deirdre knew more than one or two either because she'd complain that she could never get a message to him. That she had to wait for him to come calling for her. It was romantic at first, his being like … like he was, a soldier. A rebel. But it wore away after a time. The romance of it.'

'Did Connors ever tell Deirdre what he did for the Volunteers? The men he worked with? What he got up to?'

'Not that she told me. I think all the secrets were part of why she liked him, in a way.'

O'Keefe said, 'There are no secrets for Deirdre any more, Anne. Anything you say will help us find who murdered her. Do you understand?'

She nodded. 'I don't know anything about houses – where he stayed, what he did. We never spoke about such things. I told her she was a fool for seeing him in the first place. You have to believe me.'

'We believe you, Anne.'

Shafts of watery sunlight cut through cloud as the four left the factory. Eakins stood up from where he'd been leaning on the Ford's bonnet. Approaching the car, the men turned at the sound of another motor. It was a black Rolls Royce, more than a few years old, O'Keefe noticed, but well maintained. Almost instinctively, O'Keefe's hand went inside his jacket to his gun. He removed it when he saw who it was. The rear window glass rolled down.

'Did you get everything you needed, Sergeant?'

O'Keefe leaned into the window, noticing that the Rolls' driver was turned in his seat and looking back at him. He thought it strange; most chauffeurs maintained a studied indifference concerning their boss's affairs. But Barton didn't appear to notice or object to his driver's attention.

'We did, Mr Barton. Thank you. I don't imagine Miss Duffy will be in any fit state to continue work today.'

'Of course, of course. I'll arrange for her to be sent home. Full day's wages.' He extended a gloved hand out of the window. 'I wish you all the best in your endeavours, Sergeant. Anything we can do here to help, please don't hesitate to ask.'

O'Keefe shook hands with the man, the feel of the calfskin glove leather dry and dead to his own hand.

———

Stephen McGowan was a thin, neatly dressed man in his forties who never seemed to smile. His hair was short and side-parted. Eyeglasses, trimmed moustache – the perfect picture of a small town Irish solicitor.

Liam Farrell had been expecting a comrade like the men in the flying column. Hale and hearty. Someone with whom he could share his experiences of Drumdoolin. Instead, Farrell felt as if he was being interviewed for an actual clerkship. McGowan showed Farrell the offices and library, his family home at the back of the offices and the room at the top of the stairs where Farrell would sleep.

'My wife and the children are staying in Cork with her sister until things are safe to return. I've a girl comes in to cook and clean. Dinner's at seven. You can fend for yourself for breakfast and lunch. You'll be getting a small wage from me, so you'll be expected to work.'

Farrell nodded, though he wasn't sure what kind of work McGowan had in mind.

'You can start by finding any cases involving motor car accidents and stray sheep. The vehicle needn't be motorised. I'm sure there's precedent with horse and trap. Compensation, awards, liability. You were reading law, weren't you?'

It seemed like another life to Farrell. 'Yes. Yes, I was.'

'Good. You should have no problem then.'

'Mr McGowan, is this case to be tried in the republican courts?'

McGowan frowned. 'Of course. The magistrate's court hasn't sat for months and no man, Catholic or Protestant, would attend it anyway.'

'Even Protestant?'

'The republican courts are the courts of the land now, son. Loyalist and republican alike recognise fairness, no matter what their political outlook. Besides,' McGowan turned away into his private office to the right of the stairway, 'no one has a mind to get shot looking for a small cut of compensation.'

Three hours later, stacks of open law books on the table in front of him, Farrell still hadn't found what he was looking for. He held his head in his hands. If this was what practising law meant, then he'd stick with the soldiering … spying … policing … whatever it was that Brennan had him doing, he thought.

He hadn't wanted to read law in the first place, but his father had insisted. His eldest brother Cian would take over the draper's business, his youngest brother Patrick would be a priest, Liam would study the law, and his sister Mary would become a teacher. As if any of them had any choice in the matter. As Farrell thought of his father, a wave of bitterness washed over him. The tyrant who could rule any kingdom but the self. Forever subject to the clamouring whims of drink. Irish fathers. Bad as the Crown in their own way, he thought. Between the two, there was no liberty to be had in the country.

There was a knock on the library door. A young woman came part way into the room. 'Mr Farrell, there's a man to see you, sir.'

Farrell looked up. The girl had wide, dark eyes and long, brown lashes. Her brown hair was tied back off her face with a loose ribbon and she wore an apron as if she'd been called out of the kitchen.

'What's your name?'

The girl blushed and colour rushed to her cheeks. 'Maureen O'Connell, sir. He's waiting – the man to see you.'

Farrell leaned back in the chair and put his hands behind his head. He would have liked to confide in pretty Maureen that he was more than just some lowly clerk working for McGowan, but realised that it would be reckless.

'Show him in, Maureen. And thank you.' He gave her a smile he thought was warm, conspiratorial. The girl ignored it and turned away.

The man was in his sixties, white hair combed back neatly. He was big, with a lined face and forehead. He wore no jacket, as if he'd just stepped out.

'You the new man, are you?' No formalities. No introductions.

Farrell said, 'What do you mean "new man"?'

The visitor frowned. 'Don't you be smart with me, sonny Jim. I'm risking my neck coming to you.'

Farrell dropped his hands from behind his head and sat forward. 'I'm sorry … I didn't mean to imply that –'

'Just you put a stopper in it and listen here. The dead girl from the hillside. Her name's Deirdre, Deirdre Costelloe, and she's from Ballincollig. Her parents were visited in the days after her death by some chap going by the name of Seamus. Might be one of yours.'

Farrell began to write the information on a sheet of notepaper.

'Jesus, don't write it down, you cabbage.' The older man's voice was stern, as if he was used to telling people what to do. Farrell was offended by the order but scratched out the words he had written.

'The murder's being investigated by Sergeant O'Keefe. Seán O'Keefe. A Dublin lad. Good man; fair. And there's another fella, Mathew-Pare. He's two lads with him as well. English. Heavy boys, they look. Word is they're from Scotland Yard. I'll try to get more, but it will mean sneaking a poke around the murder book. O'Keefe, the sergeant, is keeping fierce close about the whole show. You got all that now?'

Farrell nodded, then said, 'Repeat the names.'

The old man repeated them and one was familiar to Farrell. It couldn't be the same one. No. It had been seven or eight years at least.

The man stood up to go. 'One more thing. If you see me on the street, you be polite and say hello. I'm a client of McGowan's; he's handling the sale of my land. That's why I can come and go here as I please. And you can get word to me in the barracks if you must. Say that McGowan's finished the contracts on the land or needs more details to finish them. Something like that. Right, son?'

'The barracks? Are you a Pee – a policeman?'

The old man winked and smiled for the first time. 'I was.'

Farrell stood up and held out his hand to the man. 'Thank you. Thank you for your help, Mr …'

'Reilly. Tom Reilly. Sure, as long as no fella catches a bullet on account of my help, I don't mind giving it.'

The barrack orderly at Tuckey Street barracks had told them with a smirk that Lorcan Connolly – the Crimes Special Branch sergeant who had wired O'Keefe that morning about the recent killing of a known prostitute in the city – could be found on personal protection detail in Sutton's Tavern. When they entered Sutton's, the Branch man saw them first. 'Now, I know ye fellas can only be Peelers, just by the cut of you' – the voice had come from behind them as they faced the bar – 'but take out your personals all the same, just so Johnny Sutton there can tell the bossman I do some work round the place.'

When O'Keefe turned around with his constabulary identity card, the Branch man had a Colt automatic pointed at his chest. Lorcan Connolly, O'Keefe recalled, had been a legend in Cork since before the war. Crimes Special Branch men primarily served as intelligence-gatherers within the constabulary. Many of them spent a good deal more time searching train stations and Irish-language classes for 'disaffected subjects' than they ever did prosecuting genuine criminals. Connolly, however, had a reputation for working the streets and backrooms, the laneways, bookmakers, docks and brothels. It was said he had more touts on the ear than most men had hair on their arse.

In his forties, big, like most old-time Peelers, Connolly was dressed every bit like the dandy O'Keefe had heard he was. He wore a fitted, light woollen suit jacket and waistcoat, and a bright-red tie under a starched, fashionably wide, white collar. His hair looked to be meticulously dyed an unnatural shade of brown and his thick eyebrows were combed out and upwards as if he had been cycling into a strong wind.

The Crimes Special man squinted for a moment, appearing to study O'Keefe's identity card, then smiled and set the Colt on the table next to his Sweet Aftons. 'So what'll it be, lads? Drinks are on me today.'

Joining Connolly at the table with Mathew-Pare, while Keane and Mathew-Pare's men went to the bar, O'Keefe asked, 'So what did Mr Sutton do to deserve the personalised protection of a famous Branch man like yourself?'

The publican, Connolly explained after he'd finished chuckling, was an outspoken defender of the King and Crown in Ireland. He had lost two sons in Flanders and wasn't about to let a shower of criminals too windy to serve in a real war tell him what to do and whom to serve in his pub. He had a need to feel that his sons had died for something and that something was the British Empire. So he served police, soldiers, Tans and Auxies in his pub. This made him a marked man and thus he was afforded a protection detail twenty-four hours a day, seven days a week. Connolly punctuated the story by emptying the dregs from his bottle of Wrastler stout and calling for Sutton to set the men up with more of the same. Turning back to O'Keefe, he winked and said, 'Besides, a fella of my reputation just might be of use to somebody down the road. Can't have me out getting shot at every auld day, so brass gives me a bit of a hollier. Good as a fortnight's leave, this number here. I've not been sober since I started, nor put my hand in my fucking pocket except to throw copper after nags. Sure, there's lads who'd stick a knife in you to get a week of PP detail here in Sutton's. Need to be cosy with the high hats, I'm tellin' you, Seán …' he winked for a second time and O'Keefe wondered was it a nervous tick of some sort, 'or know where they've buried the bodies, to get a *day* of this detail, never mind a week!'

The three men laughed. O'Keefe stole a glance at the four empty bottles on the table in front of Connolly and wondered did Sutton ever question the logic of supplying the man who was assigned to protect his life with free drink all day. He turned and watched as Sutton – a short, thick-set man with a shining bald dome of a head and thick spectacles – served the men at the bar and then came to their table carrying large bottles of stout and three glasses.

Connolly seemed thoroughly pleased with himself, clapping and rubbing his hands in anticipation of the drinks. The publican went away and returned, setting three generous whiskeys on the table to accompany the stout. 'Sure, isn't that right, John?' Connolly said, clapping Sutton on the arm. 'A week here looking after your auld wreck of a body, Johnny boy – better than a week in the finest hotel, I'm telling yeh.'

The publican gave a weak smile. O'Keefe imagined the man was reaching a point where he was willing to risk being shot to make up for the money he was losing in free booze to Connolly and his Peeler friends. As they poured their beer, a young boy of about ten – barefoot, with dark circles under his eyes, a pale, thin face that spoke of rare meals and harsh tenement winters – entered the pub and turned straight for

the table, stopping in front of the Branch man. He didn't
bother removing his tattered flat cap. 'First Class fell at the
third, Mr Connolly, the fuckin' bastard. Leading by two
lengths as well.'

Connolly grinned at the boy. 'Ah sure Denis, better luck
on the next.' He picked up his racing sheet, dug into his
pocket and came out with some coins. 'Put that on Western
Beauty in the 2.15. And get yourself another lemonade there.'
The boy took the money with a serious look on his face and
went out the door again.

'Now, lads,' Connolly said, when the boy had left. 'You've
a murder there and you're wanting to know about one of ours.
Not, I should tell you, that there's much in common between
the two, from what I can gather, but that you'd evidence of
strangulation and so did we. And I suppose you could stretch
to a possible sex motive in ours, if you were so inclined, but
it's a fair stretch.' He took a sip of whiskey and then a long
swig of stout.

O'Keefe nodded and swallowed some of his own. 'You
said in your message the murdered girl was on the cobbles?'

'She was. A grand girl too. Not a bad bone in the poor
crathur, 'cept some of them she was paid to have in her. Not
the sharpest tool in the box she wasn't and fierce fond of the
gin – of all your poisons – but not a bad girl. Janey Plunkett.
From the Barracka laneways. Mother was the same 'til she
fell off the harbour wall in Queenstown and drowned, stone
drunk with the *Invincible* in port. In 1915, I think it was. Sure,
she was rich that week, the mother, though she'd never been

Peeler

an oil painting. Sailors in wartime would ride anything with a hole in it. No, there was no way the daughter wouldn't go into the same trade. Luck and birthrights and all that, lads.'

'You knew her well?' Mathew-Pare asked.

Connolly winked again and sipped his whiskey. 'Mother and daughter and many more like them. Two of my better working girls, the Plunketts. When the mother was sober, she had as grand an ear for conspiracy as any Peeler. The daughter, like I said, was a bit loo-laa, but now and again came up with the odd bit of info.'

'And the cause of death was manual strangulation?'

'One last embrace, so the song goes.' He lit one of his Sweet Aftons, holding the pack out to O'Keefe and Mathew-Pare. They both accepted and lit up.

'Was there a proper inquest held?'

The Branch man appeared amused. 'On a dead doxie? You're joking. Maybe before …' he waved his cigarette around vaguely, 'the lead started flying. In fact, there *would* have been. I would have made sure of it myself, but now? Not a chance, Seán, you know that as well as me. As it was, we were lucky to get one of the sawbones from the Vic Army Hospital to give her a poke and a prod and pronounce cause of death. She was put in the ground a day after she was found.'

O'Keefe nodded, knowing exactly how such a case would be dealt with in a city at war with itself. 'Is there a file I could look at?'

'There is. As far as suspects go, I went and pumped her whoremaster. Fella called Noonan. Jackeen runs a house in the Marsh where Janey used to set up. Mind, she worked the docks and corners as well.'

O'Keefe looked to Mathew-Pare and he took over. 'Did you get anything from him?'

Connolly shook his head and swallowed another mouthful of beer. 'No. Said she'd been doing private parties for some swells in the country. And that she'd been working the streets more than usual to keep herself in gin. Was acting more cracked by the day. Galloping syphilis, no doubt, and half-pickled in gin. Pity to the punters, though it serves them right.'

'Any name on the private parties?' Mathew-Pare asked.

'No. Noonan said he didn't know. I thought about pushing it, but she was found down on Merchants' Quay where she was known to work, her skirts bunched up around her waist, so I reckoned it to be some fella'd picked her up there and lost the run of himself. I never had a chance to work any further with it. I was on to the Smyth shooting shortly after, same as every detective in the city. Never got anybody on that either, though every mutt in town knows who the shooter was.'

Lieutenant Colonel Smyth, a one-armed war veteran, a King's Own Scottish Borderer, had been made Divisional Police Commissioner for Munster earlier in the year. He had become famous for instigating the first known mutiny in the RIC since the beginning of the Troubles, having given a speech to Listowel barracks in June, telling the boys that they would please him mightily the more Irishmen they shot. Naturally enough, being Irishmen, the local constables took offence and handed in belts, swords, guns and caps, calling the man a bloody-minded murderer. A month later, Smyth was shot dead by the IRA in the City and County Club in Cork. O'Keefe wasn't alone in the constabulary in thinking the man might have had it coming, but he kept such thoughts to himself. So it was no mystery to him how the murder of a young prostitute could be neglected in the wake of Smyth's shooting. 'Only one gunman? I thought a mob of fellas plugged him,' he said.

'Oh, there was a gang with him all right, but sure the shooter, Connors, needs no help, the bastard. Cool as Christmas Eve, that fella.'

'Connors?' O'Keefe said. 'What's the Christian name?'

Connolly looked at him now, seriously, for the first time since they had come in. 'Seamus. Seamus Connors.'

Mathew-Pare was smiling again, brighter this time, as if his face actually meant it. 'Jesus, that's the second time today we've come across that name.'

'Long as you don't come across him in person, you'll be all right. How'd he come up?' Connolly asked.

O'Keefe explained to him what Anne Duffy had said about Connors and how it was most likely he who had visited the Costelloe farm in the days after the girl had gone missing. Connolly lit another Sweet Afton and slid the packet across to them. 'That sounds like him all right. You fancy him for killing the girl you found?'

'I don't know, but if he's as bad as everybody seems to think he is ...' O'Keefe shrugged. 'I'm willing to point the

Peeler

dogs that way, but one thing bothers me.' He was thinking aloud now. 'Why did Connors visit the girl's parents and claim to be looking for her if he'd killed her?'

The three were silent for a long moment. Connolly spoke first. 'Guilt? Or maybe he wanted to deflect interest in himself by going there, acting as if he didn't know she was dead.'

O'Keefe considered it, sipping some whiskey and chasing it with stout. Mathew-Pare turned to the Branch man. 'This Connors – did he fight in the war?'

Connolly laughed. 'Did he fuck! That boy was too busy making plans for his own war right here in Cork. He was a medical student in the college, if you can believe it. From a decent family, the word is. Republican family, sure enough, but respectable like. Brother's a padre in King's County and the two sisters are schoolteachers. Big farm this side of Crossbarry. Don't know where he got it from, but he's good, our Seamus. V-A-B, that fella. No sight of him since the Smyth job though. The gossip is he's gone to the hills to shoot in one of the new mobile units they're forming.'

O'Keefe noted all this in his diary as Connolly spoke, copying down the commonly used but unofficial RIC acronym. VAB. *Very Active Bastard.* He particularly noted Connors' background in medicine. A medical student would be aware of how to kill someone with one blow, wouldn't he? He thought of the mutilation of the breasts, the reasonably clean cuts.

Connolly asked, 'Why do you ask did he serve?' He gulped more whiskey and followed it with the Wrastler.

214

O'Keefe looked up from his notes. 'I mentioned the wound that killed our victim. She had bruising on her neck as well, mutilation to the chest – the victim's breasts were cut off. Initially I thought throttling was the cause of death, but the surgeon found a puncture wound at the base of the girl's skull that actually killed her. He thought it looked like the wound a professional would make. A veteran, possibly with hand-to-hand combat experience. Trench raiding, that sort of thing. Just speculation, mind.'

Mathew-Pare was silent, smoking. Connolly took more stout and seemed to think it over. 'Fairly wide pool of suspects – fellas with hand-fighting experience. War vets. Must be hundreds of them in County Cork alone. Sure, half the Tans and every bloody Auxie in the place fits that bill. Can't imagine brass would like it to be one of them anyway. Not when you have Seamus Connors as the last known jockey for your horse.'

O'Keefe took another sip of whiskey. Connolly was right. 'It doesn't work for me as a passion killing. A scrap between lovers that took a turn. It's too ...' he gestured a box with his hands, 'squared away somehow. The way she was laid out on the hill. The single puncture wound.'

'Your wire said she was labelled. I'll see if I can dig up anything on her as a mouth. Thing is, there's more operators in this town than there are tits on a sow. She could have been touting for anyone – Red Tabs, Auxies, Secret Service, Division Intelligence. Even my own esteemed colleagues in Crimes Special.' He drank and then burped. 'Or maybe she just broke Connors' heart of stone, lads, and he didn't like it.'

O'Keefe considered it again. It was possible – a crime of passion made to look like something political. But what of the feathering? The single blow that caused her death? There was too much that was clinical about the killing itself. If Connors had loved the girl and been enraged at her dismissal of him, she would have shown the marks of his rage. Severe bruising. Multiple stab wounds. *But there was the strangulation and the mutilation of the chest.* O'Keefe reckoned that despite his misgivings, Connors still seemed as likely a suspect as any for it, crime of passion or otherwise.

He asked Connolly if he could get the murder book for the prostitute Janey Plunkett and, to his surprise, the man reached under the table and took it out. It was in a brown cardboard folder. Thin for a murder book. It seemed to sum up a young and wasted life. Connolly opened it and took out a police photo of a young girl. Dark, unwashed hair, acne scars. Tired, childish brown eyes that seemed to register disbelief at the harshness of the world. O'Keefe thought of another question.

'And your Janey Plunkett, was it possible she knew Connors as well? Could Connors have been the swell booking her for the private parties you spoke of?'

Connolly thought about it. 'No way of telling. I've no doubt she was touting for the Shinners as well as for me. A girl in her position would have had to. At the same time, some of these IRA fellas are fierce puritanical about matters carnal.

Country lads a lot of them. Wouldn't know a fanny from a hole in the hedge and fear it all the same. The Volunteers can be rough on the whores unless there's information or money to be had from them. Working girls have become great ones for Republican Bonds and donations to the IRA arms fund, so it goes in the lanes and knocking shops.'

The door to the pub opened again. Still smiling, Connolly moved for the Colt. He saw it was young Denis and opted instead for his whiskey glass. 'Denis, my boy. It's more like a lemon you're looking every time I see you.'

The boy smiled and opened a clenched fist holding a wad of notes and coins. 'Bastard came in at sixteen, I'm telling you sir. By a bloody mile, he did. Here's your winnings.'

Connolly grinned and mussed the boy's hair. He then dipped into the lad's hand and withdrew most of the smaller notes and coins, leaving a pound note. An Auxie's *per diem*, O'Keefe thought, and a fortune for the young cornerboy.

'That's yours, Denis. Buy the mother something nice, Young Lemon. She deserves it she does, rearing the likes of you.'

The boy grinned. 'I'll be fucked if I'd buy her a tin button, sir. I'm going back to the bookies!' The boy turned and ran out of the pub.

'I've a gift for education, I do.'

'Any chance you could educate us further?' O'Keefe asked, smiling.

'My mission in life, son. And what further wisdom can I provide you with?'

'The address of the brothel Janey Plunkett worked in.'

Connolly smiled and winked. 'An honour and a pleasure, lads. An honour and a pleasure.'

They left the car on the South Mall, within walking distance of the city centre area known as the Marsh. Had they driven the Ford into the warren of narrow, tenement-lined lanes, they would have been spotted for who they were in seconds and word would have drummed down the alley telegraph faster than rumours of free drink.

Leaving the bright main street chorus of rattling, bell-ringing tramcars and hawking newspaper boys, for the back lane sounds of clopping dray horses hauling beer barrels and coal, the streets they now entered were filled with the smells of rotting refuse, of boiling cabbage, coal smoke and horse piss. Crumbling tenements braced the narrow lanes, families of ten to a room not uncommon. Faded grey laundry flapped gently in the wind, hanging from lines strung across the street to windows in buildings opposite. Gangs of barefoot children played, oblivious to the deprivation in which they lived. Shawlies, old women of indeterminate age, sat on stoops beckoning passers-by, selling matches, cigarettes, religious pictures and bawdy postcards.

O'Keefe kept his right hand on his Webley inside his trenchcoat. His briefcase dangled from his left. Like any old travelling salesman or debt collector he hoped, knowing he looked like nothing of the sort.

Light was fading and they spread themselves on either side of the street as they walked, pacing each other, front and behind. They passed a British army recruiting poster with an illustration of a Tommy standing watch in front of the pyramids of Egypt. The legend read 'Join the Army and See the World'. Underneath this, someone had scrawled 'Join the RIC and See the Next!'

The gas lamps on the lane, O'Keefe noticed, had been shot out, most likely by the rebels, eager to embrace night's darkness as their own. The house they were looking for was in the middle of a terrace of four redbrick Georgians. The other three were occupied O'Keefe knew, without having to enter them, by innumerable families sleeping head to toe in mould-coated pallet beds. The people of the Marsh were hard working and poor, men daily breaking their backs on the docks while their children starved and coughed in cold, damp flats, skin red raw from lice, bedbugs and fleas, eaten from the inside by consumption.

'Will I send one of the boys round the back, then?'

O'Keefe considered Mathew-Pare's offer and decided against it – too dangerous to have a man standing on his own in an alley as night fell.

'No, I don't think yer man'll scarper. What's he to be afraid of, sure? He's a businessman. He'll know well how to deal with the likes of us.'

The brothel was called Madam Grace's, but Connolly had told them that Grace had died of the Spanish flu two years before. According to the Branch man, a whoremaster named Noonan ran the shop now, without any of the titular grace the house's former madam had brought to her place of business. Times had changed, O'Keefe thought. Things were harder now, faster. A quick coin more important than form or style.

They mounted the steps and pressed the bell. O'Keefe leaned out over the iron railing and tried to look into the front window. Thick red curtains obscured his view. Below street level and underneath the steps where they were standing were a basement entrance and another window also obscured by crimson curtains. A moment later they heard the sound of heavy boots from inside.

'Sounds a right carthorse,' said Mathew-Pare's man, Eakins. Keane looked to O'Keefe for permission to smile. Eakins hadn't spoken much so far and had gone about the day in a display of professional boredom. Now there was a light in his eyes and what O'Keefe took to be a smile of anticipation on his face. O'Keefe figured the man knew his way around knocking shops.

The door opened. No carthorse. A bull. *Mr Eakins*, O'Keefe thought, *meet your match*. The man who greeted them was well over six feet tall and packed with muscle. His chest had the dimensions of a Guinness keg and his nose appeared to have been broken more than once. He wore braces over a cotton vest, holding up expensive, chequered woollen breeches. He held the door half-open, blinking in the fading daylight and recognising in an instant that the men in front of him were police. 'We've already paid you shower. Now fuck off and don't be greedy.' He tried to shut the door.

Eakins slipped past O'Keefe with surprising agility for a big man, wedging a brogue between the door and the frame to prevent it from closing. 'Now hang on a minute, mate.' He smiled like a drunken punter. 'We're only looking for a nice roll.' He gave the door a shove, catching the doorman off balance.

'I fucking told you …' Rage flashed on the doorman's face and he let go of the door to swing a punch at Eakins. His fist was halfway to its destination when Eakins landed his free foot in the man's groin, doubling him over as though someone had jerked him forward with a rope. Starkson stepped past O'Keefe, taking as he did a short, lead-weighted leather club from his overcoat pocket. The door swung wide and O'Keefe watched Eakins sidestep the doorman – still doubled up and gasping for air – and grab his wrist, twisting it up and behind his back. The doorman grunted and stumbled forward. Starkson clubbed him on the back of the head and the man dropped heavily to the floor.

Mathew-Pare smiled at O'Keefe. 'Don't like cheek, my lads. Can't abide it.'

O'Keefe had rarely seen violence so swiftly and professionally delivered, though he thought it was probably excessive. They might have pumped the big man later for information his boss wouldn't give them. As they entered the brothel, Starkson was using the doorman's braces to tie his hands behind his back. There wasn't a trick those two fellas didn't know, O'Keefe thought.

The front hallway of Madam Grace's was painted red. A cheap and dusty chandelier hung from the ceiling, casting a dull glow. Mirrors on both sides of the entry hall cast their reflections back at them, filling the entryway with suited men. In front of them a stairway led to the upper floors, and to its side the hallway continued, ending at an open door that led down another set of stairs to what O'Keefe assumed to be the kitchen. Mathew-Pare made his way to a set of double doors just across from the stairway and found a large salon with a piano, a small bar, comfortable stuffed chairs and sofas. The room was empty and dark, smelling of stale perfume and tobacco. O'Keefe started upstairs. He was halfway up when a voice greeted him from the top.

'I see you lads have met Tadhg. Fat fucking use he is to me.'

The whoremonger was dressed in a billowing white shirt that was gathered tight to his body by a satin, bright-red waistcoat that matched the predominant colour of his house and his trade. He was consumptively thin, with long, black, oiled hair. His trousers were tapered tight at the ankles and his boots shone black. His accent was Dublin. This wasn't unusual. Jackeens made good pimps. The city exported them throughout the Empire. Some of O'Keefe's fellow Dubliners were proud of the fact.

'The dozy bastard must've told yis I made your wages last week,' the pimp continued.

O'Keefe resumed climbing the stairs. 'We're not here for your payoff, Noonan. We want to ask you some questions.' He reached the top and the man stood politely aside, gesturing to a room at the end of another short hallway.

'My office, Constable.'

'Sergeant.'

'Sergeant, of course.' There was an amused pout on the pimp's face. O'Keefe was tempted to shut down the smile with his fist, but the urge passed.

As Noonan led them down the hall, a girl in her late teens emerged from one of the bedrooms, carrying a chamberpot covered with a dishtowel. Noticing the men in the hallway, the girl said, 'Bit early for knocking now, isn't it, Davey?' The girl looked as though she had been sleeping, dressed in a pale-pink, silky morning gown fastened around her waist. O'Keefe could see the outline of her full breasts and the nub of her nipples through the thin material. Her face bore the warm red imprint of a pillow and her mass of black ringlets was flattened on one side. The effect of her recent waking made her appear younger and more vulnerable than she would look, he thought, when she was made up and touting for custom. O'Keefe wondered at what age she'd started whoring and gave her another five years before her price dropped and her life would begin its slow slide towards the dark, damp of Queenstown harbour or the quays. Only the youngest, the prettiest or most uniquely talented girls kept rooms in houses like these. The rest used the lanes and backstreets, cowsheds or rooms rented from war widows, who didn't mind the noise and who needed the money.

On impulse, O'Keefe stopped her, taking the photograph of Deirdre Costelloe from inside his coat pocket and holding it out to her. 'Do you recognise this girl, Miss?'

She studied the photograph – a shot of Deirdre's head and shoulders that O'Keefe had taken the previous evening after the undertaker Casey had done his work.

O'Keefe watched her as she examined the photo. A flare of recognition in her eyes? No. More likely horror, O'Keefe decided, when she realised she was looking at a dead girl. She handed the photograph back to O'Keefe without comment and continued on down the hall. Noonan watched her go, the pimp's eyes following her figure on the stairs like a dairyman appraising a prize heifer.

Noonan's office held an oversized desk and a sofa covered in discarded clothing. It somehow reminded O'Keefe of Councillor Ryan's office. Everybody wanted to be seen as the big man, he thought – a man's desk a mark of his importance. Noonan sat behind it and indicated the chair in front for O'Keefe, who declined and walked around to the pimp's side of the desk, leaning in over his shoulder, crowding him. Keane, Mathew-Pare and his two men came into the room too, closing the door behind them. Normally, O'Keefe wouldn't have so many men in a room when he was questioning someone. It distracted the person being interrogated when O'Keefe needed their attention focused solely on him. This time, however, he didn't mind. The pimp might not need a going over like his doorman, but a bit of a frightener never hurt any whoremaster he had dealt with in the past. He took another photo, from his briefcase this time, and leaned in closer over the pimp, inhaling the pungent odour of hair oil, mingled with the scent of cologne and sour sweat. Stale sweat, O'Keefe noted, rather than the reek of fear. The man was used to Peelers. He wasn't scared. Not yet anyway.

He dropped the photo of Deirdre Costelloe on the desk in front of him. It was a crime scene shot, her injuries clear to see, her pose as sad and pornographic as when he had first found her. 'Mr Noonan?' O'Keefe waited for a reaction.

'Call me Davey, Sergeant. Everybody does.' He looked back over his shoulder. Then he picked up the photograph and let out a low whistle. 'The things,' he said, 'some lads get up to.'

'Lads like yerself, Mr Noonan?'

'Tsk, tsk, Sergeant. Too obvious by half. If yis thought I done this, yis wouldn't be asking me questions here now, would yeh? Yis would've hauled me into the Victoria barracks and had the clamps on me monkey nuts by now, yis would.' He smiled.

'What makes you think I won't put you on that desk and stomp all over your monkey nuts right now?'

'Because yis know I didn't do this, but think I might have something to give yis on it. Really now, I'd expect more from our constabulary. Are you new to the job? I'd heard they were dropping standards, wha'?'

O'Keefe ignored him. He sensed Starkson smiling from where he was lounging on the sofa in the corner, having shoved the soiled laundry to the floor. It occurred to him that

Starkson and his bull-necked partner Eakins probably spent most of their working lives lounging on sofas in offices, just being there as a reminder to people of what could happen if they didn't give Mathew-Pare what he wanted.

Shifting tack, O'Keefe took the murder book on Janey Plunkett from his briefcase and extracted the old booking photo of the girl – taken a year and two months before her death when she had been arrested for public drunkenness. This he laid on the table next to the crime scene photo from the hillside. He tapped the print with his finger. 'You know who *she* is though, don't you, Noonan?'

'Was, yeh mean. Know who she *was*.' Again, the glance over the shoulder and the smirk. Noonan caught the look in O'Keefe's eyes this time and closed down his smile. Turning back to the photo, he said, 'Janey Plunkett. Had a room here for half a year, maybe eight months. Sure, yis fuckin' well know I'd nothing to do with her death. You know full well 'cause Connolly told yis, gave yeh the book on her as well, I'd bet.'

Taking Deirdre's death portrait, O'Keefe placed it beside Janey's booking photo. As he did, he was struck by something that had escaped him the first time he had looked at the prostitute's photo back in Sutton's when Connolly had handed over the file. The girl found dead in the alleyway bore a notable resemblance to Deirdre Costelloe. She had the same dark hair, round face and high cheekbones. You wouldn't say they were sisters, O'Keefe thought, but there was a likeness.

O'Keefe stayed silent, hoping for a reaction from Noonan. Admittedly, he hadn't picked the best place from which to observe his face, but he noticed Mathew-Pare staring hard at the pimp and knew he was looking for the same thing. It pleased and surprised O'Keefe in equal measure. The man had been forced on him and yet here they were, working much like partners.

'Who's this?' Noonan asked. 'Is she why yis're here?'

'Never seen her before, have you not?' O'Keefe said.

'Never in me life.'

'You sure about that, Noonan? Won't go well for you now, if you don't admit to knowing her and we find out later that you did.'

The man looked over his shoulder again. There wasn't fear in his eyes – not exactly – but there was concern. He seemed to be thinking, trying to gauge how serious things were. How badly did the Peelers want someone for the girl's death? Was it bad enough to fix someone like himself up for it? The pimp was aware it would be hard to frame him for a murder like this, but he knew that O'Keefe could have him interned for several days if not indefinitely, under the Restoration of Order Act, Cork being a Special Military Area.

O'Keefe waited, considering his own options. At the very least he could cost the bastard money, leave his untended business vulnerable to takeover. On the other hand, Noonan no doubt had friends in high places; all pimps and madams did. No whoremonger could run his shop without them. Brothels were tolerated, even encouraged, throughout Ireland

and the rest of the Empire. O'Keefe had read once that Saint Thomas Aquinas himself had written that they were as vital to any city as its sewers, and Whitehall and the Crown Courts seemed to agree. But they existed in a grey world legally. Men like Noonan stayed on the right side of the police and the powers that be – stayed open – by being useful, not merely as a means of allowing soldiers far from home an outlet for their physical needs, but by passing information and cash payments to favoured detectives, army officers and public officials. In city police barracks from London to Cork to Calcutta, it was a commonly accepted fact that if you wanted to know the most likely men to be promoted, find out who the pimps and madams were handing the fattest envelopes to. Inside information was as much part of the trade as fresh whores. Their survival depended on it. And in times such as these, this applied doubly, because now the whoremongers had a new master to appease.

The IRA allowed the brothels to operate for their own purposes: funding and information. As Connolly had said, there was a strongly puritanical streak among many of the leading members of the IRA and Sinn Féin, but obviously there was a practical streak too. O'Keefe imagined that more than one ambush on some poor army patrol had had its genesis under knocking-shop sheets.

Noonan was now deciding if, or how, he would disappoint his masters by giving information to O'Keefe. Weighing it all up. Bother the Peelers, get shut down, locked up for a week and lose his whores to another house maybe. Bother the Shinners and catch a bullet. No choice really. He looked back at the photographs. 'Is this girl,' pointing at the crime scene photo of Deirdre Costelloe, 'the dead one?'

'She is.'

He shook his head. 'Who do yis want for it?'

At his question, Mathew-Pare cracked a half-smile. Noonan was a smarter man than O'Keefe had thought. Who was wanted for it and who actually did it. Maybe two separate issues altogether.

'We want who killed her. No politics here, Noonan. And I'm not here to tether you up for something you had no part in. I want to find who killed this girl. Maybe find who killed Janey Plunkett in the bargain. Whoever did Janey cost you her wages, don't forget.'

The whoremonger smiled a little at that. 'Not much, mind. She was losing me money the amount she was pissed on gin. Not able for work half the fuckin' time. Hadn't the heart to run her off, though.'

Starkson laughed out loud at this and O'Keefe looked hard at him. The man stifled his laughter but continued to smile. Noonan responded defensively, surprising O'Keefe. 'You might think it's a laugh but she was ... there was something about her. Anyway, she's dead now. I told that peacock Connolly she was working the lanes and the quays as well. Giving it away for a tot. For fuck all. Any loony could've choked her if she said something smart to him. I don't see –'

'You told Connolly about the girl doing private parties for a gentleman punter. Out in the country some place.'

Noonan looked up at O'Keefe. 'I did?'

'You did.'

'I must have then. Posh fella. Private parties, card games out in some pile. A social evening for select gentlemen. Connolly never came back to me on it, mind you. And Janey came back from the parties in one piece, so I didn't see the point –'

'How often were these parties held?'

Noonan shrugged. 'Once a month maybe? I don't know. The girls liked going, they did. Money for old rope. Gentlemen players. Played cards and then played with the girls. A fine time had by all, by all accounts.'

'I need a name.'

Noonan shook his head, delivering a regretful smile. 'Don't have a name. Only came himself the once. The first time. Picked out the girls and then sent his man to collect them each time after that.'

'When was the last time?' O'Keefe asked.

'Two, maybe three, months ago. Always paid up, always brought my girls back in one piece.'

'And what did he look like, this gentleman?'

'Never laid peepers on him, meself. Tadhg dealt with him. Ask him yerself if yis didn't crack his loaf.'

O'Keefe took out his notebook. 'I need the names of the girls he used.'

Again, the rueful smile. 'Jaysus lads, you don't want much, do yis? Right. Janey's dead, sure. The others ...' he made a show of trawling his memory, 'one of them is back up in

Dublin in the Monto. The other married a navy fella. Fierce religious chap from Plymouth or Portsmouth – some place 'cross the water.' He smiled and held out his hands. 'I could give you their names, I could. Yis could track 'em down if yis liked.'

'Seamus Connors,' Mathew-Pare said, from his place on the sofa.

Noonan didn't even blink. 'Never heard of him.'

'Not one of the Volunteers you pay off?'

Noonan shook his head. 'Pay off? Sure, I've hardly a ha'penny left after what I pay you grasping fuckers.'

O'Keefe closed his notebook and lifted the photographs from the desk, placing them back in their files and into his briefcase. 'Let's go.' He made his way around the desk to the door.

The other men stood. The pimp remained seated at his desk. He leaned back, linking his hands behind his head. Safe as houses. Protected. If not by some high-ranking cop or army officer, then by the IRA. 'Sorry I couldn't be more help. Come back if you think of anything else.'

O'Keefe stopped and turned back to him. 'One more thing, Noonan. The car. The gentleman's car. You see what kind it was?'

There was a flicker in the pimp's eyes. It was there and then gone. 'A Model T, maybe? Nothing special, like. Not that I saw. Anything else?'

On the street in front of the brothel, darkness had settled, though it wasn't yet five o'clock. The air was cold and moist. Mathew-Pare's cigarette glowed orange.

'He knew more than he was telling.'

O'Keefe nodded. 'He did, but he thought better of telling us. It might not be the same fella, anyway.'

Mathew-Pare considered this. 'No, I think it is. "Card sharpie"? Card games in the country? And the car. You notice how Noonan made a point of playing down the car?'

'Yes, the car and the name. He has both I'd bet. Still, won't be hard to find out who the fella is. Flash car. Card player. Someone in this town will point us in the right direction.'

'Point us toward Seamus Connors?'

'Point us wherever we need to go. I can't see Connors playing cards with gentlemen at some Big House. What we need to know is whether or not Connors knew Deirdre was stepping out with the card player. That would give us good motive. It occurred to me to ask the pimp about him, but you know yourself what his answer would have been.'

Mathew-Pare exhaled smoke. 'Connors was a med student. Been known to play the odd hand of cards, Sergeant, student chaps. College? Sounds every bloody bit the young gentleman to me. They could be best pals – Connors and our mysterious card sharp. Or maybe the girl, Anne Duffy, got her facts wrong. Maybe there was no "posh fella" and it was Connors the whole time. Maybe the two are one?' He smiled as if at his own joke.

'No, she was clear about it. Connors used to come to

the flat. Why would he stop coming, just because he got a car somewhere? No, they're two different people. One girl, wanted by both. We need to find the card player first. See is there any connection.'

Keane spoke up, his voice not confident in the company of the other, senior men but willing nonetheless. 'What does … I mean, what's the point of following up the card games? Connors has the motive, you said it yourself. Shouldn't we shake the trees and see if he falls out? The Branch man said he was running with the West Cork Brigade flying units. Couldn't we step up raiding in and around the country areas until we get someone to give him up?'

O'Keefe thought about it and then shook his head. 'No. We need something firmer. West Cork is a big place. We'd need to involve hundreds of troops and all we'd end up with is a series of ruined houses and raised IRA recruitment in the area. And all for the sake of a "maybe".'

Mathew-Pare said with his half-smile, 'Do you think there's any young chap in West Cork who hasn't already been recruited? Kitchener couldn't have done half what the IRA has done to motivate idle boys to pick up rifles for the cause. Far better than any conscription.'

'Like I said, we only have a "maybe" on Connors. Sure, we could destroy the whole of the county looking for him.'

'It's a pretty fair "maybe" though. He had the motivation, and he's wanted for any number of murders. Lieutenant Colonel Smyth for one,' Mathew-Pare said.

'Look, other murders aren't my problem. If I think he's

good for our murder, I'll rifle every house in the county to get him, tap every tout in Christendom …'

'What, all three of them?'

O'Keefe smiled. Unlike past insurrections against the Crown in Ireland, there were virtually no informers to be found within the IRA and almost as few amongst the general and criminal populations. The IRA was a tighter, more ruthless ship this time around, and citizen and rogue alike were terrified of being marked as traitors to the cause. He continued, 'I'm telling you, if we put Connors up as our number one suspect, that's it for the investigation. The brass will run with it and, when he's found, charge him with Deirdre Costelloe's murder whether or not he's done it and we'll be fobbed off to other things.'

The Englishman's face was as bland as ever. 'So they'll charge him with it. Case cleared. Connors gets the rope or a bullet and the world gets shot of a bad fucking article, making West Cork a safer place to live for you and me.'

'Safer for young women?'

'We don't know if our killer had anything to do with the whore's murder.'

'Exactly. Which is why we need an exhumation order.'

Mathew-Pare dropped his cigarette and crushed it under his boot. 'I could take Starkson in there right now and have the name for you in five minutes. We would know any connection Connors might have with this house and the card player, whether Connors knew our victim was seeing him. Five minutes. You know that, don't you?'

O'Keefe held his gaze. 'You'd want to be willing to kill him outright. He's more afraid of the IRA than he is of us.'

'He'd fear Starkson more than Satan himself, after five minutes. It's an option, Sergeant. I'm no more for violating the rights of ordinary citizens in ordinary times than you are, but …'

The Detective gave that half-smile again as he said this and a chill washed over O'Keefe. He suddenly felt the weight of violence, of brutality, that Mathew-Pare and his men represented and it struck him that they were the embodiment of the way the British had always worked in Ireland. Civil at first, pronouncing upon the value of rights and citizenship in an Empire bigger and more modern than the world had ever seen. But when the people of the country refused the Empire something, anything, there were men like Starkson and Eakins around to slap them back into line. O'Keefe wanted no part of the man's methods, the methods of the Empire. 'No,' he said. 'No heavy stuff.'

Mathew-Pare shrugged. 'Suit yourself. Where to now then, Sergeant?'

It was over. Like that. Something in O'Keefe knew it had been too easy. He thought for a minute. 'Why don't I drop you lads at the Victoria barracks? Then I'll head over to Anne and Deirdre's rooms. Give them the once-over. You could get something to eat and maybe ask after the procedure for exhumation. We'll head back after that.'

'Exhume the whore? The Plunkett girl?'

'Yes. I'm not sure if it's worth it or even possible, but it wouldn't hurt to ask Division about it.'

Smiling, Mathew-Pare said, 'Anything to help, Sergeant. Anything at all.'

———

'There,' O'Keefe said, shutting down Mathew-Pare's Ford. 'From Cork to Ballycarleton in under two hours without a shot fired or barricade crossed. I'll put us in for a commendation, Keane, what do you think?'

It was obvious that Keane wasn't sure if he was joking. To be fair to Keane, O'Keefe thought, it was something he rarely did any more. Not since the war. And it struck him that there was something about life, an axiom which held that the longer one lived, the less there was to laugh about. But then he thought of his mother and father downstairs in the evenings of his childhood, sometimes alone together, other times with friends or relations, as Peter and he lay awake in their shared bed listening to them laugh. The deep, rich bass of their father's laugh. The light, sweet stutter of their mother's and her feigned disapproval of some off-colour joke. Their parents' laughter that had made him – them, as he was certain Peter felt it too – feel all the warmer and safer in their beds. But then again, he didn't imagine that either of his parents laughed much now, since Peter's death. So the axiom held – life as a continuum, a shifting through days and ever-increasing gravity and pain that was the lot of the living. And where did that leave the children who were poor and mistreated from birth? Girls like Janey Plunkett, whoring at the age of twelve or fourteen? A steeper slide towards adult misery. They died younger, so the slide started earlier?

O'Keefe shrugged off the run of morbid thought, cursing himself. Maybe it was the Jesuits who had ripened his mind for such gloom with their brutal logic and constant exhortations against the evil they believed was so rampant in the world. And how right they were, about evil. My poor auld fella, he thought. Sending me to the best school he could afford on a policeman's wages and all I came away with was an icy reliance on the logic of pain. He smiled at Keane, letting him in on the joke that had now faded.

Keane smiled back. 'Good thing, aye. Hands like claws so I have, with the cold. Couldn't pull a trigger if I tried.'

It was nearly ten. Mathew-Pare, Eakins and Starkson had told Keane and O'Keefe to take the car back without them; they were going to paint Cork red. They had asked O'Keefe and Keane to join them, but there was something about Mathew-Pare's offer that made O'Keefe think it was perfunctory. Not that he had any intention of joining them anyway. He wasn't sure if he'd take to the way those three laid on the red paint. Besides, he had work to do.

His search of the rooms Deirdre Costelloe had shared with Anne Duffy had revealed little, but he had managed to find a cloth-covered notebook in a drawer that seemed to serve as Deirdre's diary. He had given it a cursory read, sitting in the girls' flat, and had seen nothing of interest in it, but then it had been impossible to concentrate with the girls' landlord,

Mr Timulty, standing over him. The man had insisted on being present while O'Keefe searched the room, as was his right. Since the raiding of houses in search of republican suspects had started in earnest over a year before, complaints against the army and the RIC for theft had shot up. Dublin Castle, in all its wisdom, had drafted regulations for searches, which they then made public, assuring the citizenry that a police constable would be present during all searches led by the army, and that a senior ranking constable would supervise at all police searches, to ensure the lower ranks weren't filling their tunics with the family silver. The regulations allowed the owner of the home in question to be present during the search. O'Keefe had no gripe with the principle of the regulations, but the practicality was a different matter. After about five minutes, he was feeling some sympathy with Seamus Connors' threat to shoot the landlord. When he had questioned the landlord, the man had refused to answer any questions, claiming that the police had never done him any favours, so why should he help them? O'Keefe had stared at the landlord until discomfort sent the man scuttling down the stairs. In any case, his search and questioning of Mr Timulty was quicker and less thorough than it might have been. Still, he had found the diary and taken it away.

Now he and Keane made their way across the yard, boots scuffing the cobbles, breath billowing in the night air. Squares of light showed through the firing slits in the shuttered windows. Trapped inside for days on end, most of the men had come to hate the barracks, the Tans in particular. 'Like a bloody prison, innit?' O'Keefe had heard one of them say. Finch, he thought it was – a man who probably belonged in prison. And it was like a jail in some ways. These men had no experience of barracks life before the Troubles. Back then – it seemed a lifetime ago – an RIC barracks could be a happy, sociable place, depending on the officer or sergeant in charge. People from the town, while not entirely comfortable within its walls, would come to have their forms read for them and signed if they couldn't read or write. They were often offered tea while the sergeant – citizens rarely trusted anyone of lower rank than a sergeant with personal or legal affairs – read them letters from their sons and husbands at the Front, or the forms for claiming death pensions when these sons and husbands were killed.

In O'Keefe's first barracks, in Navan, County Meath, there was an old bachelor farmer who would bring the *Meath Chronicle* to the barracks once a week and ask for O'Keefe to read the Gaelic football and soccer results to him. He always asked for him personally, telling the barracks sergeant that O'Keefe had the voice of a schoolmaster. He told O'Keefe once that his sister, who shared the farm with him, could read, but that the GAA and the soccer was 'man's business' and so he preferred Constable O'Keefe to read it to him. And every Christmas a pint bottle of the bachelor's home-distilled poitín would find its way into O'Keefe's possession. O'Keefe believed the farmer also spared a bottle for the head constable. Finer drink he'd rarely drunk and unsurprisingly the old man's still was never raided.

All this had changed. Gone forever, O'Keefe imagined. Still, on a cold night, even behind steel shutters and rolls of concertina wire, there was always a pot of tea and a warm fire going in the barracks.

As they entered through the rear door, O'Keefe said to Keane, 'Go up and tell Jim … Sergeant Daly, to take you off the patrol roster for tonight and the rest of the week. You've been hard at it and I could use you for the next couple of days.'

Keane beamed. His face was bright red from the drive and his hands were smeared with grime from the starter crank on the Ford, but his smile was bright enough to light up a building. He took off his cap, revealing that his hair was pressed awkwardly against his head, making him look more like a schoolboy than a police constable. 'Are you sure, Sergeant? I can do my lates and work with you in the days.'

'No, I need you fresh. Fall in for inspection and drill, and take school in the morning with the rest of the lads. Then change back into mufti and report to me.'

Keane started down the steps, paused and looked back.

'Something else, Keane?'

'Yes, Sergeant. I was wondering …'

'Spit it out, Keane. My belly thinks my throat's been cut with the hunger.'

'Well, since you said I'd be working in my civvies …'

O'Keefe nodded.

'Do you think there's any chance of me getting the

Working in Plain Clothes Allowance? Fierce hard on the rags, working plain clothes is, Sergeant, so it's said.'

O'Keefe stopped himself from smiling. Jesus, what Jim and a few others hadn't started with their union organising. Now, even young cons like Keane, green as grass on the job, were looking for *per diems* and allowances. When O'Keefe was Keane's age, he would never have dreamed of asking his sergeant for the Plain Clothes Allowance, although there had been times when he had been entitled to it.

'I'll see what I can do.'

The young constable smiled his thanks and said something in Irish.

'What does that mean?'

'It's a thing my mother always said. It means: *If you want, you must start by asking.*'

'Put the kettle on, would you Constable?' O'Keefe said, remembering a phrase his policeman father had liked to say to him and his brother when they were young: *Want with one hand, shite in the other, see which fills up first.* He imagined it would have sounded better in Irish.

In his office O'Keefe shrugged off his trenchcoat and stabbed at the ashy turf embers in the grate. He crouched and warmed his hands in the faint glow, thinking of the welcoming fire in the hearth of Katherine Sheehan's house. And then he remembered her husband beside the fire. There but for the grace of God …

His stomach growled and he realised he hadn't eaten since breakfast, his only nourishment being the two large bottles of stout and the short whiskeys in Sutton's tavern. He thought of heading down to forage for a meal but then reconsidered, wearied by the idea of having to endure the banter of the barracks kitchen. He could picture Keane gossiping away with his Tan friend, Heatherfield – the table tennis ambassador – recounting Eakins' beating of the doorman at the brothel and the beautiful young whore in the hallway of Madam Grace's. Or maybe he was underestimating Keane and the young lad was the soul of discretion. Still, he should have told the young constable to keep a lid on things.

To hell with it. He took the quarter bottle of the army surgeon's black-market Bushmills from his desk drawer and poured himself a glass. He shook a Player from the dented tin on his desk and lit up. The whiskey and smoke dampened his hunger, settled his nerves. Food could wait. Now, two days after receiving it, he took out the letter from his sister and read it.

Dear brother,
I hope this letter finds you well and in good health. Forgive me
for not writing sooner. Things have been so busy and you surely
heard what happened here, with the sacking of the town by
Crown forces.

'Crown forces'? Irritation rose in O'Keefe. When, exactly, Sally, did you start using the language of the republican Press in your letters to your brother, a member of the 'Crown forces'. He read on.

In a strange way, those awful events have much to do with what I must tell you. I had hoped this would be joyous news, for it is to me a joyous announcement. But it is tinged with sadness. I am to be married, Seánín. To a fine man from a fine family, the Gilshannons …

O'Keefe knew the family vaguely from his past visits to see his sister in Balbriggan. One or other of the many Gilshannon lads were forever offering help to Sally, weeding the garden, digging up spuds from the small plot that came with the teacher's house, bringing eggs from their mother's hens. They were handsome boys – men, he realised now. He wondered which of the brothers had managed to win his sister's heart.

… but in great sadness, dear brother, I must ask that you not attend the wedding. Colm's family have suffered greatly at the hands of the police and are of a mind that they …

O'Keefe noted the 'they' and read 'you'.

… have outstayed their welcome in an Ireland striving to hold itself as an independent and proud sovereign nation. Perhaps if you were to leave the police you could come, as I want nothing more than for my brother to be with me on the day I marry. Please, Seánín, don't think me cruel.

He tossed the letter onto the desk and threw his cigarette into the fireplace. *Cruel?* What kind of family are you marrying into, he thought, wondering then if he could access the file on the Gilshannons that DI Masterson had. Bitterness filled him. He took a long drink of whiskey. There was a knock on the door.

'It's open.'

Old Reilly put his head around the door. 'Drinking alone, Sergeant O'Keefe? In my day, any drinking at all would get you docked by the Head. Drinking alone, though? Not done, no.'

Someone had once told O'Keefe that the word 'chat' had come from the trench slang for louse. Buddies would comb the nits and lice out of each other's hair in the hours between shelling, all the while nattering away. Chatting. O'Keefe wondered how obvious it looked that he didn't want to chat. Reilly appeared oblivious, however, and entered the office. O'Keefe scratched his head reflexively and wondered how to get rid of him.

'Just thinking about the case, Reilly. Sure, y'know yerself, a man needs a bit of quiet now and again.'

Reilly took this as an invitation and sat down in Daly's chair, leaning back, making himself at home. Wind rattled the steel shutters and a draught snaked its way through a gap in the window frame.

'Fierce night all the same. No rain though, thank God,' Reilly said, eyeing the bottle on the desk.

O'Keefe flipped up the collar of his suit jacket against the draught and resigned himself. 'Has the coal lorry come today?' The army now supplied RIC barracks with coal.

'Did you order coal?'

Frowning, O'Keefe tried to remember. Maybe Jim had ordered it. More likely he hadn't. He shrugged and leaned forward, took a second glass from his desk and passed it over to Reilly. 'Help yourself.'

He did, a generous portion. As O'Keefe got up and checked the coal scuttle, he wondered was the old man naturally avaricious or did a retired police constable's pension not stretch to good whiskey. If it was the latter, he felt a touch guilty. Reilly was his father's age, give or take a few years. He was from Louth or Monaghan, O'Keefe couldn't remember which, but had been barracked in West Cork for most of his days. O'Keefe had no idea what kind of constable he had been and didn't much care one way or the other. The coal scuttle was empty and he returned to his chair.

'How come you never went home when you retired, Reilly?'

The man took a gulp of whiskey and let it slide down his throat, relishing it as if he was remembering the taste from some fine day in the past.

'Never had no mind to. Bought a plot of land near Upton and was going to farm it, so I was.'

'Threats then, from our friends?'

'There was. Blocked the chimney on me one night last year. Accused me of all sorts – things done during the Land War days. Claimed I'd topped one of their fathers during a march on the house of a landlord's agent in Toureen.'

'And did you?'

Reilly shook his head. 'Years – ten years easy – before my time. Not to say that the land agitating ended round here once the Land Acts came in. No. There was many the cattle drive and the odd man shot or house burned down through the days since. But I never done nothing to no one that didn't have it coming, and fellas may think what they want to think and fuck them. Still, I thought I'd better not take a chance, once the shooting started.' He took another sup.

O'Keefe nodded, selecting a cigarette and offering the tin to Reilly, who took one. 'You ever work on a murder case, Reilly?'

Striking a match and holding it out to O'Keefe, he replied, 'Aye, three big ones. Worked thirds to my Head and Sergeant in Upton. Head was a fella by the name of McMartin. The O'Connell case there, back in the summer of 1904. Poor wee girl beaten to death by her fiancé. He was a daft cunt, so he was. She gave him the shove. He couldn't think of living without her, so he killed her, then slept next to her body in the nettles by a stream. Tried to hang himself next day, but picked a branch too ripe and full of bend in it. Spent hours trying to do away wi' himself.' Reilly smiled, picturing the scene. 'Bouncing up and down with the flex in that branch. It was too high, and him too knackered to climb again and untie the rope, see, and find another branch. So he flung himself this way and that, running to the rope's end like a mad dog on a staked chain. Got fed up finally and decided God didn't want him dead. Went home for his tea, none the worse but for a half-stretched neck, nettle rash and a fierce hunger for his mother's bacon and cabbage.'

O'Keefe gave him a tired smile. 'The things people do for love.'

Reilly nodded and drank. 'You think it was love did for your girl there on the hill?'

'No.' O'Keefe said. 'Crimes of passion, love killings – whatever you call them – are more violent. Like your case there. The lover's head bashed in or fifty stab wounds to the offending heart. This one seems too cool, too deliberate for a passion crime.'

'The boyos, then?'

'Don't know. She was courting a fairly heavy fella from the 1st Corks. A shooter. Bit of an article, so her friend said.' O'Keefe drank more, feeling himself relax, the whiskey working on his empty stomach. 'And she'd chucked him over not too long before, for some swell with a flash motor.'

'Dangerous business, that. You get the fella's name?'

O'Keefe was about to tell him about Connors when he remembered what he should have told Keane about keeping his mouth shut but hadn't. He shook his head. 'No, didn't get it. Should do, though.'

'Didn't get it, aye.' There was disappointment and a hint of annoyance in Reilly's voice, as if he knew O'Keefe was withholding details. 'Slippery feckers, them 1st Cork lads. Don't have names to faces for half of 'em.'

The old man finished his whiskey and stood up. Conversation over. O'Keefe was sorry he had offended him. Not much of a life, retirement, and living alongside men doing the job you had done for years. Alongside but outside.

O'Keefe reckoned he would risk a bullet rather than lead the life Reilly led now.

'Well, you'll get it, the name, so you will. No doubt about that, Sergeant.'

'Hope so. Sounds a terror, this fella. Someone'll hate him enough to give him up.'

Reilly nodded, not looking him in the eye. 'I meant to say,' he said, his eyes flitting from the desk top to the dead ashes of the fire, 'DI said he wanted to see you when you came in.'

And then he turned and went, leaving O'Keefe alone again.

———

O'Keefe was surprised the DI was in, but maybe even Masterson couldn't dodge his duties during a murder investigation. Or maybe, he thought, the man had finally seen sense and realised that Head Constable Murray wasn't coming back or was dead, and that he would have to start doing his own paperwork now; that it was all well and good having your head constable fill out your half-sheets and weekly reports for the County Inspector while you dined out with your club chums, but it was another thing altogether leaving it to two barrack sergeants – one acting and unproven and the other known to all for his profound hatred of anything resembling labour.

'Sit down, Sergeant O'Keefe, sit down. There you are,' Masterson said, making a fuss of him, sliding an antique-looking chair over from its place against the wall to just in front of his desk. In a similar chair to his right, an arm's reach away from a half-full crystal decanter, glass and cigar in one hand, was an army officer, a colonel by his shoulder boards. He was leaning back casually in the chair as if he was familiar with the office. He stared intently at O'Keefe and O'Keefe turned to him, unsure whether or not to salute. Army ways died hard in ex-soldiers.

The man extended a hand. 'Colonel Owen Prentice, 3rd West Kents, Sergeant.' He smiled underneath a neatly trimmed moustache. The Colonel was lean, confident in his fitted, olive army uniform, his hat on the DI's desk, his hair oiled and neatly combed. He wore cavalry officer's jodhpurs, shining, knee-high, black boots and his legs were crossed at the knee. His eyes were dark, assessing.

O'Keefe took his hand. It was soft.

'Pleased to meet you, Colonel.'

Masterson introduced him. 'This is Acting Sergeant Seán O'Keefe. He's the chap I've been telling you about.'

O'Keefe wondered had the DI been telling the Colonel about his 'suspect loyalties' and anger forged itself under his ribcage. Then he thought of his sister's letter and a sadness welded itself to the anger.

The Colonel said, 'Ah, right-o. Running the show on the hillside murder, is it?'

His voice was that careless, rumbling muddle that only the most gentlemanly of Englishmen could get away with: sloppily emphasised consonants bracing randomly drawn and flattened vowels. O'Keefe pictured paintings on the wall of the Colonel's ancestral estate: his father, grandfather, great-grandfather in West Kent regimental garb.

'The victim wasn't murdered on the hillside itself,' O'Keefe said. 'She was transported there, we believe.'

The officer took a pull of his cigar and then a sip of what O'Keefe assumed to be brandy. 'Indeed, somewhere else.' He looked pointedly across at the DI.

'I was just telling the Colonel about it,' Masterson said. 'Nasty business altogether. A woman murdered in cold blood and left like that on the hill. Shocking. An outrage.'

The DI could be writing headlines, O'Keefe thought, wondering why he had been summoned to this meeting. Masterson continued, looking over at the Colonel.

'Of course, most of these killings go unsolved you know, Owen. The cornerboys have the people so terrified no one will answer questions, let alone testify before a jury – military *or* civilian – for fear of their lives. The state of our nation, sadly, as it is under the law of these … thugs.' He spat out the word, but there was something about his argument that struck O'Keefe as odd. On the one hand, the murder of a woman in such circumstances *was* outrageous and shocking. And yet, on the other, Masterson seemed to be trying to convince the Colonel that solving the crime would not be possible.

It occurred to O'Keefe that, although the Colonel and the DI were obviously friends – he had noticed a photograph of the Colonel and Masterson in hunting gear and holding rifles on the wall behind Masterson's desk – perhaps the

Colonel was applying some kind of external pressure from higher up to solve the murder. Castle to Division to Regiment to pal's police barracks. If this was the case, then maybe the DI was simply advising the Colonel to let it be known that Deirdre Costelloe's murderer might never be found. That there was nothing Masterson could do about it, much as he'd like to.

'Of course, Walter,' the Colonel said, turning to O'Keefe. 'I know how hard it is for you chaps. No help at all from the peasantry, makes the job a damn sight harder, I'd imagine.'

O'Keefe tried to think of the last time he had heard the people of Ireland referred to as 'peasantry'. How far, exactly, did this Colonel Prentice imagine O'Keefe himself was from being a peasant? 'It can be difficult, sir.' He turned to the DI. 'But we've made progress today. We spoke to the victim's friend. They shared rooms –'

'And did she give you anything you can use?' There was an over-eager quality to Masterson's voice as he asked the question.

Maybe, thought O'Keefe, the man really was under the boot to solve this murder. He said, 'I have a couple of lines of enquiry I'd like to pursue.'

'And what did she give you, this girl?' the Colonel asked.

O'Keefe looked to the DI for permission to answer. The DI gave an exaggerated nod to indicate he was among friends. 'Speak freely, Sergeant.'

O'Keefe told them about Anne Duffy's interview and his meeting with Connolly and how the name of Seamus

Connors had come up, leaving out the fact that Connors was wanted for the Smyth shooting in Cork, realising that even though Connors was a legitimate suspect for Deirdre Costelloe's murder, he would become the only suspect if Masterson was aware of his link to Smyth's assassination. He was banking on the fact that Masterson hadn't heard of Connors before now. 'In fact,' he said, 'I was going to ask if you could get on to the Raid Bureau in "I" Division yourself, sir, to expedite any file they might have on this Seamus Connors. We've put in a request on the wire, but a nudge in the right direction wouldn't hurt.'

Masterson noted his request in a leather-bound diary on his desk. 'Of course, Sergeant. Good work. Two days in and you've a plausible suspect. Impressive.' He looked up and smiled at the Colonel, like a proud father boasting of a son's exploits on the football pitch.

O'Keefe's face remained impassive. Masterson's praise had never meant much to him. After questioning his loyalty to the RIC, it now stood for nothing.

'A drink, Sergeant?' the Colonel asked, studying O'Keefe.

'No sir, thank you.' O'Keefe looked back to the DI. 'Keane suggested having the Raid Bureau cross-reference the name Seamus with the general description of the visitor who'd called to the Costelloe's farm in the days when the girl was missing.'

'Keane, Keane …' The DI scanned his memory. 'Ah yes. Young lad from Donegal?'

O'Keefe was grudgingly impressed. He would have bet a

month's wage Masterson wouldn't remember who the young constable was.

'Yes, sir. He's been a great help to the investigation. I was wondering if I could have him removed from patrol and orderly duty for the time being and have him assigned to me full-time.'

'Of course. Anything you need, Sergeant.'

'And he'd be entitled to the Working in Plain Clothes Allowance, sir?' O'Keefe added, as an afterthought.

'Absolutely. As are you, Sergeant, certainly. Have you applied for it yet yourself?'

O'Keefe told him he hadn't.

'Well then, get the forms and I'll sign off on them. Anything you need to get this fellow.'

'There is one more thing I need, sir.'

'Sergeant?'

'I need an exhumation order. Mathew-Pare enquired at Division earlier, but no one seemed to know whether it could be authorised or not. Best anyone could come up with was requesting a petition from the County Inspector. It also might be of use to file a request with the diocese or even Cork Corporation because the girl's buried in –'

'Just a moment, Sergeant,' the DI said. 'Why exactly do you need this *exhumation* order?' He spoke the word as if it disgusted him.

O'Keefe explained the possible connection between the murdered prostitute and Deirdre Costelloe. 'It comes down to cause of death, sir. The doctor who did the post-mortem on this Jane Plunkett did a rush job. He saw bruising of the throat, knew of her background and just assumed asphyxiation by strangulation to be the cause.'

'Which it most likely was,' the Colonel said.

O'Keefe tried to keep the annoyance out of his voice. 'Well yes, probably. But we have another possible link, you see. Anne Duffy told us that Deirdre had given Seamus Connors over for a rich chap in a blue motor. A card player.'

'But what does this have to do with some doxie you want dug up, Sergeant?' It was the Colonel again and there was something about the way he said 'Sergeant' – a tightness to his voice – that made O'Keefe think he was very close to pulling rank.

He turned his appeal to the DI. 'Look, sir, if you'd allow me to finish …' O'Keefe realised he was on the defensive.

'Go on,' Masterson said, but without conviction.

'Sir, this Jane Plunkett was employed to … to entertain at parties. She was hired by an unknown gentleman. He took several girls each time from a brothel in the Marsh. I believe there's a good chance Deirdre Costelloe's card player may have attended as well. If we could determine that Miss Plunkett was killed by the same type of stabbing blow and not by strangulation, then we have a vital link to where, and possibly who, killed Deirdre Costelloe.'

'And Seamus Connors. How will this exhumation bring you closer to finding him?' Masterson asked.

O'Keefe realised he was wise in not highlighting Connors' connection to the Smyth shooting. An IRA man as killer of a young woman would suit the bureaucrats perfectly, particularly if the copper who put the bracelets on him was Irish, Catholic and had a sister married into a known republican family. It occurred to O'Keefe that his 'suspect loyalties' might make him the ideal man to catch a republican murderer. He swallowed down the bitterness of the revelation and clasped his hands in his lap like a supplicant. If he was going to find out the truth about Deirdre Costelloe's murder, he knew he would have to at least appear to keep Connors in the frame, if only to satisfy Masterson and his masters.

'Sir, if there is a link between Connors and the Plunkett girl and Deirdre Costelloe, we need to find it. If there is no connection, then maybe it's only a matter of ruling it out so we can direct our energies elsewhere. Connors has sound motive for murdering the Costelloe girl but what if she is not the only girl he has murdered?' He quoted from the RIC investigations manual: '"Ruling something out in a criminal investigation is often as vital to eventual conviction as is the discovery of new evidence".'

'Indeed. You've got the book down have you, Sergeant?' Masterson glanced over at his friend. 'Didn't I tell you O'Keefe was the man for the job, Owen?'

O'Keefe said, 'About the exhumation, sir.'

'All right, Sergeant. I'll do my best. I'll contact the County Inspector. But you realise, of course, that he has the final say on it. I suggest you half-sheet your reasons and I'll pass them up. After that …' The DI held out his hands.

'Thank you, sir. Is there anything else?'

'The letter, Walter. You forgot to show the Sergeant the letter,' the Colonel interjected.

'Sir?'

The DI said, 'Ah, how could I forget? One of the reasons I called you in.' He produced a letter from inside a cardboard file marked with a red ink 'Classified' stamp and handed it to O'Keefe. Colonel Prentice scrutinised him as he read.

'We got it in a raid in Cork,' Prentice said, 'three days ago. I brought it here myself when I heard of your murder, Sergeant.'

'Can I have a transcription of this, sir?' O'Keefe directed his question to Masterson but the Colonel answered.

'Certainly. For the murder book, eh? Get your batman to type up a transcription there, won't you Walter?'

'On your desk later this evening. Constable Senior is out on patrol at the moment. When he comes back, I'll have him tap it out for you, Sergeant.'

O'Keefe looked up from the letter. 'Senior's on patrol, sir?'

Masterson looked as amused as O'Keefe was puzzled by the fact. 'He insisted. Said everyone needed to do his part fighting republican terror.'

Prentice nodded. 'Damn right, too. If the bastards in Whitehall would do their part and declare proper martial law on this godforsaken country, the insurrection would be over in days. No stomach for it, I tell you. No iron at all.'

'Will there be anything else, sir?'

The DI rose and indicated the door. 'Catch him, Sergeant. That's all we ask.'

———

O'Keefe read the letter again, seated at his desk.

A cara, Micheál,

It is with the greatest urgency I appeal to your leadership in the matter of women spies. Concern has been expressed by Volunteers as to the rectitude of their execution. There is one case in particular, originating in your own part of the world, which has caused particular concern among committed officers and men. And yet, certainly the act shows a passionate commitment to our cause among units in West Cork and could serve to deter fraternisation with the enemy among women so inclined. We are certain there have been cases of information being passed from women in the towns and city to soldiers which has been used to effect searches and, in a few known cases, the arrest of Volunteers and the capture of arms and documents. The possible deterrent effect such trial and execution of women spies may have, however, must be weighed against the reaction in the British and Irish Press.

Thus, your counsel is required forthwith. Shall we say (a) the execution of women spies is forbidden and that this woman in Cork, of whom I dare say you will soon hear a great deal, was not killed by the IRA? Or, (b) this woman was killed in contravention of orders by the IRA and that the woman was a victim of common murder committed by member(s) of the

Crown forces? Or (c) that this woman and others who may require similar sanction was arrested, tried and executed by the IRA as a traitor to her nation and people?

Awaiting your instructions. As always, I wish you luck in the gruelling task you have so willingly borne on behalf of the people of Ireland.

Mise le meas,

Erskine Childers, Dáil Director of Publicity

It *had* to refer to the case, O'Keefe thought. A surge of optimism washed through his tired mind. IRA brass were worried. And if they were worried at the top of the IRA, it meant that the local Volunteers who may have committed the murder would be twice as scared. This meant that he now had some leverage. Of course, it pointed him back to Seamus Connors. Connors' motive might not have been strictly 'for the cause', but then again maybe he had got sanction. Or maybe not. Childers to Collins? Heavy boys to be crossing if they disapproved of your means and methods.

O'Keefe was well aware that IRA units around Ireland were given a degree of independence unusual in conventional armies, but still there were actions that were punishable. And rumours abounded of Volunteers who had fallen foul of Collins and HQ staff in Dublin. Rumours of men from Collins' own active Squad who had been sent into country towns to plug some disobedient Shinner, the Squad men disguised in RIC greatcoats or British army uniforms. The 'removal' of recalcitrant IRA members gussied up to look like the work of Crown assassin squads. Rumours only, but in a war like this one, rumours carried the force of truth. There were so many rival hit squads in the country that sometimes it was impossible to tell who had killed whom and for what reason. Nonetheless, no one deserved to die like Deirdre Costelloe. There was something so cynical about the letter. To seek to deny involvement in the killing seemed to O'Keefe to be an admission that the IRA *had* committed the murder; equally, the suggestion that the murder be framed as the work of soldiers or police. But the most frightening thing to him was the possibility that this type of killing could be considered as a just punishment for a traitor. As he had said to Mathew-Pare, there were rules to this conflict and it was incumbent upon them to figure out what they were. He wondered now: was he reading the IRA's attempt to draft the rule book? And was there anywhere a similar document in the British army archives that authorised the murder, mutilation and rape of female combatants and spies? He wouldn't bet against it.

He scanned through the letter a final time and then filed it in the murder book, less optimistic than he had been half-an-hour before. In itself, the missive was proof of nothing. It was hearsay or speculative, circumstantial evidence of IRA involvement.

His brain was tired and he pressed the heels of his hands to his eyes. Nothing was ever simple. Nothing. The unpopular Rising of Easter 1916 turned into an heroic struggle overnight by the act of executing James Connolly, wounded and tied to a chair, at Kilmainham Gaol. Hundreds of thousands of obedient soldiers lying unprotesting in trenches under a never-ending rain of shells, then sent over the top to their deaths by men worthy of neither love nor respect. Obedient soldiers like himself, his brother Peter, wading unprotesting headlong into the maelstrom of Turkish machine-gun bullets. A young woman stripped and butchered and laid out on a hillside. A young girl dead in an alleyway, her life not worth the hours it would take to investigate. None of it made sense and O'Keefe wondered if it ever would.

He poured himself a large measure of Bushmills and drank.

———

Mathew-Pare and his two men sat Davey Noonan in a hard-back chair at a wooden table in a room with lead-lined walls, deep within in the former quayside meat-packing warehouse rented by 6th Division Army Intelligence.

Noonan was shaking. He sniffed and winced. His nose had been broken. Mathew-Pare lifted his blindfold and Noonan blinked as his eyes adjusted to the bright overhead light. A refrigeration unit hummed from another room.

The pimp recognised his interrogator. The English bastard from earlier that evening. The one who had sat smiling while the Peeler questioned him. He cursed himself now for not having spotted him for what he was. All the Peeler's talk about crushing his monkey nuts when here, now, he was talking to the organ grinder. Still, he had been in the business long enough to know that there was always a way out of a dodgy spot. Throw the monkey some nuts. Throw the grinder something shiny.

'Yis can take off the goggles, lads,' Noonan said. 'We can settle this like the gentlemen we are.'

Mathew-Pare laughed, took off his motorcycle goggles, stuffed them in his pocket and lit a cigarette. 'Hear that, boys? Mr Noonan has said we can remove our goggles.'

Starkson and Eakins removed their goggles. Eakins took a chair outside the halo of light cast by the single hanging bulb while Starkson joined his boss at the table. Mathew-Pare sucked hard on his cigarette and without preamble held it close to Noonan's left eye. 'I'll start with your left. Then I'll do your right, Mr Noonan.'

Fear contorted his features and Noonan turned his head away from the glowing ember.

'Jaysus fuck, lads. What do yis need know? Yis only need ask, for Christ's sake.'

'Who rents the girls for the parties?' Mathew-Pare withdrew the cigarette and took a long, relaxed drag.

Calmed by this, Noonan considered the question. 'Are yis gonna plug him? 'Cause if you don't, there's no fuckin' difference between what ye could do to me and what that mad fella he has working for him would do. Sure, he finds out I told yis and I'm as good as dead.'

'You'll be taken care of, Mr Noonan.' Mathew-Pare offered the pimp a cigarette and lit it for him. 'A name, please.'

Noonan sighed with relief, looking up eagerly at Mathew-

Pare. He gave them a name. 'Gentleman-fella. Doesn't even use the girls himself. Hires them for his pals in his gentleman's mob is all. Lives in Montenotte. And his friend, his man – Bill something – lives there with him. Acts queer for yer man. Does anything the boss says. Puts the fear of God in me, I'm tellin' yis, that Bill fella.'

'And the girls he brought to the parties?'

'I told yis the truth on that. Two of 'em gone away, one dead, and Bella. All right, all right, I neglected to mention Bella. She's back at the shop. You're not gonna mark her face, are yis? She'll be worth fuck all to me with a marked face.'

He looked at Mathew-Pare and then at Starkson. Mathew-Pare stubbed out his cigarette on the scarred wooden table. Noonan swelled with confidence, dragging on his own smoke. 'Yis know I can work for you lads, if yis need ears. Loads of all sorts use my shop. IRA lads, priests, your lot. I scratch yer bollocks, yis scratch mine, right?'

Eakins stood up from his chair and stepped out of the shadows. Mathew-Pare and Starkson stepped back.

'That's a very generous offer, Mr Noonan.'

'I'm telling yis, I can …'

Even if there were passers-by – so long past curfew, so far down the quays – the shot would have sounded like a slammed door inside the darkened warehouse. They would have taken no notice.

In the dream, his brother Peter clutches his hand, smiling,

pulling him forward. They are on the *River Clyde*, though the deck is elongated, an impossible distance to the pontoon bridge that will take them to shore. In the dream, the one he knows by heart but is powerless to stop, his legs are weighed down by the dread of what is coming and yet he moves forward, along the deck of the ship. He can make no sound, pass no word of warning to his brother. There are men behind him, more in front, all heavy-stepping into the gnashing teeth of Turkish bullets. Men moving forward, knowing but still moving, like cattle down the chute in an abattoir. The Turkish machine-gun fire beats distant and oddly regular, like a snare drum or blacksmith's hammer. Peter smiles and says, 'Come on, Seán, for the sake of Jesus. You're stalling, man.'

Now he is in the water, the weight of his pack dragging him under. Something, someone grabs his arm and tries to pull him down into the rust-coloured foam. Peter. He cannot see his face, but he knows it is his brother. He lashes out, kicks him away.

'It's me, boy! Jesus, go easy.'

A large hand slapped his cheek, the blow exploding O'Keefe into consciousness. He opened his eyes.

Constable Logan had a forearm across O'Keefe's chest, pinning him to the bed.

'I'm awake, Logan.'

The constable released him and O'Keefe sat up. He lifted his watch from the empty bully beef crate that served as a bedside table. It was a quarter past two in the morning. He had been asleep for no more than an hour.

Logan relaxed and lifted his pipe from where he had set it on the crate. He struck and held a match to the bowl and fragrant smoke filled the room. 'I'd hate to be your missus, Seán. You'd surely kill her in your sleep.'

'I'd kill you awake if you were my missus, Logan.'

The older man chuckled. 'Much too good for the likes of you, filthy jackeen git. A good country girl like myself would never have you.'

O'Keefe smiled, the terror of his dream ebbing in the comforting presence of the old con.

'Sorry to wake you, young Seánín, only you're wanted on the blower.'

O'Keefe rubbed his eyes and pulled on his shirt without buttoning it. 'Who is it?'

'Didn't say, only that he'd speak to you and nobody else and to be quick about it. Pushy fecker. Must be brass.'

The barracks reception room was to the left of the front door. O'Keefe imagined it had once been the parlour, the wife's best room, used only when the parish priest visited, or maybe when the eldest son brought a girl from a good family back to the house for the first time. A girl from a family with a bit of land. Now the room was bisected by a long counter and the walls papered with wanted posters, yellowing with age, some of the suspects long since dead or captured, others still at large. There were ordnance survey maps of the local area, as well as a locked gun rack holding six Enfield carbines. A photograph of the King hung over the fireplace. Like the rest of the barracks, reception had fallen into a state of shabbiness that would never have been tolerated in the past. Dust accumulated in the corners, ash spilling out of the hearth.

O'Keefe took a seat at the desk behind the counter and picked up the phone. Logan moved his chair closer to the fire and made a show of reading his newspaper.

'Sergeant O'Keefe speaking.'

The voice on the line had a strong West Cork accent. 'Twenty minutes,' the caller said. 'The Kinsale–Toureen crossroads. Come alone. And our friend says bring the photographs.'

O'Keefe was wide awake. 'Do you have the –'

'Bring the photographs. Come alone. You'll be watched. If we see anybody leave that barracks other than you in the next half hour, you've just had your last sleep, Sergeant.'

———

The night air was cold and damp but the wind had kept the frost at bay. O'Keefe wore gloves, a neck scarf and a woollen watch cap. His uniform-issue greatcoat in standard bottle green was warmer than his trenchcoat and he shrugged it on as he headed for the row of barracks' bicycles, protected from the weather under their oiled canvas covers. A curious Logan followed.

'You put this little trip into the Occ Book, Seán?'

Every RIC barracks in Ireland had an Occurrence Book, in which were logged the events of each day as they affected the local constabulary. In it were transcribed the most minor details of barracks life – including the weather and the phase of moon, much like a ship's log – up to the most grievous of crimes committed in the district. The comings and goings of every constable and officer were to be logged as well, though this had slackened a great deal with the advent of the Troubles. Still, O'Keefe knew how old cons like Logan were sticklers about the ledger. To some of them, he thought, it was as if the weather outside didn't really exist until it had been logged in the Occ Book.

'No,' he said. 'I didn't log it. This is private business I've to take care of, Logan. I wouldn't want the DI finding out about it, right?'

The older man didn't appear too happy about O'Keefe's disregard for RIC regulations, but his disdain for ranking officers – Masterson in particular – was stronger than his objection. 'Problem with a lady friend, Seán?'

O'Keefe removed the cover from one of the bicycles, checked the tyres for air and mounted. 'Sure, y'know yerself.'

Soon, the sound of the wind was in his ears and the crunching of the bicycle's tyres on the crushed gravel road. The surface was compacted, but beginning to soften with the early winter's rain.

As his right leg came up and around, propelling him towards the crossroads three miles away from the barracks, he patted at his ankle and felt the small .32 automatic he had fitted into his loosened boot, held safe with a wrap of bandage. Seven rounds in the small pistol. Enough to stop your average assassin, O'Keefe reckoned, if he was standing stock still less than twenty feet away, in good light. In his shoulder holster, he carried a Colt .45 automatic with a bent hammer. From any distance, it wouldn't stop anyone, a fact he was counting on.

As he neared the crossroads, he coasted to a stop and dismounted, his eyes scanning the darkness. Ten yards from where the sign pointing towards Kinsale had once stood – the IRA had removed it – he stopped and listened, straining to hear any sound. His heartbeat sounded faintly in his ears. The dying wind. A dry-stone wall marking the border of a farmer's field on his right and he propped the bicycle against it. On the other side of the road was a low ditch rising to a scrabbly whitethorn hedge, the wind nudging its branches, whispering in the grass. He sensed a presence behind him.

'Put your fucking hands up, Peeler.'

O'Keefe raised his arms slowly, keeping his eyes forward. If the man behind him wanted to be seen, he'd let him know. Rough hands went to work, patting down his waist, his shoulders, under his arms.

'What's this?' the voice said, feigning surprise.

O'Keefe felt the .45 slide from its holster. 'Christmas come early for you lads,' O'Keefe said, before he could stop himself. He expected a blow in response to his sarcasm. Instead he heard laughter, low and confident. The man had done this before.

'Happy Christmas to you too, Peeler.'

A second voice from behind, this one nervous, edgy. 'What is it?'

O'Keefe heard the slide go back on the Colt and then snap back into place. 'Donation to the arms fund, courtesy of the RIC.'

Then he felt the barrel of a gun at the back of his neck and hoped it was the disabled Colt. The barrel shoved him forward. 'Move,' the second voice said.

'Lemme put on my shoes, boy. Fuck sake …' It was the first voice and his words explained the silence of their approach. O'Keefe waited while they pulled on their boots.

'Where are we going?'

'You'll see soon enough, Peeler.'

Peeler. The way the Volunteer said it made it sound like *Traitor*, and O'Keefe thought of the sign hung round Deirdre Costelloe's neck.

'Over the wall there, boy, and keep it steady. I'll give you a bullet here as soon as any place, ye Tan bastard.'

O'Keefe climbed over the wall, his movements slow and deliberate. 'I'm no Tan, if it matters any. *Peeler* I'll take, but –'

'Shut up and walk. Mind your step. You break an ankle, I'll shoot you, boy. You'll not be a weight on my back.'

The terrain was soft underfoot. In the intermittent moonlight O'Keefe could make out that they were following the course of a long, dry-stone wall separating two fields, and were hiking steadily away from the crossroads, north towards the mountains. He stumbled occasionally and was wrenched roughly back to his feet.

'Keep it steady.'

Soon, they crossed over the wall and were on wet, boggy

ground. The land was rising and the terrain tougher to cross. O'Keefe's boots made a sucking sound in the earth. Once, they disturbed a nesting bird and heard the flapping of wings, the rasping, frightened caw.

The climb levelled off at the top of a low hill and they began to descend along an established path through a steep ravine. O'Keefe could hear running water – a small stream probably – working its way down from the mountains.

They came to the water and splashed through it, icy cold seeping into O'Keefe's boots. He thought of the loaded .32 and prayed it hadn't become fouled in the stream.

Minutes later O'Keefe felt the gun barrel on his neck again.

'Stop.'

The other voice now, louder. 'It's us, boys. We've got him with us.'

A voice came from behind the rocks. It was a cave of some sort, the entrance hidden behind a boulder, reminding O'Keefe of Christ's tomb as depicted in the stations of the cross. From behind the boulder came a Volunteer, an Enfield rifle over his shoulder.

O'Keefe suffered his first burn of real fear and wondered whether he would come out of the cave alive if he entered. He doused the fear with resignation. Done was done. He had gone and threatened Ryan, hoping the Councillor would come up trumps with the men who had harmed Katherine Sheehan. He'd given up on them as suspects in Deirdre Costelloe's killing, but there was always the possibility that they might know something. In for a penny, in for the hard road. He preceded his guards into the cave.

The interior of the cave had the dimensions of a small public house. A paraffin lamp hung from a hook drilled into the low ceiling and along the walls were several men, their faces covered with scarves or handkerchiefs, two holding lanterns. One of them stepped forward. A working man wearing rough corduroy trousers, hobnailed boots and an oversized, mushroom-shaped cap. Covering his mouth and nose was a white handkerchief. His eyebrows, thick and brown, met in the centre of his brow. When he spoke, it was with a local accent, perhaps Ballycarleton, Bandon or Drumdoolin – all towns with active IRA units.

'Bring them over,' the man ordered.

Another Volunteer, his face hidden by a woollen scarf, shoved forward two young men into the circle of light, their faces bare. The Skelly brothers. O'Keefe recognised them from their photographs in the file he had been sent from Bandon barracks. A third man – young, slender, blue eyes nervously flickering above his mask – hovered behind the brothers. O'Keefe noted the soft hands, the cut of his jacket and cashmere scarf. Though he was obviously a Volunteer, he looked as if he had unwillingly fallen in with rough company.

The man in the mushroom cap spoke first. 'You asked Mr Ryan to help locate these men. He done it. These men were involved in an act that the IRA had given no sanction to. We'll deal with that. You've five minutes to ask these fools what you want to know. They'll answer your questions.'

The Skelly brothers were a desperate pair from a long line of miscreants. The family was well known in West Cork. O'Keefe recalled that their father and uncles had all spent time in Cork prison for various offences. It was rumoured that, in the Skelly family, sisters did for wives when there were no women about. William Skelly, the elder, looked as if he'd been beaten. His eye was swelling shut and there was a smear on his chin as if blood had been hastily wiped away with a sleeve. Both had dark brown hair and dark, close-set eyes. The younger brother's hair was wild, long, and he had a dusty fuzz of whiskers on his face, making him appear younger than the nineteen years old O'Keefe knew him to be. The elder Skelly's hair had been recently cut and oiled, and he was clean-shaven.

O'Keefe felt a brief flash of pity for them. Poor sods. And then he remembered what the two were assumed to have done. Both were big and strong enough to hold down a woman like Katherine Sheehan. Like Deirdre Costelloe.

The Volunteers who had brought O'Keefe to the cave stepped back and the gun was lowered from his neck.

O'Keefe nodded. 'Thank you,' he said to the mushroom-capped man and sensed the smile behind the handkerchief.

'Don't be thanking me, Sergeant. I'd shoot you down as soon as look at ye but orders is orders. Right, lads?' He directed the question to the two prisoners, slapping the younger Skelly brother hard on the back. Neither of them looked at him, but both nodded.

Taking a photograph of Deirdre Costelloe laid out on the butcher's table from inside his coat, O'Keefe handed the picture to the younger brother and watched for his reaction. It wasn't long in coming.

'Jesus Christ have mercy, Sergeant. You think I done … we done that? You're mad, you are.' He looked away sharply from the gruesome image. His reaction was convincing.

'Give it to your brother.'

'I needn't look at no fucking photograph of no dead girl to tell you I didn't do nothing to her. I been in Millstreet barracks these past days and only raised my head out of it yesterday. Even these know that. Ask fucking them, boy, if you don't believe me.' He held O'Keefe's gaze as he spoke.

O'Keefe turned to the Volunteer in the expensive scarf. 'Is he telling the truth?'

The young man nodded. His voice was cultured, the accent different from the other men in the cave. 'It's true, we checked.'

O'Keefe held the Volunteer's gaze until he looked away.

'Why'd they let him out of Millstreet? He's up for enough to fill a cabinet back in barracks. Surely someone would have notified Ballycarleton or Bandon …' Realisation dawned slowly.

The well-dressed Volunteer didn't look at O'Keefe as he spoke. 'We've to assume that he was informing. Or that he had offered to inform, in order to secure his release.'

O'Keefe sensed uncertainty in the Volunteer. Saw it in his eyes. Not every IRA man was as committed to bloodshed as Division and RIC Intelligence believed. Or maybe this man, this boy, was new to the game.

O'Keefe turned to the younger Skelly brother. 'Look, if you know anything about this, you'd better tell me now. God won't look kindly on the killing of a young woman.'

'I swear on me dead baby sister gone these nine years, I never killed no girl. I swear to Jesus and all the saints, so help me God.' A sob broke his voice and he scrubbed the welling tears in his eyes with the back of his hand.

The Volunteer with the mushroom cap spoke up. 'There's no need to be calling on God, Mutton. Sure, when's the last time he helped the likes of ye?'

The other Volunteers laughed, though some of the laughter sounded forced.

O'Keefe ignored the banter. 'But you assaulted the egg woman on the Timoleague Road, didn't you? Put a pig ring in her backside?'

The boy hung his head.

'And did you do other things to her, Thomas?' He remembered the boy's Christian name was Thomas, though he seemed to go by Mutton. 'Did you?'

'We was told do it –'

Mushroom cap cut in. 'You were to fuck told do what you done to her, ye lying cunt. You were ordered to warn her off. That's all.'

'Who ordered you to do it, young Thomas?' O'Keefe asked.

'Don't answer that!' mushroom cap ordered.

O'Keefe turned to William Skelly, his voice raised. 'Who ordered you to do it?' A gun barrel dug into his back.

'You want to know who ordered it, Peeler?' The voice under the white handkerchief was hard. 'The Irish Republican Army ordered it. The woman was a traitor, aiding the enemies of Ireland, providing sustenance to the Crown. The IRA ordered her to be *warned*. These two ingrates took things too far. That's war for you. People make a balls of things sometimes, boy.' He pointed at the brothers. 'They'll fucking pay for it. Understand, Peeler. Just like you'll pay, one of these days.'

'And did the Irish Republican Army order that the girl left up on the hillside get a warning, as well? Did someone take things too far with her too, did they?'

The barrel pressed harder into his back and O'Keefe recognised the voice of the first man who had collected him at the crossroads. 'Easy, boy. Go easy now.'

The eyes over the white handkerchief looked away from O'Keefe. 'We'd nothing to do with that. No one here did. No one in the IRA had a thing to do with that ... that *yoke* on the hillside. You take that back with ye, boy, and tell your bosses the IRA had nothing to do with that business. I'm letting you walk out of here alive; that's as good as my word on anything. Not one thing did the Volunteers have to do with that girl and neither did these two fucking *dahs*.' He turned his eyes back to O'Keefe.

'You believe them?' O'Keefe asked.

'Course I believe them. Sure, what have they to gain by lying?'

'Their lives?'

'Their lives aren't worth the bullets, don't you think, Sergeant?'

O'Keefe shrugged, feeling cold, beginning to shake with it.

'Now,' the Volunteer said, taking off his cap and scratching his thick head of brown hair. 'I don't suppose you've some photographs for me?'

His bluff called, O'Keefe swallowed. 'I've no photos for you. There never were any.'

The Volunteer laughed. 'No photographs. *Never were any.* You know something, Peeler?'

'What's that?'

'I said them very same words to that fool Ryan, I did.'

'Clever man, you are.'

'Not clever enough to ask him could I plug you if you didn't bring them. Ryan, see, he thought you'd keep your end of the bargain. He thought, down under the arm-twisting, there was something of the decent skin about you, Sergeant.'

'Maybe we kept our end of the bargain seven years ago. Burned the prints back when we said we would.'

'Maybe you did, but I doubt it.'

'You'll never know though, will ye? There's always a chance I've left them to be sent on to Mrs Ryan if I get shot. Sure, the creamery is still in her name, I hear.'

'Better mind yourself then, Sergeant.'

'Councillor Ryan should mind I do.'

Mushroom cap laughed and signalled the man behind O'Keefe to lower the gun from his back. He stepped over to O'Keefe and put an arm around his shoulders, escorting him back to the entrance of the cave. 'What's in those photos anyway, Sergeant, just between yourself and myself?'

O'Keefe stopped, as if considering the question. 'Just between the two of us?'

The man nodded, eyes shining with anticipation.

'Ah now, what kind of man would I be, describing the private …' O'Keefe paused, 'peculiarities of our democratically elected representatives?'

The Volunteer laughed again. 'It'd be a grand shame to have to plug you, boy. You're a gas man.'

'Be a grand shame for Councillor Ryan.'

There was a smile in the Volunteer's eyes. 'Democracy's a queer thing, Sergeant. People are fierce fickle. There might come a time when it won't matter any more what Ryan sticks his mickey into or who sees the pictures.'

'Time will tell.' O'Keefe nodded over at the Skelly brothers. 'What'll happen to those two?'

The Volunteer followed O'Keefe's gaze and the smile in his eyes faded. 'Them two'll be grand. Don't you worry yourself about them two soft bastards, Sergeant.'

———

After the Peeler had gone, Liam Farrell took the Peter the Painter in his hand. Watched his own shadow on the cave wall as if he were watching another person altogether – a stranger with a shadow gun. He hefted it, noting the boxy shape, the long thin barrel. 'Peter' had been an anarchist painter who had shot a policeman in London with the same type of Mauser pistol during a bank robbery some years before, hence the gun's common name. There was a popular children's rhyme that followed the event and it came to him now. *Peter the Painter, paint your head red ...*

'Is it loaded?'

Eamonn Halloran pulled the white handkerchief from his face and stuck it in his pocket. 'Wouldn't be much use if it wasn't.'

One of the Volunteers said, 'He could club the fuckers to death with it, sure.'

The younger Skelly brother, Mutton, was crying. The older brother stared at the shadows on the cave wall. He cleared his throat occasionally and spat a mixture of blood and phlegm onto the packed earth floor.

Taking a watch on a broken chain from his pocket, Halloran said, 'Tonight, boy. Sorry ... *sir*. We need to get a move on while the country's still in darkness.'

Farrell caught the barb. *Sir*. He was nominally in charge of this interrogation, although he'd known nothing of it until Halloran and his men had called for him at McGowan's that evening. He was the Intelligence Officer. It was his investigation, and he had done his part, he told himself. He had questioned these two lads and had been satisfied that they'd had nothing to do with the body on the hillside. As for the egg woman, they'd got carried away. They were a foul lot, the Skellys, and these two should never have been used by the IRA for anything at all. But did they deserve to die for it?

'I still don't see why ...'

Halloran said, 'Farrell, I've told you, and I'll not tell you again: why in the name of sweet fuck do you think that grasping bastard was cut loose out of Millstreet? You heard the Peeler. They've enough paper on the boy to bury him and yet four days inside and he's out? Use the loaf, boy, and if that don't work, use the nose and smell the rat.'

The older Skelly brother looked over at them. 'I'm no rat.' But he said it without conviction, as if he had learned some time in his life that this was what – as an Irishman or a lifelong criminal or both – he was supposed to say.

Halloran was right. Farrell knew he was wasting his breath trying to spare the Skellys. He had a job to do. He stepped behind the two brothers and raised the Mauser. His hand was shaking. He had never pictured it quite like this, killing for his country. Putting bullets in the brains of two unarmed men had never featured in any of the heroic scenes he had screened in his imagination.

His index finger brushed the trigger guard and as if aware, the younger Skelly brother found his voice.

'I didn't do nothing. I didn't. I'm no rat. I swear it. Please.' His words were choked with sobs. 'I done nothing.'

Halloran said, 'You hurt that woman. You done that, you fucker. Who told you do that, Mutton?'

The older Skelly was unmoved. He hacked and spat again, saying nothing and Farrell was seized by sudden terror. *Jesus. I can't do this. This is not what … not how …*

He turned, handed the gun to Halloran and ducked out of the cave.

Eamonn Halloran shook his head, partly in disgust, partly in sympathy. Out of his depth, Farrell was. Should have stayed in college. No business in the fray, poor bastard. He checked the load in the Mauser and raised it.

'Any prayers, lads, before we get down to it?'

The elder Skelly brother cleared his throat and said, 'Fuck all o' ye cunts.'

The younger brother wept.

Climbing out of the ravine, O'Keefe and his escort of gunmen heard the shots. Faint pops in the night. Almost as if they hadn't happened.

———

When the serving maid left, he found another house, this one in a less salubrious area, where he would perch on the roof of a coal shed and watch as a girl, maybe eighteen, nineteen, brought in soldiers from the barracks. Sometimes they left the light on, at other times it was off, but always, once the men had left, the whore put it on and he watched as she squatted over her chamber pot, usually naked but sometimes with her shift bunched about her hips held in one hand while she cleaned herself with the other. Her bunched shift white, her buttocks a warm pink from fucking. She was a hen. He was a hawk, perched on the coal shed. Watching. Waiting.

Tuesday
30 November 1920

O'Keefe had one more thing to do before he left the barracks. He descended the stairs to the lower ground floor, entered the kitchen and cut a thick slice of brown bread, thinking of Daly's words when he'd told him earlier that he'd be visiting the Sheehan woman again. Daly had accused him of looking for a cut off another man's loaf and O'Keefe shook his head now in disgust, as much at himself and his odd brew of feelings for the woman as at Daly's lewd insinuation. He made tea, buttered the bread and topped it with a greasy fried egg from a tin tray that had been prepared hours before, and ate and drank without relish. Then he poured a second, sweet, milky cup of tea and carried it with him.

Dunn was at the desk in the hallway containing the barracks' three cells, reading a copy of the racing pages.

'Any tips?' O'Keefe asked him.

The jailer looked up. 'None worth a bullet on the way to the bookmaker's.'

'How's our friend?'

'Quiet.'

'May I?' O'Keefe pointed at the open packet of Sweet Aftons on the desk.

'Work away.'

He took the cigarettes and the cup of tea down to cell three. Behind the bars, Finch lay on the iron cot fixed to the wall, hands behind his head.

'You come up with your list of charges yet?' O'Keefe asked him.

The Tan laughed. ''Ard to make a list when you can't

remember 'alf of what you done, Sergeant.' He didn't get up, but he didn't turn away either.

'Here.' O'Keefe held out the cup of tea and shook a cigarette from the packet.

Finch waited a moment, then rose and accepted the tea and smoke. O'Keefe lit the cigarette through the bars.

'You eaten yet?'

'Not yet, Sergeant.'

O'Keefe noted the use of Sergeant and reckoned that Finch had had enough of his cell time. 'Right, Finch. Forget about Sergeant Daly's list of charges. Court-martial's off if you can give me a dig out with something.'

'Dig out?'

'If you can help me with this case. The girl who was murdered.'

Finch nodded and sipped his tea. 'What do you need, Sergeant?'

'Our garage man Morton told me you know cars nearly as well as he does. Told me you're saving every penny you make over here for a flash motor when you get back across the water.'

'That's true, Sergeant.'

O'Keefe lit a cigarette for himself. 'Tell me this then.' Setting his briefcase on the floor, he took out his investigation diary and opened it to the notes from his interview with Anne Duffy, Deirdre Costelloe's friend and flatmate. Then he picked up Deirdre's diary.

He had spent the previous evening – before he'd been

summoned to the crossroads – reading the journal. It was sporadically kept. Many days she had written nothing, while on others there were several pages on the gossipy doings of workmates and friends. Which fella was courting which girl and the like. Which of the typists or clerks was in with Mr Barton and why. When writing of her own relationships, the young woman was discreet, using initials for the names of men. O'Keefe had discovered this when he reached the part in the diaries where she had begun seeing Seamus Connors – SC – after meeting him at an Irish language class.

The Irish language, after many years of decline throughout most of the country, had come back into fashion, with young and old alike taking lessons set up in church halls or sports clubs by the Gaelic League. Contrary to myth, the British had never actually banned the language – Keane for example, was a fluent speaker from a Gaeltacht in Donegal – but it had died out in most places through parents wanting their children to speak English so that they might get ahead in the world. More effective than banning the language, the Crown had convinced the Irish people to see it as a hindrance.

Most of those who attended lessons genuinely wanted to learn Irish but, to the chagrin of the committed and monkish instructors of the Gaelic League, there were others who looked upon the lessons as a means of meeting eligible members of the opposite sex. Personally, O'Keefe didn't see any conflict between the two aims. Obviously, Deirdre Costelloe hadn't either. Nor Seamus Connors, though O'Keefe imagined he hadn't attended many classes after the shooting had started. The classes themselves were technically banned under the Restoration of Order Ireland Act as subversive gatherings, but in practice they were allowed to continue and were known to be riddled with Crown agents and spies.

Deirdre's diary charted a year and a half relationship with SC, with references to dances attended, hotels visited – for meals only it seemed – and coy admissions of SC's desire to consummate the affair. According to the diary, Deirdre had let Connors have his way to a point, stopping him short of any activity that might risk pregnancy. This, O'Keefe gathered, reading between the lines, was done more from this fear than from any great sense of moral virtue. She also claimed that Connors had repeatedly asked her to marry him and she had refused, reluctant to spoil the fun she was having living as a single girl in the city. In her diary Deirdre came across as one of the new breed of Irish women trying to shake off the shackles of Victorian morality and religious inhibition – hard working, independent and liberated.

Connors, on the other hand, and to O'Keefe's surprise, was portrayed in the diary as rather conventional, stuffy even, despite his ardent physical desire for Deirdre, and nothing like the menacing presence described by Anne Duffy and Connolly, the Crimes Special Branch man. His intentions towards Deirdre appeared honourable. He had proposed marriage half-a-dozen times, if the diary entries were to be believed. There were references to Connors' growing frustration at this state of affairs. Entries such as *'SC sulking because I put the bridle on him in the Miller's field after the dance and wouldn't let him have what he's after wanting for ages'* led O'Keefe to believe that after two years Connors strongly wanted to consummate the courtship, but nowhere in the journal was there a hint of violence or evidence of the searcher of 'dark souls' Anne Duffy had spoken of. Clearly, Deirdre was unafraid of Seamus Connors.

The reason O'Keefe had come to see Finch was a recent reference in the diary to Deirdre's new man, the card player. The entry was dated two months earlier, 14 September 1920, and was written after a month-long gap in entries, during which, O'Keefe assumed, Deirdre had met 'D'. There was no mention of their first meeting.

O'Keefe read aloud to Finch:

D collected me today in his beautiful motor. The seats are of the softest, vermillion-coloured leather and the top is soft calfskin. It's as long as a Galway currach and bluer than the sky. He calls it the Spaniard, for some reason. What a car! What a rogue! D makes SC seem the dreary boy that he is. All talk about the great republic, all the while trying to throw his leg over mine. D has been the perfect gent so far but there's something dangerous about him and his friends. He told me today that if I was very, very good, he'd take me to his club! Very wicked of him to insist on my being so very good! Delightful and dangerous is my D! Just what a girl needs in these days of shootings and misery. If only I didn't have to work!'

He pointed out the section and handed the journal to Finch through the bars. After a long pause, the Tan said, 'Ver … verm – what in fuck is that word? Sorry.'

'Vermillion. It's like maroon.'

Finch shrugged.

'The colour of red wine.'

'Oh, right. I got you.'

'A long car, shaped like a boat. Tan calfskin cover, sky blue painted body. Swanky motor, her friend said. Any ideas what kind it might be?'

Finch mulled it over, taking long, leisurely drags on his cigarette. 'Well, it's no Rolls that I can think of 'less the paint's a special job. The 'Spaniard' bit though. Only thing I can think of is an Hispano-Suiza. Sounds like the H6B. Came out in red and blue and black, I think. But that's a French motor. Made in Barcelona.'

'Barcelona is in Spain, Finch.'

'It is? Learn something every day, don't you? They're made in France as well, I do know that. They was carriage-makers before the war. If it is an 'ispano.'

O'Keefe noted: *Hispano-Suiza.* 'Is this a popular car, Finch?'

'Not at all, Sergeant. Right squodge it'd cost you. Never even seen one up in Dublin, let alone Cork. Rich man's motor. Stuck a bloody aeroplane engine in it. Same one they used in the Spad biplane – 150 horses under the bonnet. Runs like a bullet, so I've 'eard.'

O'Keefe jotted down the information. Shouldn't be that

hard to track this 'D' down with a car like that, he thought. He underlined Hispano-Suiza, H6B twice and then called down to Dunn for the key to the cell. He turned back to Finch.

'You're on lates until I tell you otherwise. Patrols if they're going. If I ever see you drunk in barracks again or disobeying a direct order, you're done for, Finch. You want that motor you're saving for so badly, you'll keep the head down and get on with the job.'

Finch grunted. 'Yes, Sergeant.'

As he turned away, O'Keefe thought of something he had always wanted to ask one of the Tans. Now seemed as good a time as any. 'Why'd you come over here, Finch, if you don't mind my asking. Was it the money?'

Finch shrugged. 'For the few bob, yeah, that was mainly it. But then, you'd need to see London to know it's the kind of place a man needs to get shot of. Four years in the mud and come 'ome to that place? Do me a favour. Bloody veteran soldiers, officers even, begging on the streets, begging for any kind of work. Doing awful things for a few quid, their decorations pinned to barrel organs, in the lanes selling toys and matches with their pittance of demob money spent. A "land fit for 'eroes"? 'Ardly. Ireland seemed a fine way out of it all. Besides …'

'Besides what?'

'It's the only thing I'm any good at.'

'Policing?'

Finch laughed. 'Fuck no. Fighting.'

Liam Farrell stepped out of Garvey's bakery into the milky morning sunlight, a fresh warm loaf under his arm, his eyes smarting from lack of sleep.

Away all night presiding over the interrogation – no, he decided, call a spade a shovel – presiding over the execution of two young men and McGowan had the nerve to send him, like some errand boy, to the bakery. He'd been tempted to ask the man what Maureen was doing that she couldn't fetch the bread herself, but he hadn't had the nerve. There was something about McGowan he found daunting, despite the man's reserve. It was an instinct only but it was there all the same. He sensed that men such as McGowan – every bit as much as gunmen like Barry – would have a major role in the new republic when the time came. Better an ally than an enemy.

A man appeared from out of the doorway of McManus's pub and stopped in front of Farrell as he made his way toward the solicitor's.

'Have a drink, Liam?'

Eamonn Halloran. A tight, sick feeling gripped Farrell's insides, an almost electric charge of fear sparked by Halloran and the air of good-natured menace he wore about him like an old coat. He said, 'What do you mean, have a drink? I –'

'Step inside here, Liam.' This time Halloran wasn't asking.

Farrell followed him into the pub. It was quiet and cold and smelled of old beer and tobacco. The light in the bar was tinted amber by the pub's coloured windows, as if it were filtered through a pint of lager. A fresh turf fire was crackling to life in the fireplace. McManus, in a white shirt and apron, was washing pint glasses in a basin behind the bar. Memory rose up. Ages ago it seemed, and it was. Seven long years past and his father, banned from every pub in Newcestown, had taken to travelling the eight miles to Ballycarleton for his binges. Seven years at least it had been, since the night Liam Farrell had found his father in McManus's, vomit on his shirt, a shattered mirror behind the bar, two police constables standing over him. One of them had been a young Constable O'Keefe. The same O'Keefe – older now, his face harder, more angular and rent by a long purple scar, but the same man – who had come to the cave to question the Skelly brothers the night before. The same man leading the investigation into Deirdre Costelloe's murder. Farrell's face burned. The Peeler hadn't recognised him behind his scarf and surely nor would the publican now, after all the years. Or would he?

Halloran sat down at a small table by the fire and leaned across it. Farrell set the loaf on an empty stool and leaned in as well, meeting the man halfway. 'What's this about? I've work to do for McGowan. Is it about last night?'

'Never mind about last night,' Halloran said. 'Last night's done and dusted. Now you listen, Liam.' He looked around the empty pub and then back at Farrell. 'First: leave out the fucking funny codes. That's an order. Might as well be reading Greek, they say, your poxy messages.'

'I sent them a key.'

'Knock the queer stuff on the head, Liam, and do your job.' The man looked up and called for two pints of stout.

McManus began to pump the Murphy's tap.

'Next, you need to get out and find this Seamus Connors fella. He's one of Barry's flying column boys.'

'Yes, I know him.'

Farrell pictured Connors driving a bayonet into a wounded Auxie on the road near Kilmichael. *Like a spade into soft ground.* Remembered O'Sullivan's shed and his questions about the missing girl. 'Did he know the dead girl – Deirdre Costelloe?'

McManus came over to the table carrying two pints of stout. Farrell looked away when he came, but the publican ignored him. McManus's was a Volunteer-friendly house, but it was better for the publican to sympathise from a distance.

Halloran took two long draughts of his pint. 'He knew her. He was courting her in Cork. He put in a good long stretch with the girl before she gave him the push. Word is he took it fairly hard.'

'What do I do when I find him?' Farrell tried to sound nonchalant, feeling weak and small inside under the awareness that the man across from him wasn't afraid of anyone. Halloran's eyes, watery blue under his cap brim, were full of pitiless good cheer.

'You're to bring him to Inchigeela. To O'Sullivan's. The boys want a word with him.'

'And what if I can't find him? Or he won't come with me?'

Halloran finished the rest of his pint in long, thirsty gulps. Farrell's stout sat untouched.

'You're one of the Intelligence boys. You're supposed to be intelligent.' Halloran stood and clapped Liam on the shoulder.

'Wouldn't …' Farrell lifted his stout and then set it back down, unable to meet Halloran's eyes, 'wouldn't they be better sending someone like yourself to collect him. I'm not certain …' There was too much he was uncertain about to continue.

'Sure, if they sent someone like me, Liam, he'd know what was coming and we'd never see him again. You, he might talk to. You're meant to be a good man with the words, boy. Now's the time to use them.'

He turned then and left Farrell staring at his untouched pint.

———

Katherine Sheehan rounded the corner of her cottage, coming from the direction of her sheds as O'Keefe was leaning the Trusty on its stand in front of the stone wall. The sun had broken through the clouds, lending some brief warmth to the day. He paused to adjust his collar and button his jacket.

She didn't see him immediately and O'Keefe watched her as she walked up the path, smiling to herself as if she were remembering something fine and light in the past, swinging the bucket she carried in rhythm with her stride. She was a beautiful woman, he thought for a second time in as many days; graceful, unadorned. He tried to picture her in a stylish hobble skirt and patent leather pumps, her hair swept off her face, a faint dusting of rouge and lip paint, and decided she would look no finer dressed to the nines than she did in the patched, heavy work skirt and man's collarless shirt she was now wearing. Sensing his gaze, she turned and recognition stole her smile, banished the fond memory that had put it there.

'It's you back,' she said, as if she were speaking to a husband returned from a three-day skite, wages gone, a shoe missing.

O'Keefe's spirits plummeted. He had hoped she would be happier to see him. But then, why should she be? What had he brought her the last time he had come here but a cold reminder of the evil that guttered outside her door? He was a fool. He could have sent Keane if he really wanted to ask the woman about the feathers found on Deirdre Costelloe's body. And as for the Skelly brothers, he had yet to decide what to tell her about them.

'It's me back,' he said, taking a cake box from where it was hanging on the Trusty's handlebars with one hand, his briefcase dangling from the other, waiting for an invitation to open the gate. 'I was wondering if you could help me. It's about the girl we found.'

Katherine Sheehan put her hands on her hips. She looked as if she was about to order him away from her property. 'Was the help I gave you last time so good you've come for more?'

O'Keefe nodded. 'It might have clarified a few things. I'm not sure yet.'

'What help is it you need this time?' Her voice was sharp, with no warmth in it.

He fumbled with his briefcase, the cake box cradled in one arm. 'Would you take this, Mrs Sheehan? I brought it for you, for your family. In return for your kindness the last time I called. I ...' He ran out of words and smiled dumbly.

'And you expect me to fetch it from you?'

'No, no.' He tried to open the gate but again his full hands prevented him. Balancing his briefcase between his raised knee and elbow, he tried once more and dropped the briefcase, spilling some papers onto the road. 'Sorry,' he said, setting the cake down in the gravel and replacing the papers in the briefcase as neatly as he could.

Katherine Sheehan shook her head, amusement, if not yet warmth, showing on her face. 'Stay where you are and I'll get the gate. Whatever you've brought will be in bits if I don't take it from you.'

She opened the gate and held it for him. O'Keefe handed her the box. 'For you and the boy, Mrs Sheehan ... and Mr Sheehan.'

'I'll put this inside and you can ask me your questions in the sheds. I've work to do, Sergeant.' O'Keefe waited outside the cottage while she went inside. When she returned, he followed her silently to the cowsheds. Entering, she picked up a pitchfork from where it was leaning against the wall and began to muck out the stall, turning over the stale bedding and then tossing it in the general direction of the doorway where he was standing. He moved out of her way.

She heaved another forkful in his direction. 'You could make yourself useful and find the barrow.'

O'Keefe set his briefcase down and retrieved the wheelbarrow from its resting place against the hen house. Hens pecked in the dirt between the stones in the yard. 'Have you a shovel or another fork? I could give you a hand.'

'You'll get no wages working here, Sergeant.'

He smiled. 'I don't mind. Sure, it's seldom enough I get outdoors for any exercise.'

'And you'll ruin that fine suit of clothes.'

'No bother, Mrs Sheehan. Where should I toss it?'

She stopped to wipe her brow with her forearm. 'There's a shovel in the last stall, and you can empty the barrow around the back. Hang your jacket on the post if you've ever a mind to visit a dance hall again.'

O'Keefe laughed. 'Dances are much too dangerous for Peelers these days.'

'Sure weren't they always, Sergeant?'

They worked together without speaking until Katherine Sheehan set her fork against the slat board wall and O'Keefe did the same with his shovel. The stall now smelled of fresh bedding, a rich, wheaten odour that reminded him of the horse stables at his father's Dublin Metropolitan Police barracks when he was a child.

She turned to O'Keefe and, for the first time since she had opened the gate, looked directly at him. 'Hope the work didn't raise any blisters, Sergeant?' Her voice was light and cut through with gentle mocking.

'I'm a regular beast of burden, Mrs Sheehan. That's why they made me acting sergeant.' He held up his hands for inspection and to his surprise she took them in her own to examine them.

'Fine soft hands, Sergeant. You've never done an honest day's labour in your life until today.'

'Not since I was a boy, and even then I dodged it best I could. Why else become a copper?'

She smiled and then the smile faded. 'I read that men from the cities and towns, men with soft hands like yours, when they went to the war, they raised blisters on the inside of their trigger fingers.' She made her thumb and forefinger into a gun and fired. 'And these blisters hardened to calluses over the months. And they say these calluses take years to go away, so that even now, back at their desks, they can still feel the weight of their guns, the weight of every time they pulled the trigger when they lift their pens.'

She lightly brushed her thumbs over the pads of his index fingers.

'I wasn't there long enough to get the calluses. I was wounded two and a half weeks after the landing and was laid up for a nearly a year with blood poisoning in the Army Hospital in Cork. Spent more time in bed than I ever did fighting.'

She nodded and looked up at him. 'You've the calluses, still, Sergeant. Just not on your hands.'

He didn't know what to say.

She squeezed his hands. 'When you're able, you'll tell me.

I want to know what happened at V Beach. What happened to my Gerard.'

He looked into her eyes and nodded. After a moment, she smiled again and said, 'Come on then and we'll cut that cake. I had a peek at it and it looked scrumptious.' She smiled and laughed. 'I've never any call to use that word. *Scrumptious!*'

The smile was like a blow to the chest for O'Keefe and he thought suddenly that there was very little he wouldn't do to make Katherine Sheehan happy.

'I hope it tastes as good, considering the trouble I had buying it.' He smiled at her. 'Nobody in the bakery would serve me so I took it from the case and boxed it myself, leaving its cost on the counter.'

She laughed again. 'Victims of the same boycott, Sergeant. Yourself and myself.'

Her husband was sitting at the fire and took no notice of their coming into the cottage.

'Fine day,' O'Keefe said to him and received no response.

He felt a pang of guilt entering the man's house, sitting down in anticipation of sharing the cake he had brought, not for him or even, if he was honest, for his son, but for Katherine Sheehan. He watched her as she prepared the tea, his eyes following the graceful slope of her shoulders, the strong, straight back, the narrow waist and full, round hips.

'I've nothing better than tea to offer you, Sergeant.'

'Tea's grand, Mrs Sheehan.'

Shifting his gaze back to Gerard Sheehan, O'Keefe noted he was still a handsome man, despite the vacancy in his eyes.

He looked like a full-forward on a Gaelic football team – long and rangy, likely to be quick in the turn. His hair was combed, neatly parted and he'd been shaved recently. Katherine Sheehan took good care of her husband. His admiration for the woman increased, along with the guilt that had wedged itself under his ribs. They ate in silence, constrained by the brooding presence of the man by the hearth. O'Keefe wondered if he was using the husband's mug.

At one point Katherine Sheehan said, 'I saw the paper. About the girl on the hill. Is it true, what was written?'

He told her it was, more or less.

'And will you find him?'

'If I'm lucky or I'm let.'

He didn't elaborate and Katherine Sheehan finished her tea without speaking. She walked him to the gate.

'You never asked me what you came for, Sergeant.'

Resting his briefcase on the seat of the Trusty, he took out a manila envelope holding samples of the feathers taken from Deirdre Costelloe's body. He handed them to her.

'These feathers were found with the body. I was wondering what kind of bird they came from. Birds. The surgeon thought they came from different birds.'

The sun succumbed to afternoon cloud. O'Keefe buttoned his jacket against the cold as she turned over the feathers, examining each one closely.

'I don't know these feathers, Sergeant. I only keep common laying hens, myself. Perhaps they're from some other type of fowl?'

'I'm a city lad, Mrs Sheehan. I might know if they were from pigeons.'

She smiled at that. 'A city lad. And now so far from the city.'

'Your son's coming up the road.'

'Back for his tea from my sister's. He loves it over there. Life is normal. There's a baby just starting to walk and an uncle who's kind to him.' She watched the boy's approach, a tiny figure on the empty road, seeming to have forgotten about the feathers in her hand. 'I pity the poor dote. He's a lonely child with no brothers or sisters of his own.'

'More cake for him, so.' O'Keefe smiled and she looked at him and smiled back sadly.

'You might try asking at Burleigh House about the feathers. I'm sure you know it. Just outside of Upton. The Major keeps exotic fowl. He might be able tell you where these came from. Or else the big poultry house on the Toureen road. They might know.'

The boy saw them and stopped, some hundred yards away, watching. O'Keefe returned the feathers to the envelope. 'There was another reason I wanted to see you, Mrs Sheehan.'

'Call me Kate,' she said, with sudden urgency. 'Just now. Before the boy comes. Call me Kate.'

'The men who … who hurt you …'

'Say my name, Seán.'

'I found them, Kate.'

She put her finger to his lips, silencing him. 'That's all I need to know.'

He nodded. He understood. Katherine Sheehan stepped away and called out to her son. Without looking at O'Keefe, she said, 'Go now, Seán. Find the ones who killed that poor girl on the hill.'

———

In the end, it was Seamus Connors who found Farrell.

Farrell had visited the Connors farm outside Crossbarry where Seamus' parents, having denied seeing their son in months, fed him tea and shortcake biscuits in their homey kitchen. 'Sure, why would he be mad enough to come home?' they asked him, with the countryside round their prosperous farm riddled with Tommies and Tans. The last thing their Seamus would want was for them to be burned out, for some auld thing they claimed he'd done. But he had come home.

'Farrell.'

Farrell heard his name called as he cycled past a derelict cottage on the side of the Kinsale road. Bringing the bicycle to a squeaking stop, Farrell turned in the saddle to see the man standing on the road under a cloud-mottled sky, openly, as an innocent man might. Farrell had a mind to peddle away. Let the Peelers or one of the hard men like Halloran apprehend him. But curiosity, as much as a sense of duty or pride, compelled him to stay.

He wheeled his bike over to Connors. Up close, there was something feral about the man, as if he had cast away a small bit of his humanity with each man he'd killed. There were dark circles under his eyes and his skin was the colour of putty. He was dressed in mud-spattered corduroy trousers and the same British army tunic he'd been wearing at the training camp. The tunic had wine-dark stains on the sleeves which told Farrell that he had worn it at Kilmichael as well. His angular chin and jawbone were shadowed in grey-flecked whiskers.

'Looking for me, Farrell?'

'Yes, I was.' Farrell cleared his throat. 'Your mother and father – they're afraid their house will be burned in reprisal for some of the things you've done.' He corrected himself. 'For some of the things they say you've done.'

'Some of the things I've done.' Connors turned his back on Farrell and disappeared into the derelict cottage. Farrell followed, wheeling his bicycle off the road and concealing it behind the overgrown hedgerow. For all he knew, the lanes and boreens in the district were still thick with Crown forces.

Connors sat down on the lip of the hearth. There were recent ashes in the grate, as if the cottage was used by wandering men, itinerants looking for shelter from the weather. To Farrell, it was exactly the kind of place patrols would search first in any sweep of the countryside. Connors took a half-full bottle from his pocket, uncorked it and drank deeply, gasping as he lowered it.

'I haven't had a drink for two years, boy.' He held the bottle out, but Farrell waved it away.

'Your mother and father said the fields are riddled with soldiers. This place isn't safe.'

'But you found me, not them.'

'Yes.'

'And you've come to take me in.'

'I've been asked … ordered … to have you follow me to Inchigeela. To O'Sullivan's.'

Connors gave a short laugh.

'It's orders, Connors. From the bossman himself like.' Farrell heard himself using Halloran's word – *bossman*. As if some of the man's courage might accompany its utterance. 'He and Brennan want a chat is all … I think.' He tried his best to sound reasonable, persuasive.

'You *think*, do you? What do you think of this war then? After all your fine words in the lecture halls and pubs. What do you think of it now, Farrell, from inside its belly?'

Farrell searched the cobwebbed corners of the cottage as if he would find an answer scored onto the wall. 'I hate the killing, Seamus,' he said, finally. 'But I hate the English more for making it necessary.'

Connors nodded. There was a long silence before he spoke again. 'I thought that once, but you don't have to hate a man to kill him. It helps. But it's not important after a while. It gets …' he shrugged and drank again from the bottle, 'easy.'

'It's a soldier's work, Seamus. You're a soldier, a bloody fine soldier.' Farrell was thinking, talking, seeking safety in words. 'We all knew it would take bloodshed to liberate Ireland. Sure, you most of all. How much blood was shed in its suppression? How many died in the Great Hunger? We're fighting for them, Seamus. For every one of those Irish dead with their hungry mouths stained green from eating grass while grain was shipped from Kingstown to Liverpool. We owe it to every man cut down in 1798 and 1867; to every man evicted from the land he'd farmed all his life because he couldn't feed his children and make the rents demanded by his leeching landlords. We owe it to our own children, to all those who come after us, to leave them a nation free, independent, sovereign …'

Clapping cut him short. Connors was leaning back on the hearth edge, giving Farrell a slow, steady applause, the shadow of a smile on his lips. 'Lovely speech, Farrell. You should be up on the stump with de Valera with all your honey-sweet words, boy. You could always talk.' His face clouded over. 'But it's not about talking any more. There's things you can only feel and do, not say, Farrell. You'll never know them. Never feel or do them. All this,' and he threw his arm out, taking in the cottage, the fields, the hills, 'all of this means fuck all. Not when the people in it … not when they …'

He coughed into a soiled handkerchief, a wet, ill-sounding hack that rattled his chest. When he had finished coughing, he opened the handkerchief and examined its contents. He shot his dead smile again. 'I don't hate you Farrell, but I could kill you, just like that and not lose a moment's sleep. That's how it gets. Easy.'

Farrell shoved his hands in his pockets, hoping that Connors hadn't noticed that they were shaking. Connors took another swig from the bottle. Setting it down, he said, 'You ever loved a girl, Farrell?'

Anticipation rose in Farrell's chest and he cleared his throat. 'No, I haven't really,' he said. 'Not so you could say. What about you, Seamus? Have you?'

'They think I killed Deirdre, don't they?'

Too quickly, Farrell said, 'No, no, Seamus. They only want to ask you some questions is all.'

'I loved her, Farrell. So much, I could have killed her.'

'And did you?' The words came before he could stop them and Farrell's brow flashed hot in the cool dereliction of the cottage.

'I loved her, Farrell. But she'd stopped loving me.'

'*Did* you kill her?'

Connors stood up suddenly. 'You tell the *bossmen* that if they want to plug me, they'd do well to send men who're up to the job.'

Then he was gone from the cottage, leaving Farrell alone in the waning light.

———

It took O'Keefe the best part of half an hour to ride the eight or so miles from Katherine Sheehan's cottage to Burleigh House. Late afternoon light was fading as he made his way up the long, tree-lined drive. The house was typical of the Anglo-Irish estates that dotted the Irish countryside. It stood alone, a grey stone fortress, the angular walls and peaked roof shaded by ancient trees. A wide staircase fanned out from the entrance down to a circular drive of pebbled stone.

O'Keefe looked at his watch. Three forty-five. It would be dark by five. He checked the sky and for a moment watched leaden, winter clouds crowd the sun. It wasn't only the local IRA units he was worried about. The Auxiliaries would be on the warpath now, after Kilmichael. It was one thing losing a man to local rebel sections – that was to be expected. To lose fifteen, twenty men to a group of fighters you considered rank amateurs? Outrage, as the papers put it. And there had been further rumours that the dead had been mutilated. One could do better than to believe barrack room scuttlebutt, but that wouldn't stop the Auxies shooting first and asking questions later. He resolved to make his visit quick and be off the roads before the night was claimed by gunmen from both sides.

Briefcase in hand, O'Keefe mounted the stone steps to the front door. A minute or more passed before the housekeeper let him in; a white-haired, dignified old woman who led O'Keefe down the central hallway.

'I'm sorry about the wait, Sergeant. I was in the back. I promised Mrs Burleigh I'd look after the house and the Major, but it's not easy on my own, sure.'

'The other staff driven off by the boys, Mrs ...?' They reached the library.

The woman turned and smiled up at him, avoiding his question. 'Gannon, Sergeant. You can wait here while I call the Major for you. He'll be grateful for the company. He used to ride every afternoon but now ...' She shook her head sadly.

Now the man was probably too terrified to set foot out of doors, O'Keefe thought, reaching to open the library door. As he did, his briefcase opened and, for the second time that day, spilled its contents onto the floor. A headshot of Deirdre Costelloe – taken before the undertaker had done his work – came to rest on the top of the pile of papers and the old woman bent down and retrieved it.

'Oh dear.' She blessed herself as she studied the image.

'I'm sorry you had to see that, Mrs Gannon.'

'She's dead, the poor thing, isn't she?' She handed over the photograph.

O'Keefe nodded, shoving the papers and photographs back into the briefcase in the best order he could manage, cursing the case's temperamental clasps.

The woman regarded him silently for a moment. 'It's fierce hard work ye do, Sergeant. Don't mind what any man says.' She touched his arm as she spoke, in the way of the old women of the country, then left to inform the Major of his presence.

O'Keefe paced in the library while he waited, marvelling at the collection of books lining the shelves, straining his eyes to read their titles in bars of light that entered through the slats of the closed shutters. Volumes of military history. The complete works of William Shakespeare. Leather-bound sets of works of fiction. A full set of Gibbons' *The History of the Decline and Fall of the Roman Empire*. Everything in the room was covered in a fine patina of dust. Behind a massive, mahogany desk hung a red and white regimental banner, its crest depicting a knight battling a lion and underscribed with a Latin motto stitched into the centre of the red and white. Mounted underneath it, was a ceremonial cutlass. The motto read: *Sub Deus quod Flos, nos pugna una, nos intereo una*. His schoolboy Latin again: *Under God and Crown, we fight together, we die together*.

The West Kent Royals was one of the oldest and most renowned regiments in the British army. Its men had seen action in most fronts of the Great War, though O'Keefe didn't remember hearing of them in the Dardanelles.

'There you are!' A booming voice from behind him.

O'Keefe turned to see a large man in his fifties enter the room. Muscle turning to fat. He was wearing a waistcoat over a dingy white shirt and riding breeches. Fading red hair combed back, greying mutton chops, a wide, thick-lipped mouth, no moustache.

'Major, I –'

'Good God, man,' the Major bellowed over O'Keefe's introduction, marauding across a threadbare Turkish carpet, 'Bridie should have opened up the shutters, let in some light. Like a bloody tomb in here, eh?' He swept past O'Keefe, unfastened the shutters, slamming them back into their casements.

In the weak afternoon light the room looked shabby. There were full ashtrays on side tables and sallow stuffing bleeding from upholstered armchairs. A bottle of whisky – O'Keefe couldn't read the label – was open on the desk, surrounded by plates of half-eaten food studded with stubbed out cigar ends, dusty paperweights made from brass shell casings and various books splayed open, loose papers and a cigar box with the lid up.

The Major bounded back across the room, his enthusiasm unnerving in the musty confines of the library. His handshake was hale and hearty.

'Kind of you to see me unannounced, Major. I'm Acting-Sergeant Seán O'Keefe out of Ballycarleton RIC barracks.'

'You're welcome, Sergeant.' The man's breath carried the scent of strong liquor. 'Major Wallace Burleigh, First Royal West Kent Regiment, retired.' He continued pumping O'Keefe's hand, indicating the banner and cutlass on the wall, 'As you might have guessed.'

'You're very kind …'

'Damn bit of bother fitting the uniform on now, eh Sergeant?' The Major patted his belly. 'Not like yourself, fine specimen of a man you are. Could have used lads like you in the regiment. Fit lads, big. Irishmen like ourselves. Best fighters God put on earth, the Irish. If only they'd point their guns in the right direction!'

O'Keefe smiled and ignored the Major's heavy slap and then grapple of his upper arm, feeling something like a beef cow must at market. 'Would that they would, Major. I was wondering if you could lend me your expertise?'

'I won't until we share a glass, Sergeant. One fighting man to another in these hard times. It's why I keep the shutters closed. Why give the Shinner bastards a proper target, I say. Like I always told my men. "Don't make it easy for the enemy.

Heads down, eyes wide, rifles ready".' He took the whisky bottle from the desk along with two glasses and poured out two generous measures. O'Keefe saw that it was Macallan's. The Major handed a whisky to O'Keefe and raised his own glass.

'Officer's Oil, we called it, in the show.'

His eyes took on a misty, nostalgic glaze for a moment and O'Keefe felt certain that this was not the Major's first glass of the day. Nor would it be his last he suspected. O'Keefe had met men like the Major before – men who spoke of the war as if it were a fine place to which they wished to return. In O'Keefe's experience, these men tended to be those who had been furthest from the fighting. O'Keefe forced himself to smile and raised his glass. '*Sláinte*, Major.'

Burleigh clinked O'Keefe's glass and drank deeply.

'I'm here, Major, because I'm told you keep a fine collection of rare fowl on your estate. I'm investigating the death of a young woman. She was found not too far from here, on a hillside just north of Drumdoolin. You may have seen it in the papers?'

'Haven't read the papers in days, Sergeant. Too busy; too busy for my own good. Thought retirement might mean fishing and fowling. History intervenes. History intervenes.' He looked away and drank more whisky.

Too busy getting pissed, O'Keefe thought. He took out the envelope containing the feathers and handed several to the Major. 'I was hoping you might be able to identify the type of bird these feathers came from.'

'Where did you find these, Sergeant? What bearing do they have on your investigation?'

The Major had trouble with the word 'investigation'. O'Keefe looked through one of the tall windows at the draining daylight. This had been a wasted trip. A diversion for a lonely, drunken landlord holed up in his castle against the people he once believed had loved him and his kind. 'They were found with the girl's body, sir. The girl was tarred and feathered before she was murdered.'

'Murdered. Indeed.' Burleigh looked up. 'Bloody Shinners. Killing a young woman, you say?' He thrust the feathers back at O'Keefe.

'We don't know who killed the girl. We're still investigating.'

'Who bloody else could have, Sergeant?' His eyes flashed angrily at O'Keefe and then he sought solace in the dregs of his whisky.

'That's what we're trying to discover, sir,' O'Keefe said, sliding the feathers back into their envelope and into the case. 'Thank you for your …'

The Major's face reddened and his eyes went to the window this time. 'This whole bloody country's gone mad, you know. Bloody Sinn Féin and their bloody assassins. Put them up against a proper regiment of fighting men and they'd get their what's-coming, I tell you Sergeant. Bloody ill, this country is, the things happening. It's infected, the whole order of the place poisoned. Nothing's like it should be any more.' Burleigh swallowed the remains of his whisky, a sheen of tears in his eyes.

O'Keefe didn't ask him if it was possible that the order of the place – under a foreign government, under landlords like himself – might have been infected from the beginning; that what was happening now was nothing more than a form of cure. Bullet surgery, he thought. Sometimes the cure could be as bad as the disease.

'You've no idea then, sir, about the feathers?'

The Major reached for the bottle. 'Ah, the feathers. No idea, Sergeant. The birds. They were my wife's hobby. I indulged her, hoping she might stay here in Cork with me for more than a week or two at a time. A lot of bloody good it did. Won't leave England now for love nor money nor exotic fowl. Not that I'd blame her. Half our friends have joined her on the mainland, bloody cowards. Flown the coop, as it were.' He laughed bitterly.

'Was there someone who helped her with them? Someone who worked the estate for you, who might know fowl? A gamekeeper possibly?'

'All gone. Every one of them run off by the blasted Volunteers, threatened by the bullyboys with their pitchforks and cork-blackened faces. Only Bridie Gannon left. She's devoted to the Burleighs. Like her father and mother before her.'

O'Keefe left Burleigh with his bottle, his memories of a fine war and cap-tipping, devoted tenants. He was angry at the time he had wasted but couldn't think of another angle to pursue until his request for exhumation was processed or he discovered who the 'card sharpie' was. He kick-started the

Trusty and fitted on his helmet. The time would come, he thought, when pulling the shutters over and drinking himself senseless just wouldn't do any more and Major Burleigh too would have to pack himself off to England. Labelled a spy, a traitor, an interloper in a land he had thought he owned. He was a man to be pitied, but not by O'Keefe.

A few hours later, O'Keefe stood in front of Masterson's desk, his eyes drawn once again to the photograph of the DI and the Colonel in their hunting garb, fat pheasants hanging by the feet from their fists. Masterson, seated, held out a manila folder. 'Give that a gander, Sergeant. And steel yourself to catch the bastard.'

O'Keefe took the file. 'Sir?'

'A certain Mr Connors' particulars. "I" Division had it flown down today. *Flown*, O'Keefe. I think you'll find it good reading of an evening.'

O'Keefe opened the file and looked at a photograph of Seamus Connors for the first time. It was an enlargement of a college photograph. The features were blurred. Dark hair, dark eyes. There was an intensity to the gaze, but otherwise nothing that would be out of character on the face of a moderately serious medical student. Neutrally, he said, 'That was fast, sir. I'm surprised they had so much on him.'

He had imagined it would take a week at least for 'I' Division to locate a file on Connors and send it down.

'Fast indeed,' Masterson said, smiling. 'And it was Keane's wire that got them running in the first place. I had a dispatch rider go to Dublin with what we had yesterday, but we got a wire back saying they were already on it and were ready to ship it down. Remind me to make a note in young Keane's jacket: initiative and all that. What an investigation like this needs.'

'Yes, sir. Fair play to him.'

Masterson leaned back and clasped his hands over his belly. 'This Connors is a bold boy, no mistake. Did you realise he is wanted on the Smyth murder in Cork? You get him for this and you'll make a lot of people up in Dublin very happy, O'Keefe.'

'I'll do my best, sir.'

'I know you will. You've made a grand stab at it so far, not to put too fine a point on it.' The DI chuckled at the pun.

'The newspaper report today, sir. In the *Daily News*.'

'I saw it. Can only help I imagine. Stir up a sense of general outrage, get the locals to help us catch this Connors.'

'There was a fair bit of information that was privileged, sir, in the report. There were only a few of us who knew the cause of death.'

'You went barracks to barracks on it, didn't you, Sergeant?'

O'Keefe hadn't thought of that. The number of people who knew the details of the murder was far wider than he had thought. It was a basic error: seeing conspiracy where there was none. Any one of the cons who had read the wire he'd sent could have spoken to the scribblers.

'Yes sir, that's true enough.'

'No harm, Sergeant. Only good can come of it. I say

tomorrow we go public with Connors as suspect number one. Flush him out. I've put into HQ about sanctioning a reward for his arrest. Should hear in the morning. Get the touts working again, if the money weighs right.'

'It could have the opposite effect, sir. It could cause the IRA to close ranks around him, ship him out of the country. We might never get him then. Could we not wait a couple of days before releasing his name? There's a few other things we should have in place, before we go to the papers.'

Annoyance showed on Masterson's face. 'What other things, O'Keefe?'

There was the small matter of evidence to consider, O'Keefe thought. Or maybe evidence didn't matter so much any more. Connors was wanted for other things. O'Keefe wondered how much evidence there was, for example, to pin Connors for the Smyth shooting. He decided not to push it with Masterson. So much of policing the Troubles, he knew, involved hunting down men on a whiff of rumour. Rumour mattered. Hard evidence seemed to be reserved for crimes that happened in peacetime. O'Keefe didn't like it, but he knew he would have to ride with it if he didn't want to scupper his hunt for Deirdre Costelloe's killer. Masterson might even be right about Connors and if he was, O'Keefe would break his arse to pinch him for it, even if it meant making people up in Dublin happy. 'Nothing, sir. In fact, Connors looks as good as any for this.'

The DI appeared relieved.

Any doubt O'Keefe might have had that the man was

incapable of killing Deirdre Costelloe vanished after reading
the Connors file. If intelligence reports were to be believed
– and that is what the file he had in front of him essentially
was: an epitomised account of accrued information on the
IRA volunteer Seamus Connors from police, army and secret
service sources – he was a hard man, not afraid of killing.
O'Keefe read:

> *The suspect answers to the name Seamus Connors and hails from
> the village of Crossbarry, in West Cork. He is known as Young
> Seamus in his local area, his father also being called Seamus. He
> was a medical student at University College Cork, his address listed
> as 23 Patrick Street, Cork. He has not been seen at this address since
> 11/2/1918.*
>
> *The suspect is of average height and average to slim build,
> around 5' 10" and 11 stone. He is pale complexioned with black
> hair and brown eyes which are said to be of a 'piercing' or 'sinister'
> mien. He is a known and ardent teetotaller and has been said to
> wear a Pioneer Pin on his lapel, indicating his avowed abstention
> from alcohol. Connors is a regular Mass attendee and is rumoured
> to seek confession for his acts of murder.*
>
> *He is known to be armed and should be considered extremely
> dangerous. He is wanted for questioning in the murder and/or
> malicious wounding of eight serving members of the armed forces and
> police.*

The rest of the file contained reports of various incidents in
which Connors was said to have been involved. He appeared

to have a particular talent for killing soldiers and police. O'Keefe wouldn't be disappointed to see him pinched.

On the other hand, he still wasn't certain he was the man he should be focusing on exclusively for Deirdre Costelloe's murder. There was something about it that didn't seem right. The tarring and feathering. The bizarre display on the hillside. The evidence of likely sexual assault. A violent man driven by frustration or jealous rage was capable of such acts. But there was something too careful about it all. Whoever had murdered Deirdre was proud of what he had done. O'Keefe couldn't see Connors revelling in the brutal slaying or exhibition of the girl he had once loved.

He checked the battered Players tin on his desk and, finding it empty, got up and rummaged in Daly's desk for tobacco. Under a half-read guide to raising greyhounds and a set of handcuffs, he found a packet of Woodbines, took one and lit it.

The confession angle was interesting: the idea that Connors sought absolution after he killed. But then again, there was the taint of myth around that one. O'Keefe was well aware of how little British intelligence-gatherers understood about the complex relationship most Irish people had with the Church. To them, the Irish Catholic Church was exotic, a repository of superstitions long dead in an enlightened, Anglican England. In some ways, they were right, O'Keefe felt. Yet mostly the spooks were blind to the mixture of love, contempt and pragmatism with which the Irish approached the Church. O'Keefe smiled to himself. *The gunman seeking penance.* The stuff of bad fiction, more like. Still, there were stranger things in this war and if it was true, O'Keefe thought, it might be a useful bit of information if they ever got to interview Connors.

There was a knock on the office door and he looked up. It was Reilly. 'The coal lorry's come, Sergeant. Bring you up a bucket?'

'That would be grand, Reilly – balls off a brass monkey in here.'

The retired con came into the office. 'That Connors' file?' he said, nodding to where it lay open on the desk.

O'Keefe's face must have shown his surprise.

Reilly smiled. 'Oh, everybody's heard about it by now. Flown up. Imagine! Word is he's the one who done it to that poor thing on the hillside.'

He appeared to be waiting for some confirmation from O'Keefe. No doubt so that he could enlighten the rest of the barracks, confirming O'Keefe's notion that there were no greater purveyors of gossip in Ireland than the RIC. Worse than washerwomen, coppers were.

'I could do with the coal, Reilly, thank you.'

The gleam of interest faded from the old man's eyes. 'I'll be up with it shortly, Sergeant.'

O'Keefe sat smoking, thinking. If the likes of Reilly knew it, then it was only a matter of time before Connors' name hit the papers. Looked like the DI wouldn't have a say in the matter after all. It was probably Masterson himself who had blabbed about the thing being flown down in the first place, the eejit.

He went back to the file, flicking through the reports of shootings and sightings until he came to the last few pages, which contained an arrest report dating from 1917 – well before the current rebellion had started in earnest. He skimmed the report and stopped. He sat forward then and reread the arrest report carefully.

Jesus, he thought, reading it again to be sure he wasn't mistaken. Maybe the DI was right after all, about this Connors fella.

<hr />

A constable on evening rounds caught the boy one night, on the wall of a house where three girls were living with their father and six brothers. The constable had a kind heart and thought it best if the young lad were dealt with on the hoof. He brought the boy, fifteen years old now, to the front of the house and asked the brothers and father what ought to be done with him.

Three of the brothers and the father beat the boy until he coughed blood and spat teeth while the constable watched. The constable made sure things didn't get out of hand but wanted to be certain the boy would think about the beating next time the inclination took him to watch young girls undressing.

When the father and brothers were done, the constable hauled the boy to his feet and marched him home. A tough young lad, the constable thought. Not a whimper out of him during or after the pasting. A right little hard nut.

The house was empty and dark when they arrived. The

constable wasn't surprised. He knew of the house and the woman who lived there. A widow. Her husband never came back from fighting the Boers. He'd heard nearly all there was to hear about the woman and part of him felt sorry for the young fellow. Still, the constable gave the lad a final clout on the ear, a reminder of what happened to boys who toyed with themselves on garden walls.

Wednesday
1 December 1920

Shaving – careful to leave a wide razor berth around his scar – O'Keefe noticed dark circles ringing his eyes, as if he'd been punched with fatigue. There were wry glances in the kitchen when he went down for breakfast and he realised he must have been shouting in his sleep again. He brought a pot of strong tea back up to the office.

'No lie-in today, Sergeant?' Daly said, from the room beside the office where he stood over a fresh basin of hot water.

'Where were you last night?'

'The hotel. Murphy kindly locked us in. Only back an hour ago.'

To O'Keefe's eyes, Daly looked unnaturally fresh for a man who'd been drinking all night. 'So what you're saying is that I was on duty last night, without knowing it, as such.'

Daly razored the last bits of soap from his face. 'Well, I suppose you were, now you mention it. Never thought of it that way. Anything of interest, at all, at all?'

O'Keefe sat at his desk and poured tea into his mug. 'I was asleep. Who was at the hotel?'

'No one of any interest. Scribbler from the *Examiner*, one from the *Star* … Told them everything I know about the case. Thought you'd understand. They were buying.'

'Sure, you lose the power of speech after two bottles and a dram.'

Daly towelled his face. 'Well, I don't remember, but they got the story somewhere. Probably from the *News*.' He pointed to his desk where there was a fresh copy of the *Southern Star*. It was a newspaper printed in Cork and generally thought to be sympathetic to the republicans. It at least strove for fairness, despite its slant, which was more than a man could say for some of the London rags.

O'Keefe picked it up and scanned the article about Deirdre Costelloe's murder. It was accompanied by a photograph, one of a pretty girl, alive and in love with life. The journalist must have got it from her family or a friend – possibly Anne Duffy. O'Keefe realised he had never asked the girl if she had a photograph of Deirdre taken in happier times. An oversight. No doubt it wouldn't be his last.

The only difference in the *Star*'s article from the one in the *Daily News* was the fact that the *Star* article quoted republican sources as denying any Volunteer involvement in the murder of the young woman found outside Drumdoolin. No surprise there. It went on to identify Deirdre Costelloe by name and gave details of her funeral, which was being held that morning in Ballincollig.

He looked up from the paper. 'How'd you like to go to a funeral, Jim?'

Daly continued buttoning his uniform tunic. 'Sure, I've had my fill of free drink, man. Couldn't stomach another drop.'

'You won't be drinking at this one.'

The big man thought about it for a minute, then turned and looked out the window. 'Weather's fair enough. How many men should I take?'

O'Keefe considered the question. 'Bring two, in plain

clothes. If you can, why don't you take that Mathew-Pare fella and see what you make of him.'

O'Keefe claimed Keane when drill was finished. Heatherfield asked if he could come for the ride and O'Keefe told him to load his carbine and change into civvies. Finch he found in the day-room eating breakfast after a night patrol.

'Come on, Finch. Shovel it in. You're riding with me this morning.'

The Tan looked up, his mouth full of eggs and sausage.

O'Keefe said, 'Chop, chop.' He had decided to bring Finch along mainly because the man deserved to have his day ruined more than some of the other lads who had put in the same number of patrols, but it also wouldn't hurt that Finch knew his way around a rifle. The road they would travel had seen a number of ambushes recently.

'Ten minutes in the yard. In mufti, Finch. Wouldn't want anyone to know we're coppers where we're going.'

Finch swallowed. 'No chance of that, Sergeant.'

Fifteen minutes later, Finch emerged from the barracks. O'Keefe stood waiting on the cobbles, smoking by the armoured Ford with Keane and Heatherfield.

'Fucking hell, Finch,' Heatherfield said, 'where'd you pinch the rags from, then?'

Finch looked pleased with himself and stopped, resting the stock of his carbine on the cobbles and opening his beautifully cut, tan cashmere overcoat to show off its silk lining. Under the coat he wore a suit of grey, worsted wool, tailored to perfection. A red silk handkerchief peeked out in a perfect triangular fold from the breast pocket of his suit jacket. Gleaming black brogues under cuffed, razor-pleated trouser legs; his hat a stiff, black-banded trilby, worn with a rakish cock over his left eye.

'My brother,' Finch answered, as if the question had been a serious one. 'Took 'em the day I set out for this kip. Got 'em diced and stitched in Dublin. I 'alf expect the bastard to show up 'ere one day and cut my fucking throat for nicking 'em.'

'Right, lads,' O'Keefe said. 'Finch, you ride up front with me. I've my reputation to think of.'

Finch gave him a mock salute and held the rear door of the Ford Tourer open for Keane and Heatherfield in their decidedly less salubrious corduroy trousers, wool coats and soft flat caps. Heatherfield ignored him and went to the front of the Ford to crank the starter.

The road to Crossbarry was quiet, not much morning traffic after they passed through Bandon. They drove with the windows down, past high hedges and dry-stone walls, fields patched with gorse and grazing sheep, passing the occasional ass and cart on its way to market. The farmers kept their eyes on the road, no wave or nod of the head from even one of them, fear drowning out the natural affability of Corkmen.

'You gonna tell us where we're 'eaded, Sergeant?'

'Poultry farm, outside of Crossbarry. Just a whim of mine.'

'You expect trouble, Sergeant?' Keane asked. 'Is that why we're along?'

O'Keefe wasn't expecting trouble, but poultry farms, like

piggeries and creameries, were known to be meeting places for – and to employ men friendly with – the Volunteers.

'Not really. But it's no harm being careful. Sure, what else would you be doing with yourself of a morning?'

'Happy to come, Sergeant.'

O'Keefe heard Heatherfield make kissing noises to Keane in the back and he smiled to himself.

'Were you in the war, Sergeant?' Finch asked.

The Tan appeared relaxed in the seat next to O'Keefe – his carbine barrel resting on the open window frame – but his eyes never stopped scanning the roadside and hills on either side of the car, even as he was speaking.

O'Keefe told him that he was.

'Gallipoli, right?'

Eyes on the road, O'Keefe nodded. 'Close enough.'

'I 'eard it was a right tumble.'

'It was. Where were you yourself?'

'All over the Western Front. The Somme, Pasch, the Racing. Fought in all of 'em.'

'Never wounded?' O'Keefe could have ended the conversation there but, oddly, he didn't mind it with Finch, perhaps because he could understand how much of the war was still in Finch, as it was in himself: the restlessness and violence. The war was in Heatherfield as well, though the young Geordie seemed, of all the veterans in the barracks, to have been the least affected by it.

'Few knicks and scrapes. Bits of shrap and the like. Hit twice in the helmet, once by a sniper round. Fritzie put an 'ole through the brim that time.' He touched his trilby. 'Always kept that tin lid. Lucky, it was. Got soaked when it rained, through that fucking 'ole, but I always kept it, I did. Got an MG round in the breadbasket once as well, but I was wearing armour.'

O'Keefe was surprised. Some men had worn body armour in the war. Grenadiers and machine-gunners who were exposed to enemy fire more than most. But Finch didn't seem the type. 'It stopped the bullet?'

Finch grinned. 'I'm not sure it would 'ave if it hadn't 'it one of my grenades first.'

Keane leaned forward over the seat, his mouth full of ju-jubes. He offered Finch and O'Keefe the crumpled paper bag. 'And the grenade didn't go off?'

'Fucking didn't, mate,' Finch said, taking a sweet. 'Bullet left a bloody great gouge in the thing but didn't hit the fuse. Lucky bugger me. Blessed, I was. The old man upstairs 'aving plans for me, no doubt."

O'Keefe smiled and shook his head to the offer of sweets.

Heatherfield leaned forward over the seat. 'My mum sent me a vest, she did. Got it out of a catalogue and posted it to me for Christmas. Never wore the thing though. Fellas might have thought I was windy, if I wore it.'

'I never bothered what no cunt thought of me,' Finch said. 'My 'ide's worth more than my pride, I always say.'

'I got one in the thigh,' Heatherfield added. 'Wouldn't have been much help anyway, the chesty vest.'

'Bad?' O'Keefe said.

'Right through and through. Poured iodine in't for a month and I was good as new. Sent right bloody back to the shit and ditches without so much as a by your leave or kiss your arse.'

Finch pointed to the scar on O'Keefe's face. 'Shrapnel?'

It was a moment before he replied. 'Bayonet.'

'You get the bastard?'

O'Keefe nodded, eyes on the road. 'I did.'

Mulaney's Poultry Farm was a mile off the Crossbarry road down a rutted track. At the end of a long drive that cut through grazing fields, the farm consisted of a whitewashed labourer's cottage and three long sheds with roofs of corrugated tin. Beside the sheds was a field littered with rusting machinery and a pile of smouldering refuse. The wind had picked up, shoving low clouds across the sky to blur the hilltops that rose behind the farm. The air was cool and smelled of rain.

'I'll go inside myself,' O'Keefe said. 'Stay close to the car. Leave the carbines inside unless you need them. No use provoking anyone.'

Finch, Keane and Heatherfield followed O'Keefe out of the car and lit cigarettes, O'Keefe continuing on across the gravel yard to the cottage. As he walked, O'Keefe noticed that several of the labourers had gathered at the entrance to one of the sheds. They were burly country men, hard men by the looks of their heavily stubbled, weather-ruddied faces, their sleeves rolled over ham-hock forearms. One of them leaned on a pitchfork. They watched him. O'Keefe nodded at the men but got no response, and was suddenly glad he had brought reinforcements.

He knocked on the cottage door and let himself in. The interior was bright, the windows on the gable ends cut larger than normal and paned with glass. A wooden floor had been added and on it sat two desks, one facing the door and the other, perpendicular to it, closer to the fire. The walls were painted white and a calendar from a feed supply company hung on one wall. A slate board divided into a grid, showing the names of local businesses and the amounts of produce chalked in beside them – eggs, O'Keefe assumed, or possibly whole chickens – was fixed to the wall behind one of the desks.

A man in his thirties, dressed in heavy canvas trousers and a woollen pullover, came into the office from the back room of the cottage. He had a narrow, unlined face and intelligent blue eyes.

'Winter's on the way,' O'Keefe said, by way of greeting.

'Could be worse.'

O'Keefe removed his identification card and held it out. 'I'm Acting Sergeant O'Keefe, Ballycarleton barracks. I was wondering if I could beg your help on something. I was told if anyone could help me it would be you. Mr Mulaney?'

'Who told you that?' Another man materialised from the back room before the first could answer. He was older than the first by a good twenty years but the two were clearly related. His fair hair was thin and greying, and there were weathered crags around his eyes.

'I was telling this gentleman –'

'I heard you. Now I'm telling you. We don't help the police. If you've evidence of something, then take us in, but we'll not aid the police any more than we would the army.'

'Sir,' O'Keefe said, 'I'm investigating the murder of a young woman. It has nothing to do with politics. I was only hoping you could help me identify these feathers.' Before he could object further, O'Keefe set his briefcase on the desk and produced the feathers from their paper envelope.

The elder Mulaney refused to look at them but O'Keefe could tell the younger was interested. The older man said, 'I told you, Sergeant, we don't help the police. Not now, not ever. Not me or my son. I don't care a damn what case it is. We keep to our own here and run a business. We've no truck with the Crown and expect none from ye.'

'I understand that, Mr Mulaney, but I've come because I'm told you have the best knowledge of poultry in the area. A young girl was murdered and these feathers were tarred to her body. They're not feathers from your normal laying hens or chickens.'

The son spoke. '*These* feathers? These were … on herself?'

O'Keefe shifted his attention to him. 'They were. She was tarred and feathered after she was killed. Have you any idea what kind of birds they might've come from?'

'Don't answer him, Stephen.'

The younger man ignored the order and examined the

feathers. Hardened scraps of tar adhered to the quills. He looked up at O'Keefe and without preamble said, 'Danny saw her. He told the other lads and they thought he was messing, dreaming things up the way he does.'

'I told you to keep *whisht*, Stephen. Don't make me say it again.' He turned his anger on O'Keefe. 'You know what'll happen to my business if the boys in the hills find out we've spoken to ye? And how long do you think it will take for one of that shower outside to tell them? It's bad enough we can't sell to the army or the barracks because of the fucking boycott and now you coming …'

'I'm sorry for your troubles, Mr Mulaney. I don't mean to cause you any further ones.' He turned back to the son. 'Who is Danny?'

The son looked to his father and then back at O'Keefe. 'He's one of the workers here. Daniel Hooey. He doesn't do much. Sweeps up mainly. Collects eggs. He's not right in the head. Never has been. He has the job as a favour to his mother, God help her. A good woman and sister-in-law to my uncle.'

O'Keefe jotted the name into his investigation diary. 'You say he saw the body? On the hillside?'

The son nodded. 'He was going on about it to the other lads. He's always up in the hills, wandering and coming back with stories. They thought he was spoofing until some of the boys went up there. And then it was in the papers.'

'Is Daniel Hooey working today?'

Again the young man looked to his father and his father

turned away. There was disgust on the older man's face but he didn't intervene. Young Mulaney was a rare type of Irishman to defy his father so openly, O'Keefe thought. Maybe he was doing what the father knew was right but hadn't the courage to do himself.

'He is,' he said, holding out the feathers. 'This one. It comes from a mottled Javanese. At least, I think it does. And this could be from a Faverolles, the salmon-coloured feather here. It's rare enough, but I couldn't be sure of it. It's only good for show anyway, the Faverolles. Sure, we've none here at all.' He laughed at the thought of it. 'But there was a time when we'd an offer to cross our Rhode Island Reds with the Javanese. Fierce laying hens in the cross, I've heard tell. Nothing came of it in the end.'

'Who was it wanted to try this cross?'

He handed the feathers back to O'Keefe. 'Mrs Burleigh. You know the big place, Burleigh House, near Upton like? You've heard of the Major, I'm sure.'

O'Keefe scratched the information down into his notebook. He knew the Major. A connection? He doubted it. 'And when was this supposed to happen?'

'Early summer. June maybe. Mrs Burleigh left shortly after. Went back to England, I heard. Sure, we could hardly do anything for the woman anyway, with the men here and the way they go on.' He gave a bitter smile. 'She was a decent woman. No bullshit from her. No airs at all.'

O'Keefe looked up from his diary at the younger Mulaney. 'Can I talk to Mr Hooey? Would that be possible?'

The father answered him, resignation in his voice. 'We'll be burned to the ground.'

'I'll make sure that doesn't happen, Mr Mulaney. You have my word on that.'

He gave O'Keefe a hard look. 'We've had enough of your word here today. Now off with you. My son's said enough. Speak to the young *dah* yourself if ye can find him, but you've heard nothing from us.'

He turned away and went back through the door from which he'd come. Moments later he returned, pointing his finger at O'Keefe, shaking with rage, his voice a bellow as if he was shouting for the ears of all present on the property.

'And stay away from us here! Stay away to fuck from this place! Between the gunmen in the hills and yourselves in the barracks, ye'll have us all ruined, the decent people of Ireland.' He turned away, his anger spent.

O'Keefe looked to the son. 'I'm sorry.'

'It's all right. You'd better be on your way. The old man's under the whip with the business, but I don't think anything will happen. Sure, gunmen need a day's wage as much as the next fella.'

With his mind fixed on locating Daniel Hooey, O'Keefe stepped out of the Mulaney's cottage and into a mêlée. Keane was taking wild swings at one of the labourers who'd been standing by the shed when he'd entered. O'Keefe paused halfway across the yard and watched. He had his Webley in its shoulder holster but left it there, thinking that perhaps a duffing might be the best way for their visit to resolve itself amongst the workers, particularly if their man gave Keane a going over. He spotted Finch and Heatherfield leaning against the car, looking on impassively. Finch was smoking. Heatherfield seemed interested in the outcome of the scrap, but not enough to intervene.

When Keane's opponent began to try to work his fingers into Keane's eyes, O'Keefe decided that the fun was over.

'Enough, lads. Leave it out.'

Keane had forced the other man's hands away from his face and was again throwing wild punches. Some of them were connecting and the other man was striving to grapple Keane to the ground. Their feet scraped, gouging wound-like rents in the gravel yard.

O'Keefe signalled to Heatherfield and Finch. 'Pull him off.'

The two moved to break up the fight and one of the labourers stepped forward. 'We'll say when it's over, Peeler.'

The man was big and there were four others with him, as well as the man fighting Keane. The odds were about even, O'Keefe reckoned.

'It's over,' he said to the man. 'Move your men off or we'll have you up. Do you understand me, sir?'

'I'm no *sir*, Peeler.'

Finch had managed to wrest Keane from the other man's grip. He shoved the young constable roughly against the car. His opponent, bleeding from the nose, made a lunge for Keane and Finch. Heatherfield stepped in front of the man and kicked his legs out from under him.

'There,' O'Keefe said, 'the show's over. Good day to ye, lads.'

He decided to leave the questioning of Daniel Hooey for another time.

The big man spat on the ground. 'And ye fuckin' Crown stooges have it coming, so ye do. Sooner than ye think.'

O'Keefe watched him turn away. 'I'll keep it in mind.'

It wasn't the first time O'Keefe had been threatened, but most threats were idle.

Keane was bleeding from a cut over his right eye and his lip had begun to swell before the car had made it down the long drive. He was smiling by the time the Ford turned out onto the Crossbarry road.

'I had him, I did. Fucking had him.' He pulled out his crushed bag of sweets and shoved a handful into his mouth.

Heatherfield clapped him on the shoulder and dug a hand into the sweet bag. 'You did. Had him right where you wanted. Sooner or later he would have walked into one of those punches, lad.'

Finch and O'Keefe laughed.

'How'd that start?' O'Keefe asked.

'A bit of lip from the boys,' Finch said. 'Me, I don't take it personal. I never much liked coppers myself.'

''Til you became one,' Heatherfield interjected, over the noise of the Ford's four cylinder.

Finch laughed. 'Bloody right. If you can't beat 'em, join 'em. Twelve shillings a day and all in? I'll be any-fucking-body you like, mate.'

The sun had cut through a gap in the clouds and the surrounding hills shimmered like light on tin. Keane laughed as well, said the fighting had him starved.

'Me too,' Heatherfield said. 'One thing about the RIC, I told my old dear in a letter, there's good grub in it. Can't beat the grub.'

'Better than bully stew 'alf-cooked in a kerosene can,' said Finch.

'Famished, I am,' Keane said. 'Eat the bollocks off a cow through a hole in the hedge.'

'Eat the hind leg off the lamb of God, I would,' Heatherfield added.

The sound was like a pebble striking the windscreen of the Ford. O'Keefe felt the warp of air as the bullet passed by his head. Heatherfield's lower jaw disintegrated, blowing tongue and teeth and bone and blood onto Keane's face.

O'Keefe realised what had happened when Keane started screaming. He accelerated and the Ford surged forward. Ahead, a horse cart had been set to block the narrow stone bridge. He had no choice but to stop the car, jamming down on the brake, throwing Heatherfield's convulsing body forward, knocking into Finch.

Finch had his door open before the Ford had come to rest on its springs. He reached a hand over and dragged O'Keefe across the bench seat and out onto the road through his passenger door. He shoved him to the ground, the car serving as cover, as he went to the rear door and jerked it open, first wrenching Heatherfield's body out and then Keane, screaming, wiping frantically at the gore on his face. O'Keefe reached back into the car and pulled out his briefcase.

'Here,' Finch said, handing him Heatherfield's carbine. 'The rocks there.' He pointed to a set of boulders embedded in the hillside. 'The shot came from there.'

Another shot rang out from the boulders and tore through the top of the Ford. O'Keefe raised the carbine and rested it on the bonnet, then let off three quick rounds. Finch took up a position at the back of the car and began firing. O'Keefe had never seen anyone work the bolt of an Enfield as fast. The Tan had fired six shots in the time it took O'Keefe to fire four. The boulders showed eruptions of dust and stone chips. Finch worked the bolt harder and threw down the gun when it emptied. O'Keefe continued firing while Finch reached into the car and came out with Keane's carbine. He loosed three quick shots before O'Keefe realised they were no longer taking fire from the hill. O'Keefe signalled to cease firing.

The wind buffeted the car and the sound of his heartbeat pounded in his ears. He studied the boulders, waiting. It was the first time he'd had time to look at them closely, to notice their placement and distance from the road. They were about a hundred yards up the gradual incline of a gorse-covered hill. It was a good ambush spot, one that had been carefully selected.

'There!' Finch said. 'They're running.'

Finch raised his carbine and O'Keefe followed its barrel with his eyes as it tracked two figures sprinting for the crest of the hill. Finch fired and missed. O'Keefe raised his rifle and sighted on the second attacker. He fired and watched as the man collapsed, doubling over his gun. His comrade stopped and turned back to the body now sprawled in the gorse. Finch fired two rounds at him, jamming the bolt on the carbine back and slamming the next round into the chamber each time. The soil kicked up a few feet behind the attacker as he crested the hill and disappeared over it.

'Come on,' O'Keefe said, hopping the low stone wall bordering the road. Finch followed and they made their way up the hill. A few yards from the boulders, Finch stopped and signalled O'Keefe do the same. He cupped his ear in a pantomime of listening and O'Keefe followed his lead. The sound was faint, coming from behind the rocks. A keening, pleading whimper like an injured animal might make. O'Keefe thought at first that it was coming from the ambusher he had shot, but from where he stood he could see the man's body lying motionless.

Finch apparently had the same idea. He raised his rifle and fired. The prone body jerked with the impact of the bullet and then returned to stillness. Not what I would have done, O'Keefe thought, but it was well within the unwritten laws of war. The man had carried the rifle. He had killed one of their own. If he was still alive, he might have used it again. Now there was no question of that. Still, the keening came from behind the boulders.

Finch signalled for O'Keefe to approach the rocks from the left side while he took the right. O'Keefe signalled back, counting off on his fingers, *1, 2, 3*. They circled behind the boulder in silence and leapt out simultaneously. The whimpering turned to a high-pitched screaming. A young man lay with his back against the rocks, his palms up, stark terror on his face. It was difficult to assess his age with his front teeth missing, several days of thick stubble on his wind-rusted face, his left eye drifting outward in a squint.

Finch roared at him. 'Shut up, you cunt! Shut your fucking mouth or I'll put a bullet in it.' Keeping his rifle levelled at the man, Finch stepped forward and kicked him hard in the ribs.

'Leave it,' O'Keefe said. The man was unarmed and even if he was carrying, O'Keefe doubted he would possess the knowledge or will to fire on them. He crouched down, resting his carbine across his knees, and patted the man on the shoulder. The garbled words amidst the keening became clearer now.

'Don't leave me, lads. Don't leave Daniel. Don't leave Daniel.'

O'Keefe recalled the younger Mulaney's words. *He's not right in the head. Never has been.* Pleased to meet you, Daniel Hooey, he thought. He took one arm while Finch took the other, hauling the whimpering man to his feet.

He patted him on his back. 'Nobody's going to leave you now, Daniel. Don't you worry your head.'

They called out an army patrol on the wireless from Bandon barracks, leaving Heatherfield's body and Daniel Hooey there with Keane, making their way back to the ambush site with a second Ford car full of angry, heavily armed constables and Tans. There they waited for a company of King's Liverpools to arrive. They would do a sweep of the hills, but O'Keefe knew they wouldn't find a sniff of the third Volunteer who had made it over the crest of the hill.

He and Finch climbed the hill again and examined the dead gunman. He was young, most likely a farm labourer in rough, patched trousers and a canvas jacket, and had been armed with a British army model Enfield rifle, the longer version of the carbine carried by the RIC.

'I don't remember his face from Mulaney's,' O'Keefe said.

Finch shrugged and checked the dead man's rifle.

'They could've sent the soft lad to fetch them as soon as we arrived and staged the punch up with Keane to give themselves time to set up.'

He cleared the breach and detached the Enfield's box magazine, finding it empty. Then he searched the ambusher's pockets and found no further ammunition.

'Imagine kicking off an ambush with six rounds in your rifle.'

They had found six brass .303 shell casings on the ground behind the boulders.

'All it took was one,' O'Keefe said.

The Tan nodded and sighted down the long rifle barrel at the road they had travelled on. 'Bloody good shot, all the same. Moving target at over a 'undred yards with an old Smelly.' Smelly was the nickname given to the Enfield by soldiers in the war, from its designation as a 'short magazine Lee Enfield'.

'Or lucky.' O'Keefe lit a cigarette and handed Finch the packet. He thought the smoke might soothe his nerves, calm the cramping in his belly. Heatherfield dead. And he himself had killed a man, putting a bullet in his back from a hundred yards. O'Keefe had thought he was finished with killing when he'd left the army.

Finch nodded. 'You're right, Sergeant. His rate of fire was too slow. If he was as good as his first shot, he could have plugged all four of us.'

'Here's to piss poor musketry.'

Finch laughed bitterly. 'Tell that to 'eatherfield.' He was silent for a moment. 'Geordie bastard was a good skin. Kept 'imself to 'imself but he was a good boy, he was.'

The wind had gathered strength, humming off the rounded surface of the boulders. The clouds were a dark, steel grey.

Finch said, 'Keane'll take it hard.'

'He will. And then he'll get over it.'

The Tan looked at O'Keefe. 'Like you did, Sergeant?'

'You and me, Finch.'

———

The barracks was buzzing when they returned. A group of constables had gathered in the yard, some in uniform, some in shirtsleeves. Word of the ambush had reached Ballycarleton.

The men parted as Finch and O'Keefe escorted Keane from the car across the yard, into the barracks – his face still smeared with Heatherfield's blood. At the door O'Keefe pulled Reilly aside.

'Fill a hot bath for him, Reilly. New soap and fresh towels.'

The old man nodded, following Finch and Keane inside.

'What happened, Sergeant?' It was Finch's pal, Barrett.

'Ambush. Sniped at from a hill. Obstacle in the roadside on the run up to a small stone bridge. Heatherfield caught one.'

'Dead?' This was Kenzie, a Glaswegian Tan.

O'Keefe told them he was. 'It was quick. The army are on it now. We got one and lifted another of them.'

'Alive?' Barrett again.

'He's alive. Bandon has him at the moment.'

As if he'd summoned the man, the gates swung open and a Crossley filled with RIC and army pulled into the yard. The tailgate dropped and two Bandon constables helped a handcuffed prisoner down from the bed of the Tender. The Ballycarleton men moved as a group, closing on the back of the Crossley. One of them shouted, 'Is that him?'

The first punch knocked Daniel Hooey to the ground and set off the high-pitched keening Finch and O'Keefe had heard on the hillside. He repeated one word this time, and O'Keefe understood it clearly. The word was 'No.'

The kicking came next. Feet and fists raining down, the dull thud of leather and fist on flesh. The keening. *No. No.*

Daniel Hooey attempted to crawl under the Tender and rough hands dragged him back.

'Enough!' O'Keefe roared.

One or two of the men stopped. A few kept at it and O'Keefe took the carbine he was carrying from the Ford and began to swing it by the barrel. He clipped one of the men on the shoulder and the man stood up and threw a punch. A young Irish con, nineteen, twenty maybe. Turner from Wicklow, his face red with rage, had trained up in Phoenix Park with Heatherfield. O'Keefe ducked the punch and jabbed Turner in the chest with the butt of the Enfield.

Bennett, O'Keefe noticed as he lifted Daniel Hooey to a standing position, had pulled one of the other Tans away, the man's last kick missing wildly, sending him back off balance into Bennett's arms. There were rough shouts and curses, as well as the odd word to leave off and the high-pitched pleading of the man in O'Keefe's arms. Their anger spent, the men moved back, eyeing the prisoner. Sheepish, O'Keefe thought. They saw it now. It didn't take a scholar to see that the prisoner wasn't right in the head.

Leading Hooey to the barracks, O'Keefe heard laughter from across the yard: Mathew-Pare, Starkson, Eakins. They were lounging in the doorway to the cottage.

'Need some help, Sergeant?'

'I could use your lads, Detective, to take this man to the cells.'

The three walked over. Eakins tossed down his cigarette and took the prisoner by the arm. Starkson took a last drag on his and flicked it dangerously close to the group of men standing by the Crossley. He didn't even look at them. He took Hooey's other arm.

'Keys are on the hooks,' O'Keefe said. 'Make sure he doesn't come to any harm.' He turned to the group of men by the Crossley. There was something in his eyes when he spoke that made one or two of the men look away. 'I'm going to forget this happened, lads. And that's the last time it does. Is that clear?'

He said it louder. 'Is that clear?'

They mumbled, more or less as a unit. 'Yes, Sergeant.'

'Good. Now clear out.'

'You want my boys to mind the prisoners, then?' Mathew-Pare was at O'Keefe's elbow.

O'Keefe watched the Crossley pull out into the street, the gate swinging closed. He turned to Mathew-Pare.

'I'd appreciate …' He caught himself. '*Prisoners?*'

Mathew-Pare smiled. 'You didn't see Sergeant Daly yet?'

'No.'

'Connors, Sergeant. Lifted him at the funeral. Nothing to it.'

Jesus. The funeral. He'd completely forgotten. 'You lifted him? Seamus Connors?'

'Like a baby into a mother's arms. Came easy, more's the pity. Loaded parabellum stuffed down the back of his trousers. Boys would have had him full of holes before he got it out. I think he knew it.'

Excitement sparked in O'Keefe – Heatherfield, the ambush,

forgotten for the moment. Keane. The man he'd shot, forgotten. *Jesus. That was easy.* The whole thing might be over.

'He say anything yet?'

'No,' Mathew-Pare said, taking out another cigarette, cupping his hand to light it. 'But he will.'

O'Keefe went to change into his uniform. As he dressed, Daly entered the office.

'Bit of rough stuff on the road, Seán?'

'A bit. Heatherfield ...' O'Keefe swallowed, the dead constable's name like an accusation in his throat, 'young Heatherfield took one in the face.'

For once, Daly was serious. 'If it's for you, it won't go past you,' he said. 'God rest him. How's Keane taking it? They were pals, weren't they?'

O'Keefe nodded, staring at himself in the mirror. His face was older than he remembered. When had he last looked at himself? That morning? He'd grown haggard, lines at the corners of his eyes. Dark circles under his eyes like ashes tipped on snow, his scar red and inflamed. He splashed water on his face and rubbed at the circles under his eyes as if he could wipe them away.

Daly changed tack. 'I heard you put one of the fuckers in the ground yourself. A one-all draw, then.'

'Won't bring the young lad back.'

'Well,' Daly said, stuffing his pipe, lighting it. 'We got Connors for you, if it's any consolation.'

'How is he?' O'Keefe buttoned his tunic and ran a wet comb through his hair.

'Either mad with grief or just plain mad.'

'He came easy?'

'Like he wanted us to have him. Got hardy looks from some lads in the lanes after we took him though. As if perhaps we weren't the only ones looking for him.'

O'Keefe considered this. Maybe the IRA had decided that Connors had killed the girl and wanted to deal with him themselves. He remembered the letter from Childers to Collins: '… this woman was killed in contravention of orders by the IRA.'

And then the thought struck him. If Connors was guilty, Heatherfield had died for nothing. A wasted trip to the poultry farm. A whim. O'Keefe prayed – for the first time in years – that it wasn't Connors who had killed the girl. The prayer rang hollow.

There were still the feathers to consider. If they didn't get a confession from him, the feathers were evidence of a sort. If he could source them and connect Connors to their source … *Jesus, Seán, get a grip of yourself.* He had a feeling the case was over, whether he wanted it to be or not.

'By the way,' Daly said, speaking around his pipe stem. 'The DI said he couldn't wait. Off to town to be awarded the Victoria Cross or some such for catching the nefarious Seamus Connors. He said for you to have a run at the boy if you like, but not to break him up if he doesn't talk. Doesn't want the glass cracked before the Castle men take him off our hands.'

'It's not me he'd want to worrying about, the thick bastard.'

O'Keefe stopped by the day-room and found Keane. He was sitting at a table on his own, staring at a cold cup of tea, a cigarette burning down in the ashtray at his elbow. He was clean and back in uniform.

'Keane?'

He didn't look up. 'Sergeant?'

'You heard they got Connors?'

Keane nodded. 'You'll write his mam?'

'I will, Keane. I'll do it tonight. Heatherfield was a good man.' O'Keefe couldn't think of anything else to say. He hadn't known him very well. Keane picked up the cigarette and stared at its slow curls of smoke.

'A fella survives the whole bloody war and then gets killed here, on a road like the roads I've walked all my life. It doesn't make any fucking sense, Sergeant.'

'No, Keane, it doesn't. Your number's on the ticket and …' It sounded harsh. He felt that he should say something about duty and honour and the higher purpose they served in the RIC. Protecting – no, striving to protect – the people of Ireland from men who thought they had the right to murder those who disagreed with their aims. That Heatherfield died trying to stop these men and that his contribution had made a difference. But O'Keefe couldn't give voice to the lie. He tried to think of something else to say, but nothing came and he turned and headed for the cells.

'Mind if I join you, Sergeant?'

Mathew-Pare had been waiting for O'Keefe in the kitchen, across the hall from the cells on the lower-ground floor.

'No, Detective. Not at all, but could I ask you not to speak in the interview? Might put the mockers on if he hears an English accent this early in.'

'Interrogation manual. Familiar faces, voices, local knowledge. Build a bond. Works better than physical influence, so the manual says.' His smile was empty under the faded blue eyes, a cigarette in his yellowed fingers.

'I just think it would be better for now.'

'Of course, Sergeant.'

He set up in the interview room, a storage area off the kitchens just big enough for a small wooden table and three chairs. It was lit by one electric light on a wire hanging from the ceiling and, high in the wall, there was a half-window onto the yard above. From his briefcase, O'Keefe took Connors' file and his investigation diary on the Costelloe murder. He had one of the young constables bring an ashtray and a fresh packet of Player cigarettes.

Starkson and Eakins escorted Connors in and sat him behind the table. Mathew-Pare nodded for his men to leave and took a chair against the wall. O'Keefe sat opposite Connors. Studying the file photograph, O'Keefe looked up and compared it to the man sitting across from him. There was a resemblance certainly, but the man had changed in the intervening years. He was leaner, his cheekbones chiselled. Dark hollows braced his brown-black eyes and his hair, so carefully oiled and combed in the photograph, hung lank over his sweat-stained collar. His strong, angled jaw was hedged with stubble. He wore a British army tunic, threadbare at the cuffs, a white shirt and black tie. His trousers were of rough corduroy and looked to have rested in many the barn or ditch. O'Keefe offered Connors a cigarette from the packet. 'Are you well, Mr Connors? Have you been mistreated in any way?'

Connors glanced over at O'Keefe and held his gaze. He seemed then to come to some conclusion and brought his eyes up to a spot on the wall and held them there.

O'Keefe stared at him for a moment longer and began to leaf through his notes. He wasn't entirely convinced that Connors was Deirdre Costelloe's killer but the man had form. O'Keefe reckoned he'd give him a jolt by starting with something from his past. From before the Troubles had started in earnest.

He read aloud: 'March 14, 1917, complaint against one Seamus Connors for the harassing of one Judith Mackey. Also charged with breaking and entering Mackey family home, public intoxication and assault on a police constable.' Pausing, O'Keefe looked to Connors for a response and got nothing. He quoted again from the charge sheet: 'Found in possession of surgical scalpel, cleaving knife, bone saw, surgical spreader.'

No response.

O'Keefe raised his eyes from the file. 'Were you going to cut the tits off Judith Mackey the way you did Deirdre Costelloe?'

Connors' eyes flared. O'Keefe caught the flash and pushed harder.

'Because Judith chucked you over? The same way Deirdre did?'

Connor's eyes went back to the wall but he blinked twice. Bull's-eye, O'Keefe thought.

'Hard to believe a man could do the things you did to that girl. A girl you said you loved. Stick a blade, an ice pick in her head and then rape her. Cut off her breasts. Spend that much time with the body. What did you do with the breasts when you'd cut them off, Seamus?'

Seamus Connors still stared at the wall, but O'Keefe could see he was trembling. The silence in the room was punctuated by the rasp and click of Mathew-Pare's cigarette lighter.

'Did it feel good when you finally fucked her, Seamus? I'd wager you felt fierce good until it was all over. Then it hit you. What you did to the woman you loved. Stabbed her in the brain and then took what you'd wanted for so long. All those rolls in the fields after dances and she never letting you 'tween her legs. Never let you at it and then chucked you over for some swell with a cushy motor who bought her presents a gunman on the run like yourself could never have afforded, not in a thousand years.'

Still nothing. Eyes on the wall. O'Keefe noticed the tensing of the muscles of Connors' jaw.

'And so you butchered her and laid her on a hillside and labelled her the worst thing you could come up with. *Traitor*. Tarred and feathered the poor girl's privates for the world to see. It wasn't enough what you'd done to her, you had to punish her, even in death.' He paused. 'What do you see on the wall, Seamus? Do you see Deirdre's face? The way it was when she laughed, when she smiled at you and said sweet things to you laying in the grass after a hike out to the Head of Kinsale? The way her face looked when you held her at the Palace Dance Hall, her cheeks flushed with the heat of the place, her lips red and her teeth lovely and white. I saw her teeth, Seamus. I saw every bit of her when the surgeon opened her up and took out her heart and her lungs and womb. I saw inside her skull, Seamus. Saw the path the sticker you used made in her brain.' O'Keefe shifted his eyes to Mathew-Pare. The Englishman was leaning back, smoking, as if he were watching a play that only half-interested him.

'Or perhaps you see Judith Mackey's face up there, do you? *Do you?*'

Connors didn't respond. O'Keefe tossed the file onto the table.

'You never loved Deirdre. You hated her. Only hate could make a man do to someone what you did to Deirdre.'

Mathew-Pare shifted in his chair.

The gunman's voice was quiet but firm, as if he were addressing the wall of the room instead of the men inside it. 'I loved Deirdre.'

'What was that, Seamus?' O'Keefe asked.

'I said I loved her.'

'Then why did you kill her? Why did you do those things to her, man?'

Connors looked at O'Keefe. 'I never hurt a hair on that girl's head. Never in my life, so help me God.'

'Only God can help you if you did, Seamus.'

'God will judge me for the things I did do, but I would never have hurt Deirdre.'

He took a Player from the packet. Mathew-Pare leaned over and lit it for him.

Connors' eyes were intense. As a policeman, O'Keefe was used to being lied to, but if this was lying, it was one of the most convincing performances he had ever seen.

'So you loved her. Do you know why she left you, Seamus?'

'Because I no longer amused her. I loved her and she loved …' he searched for a word, 'life.' It sounded lame and broken, and as Connors swiped at his eyes with the back of his hand, he appeared to O'Keefe like any young, grief-stricken lad might. For a moment it was difficult to believe he was the assassin he was said to be.

'And she found it, with this new chap she'd been courting?'

'I never got a chance to ask her.' Connors pulled hard on the cigarette.

'Did you know the fella she'd taken up with, Seamus?'

'I know of him. I'm told he's a right hand at the cards for a Montenotte man.' He exhaled a column of smoke.

'What's his name?' The question sounded too eager. O'Keefe glanced over at Mathew-Pare, knowing the Englishman wouldn't have made the same mistake.

'That'd be telling now, wouldn't it?' Connors said. 'Aiding and abetting the Crown.'

'His name, Seamus. We want to talk to him.'

'If he hurt Deirdre, I'll take care of him.'

'So you don't know that he did?' O'Keefe said. 'And you're not exactly in a position to find out either way.'

Connors shrugged. 'Didn't have the time to get him on his own. Away from that boy of his.'

'What boy?'

Connors laughed. 'You lot think I'm a wrong 'un? You've no idea – that fella.'

'What fella, Seamus? Who are you talking about?'

Connors shook his head and sucked on the cigarette. O'Keefe took a cigarette for himself and accepted a light from Mathew-Pare. He began again.

'So you'd never have hurt Deirdre?'

Connors stubbed out the cigarette, ignoring O'Keefe as if his question was addressed to someone else.

'What about Judith Mackey? How do you explain what you were carrying when you were arrested trying to force entry into her house?'

Smiling at O'Keefe, or maybe at the memory, Connors said, 'I was a medical student, Sergeant. I was on my way home from a dissection. That set of tools cost four quid. I could hardly have left them at the college.'

'So you took them to Judith Mackey's house and tried to force your way in?'

'I was drunk, Sergeant. I drank back then. I was young.'

'You smell of drink now.'

'Wouldn't you, if the situation was reversed? If the woman you loved had been murdered?'

'How do I know you haven't been on a skite for the last week? That you didn't start drinking again and kill Deirdre?'

'I wasn't on a skite. I've been teetotal for two years. Since Judith had me up. I'd lost the run of it, drink. Lost the run of myself.'

O'Keefe leaned across the table to get closer to the man, willing Connors to confide in him. 'How do I know you didn't kill Deirdre Costelloe?'

Leaning in to meet him halfway, Connors put a hand on O'Keefe's forearm. 'Because when she was killed, I was up in Dublin, killing his lot,' he nodded towards Mathew-Pare, 'in their beds. And since then I've been down in Kilmichael, sending Auxie dogs off to meet the Devil. Sure, even if I'd wanted to kill Deirdre, I'd never have found the time.'

'I think,' Mathew-Pare said, speaking for the first time, his voice as pleasant as if he were suggesting they break for tea, 'that we should wind things up here, unless Mr Connors wants to tell us anything more about his activities in Dublin and Kilmichael. Mr Connors?'

Connors smiled at Mathew-Pare. 'I've said all I'm saying to any man, English or Irish spy. Consider yourselves privileged men.'

Mathew-Pare rose and said, 'There's more privileged men coming. They'll listen and you'll talk. They'll love to hear your story, Mr Connors.'

'Sergeant!'

O'Keefe bolted upright, unsure of where he was. After a moment, he realised his right hand was gripping Constable Finch's throat. Finch had a grip on O'Keefe's wrist. It was dark, the only light in the small room coming through the open door to the office.

'Sergeant, it's me – Finch.'

O'Keefe rubbed sleep from his eyes, his heart pounding in his chest and a cold sweat of fear on his back. He could see his breath in the dim light.

'What is it, Finch? What time is it?'

'It's after four. Only I think you need to get up and come with us, Sergeant.'

'Come where?'

Finch hesitated. 'You're needed, Sergeant. Right quick.' He paused again and O'Keefe realised he still had his hand on the man's throat. Gently, Finch removed the hand from his neck. O'Keefe looked at it as if it were something strange and wild. 'Sergeant Daly told me to rouse you. We've a problem with Keane.'

'Keane? Where is he?'

Finch took O'Keefe's civilian clothes, along with his shoulder holster and gun, from the wardrobe and handed them to him.

'Sergeant Daly has the car running. Says you need to 'op it, mate.'

———

Daly drove with the lights on, racing over the crushed

stone roads, risking ambush or accident. Through breaks in the cloud, the half-moon turned the dusting of frost on the stone walls silver. O'Keefe pulled his trenchcoat tightly around him.

'Who has he with him, Jim?' O'Keefe asked, riding up front beside Daly. Finch was in the back, a wool cap pulled low over his ears, his uniform overcoat belted tight against the cold, an Enfield carbine across his lap.

Daly shouted over the engine noise and creak of the Ford's springs. 'Bunch of Essex lads from the camp. They lost two of theirs last week. One to a sniper, one kidnapped, presumed dead. Keane met them drinking in the hotel.'

Jesus, O'Keefe thought. Drunken, angry soldiers from the Essex Regiment – reputed to be the worst regiment in Ireland for the abuse of prisoners – and young Keane.

Finch leaned over the seat. 'They took one of the Essex's Crossleys. Got one of the more sober lads to drive, I 'eard.'

As they crested a hill on the Crossbarry road and levelled out, they could see Mulaney's burning. Daly swung the car up the long drive. A small scrum of people stood in the yard, helpless against the intensity of the flames. There was a sickening stench of roasting flesh and scorched feathers in the night air; a peaty smell of burning thatch from the roof of the cottage office.

One of the men in the group walked over to them as Daly braked the car. As he neared them, O'Keefe recognised the younger Mulaney, his face black with soot. There were women and children in the group, and it occurred to O'Keefe that the cottage which served as the farm's office was also the Mulaney family home. He could see a woman holding a baby, small children clinging to the coat she was wearing over her nightclothes. In the firelight he could see the sheen of tears streaking the woman's face.

He got out of the car. 'Mr Mulaney …'

'You're too late, Sergeant. They're long gone.'

'Where'd they go? Have you any idea?'

'I expect the family of the boy you shot will have more to grieve about before the night is out.' He snorted and rage flashed in his eyes. 'All the while we worried about the boyos in the hills burning us out and in the end it was you lot. Drunk as fucking lords.'

His words were overcome by a wrenching sound as the corrugated roof of the shed nearest the cottage, glowing red from the heat, collapsed inwards on row after row of pens and cages, the wooden walls imploding in an eruption of sparks and flames and smoke, the fire raging brighter for an instant, illuminating all around them and emanating a fleeting surge of warmth. Flames danced in reflection on the black body of the Ford. Mulaney watched with O'Keefe as the shed collapsed. Then he turned and walked back to his family. There was nothing more to say about anything. There just weren't the words. Silently O'Keefe got back into the car and Daly drove off.

The village of Rathleigh was a small collection of houses off the Crossbarry road, two miles from the poultry farm. They could see the light of burning houses as they approached, the road dipping to the village on the banks of the Bandon. A Crossley Tender was parked at an angle across the road and Daly pulled up behind it. Two small labourer's cottages were burning, one on either side of the muddy thoroughfare, a hundred yards or so down from each other.

The three of them got out of the car, O'Keefe unsnapping the holster under his left arm as he walked, Daly beside him carrying a hurley, the blade resting over his right shoulder, Finch following with his carbine. They rounded the Crossley.

There appeared to be seven soldiers. O'Keefe counted three holding rifles. Lined up in the road was a large family, still in nightclothes, like the Mulaneys. There were several women and children, and an elderly couple. A scatter of their belongings lay in a forlorn and broken trail from the front of the burning cottage to where they stood.

One soldier was using his rifle to hold back a young boy who was trying to get at the burning house. The soldier was laughing, digging the butt of his gun into the boy's ribs. Another soldier staggered out of a low-built, thatched pub, his arms full of stout bottles. He made it halfway to a huddle of three laughing soldiers before he dropped the bottles and fell on his arse, sitting in the mud and beer and broken glass.

'There's the lad,' Daly said.

Keane leaned against the front of a cottage opposite one of the burning houses. His face glowed orange in the firelight and he stared at the flames as if they were the most beautiful things he had ever seen. A bottle hung from his hand.

O'Keefe started towards him. 'Constable Keane.'

A young Essex Private stepped in front of him. 'Who the fuck do you think you are, mate?'

Without stopping, O'Keefe drove his boot up into the soldier's groin and the man doubled over with a yelp of pain. One of the other Essexes saw it and started shouting. A rifle was raised but O'Keefe ignored it and kept walking. Behind him he heard Finch's voice and the warning to lower arms.

Keane turned as O'Keefe neared him. 'We got the fucking Shinner bastards, Sergeant.' His words were slurred, eyes glassy. His lip was still swollen from the fight he'd had with the farm worker earlier, before the ambush, before all this, O'Keefe thought, rage, sadness and shame warring within him. He watched as Keane took a swig from the bottle and O'Keefe could smell the scent of whiskey. Fuel for many a burning, many a killing.

'Are you armed, Keane?' O'Keefe stopped in front of him. His words seemed to take a moment to register with the constable.

Keane patted at his hip and pulled back his overcoat. It was a long, yellow-tan army trenchcoat and under it, O'Keefe noticed, he wore his uniform. Stepping closer to him, O'Keefe reached into Keane's coat and removed his sidearm from its belt holster. A Colt automatic. He sniffed the barrel and was relieved to smell that it hadn't been fired recently.

'Put the bottle down and come with me.'

Keane smiled. 'We've one more house, Sergeant. The simple boy's house. Lads are only just trying to get the mother out of it now.'

O'Keefe lashed out and felt Keane's nose snap under his knuckles. Keane dropped the bottle and held his face in his hands, blood streaming through his fingers. Stepping behind him, O'Keefe wrenched one of Keane's hands back and clipped a handcuff onto it. Pulled the other hand back and did the same.

Keane started laughing and then the laughter turned to sobs, the blood running down into his mouth, the young man sniffing and spitting in the mud as O'Keefe guided him to the Ford. Shoving the young constable forward, O'Keefe watched Daly knock the rifle from one of the soldiers with a whack of his hurl. Finch loaded the rest of the Essexes onto the Crossley at rifle point.

Once he had him in the car, O'Keefe said to Keane. 'Michael Keane, I am placing you under arrest for the wilful destruction of property by means of arson …'

Keane shouted at O'Keefe through bloody teeth, 'You fuck yourself, Sergeant! Fuck yourself and fuck this whole war and fuck these people! These filthy, fucking murdering people!' The tears rolled down his face and he lowered his head to the seat in front of him.

These people, O'Keefe thought. Your people, Keane. My people.

———

When the war came, he joined up. He went with the others from the abattoir where he worked. He had no friends there but would follow the lads. Watch what they did. Mimic their actions and rough talk, and laugh when they laughed. He was tolerated, though his awkward ways and ill-timed bursts of laughter would be met sometimes with uneasy stares and odd comments. Couldn't fault his work though. The lad was a machine. Would do your work for you if you let him.

In the eighteen months that he had worked in the abattoir, his forearms had grown thick and ropey with muscle and he was at home on the killing floor, swinging the spiked mallet, the cattle in their boxes dropping to their knees, dead before they hit the ground.

They went to the town square to see Kitchener's man in their work clothes, bloody aprons thrown over their shoulders. They would be joining a local regiment; a fighting regiment with a long, illustrious history. The young lad wondered, as the army doctor shone a light inside his mouth, was this his father's regiment? He had no one to ask now. His mother was gone too.

His hand shook a little as he scratched his signature on the papers they gave him. Thinking of his mother. How she'd had it coming, the bitch. She should never have sold his laying hens. She should never have fucking done that.

Thursday
2 December 1920

The Daly house was in an area of Cork called the Barracka, due to its nearness to the main British army barracks in the city. It was a district where many policemen had settled over the years and, despite several shootings in the surrounding streets, no Peeler had yet been killed and it remained a relatively safe place for them to live. Retired Peelers and ex-British army lived there in numbers, as did teachers, carpenters, tradesmen and their families, sharing lanes with several notorious brothels that had served the barracks for years. Children played on the cobbles, warring with gangs from other streets, playing Volunteers against the Tans, the younger lads stuck being Tans and always having to die.

O'Keefe was on two days official furlough, as ordered by the DI. He sat in the Daly kitchen sipping warm, sweet tea, watching Jim's wife Muireann roll out pastry for an apple tart, talking now and again of things her five children had done; about things that she knew would take his mind off work, off the girl found on the hillside. Muireann was a rare woman in that Daly told her almost everything that went on in his work. She told Jim she wouldn't have it any other way and Muireann Daly, the sweetest, kindest woman a man could meet, would have her way or so help you God.

O'Keefe had seen this side of her himself when she had visited him each day in the Army Hospital. There was a time when he was refusing her visits, refusing to eat the food she brought. All he had wanted was to be left alone, to live in his memories, as if the longer he looked at the horror of V Beach and the two weeks of fighting that followed, the more he might see some sense in it, come to some conclusion.

Muireann Daly had made him stop. Bullied him back into daily life. She couldn't make the memories go away, but she had got him over the worst of the days as he recovered. Forcing a baby, her youngest, Paul – now three years old – into his arms. Telling him to smile at the child, or did O'Keefe want him to grow up a sour auld sod like his father? And O'Keefe had forced himself to smile at the infant and, though it took weeks, she never stopped coming and, after some time, little Paul would smile at O'Keefe and hold his fat-ringed arms out to him, wanting to be held, so that O'Keefe couldn't refuse him. And then she made him eat.

O'Keefe smiled at the memory and his stomach growled at the thought of a home-cooked meal. Muireann heard it and smiled. 'Your belly sounds like a Crossley Tender, Seán. You'd think they never feed you boys in barracks.'

'They feed us. Fatten us for the slaughter, more like.' He instantly regretted saying it. Muireann must worry about Jim. That was only natural.

Before he could apologise, the eldest Daly child – Mary, eight years old, blonde like her mother – came into the kitchen. 'There's someone outside to see Uncle Seán, Mammy. He says he's a good pal of yours, Uncle Seán. And look,' she said, holding open her palm to O'Keefe. 'He gave me these coppers and told me to buy myself a bottle of lemonade!'

O'Keefe stood. 'I know who he is, Mary. Another Jackeen who's free with his money.'

'That money's going in the poor box, is where it's going, girl.'

'Sergeant Connolly would be fierce disappointed if you made her give it over, Muireann. He thinks the young of the country grow strong on lemonade. Thinks if we all drank more of it, there'd be Home Rule in no time.'

The Crimes Special man was waiting for O'Keefe at the gate, passing a scuffed and lopsided football back and forth with Thomas Daly, aged five.

'You Cork lads,' Connolly said to the boy, 'never could kick a ball for shite. Here ...' beckoning the boy over, 'take this like a good lad, and buy yourself ...' He dug into his pocket for more coins, '... buy all your brothers and sisters a bottle of lemonade, there.'

The boy's face exploded into a smile. 'Thank you, sir! Thanks a million!'

'And don't let me hear you spent it all on yerself now.' Mock serious, he mussed the boy's hair as he passed.

'A fine litter,' Connolly said. 'Surely they can't be Daly's.'

'He claims them, anyway.'

'Mysteries of life, Seán. Mysteries of life. Like the one brings me out here.'

'How'd you find me?'

'Jingled up the barracks and Daly himself told me.'

Connolly offered O'Keefe a Sweet Afton and a light.

Exhaling smoke, O'Keefe said, 'Mysteries, Connolly. What are you on about that you had to come interrupt the first hot meal I've had in a week?'

'Wouldn't have done it, my friend, if I didn't think you might be interested.'

'Tell me.'

The Crimes Special man smoked and watched for a moment as a woman across the road swept the footpath the length of her fence, stopping at the end of her property on each side, exactly. 'Heard you picked up Connors. Fair play to you.'

'We did. Daly and a couple of lads ... the chap you met, English fella and his boys. Lifted him at the girl's funeral.'

'He give himself up for it?' He looked at O'Keefe now, as if the answer was somehow important to him.

'He didn't, no. He said he was shooting for Collins up in Dublin that weekend. Said he had a hand in the jump at Kilmichael as well. But swore blind he never touched the girl.'

Connolly shook his head and chuckled, as if at some private joke. 'The cheeky fucker. Did he give himself up for the Smyth shooting? I could claim that if he did. Be Head Con in a week for that one.'

'Sorry.'

Connolly smiled. 'So he was in your nick since when?'

'Yesterday morning ... afternoon, really.'

'Well, young Seánín, the reason I ask is this.' He put up his hand as if O'Keefe had been about to protest his point. 'Now, I know the case is closed, shut and out of business, because you've pinched your killer and thank you very much. *And* I know you'll tell me to bugger off home and don't be filling your mind with notions, but …' He smiled and took a long drag on his cigarette.

'But what?'

'But we found a body. On my patch – in a laneway off Patrick Street. Four o'clock this morning. Just got word back a couple of hours ago on the cause of death. Care to guess?'

'Jesus, Connolly, you'd talk the arse off a cart horse and leave it none the wiser.'

'Icepick in the brain. Up through the number one vertebra. Single stroke. Professional job, I'd wager.'

'Jesus.'

'Him too. Just like your girl there, only one difference.'

'What's that?' O'Keefe dropped the cigarette on the footpath and ground it out with his boot.

'It's not a girl.'

Connolly took a manila file from inside the expensive leather case he had resting at his feet and handed it to O'Keefe. 'Post-mortem's not finished yet, still working it now, I'd say. But cause of death is plain enough to see. Extensive bruising around the entry wound. The point of the weapon fairly rammed into the fella's head. Stuck him only once. Doc told me that, barring any surprises in the autopsy, single stab wound with a long, thin pointed object would be pronounced the cause of death. Just like your victim's. Said death would have been pretty instant and, in his learned opinion, it was a professional who did it. Said to look for an ex-soldier, fella with trench-fighting experience.'

'He said that unbidden?'

'Never opened me mouth.'

O'Keefe sighed and looked across the street at the Daly boys once again kicking their football on the cobbles. The woman had gone in from her sweeping. The air was cool and damp and the sun struggled to light the earth through the haze of low cloud. He checked his watch. It was nearly half-past two, two hours or so until darkness; two hours until it wasn't safe to roam the streets of Cork investigating a crime that had already been officially solved. Two hours until the trigger-happy troops of the Crown and the flat-capped gunmen of the IRA staged their nightly theatre of malice. O'Keefe told himself, I can leave this. Nothing will be different. Nothing will change if I just do nothing.

'This could all be just a grand coincidence, Seán. You know that, don't you? I debated whether or not I should even bring it to you.'

'No,' O'Keefe said, 'I was never one for coincidences.'

'Nor I, but sometimes coincidence is handier than the truth.'

'Handier but still not the truth.' O'Keefe exhaled a long breath. 'I owe you one, Lorcan. Any leads on it? Any suspects?'

Connolly smiled. 'You think I'm gonna dig the ditch for yis Ballycarleton lads, yis've another thing coming.'

'So you've nothing.'

'Not a thing. Fella's a salesman, agricultural machinery. William McKenna. Malloy's Agricultural Wares, South-Western Sales and Representation. Some grand title means he sells ploughs and troughs and those fucking things.' He motioned something fluttery with his hands. 'I know bollix about farming. He was staying at the Central for the past week. Interviewed the staff, it's in there.' He pointed to the file. 'Seems he was in a card game last night. Interviewed one of the lads playing. Private game, big stakes. The chap we talked to burned his pile and left early. Said our dead man could play some cards, he could.'

'Card game?'

'I know what you're thinking, Seán, but it might mean sweet damn all. Coincidence and all that.' He flicked his cigarette onto the road.

'You get the names of the other players?'

'In the file.' Connolly jabbed the file with his finger. 'McKenna's wallet was gone, Seán. You should know that from the off. Could be a robbery, the whole thing. No label round the fella's neck either. Found in the lane behind the hotel. Whores are known to work it. Their ponces as well. Some of those lads are handy with a knife.'

O'Keefe closed the file. 'Handy with a fish knife in a dark laneway is one thing. Killing some chap in an instant with one blow? Not many whoremongers I know'd be up to it.'

'Your ball, Seán, it's up to you to shoot or pass. I wouldn't touch it with a drover's stick meself, but I know you ambitious career types. All boot and no bullshit.'

O'Keefe smiled at Connolly, though it was the last thing he felt like doing. 'That's me all over. You've a real grip on a man's character.'

'It comes with the job, my friend.'

O'Keefe laughed. 'Why are you back on the cobbles anyway, Connolly? Aren't you supposed to be minding Mr Sutton's tavern? I thought you had two weeks.'

Connolly removed his trilby and smoothed his hair. 'Ah jaysus, man. I jacked that in days ago. Liver might as well have taken a bullet. I can feel the scars on the poxy thing. Four days of minding Sutton's arse and a man needs a week in the spa in Baden-Baden. You want a bash at it, Seán? When this thing's done? I could swing it for you.'

Replacing his hat, the Crimes Special man winked and touched his nose.

'I'll think about it. You might not want to know me when this is over,' said O'Keefe.

'I might not want to know you now, but I know a man with steel bollocks when I see one. And the brave ones, they're the most fun to wind up and set loose.'

'I owe you.'

'Sure, you find the bastard who killed that girl and maybe pin him with Janey Plunkett, we'll call it quits.'

———

An old woman was waiting in McGowan's library. Farrell shut the door behind him.

'I'm Liam Farrell. You've been wanting to see me?'

The old woman looked up at him from her chair by the fire. 'I have. You're here now, so.'

Farrell saw a tea tray on the low table next to her. 'Can I get you something more?'

'No, no, I'm drowned in tea already. A lovely girl, working here for you and Mr McGowan.'

'She is that, Mrs …'

'Gannon.'

'Mrs Gannon. You know, surely, that Mr McGowan is the solicitor, I'm only temporary here.'

'It's not the law I'm come to talk about. My boy told me to come see you, Mr Farrell. Said you were the one I'd want to be telling.'

'Do I know your boy, Mrs Gannon?'

'No, and you don't need to be knowing him, only that I was to come to you. That you were the one to see about the poor girl.'

'Girl?'

The woman pulled her black shawl tighter around her shoulders. 'The young girl found dead up on the Drumdoolin hills.'

Farrell pulled his chair closer to the fire, his attention focused on the woman. 'You've come to the right person,' he said. 'What can you tell me, Mrs Gannon?'

'Only that she was in the house where I labour. A guest of the Major. Last week it was.'

'A guest?'

'You could call her that, I suppose.' She hesitated. 'There were … other guests that night but you'd remember her.'

'Where do you work, Mrs Gannon? It's very important.'

'Burleigh House. Sure, what other man in these parts does be called the Major?'

'And why is it only now you're coming to us with this information?'

'Sure, I didn't know a thing about it until the Sergeant came to the house. Didn't he drop his case and pictures about the place.' She looked into the fire. 'Her picture fell out. I knew her from the picture, God rest her.'

Farrell leaned forward. 'Tell me about her. About what she was doing at the Major's house.'

The old woman nodded. 'The Major, you see. He has his friends in. Officers, gentlemen. Men from his days in the army. To play cards. And to …' She frowned and Farrell waited for her to go on. 'I don't like to say, Mr Farrell, but it's a disgrace, the carry on. And here, I found this in one of the bedrooms when I done my cleaning, some days after.'

She rummaged in the folds of her skirts and came out with a small object that she reached across and placed in Farrell's hand. It was a single pearl earring. 'The poor girl. She was wearing pearl earrings. I saw them on her when she arrived. She wasn't like the other girls that came.'

When the old woman had finished her story and he'd seen her out, Farrell shrugged on his coat and left McGowan's. He needed to contact his superiors and organise for a visit to be paid to Major Burleigh.

———

The mist-blurred sun was slipping behind the houses across the road by the time O'Keefe stepped out of the Daly house.

He had maybe an hour of daylight left at best. A further four hours until curfew, when the streets would be unsafe for walking, let alone riding the Triumph. He wheeled the bike up to the front of the house and left it there. Walking would be dangerous, but if a pack of Auxies or IRA was waiting around some corner, he reckoned his chances were better if he heard them first. Taking out his revolver, he checked he had a full load of six rounds and shoved it back into the holster.

O'Keefe started with the first name on the list of players at the card game that Connolly had given him. Fintan Hanratty lived in a large, redbrick Georgian house north of the city centre on Cornmarket Street. Hanratty answered the door himself and led O'Keefe into the drawing-room. It was tastefully decorated: windows garlanded with silk tasselled curtains; overstuffed sofas and polished mahogany; Chinese porcelain on the mantelpiece and Japanese prints on the walls.

The man himself was every bit as well turned out as his rooms. He was young, in his late twenties O'Keefe imagined, and wore his blond hair carefully oiled and combed in a high side parting. He was dressed in a fitted jacket, brocade silver waistcoat and grey woollen trousers, with pleats sharp enough to slice metal. His face was as white and unmarked as fresh cream; a hint of rouge tinted his cheeks.

Without asking, Hanratty poured and handed a generous snifter of brandy to O'Keefe. He then made himself comfortable in the armchair opposite the RIC man and fitted a cigarette into a long, ivory holder. He leaned across the distance between them, holding his cigarette to his lips. It took O'Keefe a long moment to realise that he was looking for a light.

O'Keefe struck a safety match from a crushed box he found in his pocket, feeling awkward, uncouth. He was well educated, cultured enough – thanks to the money his father had spent sending him to the Jesuits and his mother's love for art and music – to appreciate the beautiful proportions of the room, the attention to detail, but he didn't feel comfortable in such surroundings and imagined he never would.

'Cigarette, Sergeant?'

He took one and now Hanratty proffered a silver lighter from the side table by his chair. O'Keefe wondered why the man hadn't lit his own smoke since he had the lighter so handy. He wrote it off to eccentricity. Hanratty raised his glass. There was a hint of amusement on his face but his words didn't seem edged with the mockery O'Keefe expected. 'To the brave men of the RIC, Sergeant. And to your continued health.'

O'Keefe raised his own glass. 'And yours.'

'Terrible business, that poor man. Seemed a genial sort, when he wasn't holding aces and kings. He was murder with the cards.' He smiled to himself. 'God forgive me. No pun intended.' He mouthed an act of contrition and made the sign of the cross with his crystal tumbler.

O'Keefe looked hard at Hanratty again, searching for sarcasm. 'Are you much of a player yourself, Mr Hanratty?'

The man drank and gestured with the cigarette holder. 'I'm said to be by some. A nice fat income helps, when it comes to cards. No one gets good at anything without the will and means to practice.'

'I played enough cards in the army and I never improved. Pontoon mostly.'

'And who did you serve with, Sergeant?'

'Royal Dublins.'

'The Bluecaps.'

O'Keefe must have looked surprised.

'Royal Irish Rifles, Lance Corporal Fintan Hanratty, at your service. Three years of trench foot, bully beef and shrapnel. Made it through without a scratch.' He smiled and drank and waited for O'Keefe's reaction. He had done this before, O'Keefe thought. Surprised people, enjoyed the mild astonishment at the contradiction before them – the effete, mannered dandy as war veteran.

'Surprised?' Hanratty asked, as if reading O'Keefe's mind.

O'Keefe shrugged. 'Only that you weren't an officer. A man of your means and education.' He looked around the room as if to emphasise his point.

Hanratty drank. 'Never. Told dear old Dad I'd only join up if I could do it as an enlisted man. I am, you see, hardly fit to lead kittens to a drowning bucket, let alone other men. I am, in fact, more easily led, truth be told.'

O'Keefe nodded. 'Must have been bad, the trenches.'

'The best of times, the worst of times. As you might imagine. You were where yourself, Sergeant?'

'Dardanelles. Two weeks of fighting and a year and a half recovering.'

Hanratty smiled and pointed to the scar on O'Keefe's face with his cigarette holder. 'All better now?'

'Good as new. Yourself?'

'Like I said, never had a scratch.'

And then O'Keefe said something he hadn't meant to. 'You ever dream? Have dreams about the war, things you saw?'

Hanratty looked at him closely. 'Nightmares, you mean?'

O'Keefe looked into the fire. 'Yes, I suppose.'

'Still have them. Waking ones. When I smell bad meat – offal – rotting in bins beside the market. The smell sets them off. I start shaking sometimes, so that I can't fit a cigarette into its holder – people looking at me on the street as if I'm a souse on the first day of a cure.'

He continued, 'Cards help. When I'm playing, the game consumes all thought. And then I play so long I'm exhausted, can't dream for need of sleep.'

'And do you often play with the gentlemen you were with last night?'

'Ah yes,' he said, taking a long, mannered drag on his cigarette, 'down to brass tacks.'

'The only kind, Mr Hanratty. Do you play often with the gentlemen from last evening?'

Hanratty considered the question. 'No, not often. Not serious enough for my liking, most of them. Like your man, the victim. He was invited in and could play, you had to give him that. But he played a gruff, country style, as if he'd learned playing over a barrel in a pub somewhere. I was invited by the host, Bannon, I'm sure you'll speak to him or have done. He's a gentleman like myself, but likes the competition. Doesn't mind taking the odd beating from a bogger like that poor fellow who was killed.' And here he blessed himself again, this time with his ivory cigarette holder.

'Others do mind?'

'One or two I can think of. Don't mind losing to their own kind, but don't take it well when some grind of a farm-ware hawker relieves them of their hard-inherited money. Easy come, easy go, I always say.'

'And were there any women present at the game last night?'

'Not many women play, Sergeant.'

'Not as players, but as entertainment perhaps?'

'Not my kind of entertainment, you may have guessed.'

O'Keefe shrugged, indicating that Hanratty's choice of entertainment was of no concern to him.

'Now that you mention it, however, I have heard tell of a club, if you like. A secret society,' Hanratty said, snickering at the notion. 'Gentlemen officers and the like. Have you ever heard of the Hellfire Club, Sergeant?'

O'Keefe told him he hadn't.

'They were a private society of debauchery. Up in Dublin in the late seventeen hundreds, shortly before the Union, I think. Gambling, whoring. The whole kit and caboodle, Sergeant. Everything short of murder and sometimes not so short, so the stories go. They had, you must realise, much greater licence to pursue their pleasures than do the wealthy sons of Éire these days. Their libation of choice was a vile potion called scalpeen – hot whiskey mixed with melted butter.'

O'Keefe made the appropriate face around a mouthful of his own brandy. Something danced in the corners of his consciousness. Something pertinent but out of reach. He turned his attention back to Hanratty's story, hoping his words might shed light upon the memory.

'And when these boys tired of jumping their horses out of windows, it used to amuse them to douse their footmen and, so goes it, their whores, with scalpeen and set them alight. They were so wealthy, fathers so powerful, that they were virtually untouchable. Of course, now and again, there would come the need to flitter. Back home to England until things cooled down. Again, no pun intended.'

'Forgive me Mr Hanratty, but what relevance does this have to the card game you played last night?' The thought that had been niggling at his mind slipped away. *Something about a club?*

'Forgive me, for rambling, Sergeant. But there is talk of a similar such mob – no doubt not as rough and tumble, I imagine, as the Hellfires. A friend of mine was invited along and it was all I could do to squeeze any tattle at all out of him. It's what made me think of it, you see. The girls. He spoke highly of them and their … talents. *Unspeakable pleasures.* His words, Sergeant. Indeed, he seemed to think the card game was of secondary concern to those present.'

O'Keefe thought about this for a moment. Deirdre didn't fit in somehow. Or did she? 'Your friend, Mr Hanratty – can I speak to him?'

'Should you care to set sail for India, of course. Serving His Majesty, Sergeant. Like yourself.'

O'Keefe smiled. 'Did your friend happen to say where this party was held?'

'In some pile in the country,' he said, 'and would say no more. Very hush-hush you see, Sergeant. Blood oaths and burnt offerings. The usual boarding school toss, but taken seriously by the members.'

'But there were no women present last night?'

'No,' Hanratty said, disappointment on his face as if his story had led them back to nowhere. 'There weren't any women present, and I was there until the very end. Did quite well.'

'At whose expense?'

The man smiled. 'Not at our poor dead friend's anyway. He'd the better of us all, while I had the better of most.'

'And who got hit the worst?'

'Well, Glendinning left early. Took a bad pasting but then he always does. I play with him from time to time, different games around town. Fine chap. Knows he's useless and plays anyway. Good company. Little better than cannon fodder, but knows it.'

'And the others?'

'Well, I suppose, now that you mention it, Dickie Barton was hit badly by your man.'

O'Keefe recognised the name. Where had he heard it? He said, 'This Mr Barton –'

'Richard Barton. Son and heir to the tractor works.'

Of course. He'd met the man when he'd interviewed Deirdre's friend Anne Duffy. Deirdre Costelloe's employer. Her boss. Heat rushed to O'Keefe's neck and his heartbeat quickened. A connection?

'How'd he take it, Barton, losing his shirt so badly?'

'It's not like he hasn't the money to burn, Sergeant.'

'So why did he resent losing if money's no object?'

'As I told you. Feels men like …?' O'Keefe gave the victim's name, '… like Mr McKenna, God rest him, are beneath him. He underestimates them. Feels that they've no mind or right to be beating him. And quite frankly, your man gave him a bad drubbing. Maybe McKenna sensed how he was seen by Barton. Bluffed him so badly it was nearly impossible not to laugh. Impossible not to admire the way McKenna baited Dickie into throwing good money after bad hands and then leading him up paths and down valleys until he had no choice but to bow out. And to top it off, he always showed his cards, particularly the weak hands he won with. Now that I think of it, he really was an exceptional player. Got somewhat erratic in the late stages of the evening, but by then he'd enough drink taken and all were beaten. I took a few hands from him at the end which allowed me to leave with my purse and pride intact.'

O'Keefe noted that the victim had most likely been intoxicated. 'And what time did you leave?'

'Around eight this morning, Sergeant. Long after, I'm told, your man was dead. So there goes me as a suspect.'

'You never were one, Mr Hanratty.'

'Fintan, please. Now that I'm not a suspect.'

'At least, not until I learned you fought in the war.'

'Oh dear. And why would my days in the mud have affected your feelings towards me?'

O'Keefe decided to tell him.

'Pig-sticking,' Hanratty said when O'Keefe had finished. 'I heard it called that in the trenches. Meant to be a fine, quick way to go if you're on the wrong end of it.'

'Can you think of anyone at the game who might have wanted McKenna pig-stuck?'

He thought about it, then shook his head. 'No. Only Barton might have had his feelings hurt, but then you can rule him out too, Sergeant. We left together this morning and had breakfast in the market café. Barton's an objectionable man – enough to nearly put a man off his sausage and eggs – but the war affected him badly. Physically. Mentally, I sometimes imagine. He's forever hinting at dark deeds, secret meetings and the like, as if he's still working behind German lines.'

'He was Intelligence? In the war?'

'That he was. All the messy sectors, up and down the line with the West Kents. Sadly, I feel he isn't aware that the war has ended.'

'Wounded? Gassed?'

'Wounded, I've heard.' Hanratty looked into the fire but

couldn't suppress a smile. 'We boys in the mud. Always said we'd rather take one in the face than the place where Barton is said to have taken his.'

O'Keefe nodded, having felt the same himself once, and realised that if Barton's injury was as Hanratty implied, Barton would hardly have been able to assault Deirdre sexually. And he had stayed on chasing cards until hours after McKenna had left and been murdered. Resignation washed over him. Disappointment. O'Keefe hauled himself to standing and thanked Hanratty for the drink and his time.

Hanratty rose with him. 'There's something I've been meaning to ask you, Sergeant.'

O'Keefe looked at him, unsure of what was coming. 'What's that?'

'What will men like us do when the republic comes?'

'How do you mean?'

'The men of the RIC, like yourself and, of course, men like me.' He gestured at his surroundings as if they might indicate what kind of man he was. 'We'll hardly be welcome, between the gunmen and the priests who'll be running this country when the republic comes.'

O'Keefe liked the comparison, despite himself. Peelers and Poofs. A close run, who was further exiled from the hearth of Irish society. 'I was always a Home Ruler, Mr Hanratty.'

'Fintan, please.'

'Besides, it's not my concern what happens, once the shooting stops. Getting the guns quiet, that's my job now.'

'There's only one way those guns will go silent and that's

when the gunmen get the republic they're gunning for and the priests can perch on the arms of government chairs and caw in the ears of those who matter. And then you'll be out of a job altogether, I suspect.'

O'Keefe laughed. 'You're probably right, Fintan.'

Hanratty appeared delighted that O'Keefe had used his Christian name. 'I've always held, Sergeant, that as bad as English rule has been for this country, it's at least kept the priests in their place. Independence will only loose them on us like a flight of vengeful bats.'

'Gunmen, priests and politicians. An unholy trinity,' O'Keefe said.

Hanratty smiled and looked to the ceiling as if searching his memory. 'Diderot spoke of kings and priests but I don't think he would disagree entirely if I were to paraphrase: "When the last politician is strangled with the entrails of the last priest, only then will we truly be free."'

O'Keefe shook the man's hand, smiling. 'Worry about the priests and the politicians when the time comes, I suppose. Worry about the gunmen now.'

'And the pig-stickers, Sergeant?'

O'Keefe's smile faded. 'And the pig-stickers.'

It was dark on the streets of Cork – only a few stragglers, moving hurriedly, heads down, rushing to get home before the curfew. Some had packages under their arms: sausages, rashers wrapped in newsprint. A bottle of whiskey or stout for the long evening indoors behind the drapes and shutters, listening to the roar of armoured cars marauding the empty streets. The sporadic crack of rifle and pistol fire. The sudden stutter of a Lewis machine-gun. O'Keefe picked up his pace.

Montenotte was an area to the north of the city. For the past century, it had been inhabited by Cork's wealthy merchants and administrators. Built on a hill, it had paved footpaths, imposing black, wrought-iron gates fronting grand, redbrick houses. Tidy lawns, trimmed privet hedges and tended gardens. The area hadn't suffered much during the Troubles, but the people were scared. It was rumoured that many Montenotte men had sent their women and children 'home' to England.

Halfway up the gravel driveway, O'Keefe saw the car. It was parked next to a black Rolls-Royce under a stone arch where once horse-drawn carriages waited out of the rain for their passengers to emerge from the house. O'Keefe remembered that Barton had been riding in the Rolls when he had spoken to him outside the tractor works.

O'Keefe approached the other motor, noting the tan top covering the interior. The shining grate of the front grill was overlaid with the inscription 'Hispano-Suiza'. The words in Deirdre's diary came back to him. *Fancy Spaniard.* He rested his hand on the smooth, sky-blue bonnet.

'You want that hand cut off?'

He turned to the voice. A silhouette in the shadows at the back of the car, its face in darkness. O'Keefe couldn't see a gun but that didn't mean the man who had spoken didn't have one.

'It'd be you doing the cutting then?' O'Keefe kept his voice as casual as he could. He slowly moved his hand from the bonnet to inside his jacket, thumbing open the leather catch on his holster.

The man stepped from the shadows. He was of average height, late twenties to early thirties. Average face, as far as O'Keefe could see – his hat brim tipped down over his eyes. 'Step away from the motor or I'll serve you up, cunt.'

O'Keefe recognised him. Barton's driver. He had been at the wheel of the Rolls outside the factory. 'Mr Barton loves his car, does he? Is the man himself in, or are you playing lord of the manor?'

He took a step forward. 'Who's asking?' Another step.

'Sergeant O'Keefe, RIC, Ballycarleton. And you can stop where you are or stop a bullet. I've a few questions I want to ask your boss.'

The man slipped something into his trousers. Maybe a gun or a club. Something to protect the bossman. O'Keefe had heard that men like Barton had hired ex-soldiers as minders and drivers, and many of them were armed. Guns of any kind had been outlawed in the country under the Restoration of Order Act – even bird guns were taken from farmers – but armed bodyguards of wealthy men loyal to the Crown were known to be tolerated by the authorities. Still, O'Keefe wondered why Barton needed one. He was son and heir to one of the biggest employers in the city. Whether

Home Ruler or republican, the people of Cork needed work. O'Keefe would have thought that this fact alone would have been enough to ensure Barton's safety.

The man said, 'I'll ask if he can see you. Wait here.'

'And your name is?'

He turned back to O'Keefe, his hand on the door. 'Wait here.'

Moments later he returned.

'This way.' O'Keefe tried to place the accent. It was English, but sounded as if some of its edge had been lost to time spent in Ireland.

O'Keefe followed him inside, up a short flight of stairs, into the bright light of a back hallway. The floor was carpeted, muffling their footsteps. Framed photographs were arranged on the walls on both sides of the passageway. Before they reached the end, O'Keefe could hear voices, a man's and a woman's, coming from the room ahead.

'Mr Barton's only got a moment. Already told everything he knows to the last one of you lot what came round. Think you'd have got the picture then.'

They stood at the closed door to the parlour.

'And what picture would that be?' O'Keefe asked, assuming someone from Connolly's squad had interviewed Barton earlier.

A smile cracked on the security man's lips as he opened the door. The light in the parlour was much dimmer than in the hallway – only a side table lamp lit, a coal fire glowing in the grate. The room was decorated in much the same style as Hanratty's, but without the warmth or intimacy. Swagged curtains and overstuffed chairs. Lounging on a loveseat, her feet tucked beneath her, pumps lying on the floor, was a young woman with blonde hair cut in a short boyish bob. The style was all the rage in London and New York, according to the papers, but O'Keefe had never seen a woman with such short hair or such red lips. No, he recalled, he had seen lips as red but only in brothels.

Barton was standing with his back to the fire. O'Keefe crossed the room and extended his hand. 'Mr Barton.'

'Sergeant. We meet again.' His handshake was weak, his palms damp and warm. Releasing O'Keefe's hand, Barton nodded to the girl on the sofa. 'This is Miss Traynor, Sergeant. She's a … family friend.'

The girl giggled. Not as worldly as O'Keefe had first thought, nor as old. Most assuredly no friend of a family like the Bartons.

'My apologies for calling so late in the evening,' O'Keefe said. 'I've a few more questions I wanted to ask you regarding Deirdre Costelloe.'

'Certainly. Anything I can do to help.' Barton clasped his hands behind his back, all business. Nothing to indicate he was at all surprised or discomfited by O'Keefe's visit, but at the mention of Deirdre's name, O'Keefe noticed the girl had glanced anxiously at Barton and then away.

'If Miss Traynor would excuse us?' O'Keefe looked pointedly at Barton, waiting for him to dismiss the young woman so that they could speak in private. Barton ignored him, lifting his glass from the mantelpiece and taking a drink.

'Drink, Sergeant?' He held up the glass.

'No thank you.' O'Keefe took out his notebook and pencil, flicking through the pages until he came to the one he wanted. Brass tacks, he thought, looking up at Barton. 'How well did you know Deirdre Costelloe?'

Barton smiled. 'You asked me that very question when you visited my office.'

'All the same, Mr Barton.'

'Have you cause to assume my answer will have changed?' When O'Keefe didn't answer, Barton said in a monotone as if he'd grown tired of some game. 'She was a typist, as I recall. A pleasant, punctual girl.'

O'Keefe looked back down to his notebook and scratched a note to himself. He looked up after a long moment. 'Did you have a relationship with Miss Costelloe?'

Barton stared at O'Keefe for a time before answering. The smile was gone from his face. 'I did not. I can't imagine why you might think I did.' He looked down at the girl on the sofa. O'Keefe followed his eyes and saw that the girl had picked up a cushion and was cradling it in her arms.

'Now, if you wouldn't mind taking your leave, Constable. I'm getting rather tired of being bothered by the police about a matter that is of no concern to me. This is the second time, no, the *third* time I've answered questions about a girl I hardly knew.'

He must have seen the flicker of surprise in O'Keefe's

eyes. The smile returned to his lips. 'Yes Constable, *third* time. You didn't know, did you?'

'I've been in the field a great deal.' O'Keefe felt the heat in his face. A bite of anger in his gut. He pressed on. 'Do you know how Deirdre Costelloe died, Mr Barton?'

'I read the papers, like every other man and dog in the street.'

'Do you know how Mr McKenna died, sir?'

'Mr McKenna?' The smile dimmed.

'The man you played cards with last night. He was murdered after he left the card game.'

'Of course, Charlie Bannon jingled earlier with the news. Dreadful.' He took a drink. 'And no, Constable, I've no idea how he died.'

'Were you in the war, Mr Barton?'

Annoyance rode hard in Barton's voice. 'What does my service in the war have to do with any of this?' He gestured with his glass and took another long drink.

'Trench raiding? Hand-to-hand fighting?' O'Keefe watched Barton's face.

'I know where you're going with this, Constable, and it's tiresome.'

'*Sergeant.*'

Barton set his glass down and stared at O'Keefe. Menace seeped from him like mustard gas. 'You know what time I left the card game, so you know I couldn't have killed the man. I wasn't happy losing to him, *Sergeant*, but it's not as if I couldn't afford the loss.'

O'Keefe rifled through his notes. 'Do you belong to a club, Mr Barton?'

'I belong to several. I'd invite you along but somehow I don't think you'd appreciate the favour.'

'Any clubs here in Cork? One hosting private parties? Girls carted in from Madam Grace's for entertainment?'

Barton laughed. 'No, but I wish I did belong to such a club! Sergeant … How did you make sergeant, anyway?'

'My predecessor was shot.'

Barton's eyes showed nothing; no amusement, no pity. 'Shame.'

'Did you have sexual relations with Deirdre Costelloe?' There was a pleasing meanness to the question and O'Keefe almost smiled, remembering what Hanratty had said of Barton's injuries from the war.

'Get out of my house, Sergeant.'

'Right, then. Thank you for your help,' O'Keefe said, shoving his investigation diary into his briefcase, snapping its faulty clasps. He started for the door.

Barton's voice was like a fusillade from a hedgerow. 'Does your DI know you're investigating a murder that's already been solved? That you're harassing loyal citizens of the Crown when you've caught the man who committed the crime of which you're accusing me? Does he, Sergeant?'

'Did I give you the impression I was accusing you of a crime, Mr Barton?'

Barton held O'Keefe's stare for a long moment, then turned back to his drink without answering.

O'Keefe left the parlour, striding past the row of framed photographs on the wall. Barton on horseback. Barton in hunting gear holding a dead stag by its antlers, cigar clenched between his teeth. Barton in his mess dress uniform. He stopped, taking a closer look at the photograph of Barton in his regimental best. Looking behind him down the empty hallway, he heard the girl's voice and the low, muffled reply. Before he could think about it, O'Keefe snatched the photograph from the wall and shoved it under his belt, buttoning his coat over it.

Twenty minutes later, O'Keefe was on Washington Street, on the fringes of the Marsh. Curfew had long since fallen. Behind him he heard a shout and pounding footsteps. He ducked into a doorway and drew his revolver.

Hard-soled shoes slapping the footpath, panting, the flapping of open trenchcoats. And then they passed, running hard, three men. A flash of steel in one of the men's hands. The whine of the armoured car engine came next. A mounted searchlight painting the street with glare. Splashing light into the doorway where O'Keefe was hiding. He pressed himself further into the shadows as the car approached and tried the door. It opened. A narrow entryway and then stairs leading up. No light on the landing. A man's voice.

'Who's that there? Who's come in now? We want no trouble here.'

O'Keefe stayed silent.

'I'm telling you, if you don't answer me I'll throw open my

window up here and shout for the police, me thinking you a common robber.'

He weighed his options. 'I'm not a robber. Just caught out after curfew is all.'

There were low voices above. 'Are you one of the proper lads then?'

Options, O'Keefe thought. Choose one. 'I am … just waiting it out. Won't be a bother to you.'

The voices again, murmur and dispute. A woman's voice joining her man's.

'You're welcome then, so. Only we've no food, boy. None we can spare if you'll forgive us. We're wanting ourselves.'

He holstered the Webley. 'I'll only be a moment, until the street is clear. I'll be no trouble to you.'

'God bless you then, son.'

The woman's voice. 'And up the republic!'

The picture frame in his trouser waist dug into his stomach, reminding him of its presence. He took it out and removed the glass by touch, putting the photograph into his briefcase. He carefully set the frame and glass against the wall at the bottom of the stairs. A small token of appreciation, he thought, smiling to himself, from the proper lads of the IRA.

He stepped out of the doorway and back onto the city's streets.

O'Keefe hadn't considered it before, but wondered now if business in the knocking shops had suffered since curfew had been imposed. He imagined it had, as he hugged the shadows of the empty, cobbled laneways of the Marsh, hand inside his trenchcoat resting on the grip of his Webley, heading for his last stop of the evening.

A wedge of light slanted through the heavy, red curtains. There was light in the crescent of glass above the doorway. O'Keefe scanned the street in both directions as he mounted the stone steps to Madam Grace's. The street was void of life and it was not yet half-past nine in the evening. Eyes were on him though. He could feel the assessing weight of them on his back.

The same bruiser as before answered the bell. He didn't seem to recognise O'Keefe.

'Ye doing any business at all?' O'Keefe asked him.

The big man stood back and held the door open. 'Always doing business, boy. No point closing when legs can always open.'

It was a practised line, delivered with a well-worn leer and O'Keefe wondered, as he entered the house, if the doorman's head was still sore from Starkson's blow.

'Right this way,' the doorman said, directing him to the parlour to the right of the stairs.

O'Keefe stepped into the room and took in the two girls lounging on sofas. The room smelled of sickly sweet perfume rather than the stale smoke and booze he had smelled three days earlier. The two girls were wearing robes of silky material and one of them smiled at him from where she was reclining on a sofa against the wall. She made no move to get up, holding her bare legs out to the fireplace.

'Care for a drink?' The doorman went behind the small bar.

'Whiskey,' O'Keefe said, stepping over to the bar. 'And I need a girl. There's a particular girl. One with curly, dark hair, big eyes, big ...'

'Bella,' the doorman said, taking a bottle from the bar shelf. 'She's working at the moment.' He studied O'Keefe more closely now. 'She'll be busy for a while, boy. One of these two won't do you?'

O'Keefe wondered when the man would suss him. 'I'm sure they would if I was looking for any girl, but tonight only Bella will do me.' He tried a smile.

Recognition flashed in the big man's eyes. 'You're one of the ...'

O'Keefe had his Webley jammed up under the man's jaw before he could swing the bottle of watered whiskey. 'Don't,' he said.

'Never crossed my mind.' The big man's speech was slurred with the pressure of the muzzle. The smiling girl looked away, but the other girl put down her magazine. Lit a cigarette. Settled in for the show.

O'Keefe hoped to disappoint her. 'I don't want to give you another beating. I need talk to Bella is all. Now where's the boss?' O'Keefe had to pause to think of his name. 'Noonan, is he upstairs?'

A smile formed over the man's gritted teeth. 'Noonan's out. For fucking good. Your lads did a right number on him, I'm telling you.'

He relaxed the revolver under the man's chin a little. 'Put down the bottle.' He watched while the doorman set the bottle gently on the bar. 'What lads are you talking about?'

'Your lads. The ones … Can you put that down?'

O'Keefe lowered the revolver and holstered it. The doorman rubbed the soft flesh under his chin, checking his hand for blood.

'The ones who came with you and gave me the hiding, two, three days ago.'

'They've been back since?'

The doorman nodded, rubbing his chin again. 'Same night. Took Noonan with them and he hasn't raised his head since.'

Mathew-Pare and his boys. And they had interviewed Barton as well.

'Who's running the shop now?'

The doorman smiled. He held out his hands, palms up. 'At your service, sir. Brendan Coffey's the name. Anything you care for, it's on the house. Bygones be bygones, I always say. Always keen to do the Peelers … the *police* a turn, I am.'

O'Keefe returned the smile. This man's promotion was similar to his own. Expedited by the sudden, violent removal of another man.

'Bella's room. Which one is it? Top on the left?'

'You've been here before then?' The newly promoted whoremaster winked and poured a dram of whiskey into the glass he had set for O'Keefe and drank it.

O'Keefe didn't bother knocking. He knew the doors were kept unlocked for the girls' safety.

The man's head snapped up as O'Keefe entered the room. He was behind Bella, naked and pink, thin red hair going to grey at the sides, a corpulent, well-fed face unmarked by wind, rain or sun. O'Keefe thought of Councillor Ryan, and a dart of anger pierced him. The man was standing, working at Bella's backside or working at himself, O'Keefe couldn't tell which. Bella was on the bed on her hands and knees, her shift pushed up, the skin of her back pale and opaque. She had a look of bored vigilance on her face, putting up with the stout man floundering behind her. A working girl earning her crust like any other, but wary of any pain the punter might cause her in the bargain.

'What's this?' The punter's voice was indignant and scared.

O'Keefe crossed the room in long strides. 'Get dressed and get out!'

Bella rolled away from the man and pressed her back against the bed's headboard, bringing her knees up to her chest and pulling her shift down to cover them.

The naked man instinctively covered his cock and balls with one hand. He raised the fist of the other. A mistake. 'Who do you think you are. I paid –'

O'Keefe jabbed him in the throat with stiff fingers and the man gasped, holding his neck, his pink face blossoming red. He gawped for air and went down on one knee.

On the bed, Bella smiled up at O'Keefe. 'You're the

copper was here about Janey and that other girl, the one from Barton's Works.'

'I am,' he told her, taking the punter's clothes up from a chair and throwing them out the open door into the hallway. He pointed at the man. 'You. Shift it!'

The man lumbered to the door and out into the hall.

O'Keefe turned to Bella. 'Sorry about that.'

She smiled brighter now. 'Don't be. I've his money already. And he'll be back. Can't stay away from Bella, he can't, curfew or no.'

He pulled the photograph of Barton in uniform from his briefcase and set it on the bed. He did the same with Deirdre's and Janey's. Bella – with her brown ringlets and full bust, cleavage white and translucent, her wide brown eyes so innocent and beguiling, O'Keefe could almost understand why the pink man would be back – picked up Barton's picture, giving it a good look. She didn't touch the girls' photographs but instead leaned over to her nightstand and took a cigarette from a tin box and lit it. Blowing out smoke, she said, 'I'll tell you what you want to know, Peeler.' The innocence faded in her eyes and her smile was hard. 'But you'll pay me, by fuck. Or I'll tell him you're on to him and he'll pay me a sight more than you ever could. Only for he's a fierce cruel bastard and that boy of his, Bill Cole, would give you the shivers in places you've never had them. Only for that I'll tell you. If you make it worth me while, Mr Peeler.'

Just as quickly as it had gone, the innocence was back

in her eyes and her smile softened. O'Keefe took his wallet from his jacket pocket. He smiled, handed her two pound notes and reckoned that Bella would get on just grand in life.

———

In the dark, he watched O'Keefe leave Madam Grace's and wondered if it wouldn't just be better to kill the copper. Drive the tip of his knuckle-duster pick up into his brain and be done with it. Done enough already though, the boss had said. Follow the bastard and make sure he's not sticking his nose in where it shouldn't go. Wouldn't have a thing to worry about if you hadn't done that card sharp last night, the boss said.

Not that he hadn't wanted it done at the time. Bloody country Joe taking the piss, winding up the boss 'til he couldn't take no more. And the girls? Why'd I have to do 'em the same way, he asks? 'Cause that's the way I do 'em, I say. You've your way, I say, I've mine, and let's leave it at that. Let me top the copper and it's bother over. Not yet, he says. Not just yet. This though, the little visit to Grace's? No, he was sure the copper hadn't stopped for a poke on his way back to the barracks.

He waited until the sound of O'Keefe's footsteps had faded in the night air. The copper knew now. Too many mouths about, telling tales out of school. Only a matter of time before the copper rumbled it. Whores. You can't trust fucking whores, not one bloody bit.

He dipped his hat brim lower. The knuckles of his right hand were covered in brass and held behind his back, the tip of the pick hidden in the folds of his trenchcoat. He mounted the steps of Madam Grace's. He pressed the bell and waited.

———

O'Keefe made it back to the Daly house without seeing another soul on the streets, sticking to the shadows, using laneways and alleys when he could. Damp pavements. Shot-out streetlamps. Distant sounds of revving engines, bursts of gunfire.

'There's the man himself,' Daly said, opening the door to O'Keefe. 'Fine chap you are, arriving back after closing time.'

O'Keefe held up a bottle of Paddy whiskey he'd bought from Brendan Coffey at Madam Grace's. He'd had to force the man to take his money, the muscle become master already seeking to cultivate his contacts in the police with a free bottle. 'I'd say it's watered a fair bit, but it'll do you.'

'Do *me*?' he said, as O'Keefe slipped into the house.

'And your good lady wife. I'm heading back to barracks. Wake up that fool of a DI and press for an arrest warrant for Barton and his man. I could use a cuppa for the ride though, if it's not too much trouble.'

'Sure, who's Barton when he's at home?'

Muireann Daly stood up from where she'd been sitting reading a novel by the fire. The kitchen of the small house was warm and well lit. A welcoming place. 'Never mind him for the moment, Séan. When did you ever go short of one in this house?'

'Never, Muireann. But it's late. I don't mean to trouble you.'

'Too late for the pub, thank God.' She smiled as she filled the kettle from a jug of water and hung it on its hook in the grate over the turf fire. 'Sit yourself down and take off your coat.'

O'Keefe pulled a chair from the table up to the fire, between Jim and Muireann's, but didn't take off his coat. 'I can't stay. I have to make it back and get my notes in order. Get things ready. That bastard Barton knows something. I have him. Once I pull him in, I can break him. I know I can.' There was something more as well – something he couldn't put his mind to that he knew would back up his arrest. Like a word one couldn't recall; there in the memory but inaccessible. It would come, he told himself, if he gave it time. It would come if he had Barton in front of him in an interview room.

'Whoa there, son. Pull the brakes a bit.' Daly sat down and stirred the coals of the fire with a poker. 'You know you're going to put the mockers on the DI's commendations, medals, knighthood and general elevation to grand poo-bah of the RIC with this. He won't take it well at all, at all.'

'No, but he won't have a choice when I lay it out for him. I have proof that Barton knew the three victims. All killed in the same manner. I can tie him to all three. Well, to two of them, killed in the same way.'

'*Three* victims?'

'One: James McKenna. Farming equipment salesman. Played cards with a shower of toffs, Barton being one of them. Mopped the flagstones with Barton, so the word is.

Found behind the Central Hotel with a tiny hole in the back of his head. Same wound as Deirdre Costelloe's. Same cause of death.'

Daly considered it.

'They were seen leaving together, this Barton and the salesman?'

'No, Barton left later. This morning in fact.'

'Time of death?'

'About three, four in the morning.'

'Working girls use that lane behind the Central, you know that don't you?'

'A working girl who can kill a man instantly, one blow with an ice pick?'

'Stranger things under the sun.'

'Come on, Jim.'

Daly shrugged, not conceding the point but not rejecting it outright.

'So who's the third body? I can see the connection between Deirdre Costelloe and this card-player. Too much of a coincidence, both jabbed in the back of the head like that. But a third?'

O'Keefe told him about Janey Plunkett. 'I don't have it for certain that she was killed with a pick like the other two, but she did know Barton. She was one of the girls he brought to the parties.'

'Barton? Are you on about Richard Barton, as in the Tractor Works' Barton?' Daly said.

'The very same.'

Daly gave a low whistle. 'You know how to choose 'em, I'll give you that. Your first whack at a murder case of your own and I pull for you the biggest assassin in all of Ireland – a man with direct ties to your victim – and what do you do? You go out and try to pin it on the son of the second or third biggest employer in Cork.'

'What kind of parties were they?' Muireann asked.

O'Keefe turned to her. 'Card parties. Some kind of a monthly drinking club. Held in a Big House in the country. Near Bandon, the girl from the Marsh reckoned.'

'*Reckoned*? She doesn't know the actual house then?' Daly scoffed.

Lighting a cigarette and holding the box out to his friend, O'Keefe shook his head. 'I don't think it's a problem, but … The link is Barton. He brought Janey, Deirdre and Bella to these parties as the entertainment.'

Daly held up his pipe in place of the offered cigarette. 'Hold on a tick. You said the Costelloe girl wasn't on the game. You said she worked at the factory. A typist or something.'

'She did and she wasn't on the game. But she liked dodgy men. Her friend told me so and Bella, the working girl at Madam Grace's, confirmed it. Said Deirdre liked the attention she got from the men at the parties and liked to see herself as one of the "fast girls". But Bella thought she didn't like what went on when the card game ended. Said she only ever went to one of the parties and she didn't go back in the same car with the other girls. And then her body's found not a week later? The killer was at the party. Barton was at the party. He knows who else was. He's the man I need to pump. I've enough now to pull him in and sit him down at least.'

Daly thought about it for a minute, puffing on his pipe, filling the room with tobacco smoke. 'So you've got it on the word of some young doxie that Barton knew Deirdre Costelloe and … who was the other girl?'

'Janey Plunkett. Connolly put me on to her, said she was doing private parties for a rich fella. Bella confirmed it. Ended up dead in a lane just over a month ago.'

'And she was stabbed in the head as well?'

'Officially? No. She was throttled, but the surgeon who did the post-mortem did it for form's sake. Never looked under her hair. With bruising at the throat, he wrote it off as a run of the mill strangulation. An angry punter or some mad-in-the-head with a thing about working girls. Of no importance.'

'So you're assuming that because the Plunkett girl knew Barton and worked these parties and is dead, she must have been killed in the same way?'

'Exactly.'

'Exactly my arse, Seán. Did Barton admit to knowing either of the girls?'

'No, but …'

'Exactly. He didn't. So, what you have is the word of a doxie against the word of a gentleman whose father employs half of Cork.'

'I believe the girl in Grace's.'

'Did you pay her?'

O'Keefe shrugged and looked away.

'You don't know how this girl died, Seán. And you're on dangerous ground speculating against a man like Barton.'

'Dangerous? You don't know dangerous, Jim. Sure, did I mention who the guests at the card parties were?'

'Tell us,' Muireann said.

'I think Bella's words were something like "a fat shower of Tommy officers and brass caps. Can spot an officer a mile off I can."' He did his best Bella impersonation.

Daly laughed. 'You're done, man; you know that, don't you? You may as well pack your kit and get used to the wind because you'll be stuck in some outpost barracks so far out in the country, you won't even know it's Ireland until the first Shinner bullet hits you.'

'Masterson will have to let me bring him in.'

'And what, you'd have Connors cut loose?'

O'Keefe shot Daly a hard look.

Daly knew the look. 'Go on, say it. Tell me to fuck off with myself. She's heard worse.'

'There'll be no hard talk in this house, boys.'

'Don't mind her. You should hear her when she gets going, Seán. Make a sailor blush, she would.'

'They don't make sailors like they used to,' Muireann said and O'Keefe smiled. The fire was warm and he took off his coat. She came over and took it from him, handing him the bottle he'd brought and three glasses. 'Here, get that into you while you're waiting on your tea. And fill my glass. I've earned it, putting up with that yoke there by the fire.'

She put a plate of bacon sandwiches on a low stool between the two men and returned to her chair. O'Keefe took a sandwich. It was wonderful. A hearty smear of butter and thick salty rasher of bacon. Soft, warm white bread. The whiskey chased it down like a whippet after a hare.

Daly said, 'You're going to want to be clever about it, Seán. This whole thing. You get transferred to some two-man outpost and you'll be no good to anyone. You got Connors. He might not have killed the girl, but he's killed others.'

O'Keefe swallowed and said, 'This is not about Connors, Jim. He didn't kill Deirdre Costelloe. Or Janey Plunkett.'

'Not that you've any idea how Janey Plunkett was killed or who killed her.'

'Nor did he kill the poor McKenna chap who got his last night. Look, Connors is a bold boy. And he's locked up where he belongs. I'm not investigating this to clear Connors. He's getting what he had coming. Not that the Turks couldn't have done me for the same thing.'

'That was different, Seán,' Muireann said. 'You were fighting a war.'

'What are the likes of Connors and his lads fighting then? And at least they see some good coming out of all the killing.'

'You'd make a fine, grand writer of editorials for the *Irish Bulletin*, Seán. Ideas like that. You're not thinking of changing sides?'

O'Keefe's eyes felt heavy. He knew he needed to move but, for the moment, the Daly kitchen was too warm, too homely, the conversation too kind and tricked with banter. He decided to wait another few minutes. The road home would be cold and maybe deadly. Dark. A few more minutes of this. This, he thought, just before his eyes closed and sleep took him, is what men need: kind company, a warm hearth, good food and whiskey. And somewhere behind this was the image of Katherine Sheehan, and bracing the image was the dull ache of knowing that he could never have this with her.

O'Keefe heard Daly say, 'I'll shift the kids into our bed.'

And Muireann then: 'Leave him where is for now. He's smiling with his eyes closed, sure.'

'He won't be smiling once tomorrow comes.'

At the edge of sleep, O'Keefe sensed that, for once, Jim Daly wasn't joking.

When he was posted to the Western Front there was a lull in the fighting. The bated calm only sporadically broken by the crack of distant sniper fire. The stench of death was everywhere, awakening his senses, making him giddy, light-headed.

His first meal in the trenches, his section spooned bully beef stew from the steaming dixie. A full tin dish of it. It never occurred to him not to like it. They fed you in the army. Three times a day. Sometimes more.

One of the older soldiers in his section, a corporal from Maidstone, called him over, during that first hot meal in the trenches. Told him to go ask the supply sergeant for the ration of beer for the men and be bloody quick about it. He went, setting his steaming tin bowl of stew on an ammunition box. The supply sergeant in a support trench was almost amused by the request. 'What you think this is, eh? The bloody King's Arms? They're having you on, mate.'

When he returned to his section, his bowl was empty, the older corporal smirking at some of the other men, one a lad he had considered a friend from the abattoir, joining him. He asked the corporal first. 'Where's my grub gone, then?'

The older man answered, 'Where's my beer, then?' Some of the others laughed openly, their spoons scraping the sides of their tin mess kits.

The man who would soon become known as Birdy was hungry. As he had been all his life. No emotion showed on his face. None had since he was a boy. His boot connected with the corporal's face as he took a bite of stew. Birdy's stew. Like the spiked hammer at the abattoir, his kick was easy, guiltless and bludgeoning. It took three men to pull him off the corporal before he had the chance to stick his bayonet in the man.

When all was done and dusted, the platoon sergeant let the matter drop, despite the corporal's blackened eyes and shattered teeth, despite Birdy's drawing of his bayonet from its scabbard. There was a big push coming and they needed the bodies. Besides, it wasn't on, taking a man's grub like that. And Corporal Dutton had always been a rum bastard, just asking for the kind of sorting the young lad had given him.

Corporal Dutton was killed some weeks later on a night patrol. Stabbed in the back of the head and left in a shell hole. No one had heard or seen it happen, but his body was found some days later when the trench line advanced.

Friday
3 December 1920

It was nearly nine the next morning when O'Keefe and Daly made it back to barracks on the Trusty.

'Where's the DI? Is he in?'

A young constable looked up from his newspaper at the day-room table. 'His office, Sergeant. He was asking after you.' The constable tried to bury his smile but couldn't. O'Keefe read in the smile what he needed to know.

Daly also saw the constable's smile and clapped O'Keefe on the back. 'Been lovely working with you, Seán. Be sure to write.'

———

'Sir?'

Masterson's door was half-open and he was sitting at his desk. He looked up and said, 'Close the door behind you, O'Keefe.' His batman, Senior, sat on the couch, his legs crossed, looking over his eyeglasses at O'Keefe as if he were a specimen from a museum or zoo.

O'Keefe stood at parade rest in front of the desk, as a dark wellspring of anger flooded the DI's face.

'Sir.' O'Keefe started, directing his eyes to the picture on the wall behind the desk, Masterson and Colonel … what was his name? *Prentice*. Best pals, hunting. 'I've had a development in the Costelloe case. You told me to keep you informed of anything that might arise in the –'

'The Costelloe case is closed, O'Keefe. Closed.'

'Sir, I have information –'

'*Closed*. And if I hear of you harassing the good citizens

of Cork again … people under daily threat of assassination, good, loyal people –'

'People like Richard Barton?'

'I'll have you up for disobeying a direct order. And quitting your post.'

'I was on leave, sir. Signed out and given leave by yourself.'

'Don't you be fucking smart, O'Keefe. Do you understand me? Connors is the killer.'

'Connors is *a* killer, sir, but he didn't kill Deirdre Costelloe. I am this close to finding out who did. Two killers off the streets, sir. One stone.'

At this point, Senior spoke up from his place on the couch. 'Have you heard any more from your sister, O'Keefe? Will you be attending the wedding?'

O'Keefe looked hard at him. He let his eyes rest on the man's face until Senior could bear it no longer and looked away. O'Keefe turned back to the DI. 'Two birds with one stone, sir.'

'You'll be breaking stones, O'Keefe, if you continue.'

'Continue doing my job, sir? Continue trying to find a killer of young women? A butcher with an ice pick, who rapes and kills women, who murders travelling salesmen?'

The DI's eyes flickered and O'Keefe realised that he hadn't heard about the most recent killing. Masterson was silent for a moment. Then he said, 'As of now you are suspended from duty and confined to barracks. You are hereby relieved of the post of acting sergeant.'

He lifted a sheet of paper from his desktop. The bastard, O'Keefe thought, seeing that Masterson had had the orders for his suspension drafted in advance of his arrival back in barracks.

'*Any further involvement of innocent civilians in unauthorised investigations will be punishable by court-martial, under which penalties are as follows: Expulsion from the constabulary. Or, immediate reposting and fine upon the salary of an amount as yet undecided.*' He looked up. 'Any questions, O'Keefe?'

'Just one, sir. Do you even care who killed the girl?'

'Yes, O'Keefe, I bloody do. And he's bloody downstairs in our bloody cells.'

'He's not the killer, sir.' Welts of anger rose on O'Keefe's cheeks, his scar beginning to spasm. 'Richard Barton knows who the killer is.'

'You're correct, O'Keefe. He does. Anyone who's read yesterday's paper knows who killed that girl.'

'Connors isn't Deirdre Costelloe's killer, sir.' If he repeated it enough times, maybe it would stick.

Masterson took a cigarette from a teak box on his desk and lit it, a smile dancing at the edges of his mouth. 'If Connors isn't the killer, why did he confess to it last night?'

It was O'Keefe's turn to stop. He confessed? Memory flashed. What was it Mathew-Pare had said? *Make the devil himself tell you what you wanted to hear.*

'Will that be all, sir?'

'Your sidearm, Constable O'Keefe. And your identity card.'

O'Keefe unholstered his Webley and set it and his RIC identity card on Masterson's desk. His dress sword was hanging in the press in his office. Senior's eyes tracked him as he left.

On the landing outside the DI's office, O'Keefe passed Reilly.

'Trouble with the bossman, Sergeant?' A smile like the young constable downstairs. Nothing like some sap with his backside on the grindstone. Grain for the cons' gossip mill. O'Keefe found it hard to be angry with the man. He'd been the same himself once.

'Sure, you know yourself Reilly.'

'That I do, Sergeant. That I do.'

O'Keefe made to pass him but Reilly grabbed his arm. 'I'll be heading up to Dublin. See a sister of mine.'

'That's grand,' O'Keefe replied, distracted.

'You should go away yourself. Take some leave.'

'I'm confined.'

'Ah, go way out of that. Boss'd be happy to be shot of you for a few days.'

'I'll give it some thought, Reilly.'

'You do that, Sergeant. Don't take too long, mind. Things happen quick these days. Sometimes it's better to be out of the way when they do.'

Back in his office, O'Keefe unlocked his desk drawer and removed the pistol he had taken from Keane, a 1911 .45 Colt automatic. He checked the load and holstered it.

Daly looked on, feet on his desk. He spoke around the

pipe tucked in the side of his mouth. 'You'll drop into us, now and again, Seán? Let us know how you're getting on. Post us a letter from Boston?'

'And you'll water the flowers on my grave, Jim?' He took a box of .45 cartridges from another drawer and emptied them into his suit jacket pocket, then pulled on his trenchcoat.

Daly said, 'There you go again, trying to make more work for a fella.'

O'Keefe didn't knock.

Mathew-Pare was jabbing out an intelligence report on an old typewriter in the converted stable cottage. Starkson and Eakins were with him, Starkson on the bed, boots on, reading a copy of the racing pages. Eakins was seated by the fire, eating beef stew from a tin for his breakfast. A large bottle of Beamish stout stood on the floor beside his chair.

Seeing O'Keefe, Mathew-Pare folded the page he was typing down out of view. He turned in his chair.

'Sergeant. This is an unexpected surprise.' The bland smile. A hint of mockery behind it.

O'Keefe said, 'You lads have had a couple of late nights of it.'

'What ever do you mean, Sergeant?'

Eakins looked up from his stew. Starkson rested the newspaper on his chest, still supine, but his legs now uncrossed. Disapproval brewed on Eakins' face, as if unable to believe someone would dare interrupt his breakfast. O'Keefe felt that he would be happy to machine-gun the three of them and then go off and get his own breakfast in comfort.

'How badly did you hurt Connors before he told you what you wanted to hear?'

Mathew-Pare lit a cigarette, the smile never leaving his face. 'Not as badly as we could have. Did we, Starksy?'

'Relatively soft, sir. Needed a bit of prompting is all.'

O'Keefe said, 'Just in from the neck down, *Detective*. Isn't that what you said? Just lending a hand where needed?'

'I was *asked* to question Connors, Sergeant. Your DI was rather insistent, in fact. Wanted credit for the confession so the scary mob in Dublin couldn't claim it, I dare say.'

'*Question* him. Is that what you're calling it these days?'

The Englishman shrugged and smiled. O'Keefe's fists clenched involuntarily and Starkson noticed. He folded his paper neatly, creasing it back for future reading.

'And did he insist you make the pimp Noonan disappear? Question Barton without telling me?'

Mathew-Pare shook his head. 'Sergeant O'Keefe, it's been a pleasure working with you. You're to be commended, you know. For netting Connors. Promoted. Posted out of this war zone. You've done well. I only hope I've helped.'

'What did Barton tell you?'

Starkson sat up on the bed. O'Keefe took a step closer to the table where Mathew-Pare was sitting. Mathew-Pare indicated to Starkson to stay where he was. He held out the packet of Gold Flakes to O'Keefe. 'Smoke, Sergeant?'

O'Keefe ignored the offer. 'I'm bringing him in. I'll find out what he knows …'

'One way or another?' Mathew-Pare smiled. 'That's where men like ourselves are necessary, Sergeant.' He gestured at Starkson and Eakins with his cigarette. 'When men like Connors – men like this Barton in your immediate case – when they don't give you what you want one way, we are the other. Let us know if you need our help.'

'You've been helping someone. I just haven't worked out who it is yet.'

Mathew-Pare cast out his palms, open to the sky. 'We're fighting the same war, Sergeant.'

'I'm investigating a crime, not fighting a war.'

'Same thing, different means, Sergeant. One day you'll understand that.'

Mathew-Pare took a satisfied drag on his cigarette before continuing. 'It's in your interest to let this go, O'Keefe. You know that, don't you? No one will reward any further examination of the subject. As far as the mandarins are concerned, Connors is your man. He confessed himself. Remember that. Signed his name to the charge.'

'I'm looking for the truth. I couldn't give two fucks what you squeezed out of Connors.'

'*Looking for the truth* …' Mathew-Pare repeated the words as if it was the first time he had considered the concept. He smiled and exhaled a thin stream of smoke. 'I'd do less of that Sergeant, if I were you.'

'Is that a threat?'

Mathew-Pare shrugged. 'Call it friendly advice from one who knows better.'

Their eyes locked for a long moment. O'Keefe could feel Eakins and Starkson, poised, ready. The small fire in the grate smouldered in the silence. O'Keefe felt the weight of Keane's gun in his holster.

'Anything else, Sergeant?' Mathew-Pare asked.

———

As O'Keefe crossed the yard, he watched the DI leave the barracks and get into his Daimler. Senior cranked the starter and sat in behind the wheel. The DI noticed O'Keefe and watched in turn as he crossed the yard, making for the barracks.

Officially confined.

If O'Keefe was going to do anything, he would have to do it now, before word of his status had done its rounds on the rumour mill, if it hadn't already. And he needed help. Daly was out of the question. He would come. He was that thick – family and home be damned – and that good a friend that O'Keefe would never ask him. The man he needed was drinking coffee with a sergeant and corporal from the Liverpool's regiment in the day-room, just in from patrol. O'Keefe beckoned him out into the hallway.

'Fancy a jaunt into town, Finch?'

Finch smiled. 'I 'eard the DI 'ad your balls for breakfast, Sergeant.'

The jungle drums had beat even louder and faster than

he thought. 'It's *Constable* now Finch. Demotion as well as castration. Are you coming or not?'

'You gonna get me shot at again?'

'I'll try my best.'

'Mufti, is it?'

O'Keefe nodded.

'Gimme five minutes to get my glad rags on.'

O'Keefe turned to go. 'Oh, and Finch? Grab two shovels from the shed, would you, please?'

Finch stopped. '*Shovels*? And I thought I'd done my bit digging trenches.'

———

As the war slugged on, the men in his section came to treat Birdy with distant respect. New men came in to replace the dead and invalided and learned who the killers in the company were. The loonies. And Birdy was top of the pile. They called him the name openly and he didn't mind. Birdy. They tolerated the fact that he spent his free time in the pigeon croft and with the laying hens; that he kept a pigeon in his dug-out with him, warm against his chest inside his greatcoat. He was half-cracked Birdy was, they said amongst themselves when he was out of earshot. But so were most of the lads in some way or another.

And they had seen Birdy work. He volunteered for every trench raid or night patrol going. One of the lads he'd joined up with from the abattoir – the spiked hammer and boning knives a distant memory now – told the others that Birdy had always been good with a blade.

It wasn't long before the young intelligence officer assigned to 'C' company took notice. An Irish chap, the young lieutenant. Not hard on the men, most thought, but a bit windy. On the lookout for someone to watch his back. Most of the men agreed that a chap like the Lieutenant would have done better to have never joined a fighting regiment such as the Royal West Kents.

———

Saint Finbar's cemetery, south-west of the city, was typical of its kind – headstones, Celtic crosses, wilting flowers, the crumbling remnants of a medieval chapel. To O'Keefe's surprise, Janey Plunkett's grave wasn't unmarked. It had a simple headstone that read: *Jane Mary Plunkett. 1903–1920. Requiescat in pace.*

It was Finch who asked the question. 'Who paid for the 'eadstone?'

Lorcan Connolly, dressed in his usual dandified style, smiled, sad and ironical at the same time. 'A sentimental gesture, sure. I indulge myself now and again. I'd known the girl since she was a snapper. And she was a fine bloody tout.'

'Never took you for the soft-hearted kind, Connolly,' O'Keefe said.

'All the best coppers are, Seán. It's what makes us different from our friends across the water – no offence, Constable Finch. The Irish are unafraid to sentimentalise the hopeless cases, the lost causes, the young dead whores of the world. The English save their tears for the King. And their dogs.'

Finch looked at Connolly and tried to decide if he was mocking him personally. He decided he wasn't. 'None taken.'

'You're a gentleman, Finch. Yet another difference. The English don't take offence with half the alacrity of us Irish. The Irishman resorts to violence at the slightest provocation. Betimes no provocation is needed at all. Someone said that once.'

Finch looked as if he had no notion of what Connolly was on about. ''Ow long's she been in the ground then?'

'Six weeks,' Connolly said, 'God rest her. Say she could use a bit of air by now.'

O'Keefe looked at Connolly. 'I thought you were a soft one.'

'Only so much heart to spare, Seán.'

O'Keefe turned to see the surgeon approaching. In the daylight, Major Wells looked close to death himself, his cheekbones gouging the ashen skin of his face. O'Keefe could smell last evening's whiskey on him from several feet away.

'Thank you for coming, Major Wells.'

'At your service, Sergeant.'

O'Keefe didn't see the need to inform the surgeon of his demotion. He was fairly certain Wells would help him for the right reasons regardless, but with drinkers, he reasoned, a fella never knew. The Major had seemed the right sort when he'd done the post-mortem in Ballycarleton. A man who felt for the dead. Like Connolly. Unlike Connolly, however, he was paying the price for his solicitude in alcohol.

'How long as she been interred?' Wells asked, after he had shaken hands and been introduced.

It was Finch who answered. 'Six weeks, Doc. Think there'll be anything left of 'er?'

Wells considered the question seriously. 'Depends on the condition of the box she was buried in, soil temperature, rain, et cetera, et cetera. Bring her up and we'll see.' And then he blessed himself.

Seeing the mild surprise on O'Keefe's face, he said, 'Yes, Sergeant. Slave to Rome, same as yourself. Why I'll never make General.' He smiled as if at the notion of something so ludicrous and indicated the shovels lying on the ground at the foot of the headstone. 'You do have authorisation for this, Sergeant?'

Connolly responded. 'Sure, as a fellow Catholic you'll understand, Major. Did Christ himself – bless His name – have authorisation when he raised Lazarus?'

The pained smile again. 'Will this help catch the killer of the girl I worked on at your barracks?'

O'Keefe answered. 'I think it will.'

'Shall we start digging then?'

Finch and O'Keefe took shovels and sliced into the damp, heavy soil. At one point, O'Keefe stopped to rest. He scanned the graveyard, seeing no living soul among the headstones in the grey autumn daylight. And yet he was certain suddenly that they were being watched, as certain as he was that day on the hillside when they had found Deirdre's body. Goose pimples washed over him and he went back to digging.

The mud-slicked lid of the coffin came off with a shrieking of nails, the wood on the surface soft and rotting, underneath hard and holding its contents firm, resisting a return to the earth.

The smell was overwhelming at first, summoning memories of the war; the constant, inescapable scent of decomposition, of mortality. Finch remained impassive, but stepped back. As with O'Keefe and Wells, the smell was a part of his past, lodged in the memory of his senses as firmly as the scent of his mother, of stale beer or London fog heavy with coal smoke. Connolly, O'Keefe noticed, turned a shade of green that would have done the Shinners proud.

'Jesus, lads,' the Crimes Special man said, covering his nose and mouth with a silk handkerchief.

The surgeon stooped to Janey Plunkett's withered body, smaller in death, sunken in on itself, skin sloughing from bone. He handled the head carefully, as if it were an heirloom. He lifted the girl's hair. It had been thick brown once but was the shade of tarnished brass now, life's colour gone, but clumps of it resolutely clinging to the mouldering scalp. Wells worked at the loose skin at the base of the skull with gloved fingers, peeling it up and back, puffing a protective veil of sweet pipe smoke in front of his face. The skin came away easily as if from a boiled onion. He pointed now at the glistening skull revealed and O'Keefe leaned in.

'There,' he said. 'Same wound.'

O'Keefe touched his shoulder. 'Thank you, Major.'

'Just find the bastard, Sergeant. Then we can sit down and finish that Bushmills.'

Wells didn't smile as he said it. He looked as if he wouldn't mind joining Janey in the ground: quiet, safe, finished with a life so steeped in violence.

———

The Hispano-Suiza was gone when O'Keefe and Finch arrived at Barton's house in Montenotte. They tried both doors of the redbrick house then stood under the coachman's archway.

'Do we wait for them, Sergeant?'

O'Keefe's idea – formulated on the ride over from the cemetery – had been to lift Barton and his man at the house and get them to Tuckey Street barracks where Connolly was softening the ground with the head constable. The man was a 'good skin', according to Connolly. Once they didn't take the piss, the head would go along with things, he had assured them: an old-style law and order type who had worked his way up to his present rank and was known to despise the cadet officer system generally, and District Inspector Masterson particularly. But the deal was only on if it was done quick. Word of O'Keefe's troubles would be general to the county by the day's end. The Tuckey Street Head Con would help, Connolly had told him, if it meant putting the screws to Masterson, but only if the man could deny his knowledge of O'Keefe's demotion and confinement to barracks.

'Police work, Finch, is as much about waiting as doing.' O'Keefe offered him a cigarette.

They hadn't waited long when a black Ford pulled up in front of the gates to the Barton house and two men in trenchcoats and scuffed boots sauntered up the drive. A third man stayed in the car with the engine idling.

'Fine day, lads,' O'Keefe said, thumbing the safety off the .45 in his holster inside his coat as the men walked towards them.

'You won't find them two here, so you won't,' the one on the left said. He wore a trilby, cocked back on his head, and the collar of his trenchcoat turned up like a London cornerboy, though it was a mild day.

'Why's that?'

'Because we're entertaining them at the moment.'

'And you are?'

'You don't know that, boy, and you're not half as clever as they say you are.'

The men stopped in front of O'Keefe and Finch.

'I've a fair idea,' O'Keefe said, resignation in his voice. 'You followed us from the graveyard?'

Trilby nodded. 'You've to come with us now. There's lads want a word.'

'Will I get to question Barton?'

The one on the right, in a flat cap, smiled. 'We're just to collect you. You can talk to the boss when we get there.'

———◦—◦———

Men armed with rifles stood watch at the gatehouse. They stared after the Ford as it sped through the open gates of Burleigh House. In another, more peaceful time, they could have been gamekeepers on guard for poachers. It all came together for O'Keefe in the Ford as they rolled up the tree-lined drive to Burleigh House – what had been eluding him, dodging his conscious mind for the past two days. Deirdre Costelloe had written in her diary that she was hoping 'D' would take her to his club. For 'D' read Dickie. How had he missed it? *She liked to run with the fast girls, but I don't think she reckoned on what she'd to do after the cards were finished*, Bella had said. Parties, the Madam Grace girl had told him. *Like a drinking club, meets once a month for a laugh or three and a bit of slap and tickle.* He remembered Hanratty's account of the party his friend had attended. *In some pile in the country.*

Once a month maybe, Bella had continued. *They had one on Sunday two weeks past. And that girl, Deirdre, was there. Not the place for her, when the fun started. After the cards. She kicked up a fierce hubbub, screaming blue murder like one of the gentleman was after trying to kill her instead of give her an honest turn. What did she think she was in for anyway? Some of the men left then, which was happy days for us with less rope to pull.* And the girl, O'Keefe had asked, did she return to Cork with ye? *No. Bill Cole said he drove her home early …*

It was the regiment that linked the men. It seemed so obvious now, he didn't know how he could have missed it. He had stood in front of the banner in Burleigh's library and then listened while Hanratty had told him that Barton had fought with the West Kents. And Masterson's friend Colonel Prentice, of course. Sitting in the DI's office selling Seamus Connors like a quare butcher pushing bad meat at the close of day, pushing Connors like there was no one else in the world who could have killed Deirdre. McKenna might still be alive if he'd seen it. Heatherfield too. Even Noonan, the pimp. Rage knotted itself in O'Keefe's gut. Someone would pay for their deaths. Theirs and Deirdre Costelloe's and Janey Plunkett's.

They stopped in the circular drive and got out. More armed men were lounging on the stone steps and patrolling the edge of the forest. All of them watched as O'Keefe and Finch were escorted up the front steps and into Burleigh House. O'Keefe didn't imagine the IRA men would take kindly to using the tradesman's entrance. Not after eight hundred years of it.

Once inside, one of the Volunteers asked them for their pistols.

'Why don't you try and take it off me, mate,' Finch said. The young Volunteer raised a Webley and pointed it in Finch's face.

'No sense of 'umour, you lot.' Finch smiled as he handed over his own Webley by the barrel. O'Keefe gave Keane's .45 to the second Volunteer.

The three Volunteers then showed them into the drawing-room, its walls covered with faded, peeling flower-print wallpaper. Dusty sheets were thrown over chairs and Ottomans, a grand piano standing silent in the corner of the room. The chairs were occupied by men like the ones who had collected them. Enfield rifles and two Winchester pump shotguns rested against the piano with their stocks on the floor. O'Keefe wondered where they had got their hands on those. Taken them after the Kilmichael ambush, most likely. Dogs knew the Auxies loved their Winchester pumps.

A fresh fire crackled in the marble fireplace and O'Keefe watched as Mrs Gannon – the old woman O'Keefe had met on his first visit to the house – entered the room and began handing out sandwiches and steaming mugs and odd china cups of tea from a large tray. Seeing him, the woman smiled warmly.

'Sergeant, there you are again. Sure, you'll have a bite, won't you? You must be starved from the long road,' she said, as if O'Keefe and Finch were invited guests. She handed O'Keefe a plate of sandwiches.

O'Keefe smiled and helped himself. 'Thank you, Mrs Gannon. I will. Finch?' Finch took two.

'I'll have tea along for you lads in a tick now. You just sit down there by the fire and make yourselves at ease.'

One of their escorts, the driver, cracked a smile. The gunman with the flat cap was angling for a sandwich. O'Keefe held the plate out of reach.

'That'd be grand, Mrs Gannon. Tea would be lovely.'

She smiled again before turning to the men in the sheet-covered chairs by the fire. 'Get up you boys and let your guests warm themselves. Have ye no manners at all on ye?'

The Volunteers at the fire looked suitably chastened

and obeyed the old woman. So this, O'Keefe thought as he scanned the room, was what a flying column looked like. The men were young, most of them, seventeen to twenty-four or twenty-five at the oldest. Their faces were smudged with the sweat and dirt of a long journey and their clothes were rumpled, as if they were used to sleeping in ditches. And yet there was a quiet confidence about them. They were fit lads, of the kind seen on hurling pitches any Sunday afternoon in Ireland. Young men like he himself was once. Before all the shooting started. These young sportsmen now hefted rifles so comfortably, so naturally, like the thousands who had fought in the Great War. It was as if God had made young men with killing in mind, O'Keefe decided, and He had loved His creation so much, He never wanted war to end.

The drawing-room door opened and the men rose as one. They didn't come to attention, as they would have in a conventional army, but they stood. This was deference, discipline and respect that men chose freely to express. Respect and discipline without the coercion of regular armies. Two men entered the room and O'Keefe and Finch instinctively stood as well.

A week earlier, O'Keefe would not have thought it possible that he would ever be standing face to face with Seán Brennan, Head of Intelligence, West Cork Brigade. The man looked older than the dated photograph of him that was posted in every RIC barracks in the county. There was a good deal known about him because he had been one of the founding members of the Volunteers in West Cork in the days before the 1916 Rising. Among other things, he was thought to be a member of the secret organisation known as the Irish Republican Brotherhood, along with Michael Collins and many of the highest-ranking members of the IRA.

With him was a younger man who looked vaguely familiar to O'Keefe. He was in his shirtsleeves, the cuffs rolled up over thin, freckled forearms. It was a boy's face on the brink of becoming a man's.

Brennan extended his hand and O'Keefe shook it. 'Sergeant,' he said, 'thank you for coming at such short notice.'

O'Keefe nodded. 'Not that I had much choice. And it's Constable now.'

Brennan shrugged, as if the whole situation was rife with absurd humour. 'Sure, you'd never have made the trip otherwise.'

The IRA man handed O'Keefe a sheaf of papers, pinned together at the corners. 'These are the signed statements of the men we have in custody. Details of the girl's murder are listed and the statements are sworn and witnessed by a serving judge of the republican courts. His name, naturally, has been left off the documents. It will be made available when circumstances allow.'

O'Keefe flicked through the pages and saw names he recognised. The card players, officers just as Bella had told him. And another name that shocked him, but perhaps should not have. He shook his head at his own innocence. Masterson. How could he not have seen it? Still, it would take time to read the statements and assess their degree of truth. Even in his haste, however, he could see that the name Barton featured prominently in the statements.

He looked up from the papers. 'I hardly think that these would hold any water in a court of law, Mr Brennan, knowing that they were made at the end of an IRA gun barrel.'

'What better incentive could there be to tell the truth than saving one's own skin, Sergeant?'

'In my experience, it gives a man more incentive to lie.'

'And was that your experience with Seamus Connors?'

O'Keefe could feel his face redden. 'Seamus Connors told me only that he didn't kill Deirdre Costelloe. He told me that he loved her and that he had a solid alibi, one that you, of all people, could probably confirm. He wasn't touched when I questioned him. There are others involved in this investigation with their own motives and means. It's not the way I work.'

Brennan nodded. 'You understand then, why it's important to us that the truth of this matter be made public.'

'I do,' O'Keefe told him, 'only why do you need me to do it? You lads seem to have the newspaper war half won.'

Brennan acknowledged the truth of this without pride.

'Yes, but we want confirmation from your end, Constable. It's all well and good for our supporters to believe that we don't go around butchering young women like that lot in there, but it's those who would never believe us who have to be convinced.'

'And what makes you think I want to push your story,

Mr Brennan? Your mob has shot friends of mine. Good Irishmen every one of them.'

'I was under the impression that you didn't think of it as a question of our story or yours. I've been led to believe that you think of it as a matter of truth or lies. That you're a good man, Constable. Is that true? Are you a good man?'

O'Keefe didn't know how to answer. He thought back to how he had broken his parent's hearts; led his brother to the slaughter of a foreign war for reasons he could hardly remember; and in that war killed many men, most of them probably good men themselves. 'No, I'm not a good man. But I try to be a fair one.'

He turned to Brennan's young subaltern. His eyes. He had seen them in the cave when he was taken to the Skelly brothers, he was certain of that, and now he remembered where he knew them from. *Farrell*. His father, the draper from Newcestown, a sot, always tearing it up in some pub, barred from most in his own town and eventually in Ballycarleton as well. How many times had he helped the son drag his father home to his wife and shame-faced daughters? Years back; it seemed another life. O'Keefe asked young Farrell, 'Did your father think I was a good man? Did *you*?'

The young man blushed. He looked to Brennan, who said nothing, and then back to O'Keefe. 'If I didn't, you wouldn't be alive now.' The bravado in his voice rang false.

O'Keefe turned back to Brennan. 'Can I question the suspects myself, Mr Brennan?'

'Of course.'

'And you'll release them to my custody so that they can be arrested and tried?'

'To be tried at court-martial, by their fellow officers, who have no evidence of their guilt and only praise for their past records?'

There wasn't a lot O'Keefe could say. 'I have evidence.'

'You have supposition and circumstantial evidence, which you've done well to get. But you've nothing that would stand up in any court without the confessions we've got.'

'Confessions at gunpoint aren't known for their weight in court.'

'And confessions obtained under torture are?'

Again, O'Keefe felt heat rise in his face.

'I take your point,' Brennan continued, 'but the stories match. The information we have confirms the truth of the confession.'

'I thought you said *confessions*.'

'We have one confession and the truth behind it.'

'You think.'

O'Keefe's eyes caught a flash of sky blue passing one of the windows outside the house. Barton's Hispano-Suiza. O'Keefe said, 'Do you mind if I search the motor?' He reached down and picked up his briefcase. The men sitting against the wall stirred.

'Anything to help, Constable.' Brennan looked amused.

O'Keefe walked past Brennan and patted young Farrell on the shoulder. 'Come with me.' Brennan followed them out.

The Hispano-Suiza was parked in front of the house on

the circular drive. O'Keefe took two photographs from his briefcase, handing them to Farrell before opening the car's luggage boot.

'What is it in the pictures?' Farrell asked.

'It's the imprint left in the mud by a plank of wood used, I'm certain, by whoever it was brought the body to the hillside. By Barton or his man, Cole is it? I'm hoping …' O'Keefe said, leaning into the Hispano's boot and rooting among the tools and blankets, shoving aside a half-full case of burgundy wine and an empty picnic basket, 'I'm hoping that I might find it in here.'

But there was no plank of wood in the boot nor inside the car. O'Keefe stood with his hands on his hips.

'I took these photographs at the site where the girl's body was found. We knew some form of transport was needed to bring the body there. One of our men spotted ruts in the ditch. The car used to transport the body had become stuck in the soft ground at the edge of the path, we assume, when it was turning to leave the hill. Deirdre Costelloe mentioned a blue-coloured car in the diary we found in her rooms. Called it his Fancy Spaniard. Barton was "D" in the diary. "Dickie", one of his acquaintances called him. For Richard. He was the card player who'd been courting her, if that's what you could call it.'

Farrell said, 'It's the same car Mrs Gannon spoke of when she came to me. A lovely blue motor. She took a lift back to her niece's in it, the night the Costelloe girl was here. The night we know she was killed.'

'Mrs Gannon was here that night?'

'Not for long,' Brennan said, 'she was visiting her niece in Bandon and returned late that night. There was a commotion of some sort and the Major asked Barton's man to drive Mrs Gannon back to her niece's. She said he didn't seem to want her about the place.'

Barton's man. Bella had called him Bill. 'One of the other girls who was at the house said that his man had taken Deirdre home early. Bill something ...'

Brennan nodded. 'Cole. Bill Cole. Driver and minder. We're holding him with the others inside. He served under Barton in the war.'

'The West Kents?' O'Keefe said.

'It would seem so.'

'There has to be proof. *Has* to be. Here,' Farrell said, 'has one of ye a lighter?'

Finch handed him his. Farrell sparked the lighter, leaned into the boot and, like O'Keefe, rummaged among the detritus, taking time to remove the picnic basket, the wine crate and the blanket, handing the last to Finch.

'Fuck it anyway,' he said, staring into the empty boot. 'We have the confession.'

'It's a weak case without any hard evidence, Mr Farrell. The defendants will claim coercion,' O'Keefe replied.

Farrell said, 'Look, we have the earring Mrs Gannon gave to me. We can prove she was here by matching it with the one that was found on her body.'

'And how would you know about that, Mr Farrell?' O'Keefe asked, but smiled.

Farrell blushed and Brennan said, 'Ways and means, boy. Ways and means.'

'Still,' O'Keefe said, 'that only proves she was here, not that anyone present killed her.'

Frustration showed on Farrell's face. 'Fuck it anyway,' he said again, taking the basket and wine case up off the ground, roughly shoving them back into the boot. Finch handed him back the blanket and brushed down his coat, sending dust and ephemera from the blanket floating into the still, damp air.

Farrell tossed the blanket in after the other things and was about to close the boot when O'Keefe said, 'Mr Farrell, take that blanket back out, would you? Carefully now, and set it out on the ground, there.' He stepped closer to Finch as he spoke. 'Don't move, Finch.' He reached out and plucked something that was clinging to the cashmere above the Finch's breast pocket, holding it up between his thumb and forefinger for the others to see.

'Now,' he said, 'Mr Farrell, could you open the blanket out? Gently, so.'

Farrell folded open the blanket on the wet gravel drive as Brennan examined what O'Keefe held in his fingers. The Intelligence man smiled.

'Is that hard enough for you, Constable O'Keefe?'

The touring blanket was a standard feature of many luxury motor cars – along with the picnic basket – and was stitched with Hispano-Suiza in a flowing script to match that of the grill work on the car. The blanket was a deep blue with gold stitching, making it all the easier to spot the stray, downy feathers that had lodged themselves in the wool weave of the blanket.

'Hard enough,' O'Keefe said, 'when you consider this as well.' He squatted beside the blanket and pointed to a glossy, black, 'C'-shaped stain on its corner.

Farrell crouched beside him and appeared confused for a moment before his face blossomed into a smile, one that exposed his youth to the world. He reminded O'Keefe of Keane – of how Keane had been once, before all this.

'Tar, boy,' Farrell said. 'It's fuckin' dry tar!'

O'Keefe couldn't help smiling. 'That's police work for you, Mr Farrell.' He took out his patrol diary and noted the find, the date, time and place, and those present on discovery. 'The smallest thing can turn a case. Something that seems unimportant at the time. Half a copper's job is documenting the details. Most of them you won't use, but some that you think are of no importance, a clever prosecutor can use in ways you never thought of.'

Farrell's expression darkened, as if he was suddenly ashamed of his excitement. 'And if you can't find any evidence, you can always fabricate some for the sake of the court-martial judge. That's police work too, Constable, wouldn't you say?'

'It happens,' O'Keefe said, 'but not on my watch.'

Brennan turned to the young man. 'I was led to believe Constable O'Keefe was more than fair to you and yours, Mr Farrell?'

Farrell's face washed red and he looked down at the blanket.

Brennan turned back to O'Keefe. 'Would you care to question the prisoners yourself now?'

'I wouldn't mind hearing their version first-hand.'

'I think you're entitled to hear it, Constable.'

———

Bill Cole killed his first prostitute on a two-day leave before the second battle of Ypres. He couldn't have said at the time why he'd done it other than it didn't seem to matter – one more death.

He had wanted to see her privates – wanted to see inside the place where, in his mind, the eggs came out and she wouldn't let him. She had taken offence somehow, though he couldn't understand a single foreign word she'd screamed at him in the roofless, shell-pocked cowshed where she'd taken him. She was once a fat girl who had grown thin on the war, her skin slack, stretch-marks etched across her belly and sagging breasts, her breath smelling of vinegary wine, between her legs reeking of garlic and fish and sweat and semen.

Yet she was proud and angry and spiteful towards him when all he had done was look at her down there. He had money after all. And he had his Boche-poker. He and some of the hardened night raiding gang had made them themselves: knuckle dusters with a welded six-inch spike fashioned from a French pig-sticker bayonet. One blow with the poker was all it took usually. Like the hammer back in the abattoir.

When the whore was dead, he took his time with her. He saw where the eggs came out and he thought how the whore reminded him of his mother and he felt good, spilling his seed into the private place where the eggs came from.

───────

Two Volunteers stood guard in the library. When O'Keefe entered the room, they went to lean against the wall and watch. The Major was tied to his desk chair. His face was red and smeared with blood, and he was shaking. O'Keefe reckoned he'd been given a slap or two but he wasn't badly injured. He guessed that forced abstinence – there was a whiskey bottle and a half-full glass just out of his reach on the desk – was the primary cause of his suffering.

A second man was bound to an upholstered chair set against the wall, bleeding from his nose, his tidy moustache stained claret, staring straight ahead, a look of fierce bullishness on his face, as if he'd said all he was going to say. Colonel Prentice. DI Masterson's hunting pal. Bearer of the Childers letter, which O'Keefe now knew was a fake.

O'Keefe nodded to the men. 'Colonel. Major.'

The Major blustered, as if he'd been rudely disturbed from sleep. 'I should have known you were one of them. Traitor to your country, to the men who died serving with you.'

'*Traitor*,' O'Keefe said. 'Isn't that what you wrote on the sign you hung around Deirdre Costelloe's neck? Misspelled it, mind.'

'I had nothing to do with that. Nothing!'

'But you knew about it, didn't you? And let it happen – let a poor girl be butchered and then helped cover it up.'

Burleigh looked away. O'Keefe turned to the Colonel.

'Colonel Prentice. You tried to strangle the girl, am I correct?'

Prentice stared straight ahead in silence and O'Keefe wondered if he had been taking lessons from Seamus Connors.

'She didn't want to do what you had in mind, Colonel? Or you went too far with things – maybe squeezed a bit too hard? That's what's written here.' He gestured to the statements taken by the IRA. 'Major Burleigh's words, Colonel, not mine – that you're the poo-bah of the club. Says that each month a different member brings you a girl as an offering. Mostly whores, the Major says, but then this time, Barton brings Deirdre Costelloe. A beautiful young woman. A virgin, I'd imagine. Only she didn't fancy being offered to you, Colonel, did she? The whole house heard the ructions. The lot of you thinking you'd killed her when she resisted – your little Hellfire club. And then you had your friend Barton and his batman clean things up for you. Is that how it went, Colonel?'

The Colonel sniffed back blood.

'Except she wasn't dead. Not yet, she wasn't.' O'Keefe said, turning back to Burleigh.

The Major pleaded from his chair, his voice high and wheedling. 'We'd no idea what that beast would do. Don't you see?'

'But none of you saw fit to come forward when you found out what he'd done.'

'You don't understand.'

'Oh, I understand. You West Kents stick together. Tight lot, you lads. And now you're going to die together.'

'You need to take us in, Sergeant. Arrest us for God's sake, man.' There was terror in Burleigh's eyes, in his voice. One of the IRA men against the wall muttered something to his comrade and they both smiled.

O'Keefe said, 'I don't think they're going to allow me do that, Major. You could have told me what you knew when I came to you three days ago. A fine young constable died because you lied to me. A businessman guilty of nothing more than beating Richard Barton at cards.'

'I didn't know what to do.' Burleigh's bloodshot eyes welled with tears.

Bile rose in O'Keefe's throat as he watched him. *How many men did this fat sot send to die in his time?* 'The feathers came from your birds, didn't they, Major?'

The Major nodded. 'But it wasn't my idea. I never knew what he'd done to her until after ... until I read about it. Like everybody else.' A sob broke in his throat. 'Jesus, I didn't know. The man's insane.'

'To do your dirty work?' O'Keefe turned. 'Colonel?'

Prentice's eyes locked on O'Keefe's and for the first and last time that day, he spoke.

'Let's get this done with, Sergeant, shall we?'

———

One morning, the sun heating the mud of no man's land, raising the stink of the dead, 'C' company of the West Kents had taken a hundred yards of German trench. And then the Germans had counterattacked and had taken it back. The fighting had been close and brutal, and Birdy's hands and forearms were drenched in blood as he dragged the young lieutenant back out of the German trench, shrapnel from a potato masher grenade riddling the young man's legs and groin.

As he pulled the lieutenant over the pocked, steaming earth, the Boche machine-guns stalked the surviving West Kents as they retreated across the waste.

Birdy dragged the lieutenant into a shell-hole deep enough for cover. Some time later, the lieutenant calmed himself and made Birdy a promise. His father, he said, was a very wealthy man, back in Ireland. He'd be taken care of, Birdy would, if only he'd help him. Birdy would never want for work again in his life if he helped the lieutenant survive the war.

And the lieutenant had kept his promise. There was always work, after all, for a man of Birdy's certain expertise.

————

In the scullery two more young IRA men watched over Richard Barton and Bill Cole. Both of them were bound with their hands behind hard-backed chairs. They had bruising on their faces and Barton had a cut on his forehead that had been bleeding heavily, blood running down his cheek and neck into his collar.

'Which of you killed her?' O'Keefe began.

Barton's man looked up and smiled. 'I killed the cunt.'

O'Keefe was stunned for a moment, as much by the tone of Cole's voice as by the admission of guilt. *The man was proud of what he'd done.* He continued, 'And did you enjoy it?'

Bill Cole smiled wider and O'Keefe studied his face. High cheekbones and close-set, blue eyes. A thin slit of a mouth and regular, straight teeth with a small gap between each one. Thinning fair hair. O'Keefe sensed the man's strength, even tied to the chair. Looking closer, he saw there was a deadness in Cole's blue eyes, a vacancy he'd seen in men in the war. A vacancy still there in some who had come back. At times he'd seen it in his own face when he looked in the mirror.

'I did,' Cole said. 'And I enjoyed doing the whores as well. Not enough time with them for my liking, but needs as needs must.'

'Janey Plunkett?'

'Don't know what her name was – a skin and bones, young brown-haired bitch is what I knew. And Bella. Curly-haired Bella.'

'Bella? You couldn't have, I was –'

'Watched you leave, Sar'nt. Popped in for an old poke. Don't mind seconds, me.'

O'Keefe felt his insides twist. He swallowed back his rage. 'And the salesman, two nights ago? The card player.'

Bill Cole turned to Barton. 'He insulted us, didn't he sir? Taking the mick, he was.'

Barton shook his head. 'I never wanted you to kill him, Bill.'

Gone was the game-cock he'd been in his home the night before. O'Keefe felt a stab of pleasure at this and then guilt. This man was going to die today and there was nothing O'Keefe could do to prevent it. 'Or the girl. I didn't, Sergeant. You have to believe me. I only asked Bill to drive her home.'

It was O'Keefe's turn to shake his head. 'But you brought her here for Prentice. Why? What did that girl think you were bringing her to?'

Some defiance came back to Barton's face, his voice. 'She *knew*. She liked it, the flirting and the bold talk.'

'Well ripe, she was,' Cole interjected, as if reminiscing. 'The fruit in her box spoiled from the mind down. The Lieutenant here,' Cole nodded at Barton, 'had her well spoilt in the mind. Only ready for a bit of poking to make her bits agree. That's us: work together, always have. The Lieutenant works on the mind, the holy Catholic souls of these butter-wouldn't-melts. And it's others get to do the actuals.'

'Shut up, Bill. Shut your fucking mouth. I never knew what you were at.'

'Course you did, back as far as the war. You knew, but you turned a blind one 'cause you knew you'd never survive without old Bill at your back. We was a great old team at tearing down the butter-wouldn't-melts and their holy Catholic cunts.'

O'Keefe had thought that Barton held the reins on Cole,

but was wondering now if, in the end, Cole had been more than Barton could handle. As if reading O'Keefe's thoughts, Barton said, 'I didn't know what he was doing. Honestly, I didn't.'

O'Keefe ignored his plea. 'Where did you kill her, Cole? When the men asked you to take care of her?'

Cole appeared pleased to be asked. 'Right there in that old cottage on the hill. Nice and cosy, it was. Every time I drove by it with Mr Barton on our way out here, I said to myself, *Bill, there's a place where you could work in peace.* Dodgy enough getting there at night with these chaps,' Cole nodded at the two Volunteers, 'all over the roads like maggots on old meat, but I got there.'

O'Keefe remembered the fresh ashes in the fireplace of the derelict cottage, the staining on the makeshift table. 'Where did you get the birds, the feathers?'

'Right here, Sar'nt. Took his last couple of beauties when I took the girl. Shame to kill them but we had a fine grub-up that night.'

'And the tar?'

'Here again, mate. What farmer with his wits about him don't have a tin of tar in the shed. "Nelson's Coal Tar for Veterinary Complaints of the Skin."' He smirked at O'Keefe.

'But why did you cut off her breasts? Why did you mutilate her?'

Cole's face brightened. 'Because I fucking could, is why. How's that serve you, Sar'nt? Because I wanted to and I could.'

O'Keefe had to stop himself from driving his fist into

Cole's mouth. He turned to Barton. 'District Inspector Masterson. Did he know about Deirdre Costelloe, Mr Barton? Was he here that night?'

Barton hesitated.

'There's no point keeping him out of it, Barton. Sure, he was no West Kent, was he? Do you want him to be the one who walks away from this with his bib clean? You're not walking away; you know that, don't you? But you can make sure that Masterson doesn't either.'

'He was here as Prentice's guest, just like all the other times. Had his man Senior drive him back to your barracks when things got out of hand. He took Prentice with him as well, with some Tommies who'd been on sentry outside, running escort. Great friends, the Inspector and the Colonel. What the Inspector wouldn't do to help his friends.'

'You're sure about this?'

Barton nodded. 'The DI loved the bints. Every time a club night was mooted, he'd ask me, *Are you bringing the lovelies, Barton?* He was like a child in a sweet-shop.'

O'Keefe thought of the DI and the Colonel, how they had pushed the Childers letter at him. He imagined them tapping a friend in the Documents Office up in Dublin Castle for a favour; the forged letter flown down special delivery with Connors' file. And it came to him now clearly: how everything they had done had served to lead him away from themselves and towards Connors. It had been a lucky break for them that Deirdre Costelloe had once been courted by the IRA man. Could a more convenient scapegoat for their mess have been invented? But O'Keefe had somehow stumbled onto the truth. With the help of the IRA.

'If it's any consolation, Mr Barton, I'll have Masterson for this as well,' he said. 'I'm afraid there's nothing more I can do for you. If you'd spoken openly to me yesterday or the first time I interviewed you …'

Bill Cole looked up at O'Keefe. 'Don't you worry about us, Sar'nt.'

One of the Volunteers shifted the rifle from his left shoulder to his right. A new recruit by the look of him, better suited to tramping hillsides than standing guard over a snivelling Barton and his deranged bodyguard.

'Have you searched these men?' O'Keefe asked the Volunteer.

The older of the two guards answered. 'You mind your business, Peeler, and we'll mind ours.'

O'Keefe persisted. 'Did you find the murder weapon? I didn't see any mention of it in the file.'

'He had a Webley and half a dozen spare rounds, Peeler, which we fucking took off him, didn't we? We know how to search –'

Bill Cole suddenly stood up, as if he had grown bored with the conversation. Somehow his hands were free from their binding and they went to the table, gripping it, lifting.

The younger of the IRA men scraped back his chair, his rifle dangling from its strap, butt against the floor. The table hit him, flipped up and over before he could get his rifle up. Cole shielded himself with the table as he moved, his right arm swinging, the colour of brass flashing, knuckle-duster sheathing his fist, lethal pick protruding, the pick driving, jabbing in lightning fast blows into the neck of the young Volunteer. Arterial blood sprayed, a red plume, drenching Barton who remained tied to his chair.

O'Keefe jumped back to avoid the table, its legs in the air, ploughing into the older IRA gunman, the man dropping his rifle in the scramble. O'Keefe went for the rifle on the floor, had it, when the IRA man wrenched it from O'Keefe's hands. O'Keefe stepped back as Cole stepped around the table legs, advancing towards O'Keefe and the Volunteer with graceful, weaving steps.

Odd, grunting silence in the struggle. Flashing images. The young Volunteer slumped on the floor, hands at his throat, the spew of blood slowing, pooling, his legs kicking in the crimson morass. Barton covered in the dying man's blood, struggling against his bonds in the centre of the storm. The older Volunteer raising his rifle. A shot, explosively loud in the scullery. The shot missing Cole. Barton's head snapping back, blood, brain and bone painting the white wall behind him. Cole now knocking the rifle aside easily, driving the pick into its owner's heart. Cole's momentum driving him forward, slamming through the scullery door and into the hall. The sound of pounding steps. A shot, two more shots.

O'Keefe sprinted down the hall and out onto the steps in pursuit of Cole. A shot cracked and split the stone beneath his feet. The IRA men watching the house had been taken by surprise and were firing at any moving figure. O'Keefe raised his hands and roared at them to cease firing.

He watched Cole's sprinting form making for the forest at the far edge of the drive. 'He's there, he's there!'

'Hands up! Keep your fucking hands up, boy!'

O'Keefe did what he was told. 'He's getting away, for Jesus sake! He's made the trees!'

'Keep your hands up. He's going nowhere.'

As Cole made the tree line – some hundred yards from where O'Keefe was standing on the steps of Burleigh House – the crack of a rifle shot sounded. A muzzle flash and puff of gunsmoke from within the shadow of the woods and Cole stumbled, then dropped as if a rope had been pulled across his path. His limp form skidded in the soft earth and came to an abrupt halt. A Volunteer emerged now from the tree line, rifle at his hip. Before others could arrive, the Volunteer pointed the barrel of his Enfield down at Cole and pulled the trigger. Bill Cole's head jumped in the mud and then was still. The Volunteer shouldered the rifle and strolled towards the house.

'I told you he was going nowhere, not with Mickeen Cope in them woods,' one of the men behind O'Keefe muttered as he escorted him back into the house.

A while later, O'Keefe stood with Brennan and Farrell in the hallway outside the scullery, watching as the bodies of the dead men were removed.

'Are we free to go?' he asked. Waves of fading adrenaline shook through his frame. He was tired, of no more use to the IRA, but confident he and Finch wouldn't be harmed.

Farrell watched Brennan carefully.

'In the morning,' Brennan told him. 'Hate to inconvenience you, but that's the way it has to be.'

'I need to question the DI. He was *here*. The night Deirdre Costelloe was murdered.'

Brennan nodded. 'The DI will be taken care of.'

'I can't allow that, sir. You know I can't.'

A bitter smile cracked on Brennan's face. 'And you've a choice in the matter?'

'He needs to be tried for his crime.'

'Which was?'

'Aiding and abetting a criminal act. Accessory to murder. Obstructing an investigation. He'll be given jail time, Mr Brennan.'

'And you can guarantee this?'

O'Keefe was silent, knowing that he could guarantee nothing.

'I thought not,' Brennan said.

'So you'll have him shot and he'll die a martyred servant of the Crown, instead of serving sentence for the crime.'

'We'll work his reputation to the best of our abilities in the Press, Constable. Otherwise, I couldn't care less how he dies. His reputation will matter very little in the new republic.'

'If it comes.'

'When it comes.'

'And the other two? The Colonel and the Major.'

'See for yourself.' Brennan turned away from the scullery door and beckoned for O'Keefe to follow him.

To his back, O'Keefe said, 'There's nothing I can do to stop you?'

Brennan paused. 'Nothing.'

The stone slabs of the yard shone wet and slick. Thick grey clouds dredged the sky, menacing further rain. The Major and Colonel were on their knees in the centre of the yard, a grim-faced Volunteer standing behind them holding a boxy Mauser pistol in his right hand. Tears cut a clean path through the smeared blood on the Major's face. The Colonel stared straight ahead, his face red with rage or fear or both. Chickens pecked the ground at the periphery of the yard.

O'Keefe watched as young Farrell walked over to the kneeling men and took a folded sheet of paper from his tweed jacket. It was a jacket cut for a larger man.

Farrell cleared his throat. 'You have been found guilty of the crime of treason against the people of Ireland. You have been found guilty of the crimes of murder and conspiracy to commit murder by a court sanctioned by the democratically elected provisional government of the Irish republic. The penalty for these crimes is death.'

He folded the paper neatly, tucked it into his jacket and walked back into the house.

The man with the Mauser stepped forward and put a bullet in the back of the Major's head. Then the Colonel's. The shots echoed off the walls of the cowsheds. Chickens stopped their pecking, ruffled their feathers and then resumed.

Brennan turned to O'Keefe. 'If you ever consider working for us, Sergeant O'Keefe, we need good men for when the republic comes. Men like yourself.'

'You make it sound like a train due in, the republic.'

'Can't you hear it coming?'

O'Keefe shrugged.

Brennan held out his hand. 'You'll get that out then.' He nodded at the briefcase at O'Keefe's feet, indicating the copies of the signed confessions and the evidence.

O'Keefe shook hands with the IRA man. 'Yes, I can do that much.'

'You're a fine policeman, Sergeant. It's been a long time since I've said that.'

'Funny how things work.'

'Strange bedfellows, boy.' Brennan turned to go. 'Enjoy your stay in Burleigh House, courtesy of the Irish Republican Army.'

———

Brennan should have known better.

Darkness descended and Mrs Gannon retreated to her rooms, leaving O'Keefe and Finch in front of the drawing room fire with more sandwiches and a fresh pot of tea. Finch had liberated the bottle of whiskey – overlooked by the departing flying column – from the Major's desk and he poured healthy measures into four tea cups. Two Volunteers, resentful at having been left to guard the Peeler and the Tan, decided to make the best of things and got stuck into the whiskey. Two hours of newspapers passed from one man to another, shared cigarettes – at first refused and then accepted grudgingly by the Volunteers – and strong drink had the desired effect.

Finch gave O'Keefe a signal. O'Keefe gestured back for him to go soft. There had been enough killing.

'Game of cards, lads?' Finch asked, standing. 'There's a deck I saw over on the table.'

He stood and strolled leisurely across the room, retrieved the pack of cards and doubled back behind the wing chairs where the Volunteers were lounging, senses dulled by the fire and the whiskey. He picked up one of the two rifles left on the floor and rested the barrel on the capped head of the Volunteer closest to the fire. 'Dear oh dear, lads. Not up to regs that, leaving loaded rifles down round the place.'

It occurred to O'Keefe that the two Volunteers might suffer for their lapse. Finch trussed them to their chairs, using their belts and braces as bindings. The Hispano-Suiza was still parked outside on the drive and Finch was grinning like a child at Christmas as he hand-cranked the engine to life.

'Mind if I drive, Sergeant?'

'Once you mind the ditches, Finch.'

It was after ten – under a half-moon in clearing skies – when they braked the Hispano-Suiza at the barracks.

Constable Barrett opened the steel gate and Finch played the lord – 'Very good chap, thank you, thank you there, my good chap.' He parked in the space next to the DI's Daimler and killed the choke. The silence was heavy after the purr of the engine.

He turned to O'Keefe. 'What's it gonna be, Sergeant?'

'I'm going to arrest him.'

'Would you not be better giving what you 'ave to your pal, Connolly? Let him and his head con pull him.'

It was the most reasonable thing to do but something told O'Keefe he might not get another chance at this. The sound of that rumbling train in the distance. *When, not if …*

Finch waited, then said, 'Or we could just go in and …'

'Only if he shoots first, Finch.'

———

Mathew-Pare and Senior were in the DI's office when O'Keefe entered.

'Ah, the man who never knocks,' Mathew-Pare said.

O'Keefe strode to the front of the desk where Masterson sat. He didn't bother with any preliminaries. He said, 'You were there, you bastard. You knew what that animal did to her. You weren't even one of them, one of their regimental pals. And you let them away with it. As if that young girl didn't deserve any better.'

'What in God's name are you on about, O'Keefe?' Masterson stood, his face reddening. 'Senior, arrest this man.'

Mathew-Pare, observed the confrontation as if he were only mildly interested.

Senior hesitated.

O'Keefe caught the batman's reluctance. He turned to Senior, keeping his voice low, steady. 'Sit down, Senior. Or I'll take you down with him.'

'You have no evidence on which to base these wild accusations, O'Keefe. None. Have you?' Senior asked the question but for once he didn't sound so sure of the answer. 'A man with known republican connections? Accusing a distinguished inspector of what exactly?'

Mathew-Pare intervened. The smooth voice of moderation. 'Sergeant O'Keefe, you know you're finished with this, don't you? This case is closed. No court-martial judge in the Empire would touch it. Not that you haven't done fine work. You could have a long career ahead of you.'

O'Keefe ignored him. 'You're not listening to me, Masterson. I've evidence against you and you are coming with me.'

'I'm sorry you feel that way, Sergeant O'Keefe.' Mathew-Pare again, cool, composed. 'You'll be a genuine loss to the Crown.'

O'Keefe turned to him. 'You may fuck the Crown. This is an Irish problem, Mathew-Pare. You've no part –'

Mathew-Pare held the small automatic pistol low, his gun hand resting on his crossed leg. He raised it now, drawing a bead on O'Keefe's heart. 'Not only an Irish problem, I'm afraid. I'm sorry, Sergeant.'

'Sorry for what?'

The DI spoke, appearing emboldened with the appearance of Mathew-Pare's gun. 'Take him down to the cells, Mathew-

Pare. Insubordination, disobeying a direct order. Senior, draft the –'

'There are signed statements, signed confessions,' O'Keefe said. 'Barton told me the whole story. About your pal Prentice and how you used Barton's man to clean up the mess he'd made with Deirdre Costelloe. And I'd wager Senior was there with you when the screaming started. Amn't I right, Senior? How'd it feel, finding out what Barton's monkey had done to the girl?'

Senior's eyes sought the ground.

'You'll have to hand over these statements, Sergeant; along with your files and any physical evidence,' Mathew-Pare said.

It was O'Keefe's turn to smile. 'You think I'd be fool enough to hold them myself?'

Masterson turned to Mathew-Pare. 'He's bluffing, isn't he? He doesn't have a thing.'

Mathew-Pare gave a lazy shrug. 'We'll find out soon enough if he is.' To O'Keefe he said, 'Shall we go now, Sergeant?'

'For a bit of a chat with you and your heavy boys, Mathew-Pare? Or are you going to shoot me? With how many other men in the barracks as witnesses?'

'I rather hope it won't come to that.'

O'Keefe raised his voice. 'What do you think, Finch? Jim? You think the *Detective* here will shoot me?'

The office door opened and Daly and Finch entered. Mathew-Pare held the automatic on O'Keefe, his face unmoved by the intrusion. Finch and Daly raised their own guns.

Masterson's face washed a paler shade of grey. 'This is outrageous. *Mutinous.* Put those guns down now or you'll be charged. Expelled from service, Sergeant Daly. Constable …' He couldn't remember Finch's name.

'Finch, sir. John Raymond Finch, number 155369, sir.' He turned his Webley on the DI.

And just then, the lower wall of the barracks exploded.

There were shouts and the anguished screaming of a man in pain. Heavy footsteps on the stairs. The crack of gunfire, from inside and outside the barracks.

Finch and Daly held their guns steady on the DI and Mathew-Pare, while Mathew-Pare held his on O'Keefe, eyes never wavering from their targets, despite the chaos below them. The DI moved slowly from his desk and lifted the telephone receiver from the box on the wall.

'It's dead.' His voice was weak and dry. 'The wireless. We can use the wireless.'

O'Keefe turned on his heel and walked out of the office. 'We're being raided, lads. We can shoot each other later.'

He heard Finch and Daly on the stairs behind him as the barracks fell into darkness.

Mathew-Pare found Starkson and Eakins waiting for him in the cottage. They had laid out their arms and were smoking.

'Gentlemen, it's time for us to scarper. Bandon will see the flares and Tommy will be here *toot-sweet.* We'll make a run into Cork then.' He took up a sheaf of papers from his desk and fed them into the fire. 'Eakins, pack up the motor. Anything you can't shoot or wear, burn it. Starksey, take care of our remaining problems, would you?'

———

Much of the front wall of the barracks had been blown in, taking part of the main steel door and most of the reception room with it.

Constable Declan Morris had been on orderly duty in reception when the charge had gone off – O'Keefe assumed it was a barrack mine, leaned up against the wall from the outside and detonated by a long line fuse – and now two men had him by the arms, ducking low themselves and dragging him down the main hallway. Bullets whizzed by and pocked the plaster of the inside walls, coming from the outside through the gaping hole. Morris' legs left a bloody wake behind him on the wooden floor.

The electric lights, having survived the initial blast, flickered and then went out, casting the barracks into darkness. For a moment O'Keefe froze, halfway to the bottom of the stairs. A wave of heat washed over his face and his memory was wrenched back to the *River Clyde*, the blood in the water and the savage hailstorm of bullets. The chaos. He squeezed his eyes shut and tried to obliterate the images. He knew he had to move. He heard Daly's voice on the steps above him; it sounded tinny and distant. 'What are we doing, Seán? Is it down or up we're going?'

O'Keefe opened his eyes and saw his brother. He was there on the stairs with him, the same panic on his face as was there in the moments before they stepped out of the steel hull of the *Clyde* and into ten thousand Turkish machine-gun rounds. O'Keefe closed his eyes again and when he opened them, Peter was gone. Finch grabbed his arm.

'We have to make it down, Sergeant, before the smoke clears.' Bullets splintered the steps below them, the sporadic impacts felt through the soles of their boots. 'You all right, mate?'

'Grand, Finch. Grand. Let's go.'

Finch leapt down the five remaining steps and swung left, passing the gaping front door, feeling the whizz of bullets pass his head as he threw himself into the day-room across the hallway from reception. He took up position behind the door and began firing his Webley out into the night, using the muzzle flashes of IRA rifles to guide his aim.

Daly headed for the back stairs and the lower ground-floor armoury. He passed a group of constables at the back of the hallway, taking cover behind the stairs. Heading down the steps, he met several others on their way up. They had lit paraffin lamps and had begun passing Enfields to the men waiting above.

O'Keefe felt a bullet nip the sleeve of his jacket under his arm as he rounded the bottom of the stairs, the smoke from the initial mine blast clearing, the Volunteers outside better able to see into the barracks' exposed innards. He made it to the cover of the back stairs behind Daly. Pounding up the lower ground-floor stairs were Barrett and Taylor, two of the Tans, both of them carrying lamps. O'Keefe stopped them. 'Has anybody manned the Lewis in the attic?'

Bullets slapped the wall across from them with deliberate regularity. They were under the front stairs and out of the line of fire but all of them flinched at the striking rounds. The shoulders of the Tans' uniforms were dusted white with plaster in the lamp-light.

'Get up there and start shooting. And set off the flares. With any luck, Bandon or Macroom will see them and give us a dig out.'

The two Tans headed for the main stairs without answering, Barrett saluting out of instinct. O'Keefe heard their boots beating the steps. The smell of smoke hit him. Burning wood and paper, over the acrid scent of cordite. Fire. *Jesus*. He jumped across the open hallway and ducked into the day-room from where Finch was firing. From this cover, he looked across the main hallway into reception and could see nothing but smoke and a faint orange glow. There was no way to put out the fire until the raiders had stopped shooting and O'Keefe wondered how well armed they were, how much ammunition they had. He thought of the column at Burleigh House and suddenly realised that they must be the attacking party. It was why Brennan had wanted him kept at Burleigh House for the night. The republican train was rolling into Ballycarleton barracks. He rapidly assessed the flying column in his mind. They were well-armed, well-trained, well-motivated. And now they had come to collect one of their own and punish one of his.

O'Keefe shouted to Finch, 'I'm going down to the cells.'

Finch knew why. 'Don't you give them that Connors bastard.' He fired two more rounds from his Webley into the darkness. 'And get me a rifle, Sergeant.'

O'Keefe ran back to cover under the main stairs calling for an Enfield. He slid it down the hall, staying under cover. A box of .303 rounds in charger clips followed. Finch gingerly reached an arm out of the day-room and retrieved them.

O'Keefe shouted again. 'You can keep them out of here, can't you?'

In the room to the left of the front door, Finch raised the Enfield and followed shadows down its sights. He fired once and his shot was returned by a fusillade.

'I've kept whole companies of Boche out of my trench. I'll keep these fuckers out.'

Daly came up the back stairs holding an Enfield and crate of ammunition. 'I'll head upstairs and see what I can pick off from the DI's front window. We have to fire from the upstairs loopholes. We can't even see them otherwise. Here, you and Finch lay down covering fire.' He took another Enfield from a constable on the stairs and handed it to O'Keefe.

O'Keefe shouted instructions to Finch and raised the Enfield, keeping his body behind the wall. He fired as fast as he could, slamming back the bolt on the rifle, his rate of fire slower than it had been during the war, but steady, driven by fear. He got off five rounds to Finch's six, Finch raising his Webley to fire twice more when his Enfield emptied.

Daly made it to the stairway, his boots skipping steps, Volunteer bullets thwacking into the stairs and the banister. O'Keefe knew that Jim was right: they had to get men into higher firing positions or they would never hold the barracks. He turned to the two constables with him beneath the stairs, each with three Enfields in their arms.

'You lads will have to make it upstairs and fire from there. Can you do it?'

They looked pale and young, but both nodded. It was the closest they would ever get to going over the top of a trench, thought O'Keefe. He fired off the final five rounds in his Enfield and then pressed a fresh charger clip into its magazine. He shouted down the hall to Finch. The chatter of the Lewis gun started up from the roof and O'Keefe thought he could make out the red phosphorous glow of the distress flares in the night sky. Now was as good a time as ever.

'Go!'

Six quick rounds, Finch's six on top and the stuttering machine-gun from above. The first young constable made it to the stairs and mounted them. One round popped in response. The second – Dawson from County Down – took the corner to the stairs too quickly, his feet slipping out from under him, the floor slick with Morris' blood. The three rifles he was holding clattered to the ground. O'Keefe reloaded and was aware of the silence of Finch's gun. When he raised his rifle again to fire down the hallway, he saw Dawson get up, bending to gather up the rifles. A bullet struck his head and he dropped. His leg slid out from under him, as if he was trying to find a comfortable position on the floor to rest.

O'Keefe wrenched back the bolt of his carbine and fired in rage, again and again, until the magazine was empty. He handed the gun to another young constable beside him – nineteen-year-old Joseph Moran from Drogheda – shoving the box of .303 cartridges closer to him with his boot. 'Take this and keep firing. Anyone comes through that hole in the front, kill him.'

Moran swallowed, nodded. 'Yes, Sergeant.'

O'Keefe slapped him on the arm as he passed, then headed down the stairs, removing the Colt automatic he'd retrieved at Burleigh House from its holster under his arm.

The lower ground floor of the barracks was strangely quiet, though above O'Keefe the floorboards sounded with thumping boots and the crack of rifle fire. Then, what sounded like a ball-bearing rolling and spinning across the boards above and sudden, panicked, roared warnings of 'Grenade!' The blast was a muffled *whump*.

O'Keefe made his way to the cells, opening the main door and pulling the keys from the ring inside. Whoever had been on watch had abandoned his post, leaving three scared men in their cells. Hearing the keys jingle as O'Keefe took them from the ring, Constable Keane shouted, 'Get us out of here, for the sake of Christ!'

He opened Keane's cell first. The young man had dark circles under his eyes and his nose was broken. He looked as if he had aged ten years in the past week.

'You're to mind Daniel Hooey. Get him up the stairs and out the back of the barracks. We'll put him and Connors in the sheds where it should be safe, right?'

Keane nodded. Moving quickly, O'Keefe unlocked Daniel Hooey's cell. The prisoner lay curled in a ball on his bunk, knees pulled to his chest, muttering something unintelligible, repeating it over and over. O'Keefe thought it was something to do with his mother but didn't bother asking, pulling him up by the arms and shoving him out the cell door. 'Go,' he said to Keane. 'Get him outside.'

Seamus Connors was standing when O'Keefe unlocked his cell door. He was smiling, but O'Keefe could sense the pain beneath the smile. Unlike Keane, he bore no outward signs of a beating. O'Keefe wondered what Mathew-Pare and his men had done to him.

He pointed the Colt at Connors and instructed, 'Come with me. Now.'

'The boys've come to collect me, Sergeant.'

'If you want to live, Connors, you'll do as I tell you.'

'Live to die a different day, Sergeant?'

'Just move, Connors. Hanging's better than burning alive.'

Connors stepped out of the cell then stopped, his gaze locking on something over O'Keefe's shoulder. O'Keefe felt the presence and turned.

In the hallway outside the cells, Starkson was raising a pistol. A German Luger, O'Keefe noticed. Better than the Webley, so it was said during the war. Amazing, he thought, how the mind keeps working. Even when you're about to die.

Starkson aimed the Luger at O'Keefe's chest. O'Keefe watched the killer's knuckle whiten as he started to pull the trigger.

Another grenade came in through the gaping front of the barracks. It skipped down the front hallway like a flat stone on water, past Finch and between the legs of Constable Moran. It hit the wall behind Moran and bounced once, twice, down the lower ground-floor stairs, sounding, for all the world, as if a child had dropped a toy. Moran shouted and covered his head with his arms. 'Grenade!'

And then Starkson was gone. The blast from the grenade took his legs first, shattering bones and piercing his body with hundreds of tiny pieces of shrapnel. O'Keefe and Connors were knocked back by the blast, but were shielded from the brunt of it by the heavy open door of the cell. There was a deafening ringing in O'Keefe's ears and plaster dust coated his eyes, nose and mouth. He spat on his hand and rubbed his eyes to clear them. Connors appeared to be struggling to regain his breath, his mouth gaping open as he tried to raise himself to his feet.

O'Keefe stood first, searching the floor for the Colt. Finding it, he said to Connors, 'Get up.'

Upstairs, Finch had decided that if the Volunteers sussed the timed fuses on the grenades, they would take the barracks. Until now they hadn't, sending the grenades sliding into the front hallway as soon as they'd pulled the pins, giving the cons time to pick them up and throw them back out. He had seen one of the young Irish lads put his foot to a rolling grenade and kick it back down the hallway and out of the barracks. Like to have that lad as a centre-half, Finch thought, and fired again.

O'Keefe made it to the top of the stairs with Connors in front of him. He had to manoeuvre around Constable Moran, who was firing as if he'd been doing it all his life. Brass shells from his Enfield clinked down the stairs in brassy, spinning arcs.

Reaching the barracks' rear door, O'Keefe pulled it open, giving Connors a hard shove into the dark stable yard and following him out.

He was closer to Connors than he should have been, in his rush to get out of the barracks. Panic was edging at his consciousness, making his movements jerky, rash, instinctive. His ears rang and his eyes burned and watered. The notion came to him too late: *I should have put the bracelets on him.* Connors' elbow suddenly hit O'Keefe high in the stomach, knocking the breath from his lungs, sending him tumbling back through the doorway into the barracks, directly into the line of fire at the back of the main hallway.

Connors turned and ran, making it to the steel security gate. He lifted up the steel catch. He was shouting before he had the gate open.

'Come on, boys, take the place! In through here!'

Eakins had been packing the Ford when he heard the shouting. He recognised the voice and followed it across the stable yard – the sound of his footsteps on the cobbles lost amidst the gunfire and shouting.

He shot Seamus Connors point blank in the back of the head. Then he closed and latched the gate again and went back to his packing. The Ford was nearly loaded and they would be leaving soon. He noticed that the barracks had begun to burn in earnest now. He stood in the cottage doorway and lit a cigarette. Not his problem. The barracks could burn and every man in it. His work was done.

———

Rough hands pulled at O'Keefe's jacket, dragging him into the cover of the back stairs. Rounds slapped the skirting boards and plaster where he'd been lying.

'You all right, Sergeant?' Moran was smiling, his eyes alight. When O'Keefe nodded, his breath returning, Moran stood and fired again. Moran hadn't fought in the war – he'd been too young, O'Keefe knew – but he was born to fight. Some men were.

O'Keefe stood up and searched the ground for the Colt. Not finding it, he squeezed back down the stairs and returned with another rifle, a box of .303 cartridges and a crate of grenades. He dumped half the ammunition and set six grenades at Moran's feet.

'Don't spend it all in one place.'

Moran smiled and squeezed off a shot. 'Not a bother, Sergeant.'

The smell of smoke was stronger as O'Keefe peered out

over Moran's shoulder. He could see flames licking up the paint of the front stairs and imagined he could feel the heat of the fire.

'We have to evacuate. This place is going to go up.'

'I'm not fucking leaving 'til those bastards leave first.'

'You'll go if you're ordered, Moran.'

The young con fired and drew back the bolt, sending a spent shell spinning at O'Keefe's chest. 'Yes, Sergeant.'

O'Keefe went out into the barracks yard. It was relatively quiet, Connors nowhere to be seen. Two Tans had pushed the DI's Daimler up to the wall and had taken sandbags from the guard hut at the gate to make a machine-gun post on the hard top of the car. They fired short bursts of repelling fire and appeared to be doing a good job of holding back any attack from the rear of the barracks. Two other constables were using Enfields to the same effect on the opposite wall. O'Keefe went to the sheds to check on Keane and Daniel Hooey. Keane stood when O'Keefe entered the shed.

'Give me a carbine, Sergeant.'

'No, but I need your help. Take the long ladder from the shed and put it up to the DI's office window. We're going to have to evacuate the barracks. It's burning. Get moving.'

———

Liam Farrell watched in awe from the upstairs window at the front of McGowan's office with Seán Brennan and McGowan himself. From their vantage point, they had an unimpeded view of the wide street in front of the barracks.

A beautiful sight to behold, Farrell thought. A glimpse of what it must have been like in the war. The muzzle flashes were like matches struck and then extinguished in the dark. The arcing tracer rounds from the machine-gun in the barracks' attic could be sparks hammered from a blacksmith's anvil. The muffled flash and then *whump* of exploding grenades was audible over the popping of the rifles and the *kakk-kakking* of the machine-guns. Emergency flares in the inky night sky descending like slow-falling stars. Make a wish, Farrell thought, amused at the way the mind worked, independent of external reality. This was beautiful. It was hard to imagine people dying out there.

He watched as Ballycarleton barracks started to burn, flames painting the outside walls to the side and front of the structure where the mine had detonated. Now and again he thought he could make out the shadows of Volunteers moving from one firing position to another in the darkened street. He knew for a fact there were three men behind the trough and water pump in the centre of the road, and several others at the corner of the warehouse, two buildings down from the barracks. One or two more were on the warehouse roof.

Brennan broke their watchful silence. 'The machine-gunners are good. Targeted bursts. Keeping our boys pinned down. Easy on the ammo, keeping the barrels cool enough. They know to hold back, that our boys don't have all night. Professionals, some of those lads.'

'We're not doing too badly ourselves, sir,' Farrell said, vaguely offended by Brennan's appraisal of the Tan gunners.

'Oh, they're doing all right. Getting better by the day, boy.'

McGowan took the pipe from his mouth. 'And Connors? Will they get him out, do you think?'

Brennan was silent for a moment watching the battle, the flames from the burning barracks casting his face in a flickering, yellow light. Finally, he said, 'I'd imagine he's dead already. God rest him, but it saves us the job.'

Farrell was about to protest when McGowan spoke again. 'Seems a shame, but he was a fierce loose cannon, that boy.'

Brennan gave a rueful smile in the flashing glare of the firefight. 'Most of the best gunmen are. Reining them in, when this,' he gestured out at the battle, 'when all this is over. That'll be the hard part. Connors …' He seemed lost for words. 'Connors, will be well missed. He'll die a hero. It was forever coming, the bullet with his name on it.'

Liam Farrell turned his attention back to the battle outside, certain he would never understand the inner workings of the cause to which he had pledged his allegiance, nor the men who were its leaders.

———

O'Keefe headed up the front stairs, Finch and Moran laying down covering fire, IRA rounds taking out chunks of plaster, dusting his hair and clothes. The wall of the stairway was hot to the touch and smoke rose with him, beginning to scorch his throat with each ragged breath. He found Daly and two other constables firing through loopholes in the day-room that faced the front of the barracks. Two others were in the DI's office, doing the same, one stopping to open the steel shutters while the other tossed grenades into the darkness.

Through his boots O'Keefe could feel the heat of the fire below and smoke was making lazy spirals up between the floorboards. It was time to leave. 'Let's go lads. Abandon ship. This place is going to burn. Grab the lads on the machine-gun from the attic and use the back window where the ladder is to get out.'

Next he went through into the DI's private room and opened the shutters onto the barracks yard. As he did, Keane set the ladder against the window frame. O'Keefe wondered suddenly where the DI had got to. He pushed the thought from his mind. Heading halfway back down the stairs, O'Keefe shouted to Finch and Moran to evacuate. He waited for their responses and the sound of their bootsteps making for the rear door of the barracks before he went back upstairs.

'Let's go, Jim.' Daly was the last one in the room.

'You hear that?'

'What?' They were both silent. At first all O'Keefe could hear was the crackling flames below. Then he noticed that the firing from outside had stopped. And in its absence he could hear the distant chug of lorry engines and the whine of armoured cars.

'The cavalry. Took their fucking time about it.'

Daly said, 'If they'd left it any later, we might have had to abandon barracks.'

O'Keefe coughed smoke. 'Get yer arse out that window.'

Saturday
4 December 1920

The men stood in the barracks yard and watched the barracks burn. It was too far gone to save, even if the fire brigade could have been persuaded to fight the blaze. Firemen had been warned off aiding the Peelers, the same as everybody else.

Another barracks burning, O'Keefe thought. Eyes and ears of the Crown, blinded, deafened. Fair enough. The men had fought well. The opposition had been determined, well-trained. Fair enough. He walked over to Finch and Daly.

'Has anyone seen Mathew-Pare or Masterson?'

Constable Moran stood behind them. 'Left about ten minutes ago. Just before you got out. Soon as the army lads showed, they flew out of here in the spooks' Ford motor.'

Spooks, O'Keefe thought. Was he the only one who had met Mathew-Pare and his men who hadn't immediately known they were agents? Maybe he *was* as thick as Masterson must have assumed when he'd assigned the case to him.

'You're sure the DI was with them?' he asked Moran.

'He was. And that prick – sorry, Sergeant. And Constable Senior.'

Finch said, 'We should've shot the bastards.'

Soldiers patrolled the streets around the town, but the flying column was long gone. Night gave way to a milky dawn, the barracks still burning, rounds of ammunition popping off in the armoury, the occasional dampened blast of a Mills bomb. The roof collapsed just before eight o'clock and they moved out to the square in front of the barracks to watch it burn, as did the people of Ballycarleton. None of the people cheered when the roof went down, though there were wry smiles exchanged between men of a certain age. They had heard about the burning of the poultry farm and the three houses in Rathleigh.

O'Keefe saw Liam Farrell standing on his own in front of McNulty's public house on the far side of the square. He made his way over to him.

'Mr Farrell.'

'Sergeant.'

'Connors is dead. I tried to move him from the barracks but he bashed me in the ribs. He was shot trying to open the gate is my guess.'

'I heard. Still, not an altogether unsuccessful raid.' He gestured toward the burning barracks.

'Not from your perspective, no.'

'And from yours?'

O'Keefe shrugged. 'The DI is gone. Went off with the two Castle spooks and his batman. I won't get him now. My files and the murder book were inside.' He took out a crushed box of Players and held it out to Farrell.

Farrell took one and accepted a light. Exhaling smoke, he asked, 'And how long ago did they leave?'

O'Keefe held the match to his own cigarette. 'An hour or so. I reckon they'll make their way to Cork and then on to Dublin.'

Farrell nodded, staring out at the flames. 'And what kind of car was it?'

'Ford Tourer.'

'Four men you say?'

'Two shades, the DI and his man.'

'Where's the other spy?'

'Dead.'

The young man nodded and crushed his cigarette under his heel. 'I'll be going so, Sergeant. Must use the telephone.'

It was O'Keefe's turn to nod. 'I hope the lines are clear.'

'They will be. We've good people working them.' He smiled at O'Keefe and walked away.

O'Keefe smoked his cigarette and watched Ballycarleton barracks burn. Daly came over to him, pipe in hand. His face was black with soot and gunpowder, his tunic riddled with tiny burnholes. He was hatless and his hair stood on end.

O'Keefe said, 'You saved your pipe and plug anyway.'

'First things first. A man has his priorities.'

'I wonder where they'll post you now. Back to Cork?'

Daly shrugged. 'Long as they keep paying the wages, I couldn't give two fucks. We're due a raise y'know, so don't you think about jacking the job in now. A *pensionable* raise, mind.'

'Somehow, I don't think I'll be collecting any kind of pension at all.'

Around his pipe stem, Daly said, 'At all, at all? Never mind. I'll stand you a drink, Seán, if you're short –'

'… at my funeral.'

'Sure, you'll outlive me by years yet, you jammy bastard.'

Acknowledgements

The author would like to thank the following: Fingal Arts Office of the Fingal County Council for the award of the bursary which allowed me to spend time completing the first draft of this novel at the Tyrone Guthrie Centre in Annaghmakerrig, County Monaghan; the staff and residents at the Tyrone Guthrie Centre for their hospitality and support; my agent, Jonathan Williams, for his expert representation and editing; Moya Nolan for her photographs; Geoffrey 'Jefe' McCarthy for his management of the ARCs; Davide Martinazzo for his printing and design of the ARCs; my first reader and editor, Juliet McCarthy; first readers, Colin McCarthy, Denis Carolan, Niall and Susan Hogan; all current and former staff of Mercier Press, especially Wendy Logue, Patrick Crowley and Eoin Purcell, for their tireless work and support; Col (ret.) Geoffrey McCarthy, Breda Dunne, Donnacha O'Leary, Alex and Giovanna Connolly, Stephanie Haller, Jonathan Grimes, Susannah and Mary McCarthy, and all those who answered any of my myriad questions on everything from laying hens to firearms to autopsies; and most especially to Gi and the girls without whom the novel would not have been possible.

This book is dedicated to my mother, Juliet McCarthy.